This is a work of fiction. All the characters and events portrayed in this book are fictitious, and any resemblance to real people or events is purely coincidental.

ELVENBLOOD

Copyright © 1995 by Andre Norton, Ltd., and Mercedes Lackey

Cover art by Boris Vallejo
Edited by James Frenkel

A Tor Book
Published by Tom Doherty Associates, LLC
175 Fifth Avenue
New York, NY 10010

www.tor.com

Tor® is a registered trademark of Tom Doherty Associates, LLC.

ISBN: 0-812-56319-0
Library of Congress Catalog Card Number: 95-5797

First edition: June 1995
First mass market edition: April 1996

Printed in the United States of America

0 9 8 7 6 5

ELVENBLOOD

ANDRE NORTON AND MERCEDES LACKEY

TOR®
fantasy

A TOM DOHERTY ASSOCIATES BOOK
NEW YORK

1

SHEYRENA HAD GROWN very weary of coos of admiration over the last hour or so. Human voices, harsh and heavy by elven standards, did not normally grate on her ears, but they did today.

"Oh, my lady, there has never been a gown so lovely, I swear!" The nameless blond slave out of her mother's household shook her head over the shimmering folds of Sheyrena's gown. She probably spoke the truth, by her own standards; it was heavy damascene silk, of peacock-blue shot through with threads of pearly iridescence. The color was far more vivid than anything ever seen in nature.

And a more wretched color for me could not be imagined. It would, of course, completely overwhelm her. She would be a ghost in the stolen costume of the living.

"Truly!" gushed another. "You will ravish the mind of every lord who sees you!"

Only if they have taste for a maiden who resembles a corpse bedecked for her funeral. No amount of careful makeup would ever give her the coloring to match that gown.

It was suitable for the vivid beauty of a human concubine, not an elven maid, and particularly not one who was pale even by the standards of her own race. It was typical of her father to have chosen something that would display, not her, but the power, *his* power, that made it possible.

Sheyrena an Treves closed her ears to the chattering of her human slaves and wished she could be anywhere but where she was. The windowless, pale blue marble walls of her dressing room were far too confining at the best of times; now, as it was crowded with the bodies of not only her own half-dozen slaves, but an additional four from her mother's retinue, she was not entirely certain there was enough air to go around. There was too much perfume and heat in here; she wished vaguely for an escape from all of it.

If only she could be outside! *Sitting watching the butterflies in that meadow Lorryn discovered—or riding along the wall around the estate—*she thought wistfully. For a long moment she was lost in her dreams of escape, her mind far from this room and all it contained, as she imagined herself riding Lorryn's spirited gelding in a headlong chase along the sandstone wall, the wind in her face, and Lorryn only a pace or two ahead of her—

Lorryn, if only you could come and rescue me from this! Oh, that is a foolish thought, you cannot even rescue yourself from the bindings of custom.

Two of her own chief attendants—castoffs from her father's harem, twin redheads whose names she could never keep straight—said something to her directly and waited for a response, shaking her out of her dreams. She shook her head slightly and emerged from her thoughts.

"Please, my lady, it is time for the undergown," the right-hand girl repeated quietly, with no expression whatsoever. Sheyrena stood up and allowed them to bring the undergown to her. The slaves were all used to the way she sank into half-trances by now, and if they felt any impatience with her, they were too well trained to show it. No slave in the household of V'layn Tylar Lord Treves would ever dare to display anything so insubordinate as impatience with one of his elven masters. Sheyrena's handmaids always wore the identical expressions of insipid and vacuous pleasantry that one would find on the face of a formal portrait. That was the way her father wanted it, but it always unnerved Sheyrena; she could never tell what they were thinking.

If I knew what they were thinking, I would at least have some idea of how to think of them. Then again, I doubt that their thoughts would be very flattering. There is not much in me, I fear, to inspire a good opinion.

Obedient to their directions, she turned toward the four who bore the gown as carefully as a holy relic, and lifted her arms. Silk slid softly against her flesh, muffling her head for a breath, as three slaves pulled the sinuous, soft folds of the sea-green undergown over her head and arms. They drew it down in place, allowing the skirt to billow out around her bare feet. The sleeves and body were cut to fit tightly with a plunging décolletage, the skirt flared out from the hips, billowing out into a long trailing train in the latest style—

So that I look like a green twig being tossed atop a wave. Very attractive. How can they keep from laughing at me? Another selection by Lord Tylar, of course, to show that his daughter was no stranger to the highest of fashion. Never mind that the highest of fashion looked ridiculous on her. On the other hand, did she really *want* to look attractive?

No. No, I don't. I don't want a husband, I don't want any changes; as pathetic as my life is now, I do not want to find myself the property of some lord like my father. And since Father chose all of this for me, he can hardly blame me for looking ridiculous. That, in and of itself, was a relief. If Sheyrena failed tonight, her father would be looking for someone or something to blame, and it would be best if she gave him no excuse to place that blame on her. Lord Tylar had made it clear to his wife and daughter that this particular fete was of paramount importance to the House of Treves. The glee on his face when he had received the invitation, not only to attend, but to present Sheyrena, had only been equaled the day that he learned that the price of grain for slave-fodder had tripled due to a blight that his fields had been spared. While Lord Tylar's lineage was good, it was not great—and his monetary wealth was due entirely to his successes in the marketplace. Lord Tylar's grandfather had been a mere pensioner, and only astute management had brought the House of Treves this far. He was *not* one of the original High Lords of the Council, but a recent appointee, and under normal circumstances, he would not ever have found himself in the company of the House of Hernalth, much less invited to their fete.

"Turn, please, my lady."

The invitation came not by teleson, but by messenger—an elven messenger, not a human slave, which showed how Lord Tylar's status had increased since the disastrous conflict with the Elvenbane. Scribed on a thin sheet of pure gold, it could only have been created magically—an indirect and subtle demonstration of the power and skill of the creator.

V'kass Ardeyn el-Lord Fortren Lord Hernalth requests the pleasure of the company of the House of Treves at a fete given in his honor by his guardian, V'sheyl Edres Lord Fortren, on the occasion of his accession to the lands and position of the House of Hernalth. He further requests the boon of the presentation of the daughter of the House of Treves at this fete. No need to mention dates or time; even the least and poorest of the pensioners on Lord Tylar's estate knew the date of Lord Ardeyn's accession-fete, just as they knew *why* the heir to the house of Fortren had inherited the House of Hernalth—over the strenuous objections of Lord Dyran's brother, it might be added.

"Please raise your arm a trifle."

Odd that his *given name is Treves.* There had been strong words between Lord Treves and Lord Edres in Council, and Lord Treves had gone off in a huff, taking what little he owned under the law, becoming a pensioner under the auspices of one of Lord Edres's opponents. She could only hope that such an unpleasant coincidence might cause Lord Ardeyn to regard her with a less than favorable eye, for by asking that she be presented, Lord Ardeyn had made it very clear that he was not only holding a celebration, he was seeking an appropriate bride.

"Turn a little more, please."

It had been nearly a year since Lord Dyran and his son and heir had died, and the inheritance had fallen into dispute. But the Council—Lord Tylar among them—had eventually ruled that the estate and title could only be inherited by the oldest surviving son—unless there were no surviving sons to inherit. And while it was presumed (since there *were* two bodies) that Dyran's heir Valyn had gone up in smoke with his father, there being no evidence to the contrary, there was still Valyn's twin alive, of sound mind and body, living in, and the designated heir to, the house of his grandfather.

That made young Ardeyn a double heir, and doubly desirable in a marriage alliance. Little matter that Lord Edres was quite vigorous and unlikely to make Ardeyn a double-Lord any time in the next several centuries; Ardeyn now had all of Lord Dyran's considerable holdings in his own right. That made him the equal of his grandfather in status and standing. Lord Tylar's support of Ardeyn's claim had been noted, and now would be rewarded—though it was vanishingly unlikely that the reward would be a wedding to Sheyrena. Lord Ardeyn was *too* highplaced for that, and Lord Tylar still an upstart, though a valued upstart.

"Lower your arm now, my lady, please."

And no doubt, every unpledged elven maiden of appropriate rank has gotten an invitation to come and show her paces for the benefit of Lord Ardeyn—or rather, his grandfather. There was no doubt in Sheyrena's mind who was going to be making the choice of a bride for Ardeyn. Only those who were fortunate enough to have no parents or guardians ever made the choice of a spouse for themselves. If the young Lord was lucky, his grandfather *might* consult him—but the probability was that he was so ruled by Lord Edres that he would tamely accept a wedding to a mule if that was what his grandfather dictated.

Just as I will tamely accept a wedding to a mule if that is what my father dictates, no matter how I feel about it, for my feelings are of no consequence, she reflected with resignation, as the maids laced the bodice of the undergown so tightly as to make it a second silken skin. The effect was not to make her somewhat meager charms seem more generous, but rather the opposite.

Although the invitation had said nothing about other maidens being presented at this fete, it didn't have to. It was the word of every bower across the land that Lord Ardeyn was looking for a bride and a profitable alliance, not necessarily in that order. There would be dozens of unwedded and unpledged elven women there tonight, from children still playing with dolls to widows with power and property of their own. There was only one Lord Ardeyn, however, which meant that it was inevitable that many other unwedded elven lords or their parents or representatives would be appearing at this fete as well, looking for prospective brides. It wasn't often that there was an occasion grand enough that all the houses could put aside their various feuds and pretend civility for one short night. Any number of alliances might come out of this fete; old conflicts might be resolved—

"—the train, my lady, please to lift your foot."

And entirely new ones created. The maids indicated that she should turn a full circle; the silken folds of the skirt swirled around her and settled again with a sigh. They held up the overgown, and once again she held still while they eased it over her head, for all the world like a giant doll they were all dressing. The heavier silk of the overgown poured down over her body and added its weight to the invisible burden of misery on her shoulders.

So I am to be trotted out like one of Father's prize mares, for all the unattached lords to check my paces and my teeth. Just as Lorryn is trotted about like a prize stallion, displayed to the fathers of all the maidens in our circle. Father's will is everything. She was too well schooled to show her distaste, but her unhappiness sat in her middle, a lump of sour ice, and made her throat ache with tension. The maids fussed with the lacings on the side of the overgown as she closed her burning eyes for a moment to fight for control and serenity.

It was hard, hard, to maintain that well-schooled serenity, especially in light of the ordeal to come. She had never been comfortable with strangers; the few times that her father had summoned her to be displayed—presumably with an eye to a possible marriage—she had wanted to crawl under the rug and hide. The prospect of being trussed into this torture device disguised as a gown and spending the entire evening displaying herself to dozens, hundreds, of strangers was enough to make her physically ill.

"—and this lacing must be tighter, please try not to breathe heavily—"

Her mother had been trying to convince her for weeks that this was going to be a golden opportunity for her. This would be her one, perhaps her only, chance to make a marriage that would satisfy her father *and* herself. This was a rare chance to actually meet some of the lords looking for brides before one of them was foisted on her. She might actually find some young elven lord there that she *liked*; someone who would allow her to continue her excursions outside the bower, rather than confining her to the space within the walls of the women's quarters as so many elven lords insisted was proper.

Her mother's arguments had included those, and many other persuasive blandishments in the same vein. Her mother claimed she understood Sheyrena's feelings of doubt, the unsettling thoughts that had been moving through her mind of late, and her reluctance to contract *any* marriage. *And what would Mother know about it? Viridina an Treves has never had an inappropriate thought in her life. She has always been the perfect, obedient Lady, pliant and pleasant, willing to be whatever her father and her Lord wished her to be....* How could someone like that ever understand the restless thoughts passing through her daughter's mind these days?

"Hold your arm here, please, my lady."

Right now Sheyrena would have given everything she owned to be able to catch some kind of illness, as the humans did in order to have an excuse to stay at home. But for all their outward fragility, elven women were as immune to such things as the males of their kind.

And it's too late for me to manufacture mind-storms like Lorryn has. No one would believe a bout of head pain coming now was anything other than a ruse.

She turned at her maids' direction, raising and lowering her arms, while they fussed with the side-lacings and drew the long, floor-sweeping sleeves of the overgown up over the tight undersleeves and fastened them to the shoulders with lacings of gold cord.

Do I look as stiff as I feel, I wonder?

She was torn by conflicting emotions. While it was humiliating to know that her father could not possibly have concocted a less flattering costume for her and that she was going to look her absolute worst in front of a horde of strangers, still, looking her worst would make it less likely that anyone would find her even remotely interesting.

Better to be thought of as the sickly looking stick than to find myself—

Find herself—what? Betrothed to someone like her father, perhaps?

Mother would say that wasn't so bad a prospect. There was resentment in that thought. *But then, Mother has never cared half as much about my welfare as she has about Lorryn's. If he stood in my place this evening, would she be so quick to urge him to be bartered off to a bride?*

"If my lady would hold still for a moment—?"

But Viridina was not her daughter. Viridina was used to her constricted lot in life. Sheyrena had a brief glimpse of a wider world in the last year or so, and she did not want to give that up.

In many ways it was much easier to be Lord Tylar's unregarded daughter than his wife. Viridina's entire existence was bound up by so many rules and customs that she could scarcely breathe without risking the breach of one or more of them. That most of those customs dated back to a more hazardous time when women were in constant danger mattered not a bit to her lord husband; they were customs, and therefore they were to be followed to the letter. But Sheyrena had little or no importance to the house until recently; her older brother Lorryn was the important one, the heir, the *male*. There were more unmarried females in Lord Tylar's social class than there were males; he was too proud to send her to wed a lesser lordling, and dared not look higher. And Lord Tylar, like all the rest of the Lords of the Council, had been very involved with first the rumor, then the fact, of the Elvenbane's existence—

"Please, lady, a step to the right."

Then had come the second Wizard War, which had occupied his attention to the exclusion of all else. So Sheyrena had been ignored, as long as she was properly dutiful, properly trained, properly behaved.

She had found that on the whole she preferred her own company to anyone else's—except, possibly, her brother's. She hadn't made any effort to find friends or companions mostly because she had no interest in the things the others of her generation occupied themselves with. Attendance at a handful of parties had quickly taught her that she was the kind who would settle into a corner and remain there during the entire duration of the event, uncomfortable and alone, wishing she could go home.

"—and this fold should go *so*—"

She didn't enjoy the loss of control that came with intoxication, she didn't see what made gossip so fascinating, she was too plain to attract male attentions, unwanted or otherwise, and the games that the others seemed to find amusing just left her wondering what it was they enjoyed so much, and why something so unchallenging to the intellect should be amusing. On the whole, she would much rather be left to find a corner of a garden, read, and dream her strange thoughts.

There had been a lot more of those strange thoughts in the last year, although they had begun the day she had first learned flower-sculpting.

"A stitch here, I think."

She had begun by resenting those trivial-seeming lessons that her father had ordered her to begin. *Lorryn learns how to shatter stone with his power. I learn flower-sculpting.*

She would never know if her magic was the equal of Lorryn's, because no elven maiden would ever be taught anything but useless skills like flower-sculpting, water-weaving, and the like. Oh, she had heard vague rumors of a few, a very few, elven women who wielded their power like a man, but she had never met any, and she doubted that any of them would be willing to share their secrets with her. Yet before that lesson, it would never have occurred to her that she had a certain power in her own hands that no elven lord would ever suspect.

For it was during the course of that lesson that she realized something strange, exciting, and a little frightening.

The same skills I used to shape the flower could be used in other ways—stopping a heart, for instance. Those useless lessons? If she ever needed that power, those lessons might not be so useless after all.

"What is this? A thread? No, cut it off."

She had not mentioned her revelation to her mother, knowing that Viridina would have been horrified. And she had not really known that the idea would work until a few days later, when she had found a bird in the garden that had flown into a window and broken its neck. Without thinking, she had moved to end the poor thing's pain—and stopped its heart.

She had run back to her own room in horror, fleeing what she had done. But the deed remained, and the power, and the knowledge of what she had done.

Since that moment she had not been able to look at anything the same way. She had surreptitiously experimented with her power, working with the sparrows and pigeons that flocked to the garden. At first she had only made tiny alterations in their color, or the length of their feathers. Then she grew bolder, until now her garden was full of exotic creatures with feathers of scarlet and blue, gold and green, with trailing tails and flaring crests, all of them tame to her hand. Something told her that making subtle changes with her power could be as important—and as dangerous—as the kinds of magic that Lorryn wielded.

And yet, at the same time, she was afraid to stretch out her hand and take the ephemeral power that beckoned her. No other elven woman had ever dared do so—perhaps there was a reason. Perhaps this beckoning power was nothing more than an illusion of strength. True, she could make a colorful bird out of a sparrow—but what good was that? What did it prove?

"If my lady could remove her foot from the sleeve, please?"

But what if it was not? What if it was real? What if she had discovered something no one else knew?

Her secret thoughts weighed in her soul and made it impossible to accept anything at face value anymore. Hardest to bear was the way her father treated her mother and herself.

This very gown was an example of how little he thought of them, how little he trusted them with anything of import. To Sheyrena's certain knowledge, the only time he ever came to Viridina's bower with a pleasant face was when he wanted her to come play the proper wife before his influential friends. In private, neither of them could ever truly please him. He preferred the company of the human slaves in his harem, and constantly compared Viridina to his latest favorites, always unfavorably.

Not that I envy them, she thought, glancing out of the corner of her eye at one of the redheads. *Father's tastes are fickle, and his favorites never last long.*

And when his favorites were out of favor, Lord Tylar seemed to take a malicious delight in sending them to serve his wife or daughter in the bower. Sheyrena had never been able to guess whether he did so to try to torment them with the still lovely presence of his former leman, or to torment the former favorite with the presence of the lawful wife who could not be displaced. Perhaps it was both.

Viridina accepted this quietly and without a single comment, ever; just as she accepted with the same serene resignation everything else that life bestowed on her. She was not envious of the harem beauties either; there was really no difference in the world of the harem and that of the bower except that Viridina could not be supplanted. They had neither more freedom than their putative mistress, nor less. As Sheyrena had gradually come to understand, the distinction between the bower and the harem was that the bower was a harem of one. Only when it came to Lorryn and Lorryn's well-being did Viridina show any signs of interest—though a furtive, obsessive, fearful anxiety, as if she was terrified that something would happen to him. She watched over Lorryn with the care and concern she could have shown if he were an invalid, rather then the healthy creature he was. Or did his attacks of *kryshein* mean he was not as healthy as Sheyrena thought? Was there some secret trouble with Lorryn, something Rena could not be told? But if that was true, then why hadn't *Lorryn* told her? He never had kept any secret from her before!

Viridina might accept her lot as an elven lady, but it was more than Sheyrena could stomach for herself.

Better to be ignored as the daughter than humiliated as the wife of someone like Father.

She was surrounded by all of the slaves now, each of them making minute adjustments to the gown, the lacings, as if she were nothing more than a mannequin inside it and the gown itself was the important guest. Sheyrena had a sudden, absurd thought, that perhaps this was the real truth—that the gown had a life and purpose of its own, and she was nothing more than the vehicle it required to propel it to the place where it would be admired!

Yet, in a sense, that was the whole truth. The gown represented Lord Tylar, his power, his wealth, his position. *She* was nothing more than the means to display all these things, a convenient banner-bearer. It was the banner that was important, not the hand that held it, after all. *Anything* would have served the same purpose.

If I'd been as feeble-witted as Ardeyn's mother, he would still have had me trussed up in this gown and sent off to the fete. And if he were as wise as any of the High Lords, he would have found a way to command my silence so as not to distract potential suitors from the message of his importance.

She and her mother were nothing more than things to Lord

Tylar—not that this was a new thought, but it had never been driven home quite so obviously before. They were possessions, game-pieces, and their whole importance lay in how they could be played to the best advantage.

She was encased in the layers of this gown as she was encased in the layers of his power over her, and nothing would ever change that. She knew that, and yet a persistent little voice deep inside kept asking, "Why not?"

Because that is the way things are, she told that little voice. *They have always been that way, and they will always be that way. Nothing will ever change them. Certainly not one insignificant female, for females are of no consequence to anyone.*

But the little voice would not accept that answer. As her slaves directed her to sit again so that they might dress her hair, it replied, "Oh no? Then what about the halfblood wizards? What about the Elvenbane? She is only one female."

Sheyrena had no answer for that. Certainly the High Lords had been certain they had disposed of all the halfbloods long ago, and had thought they had made certain no others could be born. The halfbloods, with their melding of human and elven magics, were holders of the only real power that had ever threatened the elven lords' rule over this world they had conquered so long ago. Yet despite all the precautions, more halfblooded children *had* been born—worse, had escaped to grow into their powers—and had survived to learn how to use those powers. One of those children had been a girl who had, by ill luck or conscious direction, matched the descriptions of a "savior" in human legend called "the Elvenbane." *She* had found allies the High Lords hadn't even dreamed existed.

Dragons.

Sheyrena sighed as she thought of the dragons, her chest constricted by the tightly laced dress. Not that *she* had ever seen one, but she had heard plenty of descriptions. Oh, how she would love to get just a glimpse of one! Sinuous, graceful, glistening in the sunlight with the colors of precious gems as they flew—dragons lilted through her dreams at night sometimes, leaving her yearning after them when dawn came, sometimes with her cheeks wet with tears of longing and loss.

"Turn your head this way, my lady."

It was the dragons that had turned the tide for the wizards, and made it possible for them to hold off the armies of no less than three of the High Lords. There had been a dreadful slaughter that included many elves. Chief among those was the powerful, if half-mad, Lord Dyran. Sheyrena had heard it whispered that it was his own son who had slain him. That hardly seemed possible, and yet, who would have thought that dragons were possible a year ago?

In the end, the High Lords were forced to accede to a truce. The wizards retreated out beyond the lands that the elves claimed, and the elves pledged to leave them in peace.

My father claims we drove them out, and that we only let them go because it wasn't worth pursuing them. She allowed herself a treacherous iota of contempt. *The last time he entertained guests, he went on for hours about it. They all did. You'd think we actually defeated them, from the way Father acted!*

And that little voice inside spoke up without prompting. "Maybe they aren't as much in control as they would like to think," it whispered insidiously. "Maybe they aren't anywhere near as powerful as *you* think. Maybe you aren't as insignificant as they would like to make you think."

That's all very well, she told it sullenly, *But what exactly am I supposed to do to prove how free I am?*

The voice finally went silent then, having no solutions to offer. After all, it was nothing more than her own stubborn rebellion.

Still, that was a point. Lorryn called the second Wizard War "a draw at best, a rout at worst," and he did not mean for the halfblood side. What if the power of the High Lords had weakened? Did that mean there was room for a female to make a life for herself, in the midst of the High Lords' scramble to retain what they had?

"Bend your head, please, my lady."

But how? That was the real question. How to escape the

dreary life that had been laid out for her from the moment of her birth? These plans had a life of their own, rolling along whether or not she agreed to them.

And Father can force me if he wants to. That was another fact. He could visit any number of unpleasant punishments on her if she refused to cooperate. He could confine her to a single room on starvation meals.

He could even lock a slave-collar on me, and coerce me to obey with magic. She had heard rumors of that happening to some maidens, faced with exceedingly unpleasant husbands-to-be. It was easy enough to conceal such a device in a piece of elaborate jewelry; such things were constructed for favored slaves all the time. She felt her throat close and her breath come shorter at the very idea. She quickly controlled herself, before the slaves noticed.

No, there was no escape for her—only the minimal freedom she had now, as the daughter rather than the wife. But if only there were!

Not that I have any idea what I would do, she admitted to herself. It was just that she had been feeling so stifled for such a long time, locked up in the bower, doing next to nothing, listening to the gossip of the slaves. *I want to do* something *with my life, even if I don't know what. I don't want to become another pretty puppet like Mother; that much I do know. I couldn't bear that.*

But as she watched the slaves braiding and arranging her hair in the mirror, she was struck by how much she *did* resemble her mother. And an uncomfortable thought occurred to her. Had Lady Viridina always been the perfect elven lady? Or had she been forced to pretend that she was, until the last of her spirit faded, and the pretense became reality, the facade became fact?

Could that happen to me?

A *very* uncomfortable thought, that. Sheyrena turned away from it hastily. There was not and never had been a sign that Lady Viridina was anything but what she appeared to be. Sheyrena was not her mother. Viridina could never understand her.

If only I'd been born a boy.... Another thought-path, this one worn by travel. If only she had been born a male, Lorryn's little brother instead of his sister. They were nearly as close as brothers anyway, for despite custom to the contrary, because of his mother's obsessive need to oversee his welfare, Lorryn had spent plenty of time in the bower instead of being sequestered away with a series of male tutors. Viridina encouraged this, and even dropped her fanatic watchfulness whenever her son and daughter were together. He had shared plenty of lessons with Sheyrena as they grew. She had trailed along after him countless times, dressed in his castoffs, without anyone seeming to notice. Even now he smuggled her out in disguise as a male slave, sharing rides and hunts with her, whenever their father wasn't in residence. Discipline was relaxed whenever Lord Tylar was gone; there wasn't such a close watch kept, and Lorryn's age and status kept awkward questions from being asked.

She enjoyed the rides, although the inevitable conclusion of the hunts generally made her feel sick and she avoided the kill whenever possible. It was Lorryn who had told her most of what she knew about the *real* conclusion of what he called "the second Wizard War."

"Please close your eyes, my lady."

Sheyrena obeyed the request, and continued to follow her own thoughts. She assumed Lorryn picked up most of what he knew from the other el-Lords, the young heirs and younger sons that he saw socially. Most of what Lorryn had told her, she suspected, was not anything their elders would approve of her hearing. Very little of it was flattering; Lorryn and his contemporaries did not have a high opinion of their elders' intelligence or ability.

She had the feeling that Lorryn secretly admired the now-deceased Valyn, Lord Dyran's heir, who had actually joined forces with the wizards, turning traitor to his own kind. Lorryn swore that he had done so to save his presumably halfblooded brother, Mero; though how he could know that, she hadn't a clue. He seemed obsessed with that part of the story, but as for her, *she* could not hear enough about the dragons.

Oh, the dragons ...

The slaves were working on her face now, with tiny brushes and pots of cosmetic, trying to give her some semblance of a living person. That was going to be difficult to do; her hair was the palest white-gold imaginable, and her face completely without color in its natural state, her eyes so pale a green as to seem gray. Anything they did with cosmetics was doomed to look artificial. At the best, she would resemble a porcelain statue; at worst, a clown.

At the moment, she was inclined to hope for the clown.

Lorryn had also been the one to tell her about the Elvenbane, who summoned the dragons. Some of what he had told her she had also overheard when her father had made conversation with guests, but not that. Her father never even acknowledged that any such creature existed.

That wasn't particularly surprising. The Elvenbane was female *and* halfblood, and must represent everything Lord Tylar hated and feared.

But if I could choose anything other than a boy—I would choose to be her. Oh, how *that* would shock Lady Viridina! But that was what Sheyrena dreamed, in the secret dark of the deep night: that she was the Elvenbane. Powerful in her own right, bending the world to *her* will and *her* magic, riding across the sky on a dragon; that was the way to live!

If I was the Elvenbane, there would be no father to stop me, nothing I couldn't do if I wanted to. I could go anywhere, see anything, be anything that I wished!

She settled back into her daydreams as the slaves worked on her face, tiny brushes flicking across her cheeks, lips, and eyelids with the kiss of a thousand butterflies. She envisioned herself mounted on a huge scarlet dragon, soaring under a cloudless sky, so high above the forest that the trees blurred into a mossy carpet of green and there was no sign of walls or buildings. In her dreaming, the dragon carried her toward the mountains she had never seen, which rose to meet them, towering spires sparkling with fantastic crags of crystal and rose quartz, amethyst and—

A polite cough woke her out of her dream. Regretfully she opened her eyes and regarded the handiwork of the slaves in her mirror.

It was appalling. It was also the best they could do, and she knew it. Her eyes were washed out by the heavy peacock-blue they had painted on her lids; her cheeks had hectic red circles that looked as clownlike as she had imagined, and her rosy, pouting lips simply did not look as if they belonged on her face.

She dared not approve it, but she did not disapprove either. If Lord Tylar didn't like it, let *him* be the one to say so.

When she said nothing, the slaves went back to the final arrangement of her hair.

Left alone, it was her one beauty, but they were building it into an edifice that would match the dress, and as a result, it looked like a wig made of bleached horsehair. They had piled most of it on the top of her head in stiff curls, coils, and braids, leaving only a few tendrils, stiffened with dressing and trained into wirelike spirals, to trail artificially about her face. Now they were inserting all the bejeweled hair orna-ments her father had dictated; heavy gold and emerald, of course.

If I had been dressing myself—I would have chosen the pale rose silk, with flowers and ribbons, pearls and white gold. Nothing like this. I would fade into the background, but at least I would not look like a clown.

By the time they were done, no one would ever recognize her. Which was just as well. She wouldn't want anyone to recognize her, looking like this.

It wouldn't have been so bad if only Lorryn could be with her. He'd have been able to make her laugh, he'd have helped her to keep her sense of humor about it all, and he would have kept anyone she actually disliked from getting too close. But Lorryn was subject to spells of terrible pain in his head— the one affliction that elves *were* subject to—and he had been overcome by one of those spells just this morning.

It's just as well. I wouldn't even want Lorryn to see me looking like this.

Lorryn lay on his bed, with one eye on the door, one eye on his hard-won book about an ancient and extinct tribe of humans called the Iron People, and one ear cocked for the sound of footsteps. He had carefully positioned himself so that he could drop the book to the floor and fling his arm over his eyes at the slightest sound or movement of the door to his bedroom. Fortunately, Lord Tylar was more likely to come striding into his son's chambers with a fanfare and an entourage than he was to try and catch Lorryn unawares.

He hated having to feign *kryshein*, a dreadful head pain accompanied by disorientation that had no counterpart in any human illness, and was supposedly brought on by overuse of magic. This deception meant he dared not leave his bedroom even after Lord Tylar left for the fete. He never *had* suffered from this particular affliction, though many elves did—it was considered to show either a great deal of ambition or the precocious onset of magical power in a child. Viridina had chosen to have him pretend to *kryshein* attacks long ago, precisely because such attacks were crippling, easy to counterfeit, and impossible to disprove. And because to be afflicted by *kryshein* implied that Lorryn was a powerful mage, Lord Tylar was predictably and perversely proud of the fact that his son suffered from the affliction.

He particularly hated having to feign yet another attack on this occasion. He had wanted to attend the fete—not because he was particularly looking forward to what was going to be a tedious evening at the very best, but because he had not wanted to leave poor little Rena to fend for herself. Lord Tylar would not be bothering himself about her whereabouts and welfare; he would be cultivating Lord Ardeyn's other supporters. Lorryn knew what happened at huge fetes like this one; they were too large to properly supervise, and things happened when people became intoxicated. Rena could find herself being teased or humiliated, made the butt of unpleasant or cruel jokes, or fending off the unwanted advances of half-drunk old reprobates or callow young hotheaded fools. The Ancestors knew *he* had made his share of drunken, unwanted advances when he was younger, before he learned his limits. No *real* harm would come to her, of course; there would be plenty of Lord Ardeyn's sober underlings on the watch for a male trying to carry off an unwilling or inexperienced elven maid. Before anything could *really* happen, one or more of them would move in, separate the gentleman from his quarry, and substitute a human slave-girl, before sending him on to his original destination in the garden or other secluded place. The virtue and presumed chastity of the elven maiden would remain intact. *No one worries about what the slave-girls think about the situation. Poor things.*

No, Rena would not be allowed to come to any physical harm, but she could be hurt or frightened, and he did not want to see either. She was so fragile, so vulnerable.

She'd be all right, even at a wilder affair than this, if she were just a little braver. Ancestors! I wish she'd grown a bit more spine sometimes! She acts as if she just might actually start to assert herself—then she just folds up and does what anyone tells her to do. She wouldn't need me if she'd just learn to stand up for herself!

That was an uncharitable thought, and he felt ashamed of it immediately. After all, when would Rena ever learn to stand up for herself? That was absolutely the very last thing Lord Tylar wanted her to learn. A properly submissive daughter, well bred, well trained, meekly bowing to whatever her father wanted from her—*that* was what Lord Tylar wanted.

And that was what Lord Tylar was likely to get, too. Lady Viridina was already risking her very life for the sake of her son, and she had very little time or energy to spare to worry about her daughter. . . .

A light tap at his door, two knocks, a pause, then three more, made him drop the book and slide off the bed even as Viridina opened the door a crack and slid inside. She was gowned and coiffed for the fete in silver silk and diamonds; she could have been a living statue of crystal, carved by the hand of a master.

"I cannot stay," she said in a low, urgent voice. "I only came to tell you that I overheard Tylar on the teleson, and the guess you made was right."

"So the High Lords have set a trap for any halfbloods among the youngsters attending this fete." He felt his blood run cold at the nearness of his escape. "I wondered, when Tylar gave all those orders about Rena. He could have made her look any way he wished with subtle illusions—unless there was going to be some reason why he dared not."

His mother nodded solemnly. "There is to be an entire gauntlet of illusion-banishing spells in place, cast by the most powerful members of the Council, through which every guest must pass. There is a rumor now that it was Valyn, and not his slave Mero, who was the halfblood."

"As if they couldn't believe that a fullblood would revolt against a mad sadist like Dyran." Lorryn's lip curled with contempt.

But Viridina shook her head. "No. It is just the old men, being afraid, pretending that it was not revolt, but the inherent evil and instability of a halfblood. But now, having decided that there was *one* halfblood among the young lords and el-Lords, there may be more. They are afraid, and acting out of fear."

Lorryn coughed. "They might be afraid, but they are right," he reminded her with gentle irony. "There is at least one halfblood among them."

Viridina swiftly crossed the space between them and placed a finger on his lips before he could say more. "There are ears everywhere," she whispered warningly.

"Not here," he replied, with a certainty she could not share—could not, for she was only elven. *He* was halfblood, and had the magics of both his mother and true father—and his true father had taught him how to use the latter, before Viridina had freed him and sent him away to join the outlaw humans that had escaped their lives of slavery. There was not a single mind in this manor he could not read if he wished—and he *knew* there was no one listening to them.

"I must go soon," she said then, bestowing a faint smile on

him. "I only came to tell you that you were right. And we must walk even more carefully from this moment on. I still do not know how you guessed."

He made no reply to that, only bent to kiss her hand; she turned it and laid it against his cheek for a moment in affection.

He stood up again and began to pace. "When Tylar asked me to help create Rena's ornaments with my magic, I first suspected a trap. Why go to all the effort of making real, solid creations when simple illusions would be just as effective and a great deal easier to wear?"

She nodded, slowly, the crystals woven into her hair sparkling with the movement.

His nerves were not going to be eased by pacing, but at least it gave him some release for his energy. "When I learned from you that Tylar had ordered you to lend Rena some of your maids to enhance her looks with paint and powder, the suspicion deepened into certainty. That was when I *knew*."

"I see!" she exclaimed. "An illusion laid over her features would have been much more effective—and much more flattering than anything those poor clumsy creatures can do with cosmetics. How clever of you to know that!"

He shrugged. "Not clever, simply observant. So I went out of my way to create impossibly ornate jewelry for Rena, of heavy gold filigree and emeralds; not only necklace and rings, but an elaborate belt that reached to the floor, bracelets, and hair ornaments." His constructions would last for three or even four weeks, and exerting himself gave him every excuse to have an attack of *kryshein* as a consequence. Tylar would be able to brag about his son's prowess as a mage, while offering the reason for his absence, and since the trap was supposed to be secret, no one would guess the real reason why he was not at the fete. Only Rena would suffer for this, and only a little.

That did not make him happy—but he had a great deal more to worry about than Rena's welfare. It was beginning to look as if his own secret was in jeopardy.

"He is ridiculously proud of you," she replied, curling her lip a little, the mask of serenity cracking. Then she sighed. "Your true father would be much prouder of you, and with more reason."

He started; Lady Viridina did not often mention his real father. She had conceived him by a human slave, a trusted man who had come with her from her father's estate, when Tylar became increasingly abusive over her failure to conceive at all. The man had been completely devoted to her; what her feelings had been for him, Lorryn did not know and probably would never learn, for the one mind in all of this place he refused to ever try and read was hers. Viridina did not discuss such things with her son, and he would not violate her privacy. All he *did* know was that at some point before she became Tylar's wife, she had disabled Garth's slave-collar, freeing his human magepowers of thought-reading, and that Garth had used those powers to serve and protect her.

She *had* confessed to her son that she had never expected him to live past infancy; everything she had ever heard about halfbloods made her certain he would be weak and sickly, and would die before he reached his second year.

"Do you ever regret—" he began.

"Never," she said flatly. "Never once."

Her powers of magic were at least the equal of Tylar's; they might even have been superior. When Lorryn was born, he already wore the illusion of full elven blood, and she maintained that illusion, day and night, waking and sleeping, until he was old enough and strong enough in his powers to maintain it himself.

Tylar was overjoyed at the strong, healthy son she presented him with—and if she was dismayed by Lorryn's vigor, she was too careful to show it. Ironically, she gave birth the following year to Sheyrena, Tylar's true daughter, who was as fragile in appearance as Lorryn was vigorous. Two children were enough for Tylar, who openly preferred the amorous company of his concubines; he left Viridina alone after that.

"I can never repay what you—" he whispered.

She interrupted him, fiercely. "You are my child," she said, a hint of the fiery will that had fueled the fight now showing in her eyes. "You are *my* child, all mine, not his. There is nothing to repay." The force of her words stopped him dead in his tracks.

He was not sure about that, although she could never have predicted what happened later. Everything would have been fine if events had proceeded normally. Viridina had no trouble holding her illusion on him; *he* would have had no trouble maintaining it. There would have been no need ever to worry that their secret would be discovered.

Except for the Elvenbane.

"I must go," she said then; and turned swiftly, slipping out the door before he could even reply.

He resumed his pacing. *Except for the Elvenbane. One small girl-child. And how much havoc that single child wrought. . . .*

In many ways, that small girl-child had been very good for the House of Treves. If it had not been for her, there would never have been a second Wizard War, and the ranks of the high and securely placed would remain exactly as they had been for the last half-century or more. But there *had been* a second Wizard War, and the ranks of the high were decimated by the failure of battles and policy. Lord Tylar had been waiting, ready to pounce, and pounce, he had.

But the girl had made every elven lord painfully, fearfully aware that the day of the halfbloods was *not* passed, that there had been halfbloods born, smuggled off, and hidden in the wild lands all along. The secret was out, and now, with the wizards out of reach, the elves were assuaging their fear by searching for those halfbloods they *could* punish for merely existing.

In the abstract, of course, he could not blame them. How could any of them feel anything other than fear for people who had not only the elven magics to call on, but the forbidden magics of the human slaves, magics kept in check only by the controlling collars locked around the necks of all slaves as soon as they were old enough to be trained?

In the abstract—well, there was nothing abstract about *his* situation, that was the problem. And it was all the fault of one flame-haired girl.

He could not bring himself to hate her—after all, she probably had as little control over her situation as he had over his—

But I wish she could have appeared in someone else's lifetime. Or at least, I wish she could have appeared after I found some way to dispose of Lord Tylar and was securely Lord Treves myself. . . .

A cold thought, that, but inescapable. He had been forced to watch the humiliation of his mother and sister for far too long. Lord Tylar had never shown him so much as a single instant of affection; he was another prized possession, no more, and no less. But Lord Tylar's cruelty to the possessions he no longer prized was more and more pointed, and he no longer prized Lady Viridina. It had occurred to Lorryn recently that he and Rena were not the only vehicles for alliance-by-marriage. There *was* Lord Tylar himself.

Not while Lady Viridina was alive, of course, but—

But elven women are notoriously fragile, and once Rena is wedded and out of the manor, and I am packed up to one of the liege men for more lessons in the management of an estate, there would be no awkward witnesses.

Except for human slaves, of course, but they were easily silenced.

If this had occurred to Lorryn, it had certainly occurred to Lord Tylar. Lorryn had seen the elven lord eyeing his wife with a light in his eyes that Lorryn did not particularly like, of late. So without saying anything to his mother, he had begun planning ways to turn the tables on her husband, and make him the "disposable" one.

All those plans had been overturned by the advent of the Elvenbane, of course.

He flung himself down on the bed, all interest in his book long lost. Oh, if only she could have appeared some other time!

Well, she had no choice, and neither did he. Now his plans were much different. Now they were concerned with his survival. Somehow he was going to have to negotiate this difficult time, until the older elves lost some of their fear and stopped looking for halfbloods in their own ranks.

His stomach turned over as he thought of the consequences awaiting him if they found him. *Or else—I'm going to have to plan something more basic. How to get away, and where to flee. Considering the number of times I've had to feign illness to avoid exposure lately, maybe I had better begin planning an escape right now, while I still have the leisure to plan it.*

2

THE SLAVES DREW their "mistress" to her feet, and led her over to the floor-to-ceiling mirror to survey their handiwork for herself. Rena stared at the reflection in the mirror and felt her stomach churn with dismay. The effect of hair, gown, jewelry, and cosmetics was just as dreadful as she had imagined.

No, she decided after a moment more of contemplation. *It isn't as bad as I imagined. It's worse.*

Both gowns were of silk, the undergown lighter in color and weight than the overgown. They were supposed to create a flowing line, as if she was a wave upon the sea—curving over her body gently and voluptuously, hinting at what lay beneath without actually revealing anything.

Instead, they hung upon her slight frame, falling straight from her shoulders, hinting at nothing beneath because there was, frankly, nothing there to hint at. Both gowns boasted long trains that were supposed to sweep gracefully behind her, trains that would be pure hell to manage in a crowded room. She kicked at the trains a little, sourly. *All very well if you are someone like my mother, with prestige and presence—or if you're a real beauty, like Katarina an Vittes. People notice not only you, but whether or not you're dragging six ells of fabric behind you, and they take care not to step on it. I'll be lucky if someone doesn't half-disrobe me by treading on my train while I'm walking.*

The sea-green silk of the undergown was plain, decorated only at the hems and cuffs with borders of plain gold, but the silk of the peacock-green overdress was patterned with iridescent emerald threads woven in a motif of moonbirds, the symbol of the House of Treves. If anything, this was worse on her slight body than plain silk would have been, since the pattern had been woven large, and there wasn't a *whole* moonbird visible in the dress until you got to the train. It was supposed to show that she was the pride of her House; instead, it looked rather as if someone had made her dress out of leftover drapery fabric.

Or else people are going to wonder if we've taken to displaying our symbol decapitated, detailed, or dewinged.

The darkness of the color made her pale skin appear even whiter than usual. She *did* look like a corpse. Thanks to her stiff expression, the cosmetics only made her look like a corpse that had been painted for the funeral.

Charming. Absolutely charming. But as long as I don't try to smile, at least I won't look like a clown.

Her hair—no, she didn't want to think about her hair. It was a disaster; an artificial construction cemented over her head, a monument to vanity, an architect's worst nightmare. But from her point of view, it was worse to wear than it was to look at; the emerald and gold ornaments were so weighty that she feared she would have a headache long before the fete was over. An enormous emerald necklace lay heavily on her white throat, and looked *far* too much like a slave-collar for her own comfort; huge bracelets encircled her wrists under the oversleeves, rings weighed down her hands, and a belt that clasped tightly at her waist with a long end that hung down to the ground in front made her feel chained to one place.

I hope no one asks me to dance, I can't move in all of this.

Each of the emeralds was the size of her thumbnail at least, and the gold that anchored them was often in palm-sized plates. The jewels might have been suited to a particularly vain warrior or a very vivid (and strong!) concubine; they certainly were ill suited to *her*.

She sighed and turned away from the mirror. It didn't matter anyway. *She* didn't matter. She was nothing more than a display. The very best thing she could do tonight would be to stay seated somewhere where Lord Ardeyn (or any other would-be suitor) could admire her jewels, her gown, and the power they implied—power that any children she bore would be presumed to inherit. After all, Lorryn had inherited that power, hadn't he?

The maids waited for her to say something, either in praise or blame. She waved a heavy hand at them. "My father will probably be very pleased with you," she told them, unable to offer either on her own behalf. "Myre, please stay; the rest of you may go."

The maids curtsied, with relief evident on every face, and swiftly left the room, leaving only Rena's favorite slave, Myre, behind. The girl was not one of Lord Tylar's former concubines, one of the few who wasn't, and that alone would have endeared her to Rena. Myre had other virtues, however.

There was nothing particularly distinguishing about Myre; she was neither plain nor pretty, tall nor dwarfish, her hair and eyes were an ordinary enough brown. That was the outside, an exterior that Rena now knew was purely protective. That was because Myre was the only one of all her slaves who actually *knew* some of what was going on outside the walls of the estate, although she was very mysterious and elusive about her sources of information. What was the most important, though, was that she was willing to share that knowledge with her mistress. She had begun by calling that news "tales" and "stories," but that particular pretense had been dropped a long time ago.

With the rest of the maids gone, Rena dropped her illusion

(thin as it was) of satisfaction, then chuckled as Myre made a grimace of distaste.

"I know," Rena said to the human. "I know. Dreadful, isn't it?"

"You make me think of a sacrificial virgin from one of the old religions," Myre replied, shaking her head, a sardonic smile on her lips. "Some poor little slip of a thing, all weighed down with the gifts to the gods so that she sinks properly when they push her into the gods' well—brr!"

"Not so much important for herself, but as the bearer of the gifts, yes, I was thinking much the same." Rena sat back down carefully. "Is there any way you can make these things a little more balanced? I feel as if I might fall over at any moment."

"I'll see," Myre responded readily. "You know, I think I might be able to 'lose' some of those horrid hair ornaments. I doubt Lord Tylar will bother to count them. I have never envied you, my lady, but tonight I am very glad that I do not stand in your place. The hair-sculpture must be horrible to wear, and the hair ornaments too heavy to think about." She cocked her head to one side. "Hmm. I believe I can rid you of about half of them and still keep the entire dreadful effect."

"Oh, please," Rena begged shamelessly. "Lorryn made them; they'll go away by themselves in a day or two. And you can tell me news, if you have any."

"Some." The slave carefully removed one of the ornaments, dropped it, and kicked it behind the dressing table. "I've heard that the wizards have found a new stronghold and are settling in it. That is, they've found a place where they can build a stronghold, and they've sent word so that escaping halfbloods can find them there. The dragons are actually building the stronghold for them, or so it is said. I suspect it's true."

"They are?" Rena didn't care about the wizards—but that the dragons were still with them, helping them—"How can a dragon build, though? Wouldn't that be terribly hard to do, with claws and all?"

Myre laughed, and kicked another ornament into a new hiding place. "I thought I'd told you that when I told you about the war! Dragons have magic too, besides the magic of calling lightning; they can shape rock to whatever form they like. It's as easy for them to mold rock as it is for a slave to mold clay into a pot."

Rena saw her own pale green eyes widen as she stared into the mirror. "No, you didn't tell me that—you didn't tell me they had magic. I mean, flying and calling lightning is wonderful enough, but magic of their own—they're like one of the great *dursans* from Evelon!"

Myre shrugged, as if it didn't matter much to her. "Well, I suppose it's a magic that's logical, even necessary, for something that big to have, anyway. Think about it—if you have to live in a cave, wouldn't it be a good thing to have some way to make it more livable?"

The slave disposed of another pair of hair ornaments, then loosened the necklace somewhat as Rena nodded. "I imagine you're right," Rena responded. "It's just that every new thing you tell me about them is more wonderful than the last! Oh, I would give *anything* to see one, even at a distance!"

The slave laughed dryly. "The way things are going, you're likely to get your wish, since they don't seem disposed to hide themselves. They're likely to start flying over the estates someday! You really are attracted to them, though, aren't you?"

Rena just nodded. Lorryn, now—if he were here, she knew what *he* would be asking the girl about. The Elvenbane; he was as obsessed with the halfblood wizard-girl as Rena was with dragons. Never mind that it was forbidden to even mention the name of the Elvenbane to the slaves, and that if they were overheard, the fact he had done so would get *Myre* in serious trouble!

Not that Myre would ever get herself in jeopardy; she's too canny for that. She always made sure that there was no one to overhear any of these conversations. Still, Lorryn took risks *she* never would. . . .

But Rena would rather hear about dragons, a safe enough topic even if there *was* someone to overhear.

"What's a *dursan*, anyway?" Myre asked, as she took a comb and carefully rearranged Rena's hair to disguise the fact that ornaments had been removed. "And what's Evelon?"

"Evelon's where we came from," the girl replied absently, her own thoughts caught up in a vivid image of a dragon sculpting a mountaintop into an image of itself. "I don't remember it, of course, and neither does Lord Tylar, because we were born here, but all of the really old High Lords of the Council do—like Lord Ardeyn's uncle. It's supposed to have been a dangerous place, so dangerous we had to leave or die."

"Dangerous?" Myre persisted, her eyes narrowing. "How?"

Rena shrugged. "Lorryn says it was all our own fault. Every House had at least a dozen feuds on the boil, and they *didn't* fight those feuds with armies of slaves or with gladiators because there aren't any slaves there, there aren't any humans. Houses train their children as assassins or have magic-duels, or create horrible monsters to turn against other Houses, only half the time those monsters get away and become dangerous to everyone. Some of the Houses got their emblems from the monsters they created. The *dursans* are something like a dragon, I suppose; they look like huge lizards, but they don't have wings, they'll eat anything in sight, and they breathe fire. They made dragons too—only the dragons flew away entirely. The *dursans* began to have magic, fascination magic, so the histories say, and that was one reason why they became more dangerous than before.

"Huh." Myre smoothed Rena's hair, but she wore a closed, inward-turning expression. "So was that why you all left this Evelon in the first place?"

"I suppose so. Mostly we left because we could." Rena didn't blame her grandfather for leaving either, if Evelon was as terrible as Viridina had said it was. "Lorryn thinks the Houses that left were probably the weakest, the ones with the least to lose by trying somewhere else. He says that's why there are so many lords here with very little magic."

"Every once in a while your brother makes sense," Myre replied sardonically. "So the weak ones fled and left the field to the strong—who will probably destroy themselves and everything around them as they fight each other. I don't think I would care to live in Evelon either."

"You sound like Lorryn now," Rena observed, with a tiny laugh. "That's the kind of thing he'd say."

"As I said, every once in a while he makes sense." Myre put down the comb and examined her handiwork. "So I take it that's the reason why no High Lord will ever have a direct conflict with another, why it's all done through intrigue and battles with armies of slaves or gladiators?"

Rena nodded. "It's not a law so much as an agreement—in fact, in the old days, when we were first building our estates, the High Lords would all join power so that everything was done quickly. Now, though—" it was her turn to grimace "—well, pigs will don court-gowns and play harps before someone like Lord Syndar would lend his power to help Lord Kylan. I hope that the dragons are better at working together than they are."

"I've been told they are," Myre offered. "I've been told they lend their powers to each other, and that there are never any petty quarrels between them, that only betrayal of the worst kind can force them to become enemies. They say that where the dragons are, there has been peace for thousands of years. That's supposed to be why they helped the halfbloods; the wizards were just trying to live in hiding and it was the lords who attacked them to destroy them. I suppose the dragons must have felt sorry for the halfbloods, and disliked the lords who were trying to hurt them."

"I wish we were like that," Rena sighed, and studied her reflection.

If we were like that, I wouldn't be served upon a platter to make some drooling old dotard a tasty bride, she thought glumly. *If we were like that, I could do what I wanted to do, and Father would leave me alone.*

To do what?

"What do dragons do when they aren't helping the wizards?" she wondered aloud.

"Oh, marvelous things." Myre replied immediately. "Fancy flying, playing games, exploring, using their magic to create beautiful sculptures, telling stories, all kinds of wonderful things. It would take me all day to tell you."

Rena swallowed around the lump in her throat that the vision of such freedom had conjured up. *If only I could run away, somehow, run away to the land where the dragons come from! If only I could go somewhere where I'd never have to obey Father again, where there aren't any rules*—The rules and her father's will weighed her down as truly as the terrible jewels he had created for her weighed her down. How could anyone fly beneath such a weight?

But wishing to run away was as useless as wishing for a dragon to come carry her off; one was as likely as the other. How *could* she run away? She'd never even been off the estate! She had no idea how to fend for herself—which was precisely what she would have to do to keep from being found and brought back before she got more than a foot off the grounds.

Running away was as out of the question as—as pigs donning court-gowns and playing harps!

What was more—she had already drawn these preparations out as long as she dared. Much longer, and her father would come here to find out what the delay was about, and he would not be pleased to find her completely gowned and jeweled, staring into the mirror.

She rose once again, with dignity, if not with happiness. "Don't wait up for me, Myre. Tell one of the others to wait in my rooms until I come home."

That would at least save Myre from the tedium of a long and boring evening alone in these echoing rooms.

"Who?" Myre asked, promptly.

Rena shrugged. "I don't know, and I really don't care. Pick someone you don't like. Tell her I ordered it." No slave would dare direct insolence to the daughter of the House, so if there was anyone giving Myre trouble, this would be a subtle way for the human to have a little revenge. All of the closets and drawers would be mage-locked by Rena's absence, so there would be nothing to do but sit and wait in this eternally peaceful and eternally boring dressing room until Rena returned.

Myre grinned slyly, and bowed—and if there was a touch of mockery in her bow, Rena was not going to say a word about it. Without waiting for an answer, she turned and waved her hand at the door, which opened at her signal, and stepped through it into the hallway of pink marble.

Like her rooms, the hallway had been created by the previous owner of this estate, a High Lord with *far* more power than Lord Tylar had. Every room had doors that answered only to the signals of those with elven blood, or power-curtains that would only pass those who were keyed to them. Sourceless lighting illuminated the entire manor, until and unless someone with elven blood wished a room in darkness, so there were no windows in this place, not even a skylight. Slaves lived and died here without ever seeing the sun once they were brought from the pens to be trained.

Some aspects of the manor were still as they had been when the original owner died; Lord Tylar did not have enough magic to change them. That, Rena reflected, was probably a good thing. She had visited other manors where one never knew what was going to lie just outside a door—sometimes it might be a hallway, sometimes a ballroom, sometimes a precipice. Not a *real* precipice, of course, but the illusion of one was quite enough to frighten Rena out of her wits for a moment or two—which had been the whole point of the so-called joke.

No, this was a perfectly ordinary pink marble hallway, lined with alabaster urns, which led to an ordinary pink marble staircase, which descended in a gentle curve to the next floor. Her own escort of human guards fell in behind her as she passed them just before she got to the landing of the staircase, moving silently. And hopefully Lord Tylar and Lady Viridina would be waiting for her at the foot of it, having *just* arrived there from their own preparations. Rena had been counting on her father's vanity to keep him at his preening—

She paused at the head of the stairs and took a deep, steadying breath. *Head high. Walk slowly. Try to remember that stupid train; try to forget about the stupid escort. Pause between each step. . . .*

She took each stair of the curving staircase carefully, and stopped at the halfway point to listen to the voices ahead of her. Lord Tylar was holding forth on something, but he sounded pompous, not irritated, which meant she wasn't late.

Thank goodness for small favors.

She took the rest of the stairs at the same deliberate pace, knowing that if she rushed and looked the least bit undignified, Lord Tylar would be annoyed with her. He was going to have enough to be annoyed with her about before the evening was over; best not to give him more than she could manage.

He *was* watching for her; her heart sank as she saw him turn toward the staircase as soon as she came into sight, and examine her every move with a critical eye. Her stomach tightened and she found it hard to take those deep, serene breaths.

He's going to hate the dress, the hair, the cosmetics . . . . he's going to hate how I'm walking. . . . It was an automatic reaction, one she had every time she had to confront him. How could she help it? All he ever invoked in her was dread.

He was a handsome man, even by elven standards, but even by those standards his expression and bearing were chill and detached. He stood much taller than Viridina and his daughter, by a head-and-a-half. His pale gold hair was worn as his grandfather had worn *his*, as if to invoke the memory of that formidable man; cut unfashionably short, and without the usual diadem or fillet that current mode dictated. His long, chiseled face bore no signs of emotion whatsoever, but Rena knew him well enough to be aware that the slight narrowing of his brilliant green eyes meant he was looking for faults to criticize.

He and Lady Viridina were dressed in the same colors—or rather, lack of them—of ice-white and gold. *His* costume hinted at armor without actually *being* armor; hers was a more elaborate version of the same gown Rena wore. On Lady Viridina, however, the gown of pearly-white silk with iridescent moonbirds looked beautiful. The only touch of color that either of them wore was in the emeralds and beryls of their jewels; again, the Lady's jewels were copies of Rena's, but she carried them as if she did not notice their weight in the slightest. Lord Tylar's jewels were simpler and fewer; belt, a single ring, a single armband, and a torque about his neck.

Rena paused on the last stair to wait, trembling inside, for her father to speak.

Silence stretched the moment into an eternity, as she strove to keep her trembling invisible.

"Good," he said, finally, with grudging approval. "You are actually presentable."

She kept her relief as invisible as her trembling, and took the last few steps across the marble between them. "Thank you, my Lord Father," she whispered. She hadn't *meant* to whisper, but somehow she couldn't raise her voice any further than that.

"Well, let's not stand here all night." He turned before he even finished the sentence, and strode off down yet another pink marble hallway, this time heading for his study and the Transportation Portal in it.

He could never have mustered the magic for a direct Portal to the Council Hall, but one had come with the manor. The Treves Portal would take them to the Council Hall, and from there they would use the Hernalth Portal to the estate, permitted to pass there by the magic signet impressed into the invitation. Only those who had access to such Portals would be able to take such a direct and immediate route to the fete—the ones who did not would be forced to take tedious journeys across country until they reached the estate the hard way. It was a measure of the power the House of Hernalth held that there were plenty of elven lords praying for the opportunity to make such a journey.

The ring on Rena's right index finger was *not* one of

Lorryn's creations, but a simple signet, with a moonbird carved into the beryl (not an emerald) held in the bezel. That would be her key to the Portal that would allow her to return home; without it, she would be stuck in the Council Hall until someone came to get her. While emeralds were prized for their beauty and sought after by the human slaves permitted jewels, it was the more common beryl that was truly priceless to the elven lords, for only beryls could take and hold magic power, or be used as the containers for spells. Women wore emeralds, useless, lovely emeralds. *Men* bore beryls, as the outward signature of their power.

Rena trailed along behind her father, careful not to step on the train of her mother's gown, with the guards following in her wake.

The door opened as Lord Tylar approached, and the little parade massed through it into the room beyond. There wasn't much to mark the room that her father called his "study" as anything of the kind; it really held nothing but a white marble desk and a couple of chairs—no books, certainly no papers; he left all of the tedious business of dealing with accounts and the like to his supervisors and underlings. The pink marble of the floor of the hall gave way here to soft, thick carpets of heathered gray, and the pink marble of the walls to some unidentifiable substance the pale gray of rain clouds. There were two doors to this room, both of a darker gray than the walls; the one they used to enter, and the one that stood directly across from it—but the second was no door at all, but the Portal.

Lord Tylar stopped in front of the Portal, his hand on the latch, and turned back to frown at his daughter. Rena shrank into herself a little, involuntarily.

"Hold your head up," he reminded her sharply. "And smile."

Without waiting to see if she followed his orders, he opened the door and stepped through it. He did not hesitate a moment—but then, he was used to Portals by now.

The doorway held only darkness, and it was as if he had been devoured by that darkness the moment he stepped across the threshold. Rena had never actually used this or any other Portal before, although Lorryn. who had, told her it was nothing to be afraid of. Still, something inside her quailed before the lightless *emptiness* of it, and she would have stepped back except for the presence of the guards behind her—

—*who are probably there to make sure I don't turn and bolt back to my room!*

Lady Viridina seemed oblivious to her daughter's fear; she didn't even hesitate, simply followed her husband's lead, stooped and gathered her train up gracefully, and stepped across the threshold into nothingness.

Rena froze.

One of the guards cleared his throat ostentatiously. She started, and turned to look at him, knowing her eyes were probably as wide and frightened as a rabbit's.

"If my lady would please to follow the Lady Viridina?" he said, in a voice harsh with many years of shouting orders. His bland but implacable expression left no doubt in her mind that he had been ordered to pick her up and *carry* her across if she balked.

That indignity, at least, she would spare herself. She bent as her mother had, though with none of Viridina's grace, picked up the end of her train in hands that were damp with sweat, and crushed the silk to her meager chest. Then, with her eyes shut firmly, so she would not have to *see* what she stepped into, she crossed the threshold.

Myre took a great deal of satisfaction in delivering Rena's orders to Tanhya Leis, a *particularly* nasty piece of blond work that Myre had been longing to get stirred into mischief for some time now.

Mischief, after all, was a time-honored draconid tradition, and this was one tradition Myre saw no reason to abandon.

Tanhya had been banished from the harem for deliberate sabotage, and now was trying to make everyone else's life miserable, engaging in histrionics and trickery in an effort to regain the comforts of her "rightful" place. She wouldn't get it, of course; she was far too common for the tastes of Lord

Tylar and she probably would have been disposed of soon anyway, but nothing would convince her otherwise. In fact, she was quite certain the place of Chief Concubine (now occupied by a slim and dignified brunette) was hers by *right*. Where she got that particular illusion, Myre had no idea—but forcing her to spend her evening cooling her heels in Lady Sheyrena's dressing room should give her *plenty* leisure to nurse her grievances. With any luck, she'd have come up with some plan or other to rid herself of the obstacles in her path that would be even more entertaining than her last attempt at eliminating Keri Eisa—the one that had gotten her banished in the first place.

Really, Myre chuckled to herself, as she watched Tanhya returning to the dressing chamber, her back stiff with anger, *how dense can even a two-legger be? You'd think she'd have known that stupid cook's helper of hers would be caught. And that he'd talk once he was caught. I don't care how good you are in bed, that's not going to keep your paramour from telling everything he knows when his tail is in the fire? After all, it was trying to seduce one of the guards into spoiling Keri's looks and making it look like an accident that got her sent down here in the first place.*

One more incident, and Tanhya would probably find herself sent to the breeding pens. No elven lord would ever take the quarrels between the women in his harem seriously enough to invoke the ultimate punishment on the perpetrators—but no elven lord would ever allow someone like Tanhya to inconvenience him, either. And right now, being without Keri would be a serious inconvenience for Lord Tylar.

This was all the more amusing to Myre because Keri's rise in the harem was due to her *own* interference. Keri had been simply very attractive—until Myre slipped into the harem one night, and did a little careful rearrangement of her face. From sculpting stone it was a simple matter to move to sculpting flesh, and anyone who knew how to shape-change would find it very easy to make that transition if the power was there in the first place. Next morning, Lord Tylar found himself possessed of a real beauty, and Keri's rise from nothing to Chief Concubine had upset the established order of the harem. *That* had put the idea in Tanhya's head that *she* could become Chief Concubine as easily as Keri, and the fight was on.

Strangely enough, it never occurs to the elven lords that the same powers their women use to sculpt flowers could be used to make beauties of their human slaves.

That had been very early in the game, when Myre had first insinuated herself into this particular household as only a dragon could—shape-shifted into the form of a human slave. Her only thought at the time had been to see how much she could learn, and how much trouble she could cause for the elves. She hadn't picked this House for any particular reason, other than the fact that Lord Tylar's overseers were not terribly careful about keeping track of ordinary female house-slaves.

The elder dragons would have a fit if they knew. She was not supposed to be here at all, in fact, and certainly not in the form of a human.

She was *supposed* to be shape-shifted among the wild alicorn herds; that was what the elder dragons of the Lair thought she was doing. They'd have had seizures if they knew where she really was.

Since the second Wizard War, the young dragons of the Kin—those that had not deserted the Lairs of the Kin to help the halfbloods—had orders that were not to be violated. *Stay away from the elves.* It was bad enough, so the elders thought, that the elves knew that dragons existed. It would be worse, much worse, if the elves had any idea of their shape-shifting abilities, or how easily and thoroughly their very homes could be invaded. Only the oldest and most clever of the dragons would be permitted to walk in shifted form among the elves—only those with experience in keeping themselves safe. And only for the purpose of gathering information—there would be *no* interference in the lives of human slaves or of elves.

Hah. As if alicorns had anything worth learning about.

Like Tanhya; pretty outside, crazy inside, and just about as much sense. And speaking of Tanhya—

She has her little circle of supporters, and one of them is our supervisor. If I don't want to end up doing some mindless chore until bedtime, I'd better get out of the way before Maryan finds out who delivered the bad news to Tanhya.

The best, and most entertaining, place to "get out of the way," as Myre knew from long experience, was the roof. Not that a human slave had any business being on the roof, but she wouldn't be a human slave once she got up there.

She went up two staircases and a ladder, and out the roof-top hatch, and a moment later there was one more ornamental moonbird-rainspout up on the roof than there had been before. From this vantage, Myre had an unobstructed view of the grounds of the rear of the manor—the place where things actually happened, that is. Not the pleasure garden, but the kitchen garden, the stables, the beginning of the slave quarters. With all the masters gone but Lorryn, the only activity would be among the slaves.

She watched the slaves scurrying about their business with avidity; after having *been* one, she had quite a few motions about how the Kin could use the natural abilities of humans. It would be very pleasant to have someone around to oil her skin and groom her, for instance—to heat water for a really *good* hot bath instead of making do with the odd hot spring—to hunt her kills for her and skin and prepare them in nice, bite-sized chunks—to keep her lair swept and clear of vermin.

The old ones are crazed, cowards, or both, she thought resentfully. *Just because the elves know we exist, that doesn't mean they have a clue about what we can do! They* can't *detect us when we're shape-changed among them, our magic isn't an illusion that can be broken, and unless they somehow get the idea that we shift mass into the Out, they'll never know what to look for!* Her thoughts ran down old, well-worn paths of discontent and rebellion. *With proper manipulation, the Kin could easily wear down both sides of this conflict, halfbloods and elves alike, until they were both so worn out with the struggle that we could take over both sides at once. Then we would be the ones to dictate terms and peace, and the humans would probably be so grateful that they would serve us better than slaves!*

It was a glorious thought, ripe with a hundred possibilities, all of them currently blocked by the elders' stubborn refusal to see any other path but that of caution.

Myre was not alone in her restlessness by any means; she had her own coterie of followers among the younger dragons, who chafed at the restrictions that the elders placed them under. *They* wanted the right to range freely in any shape they chose, and there were at least one or two who found the idea of having two-legger servants as pleasing as Myre did. All of them had decided that the elders were too conservative and needed to be replaced in their roles as leaders of Lair and Kin.

There was only one little problem with this.

The older a dragon became, the more powerful he grew. A dragon never really stopped growing, and with age came physical strength, skill in magic, and power of will. No one dragon, no *group* of dragons Myre's age, could ever hope to defeat an elder.

No group of dragons, maybe. If someone had looked up from the garden at that moment, he would have seen the waterspout gape its beak in something like a smile. *But it doesn't have to be a dragon, does it?*

The elders feared elves and wizards alike, and with good reason. Small and physically weaker than dragons, their magics were nevertheless quite formidable, even by draconic standards. One against one, and the dragon would win—but elves and halfbloods would never fight a dragon in a single combat.

I've seen what they can do, elves and halfbloods alike. If I could get a halfblood on my side, and trick it into helping me get rid of the older dragons, I could pack the Council with my friends. There's a lot of discontent among all of the Kin, not just the ones in my band. They don't see any reason why we need to redouble our efforts to keep in hiding now

*that we aren't a secret anymore. I don't even have to do
much, just weaken the elders, cloud their minds or something,
and take over quietly and easily. By the time they figure out
what's happening, it will be too late to stop me.*

The only dragons who *would* have opposed her were no
longer with the Kin, anyway.

But that particular observation brought her no joy, only a
sour feeling in the back of her mind. *Those* dragons—led by
her own mother, who *should* have been supporting Myre instead of agonizing over the wayward behavior of Myre's
brother Keman—were part and parcel of the cause of the very
restrictions Myre now suffered under!

*If Mother hadn't brought that damned halfblood cub
home—or if someone had just had the decency to get rid of
it instead of letting Keman make a pet out of it—none of this
would have happened.*

Now the waterspout snarled, silently.

That halfblood "cub" had grown up to absorb the attentions that Myre's mother, Alara, *should* have devoted to Myre
herself, right from the very beginning! It was all just one
more example of how everything that Keman did only caused
Alara to spoil and cosset him more, and everything Myre did
was somehow wrong. Even when the cub had *finally* over-
stepped even the generous bounds Alara's indulgence set, and
attacked Myre's best friend, it wasn't killed as it should have
been, it was only sent out into the wilderness to fend for itself. Then what did Keman do but follow it—

*And what did Mother do? Not abandon the brat to his own
devices, she followed* him! *Then, when he defies the entire
Lair and then runs away, she keeps the rest from going after
him to punish him the way he should have been in the first
place!*

Myre seethed at the memories of how Alara had spoiled
Keman and ignored her; her stomach burned with anger and
her talons clenched so hard on the stone of the roof-edge that
it began to chip beneath them. Keman, always Keman!

And even when the brat came back and Myre *finally* put
him in his place, defeating him in single combat, did Alara at

last come to realize which of her two offspring was really the superior? No! Instead, she and half of the elders went kiting off after precious little Keman, and in the process of helping protect him and his pets, revealed the existence of dragons to the very creatures they had been trying to avoid for centuries!

It was enough to make a sensible dragon want to rend things.

Anger *was* making her lose control over her shape, and with difficulty, she calmed herself down. After all, it wasn't as if she was all alone. Lori was *twice* the mother Alara had been to her. Lori thought that Myre was absolutely right in everything she had said and done—and Lori was supporting Myre in her bid to become the Lair's new shaman.

Not that Mother ever gave me one iota of training. Oh no, that was all for dear Keman and his pet!

And after all, at least now that everything was turned so upside down, there were more opportunities than ever before for an ambitious dragon to gain power in the Lair. You just had to be clever about it.

And once I've got the Lair under my talons—if Keman's very lucky, I might leave him and his pets alone. For a while.

Once she had a halfblood of her very own, it would only be a matter of time before she had the Lair. Once she had the Lair and the rest of the Kin saw how successful she was, it wouldn't take long before other Lairs followed her as leader.

Then I'll have them all, elves, halfbloods . . . and Keman and his pets. Not even Mother or Father Dragon will be able to stop me.

She had come here in the first place simply out of a spirit of rebellion, but once she actually came to realize what the situation was in the House of Treves, this great plan all fell into place for her. That was why she stayed here, cultivating Sheyrena. She knew something that poor, pathetic little Sheyrena didn't.

Rena's brother, Lorryn, was a halfblood. He had no contact with the other wizards—in fact, until the Elvenbane showed up—

Elvenbane. Pah. Trust that little nuisance Shana to come

up with a name like that for herself. Lashana wasn't good enough for her, oh no, she has to have a name like some creature out of a legend.

—he hadn't even known there *were* any other halfbloods in existence. He had no way of getting to the new Citadel now even if he had contact with them; he was too busy trying to keep from being caught.

But the odds against him were lengthening. Myre knew, even if he didn't, that the High Lords' Council had declared that all male elves of a certain age were to be tested with illusion-breaking spells. Paranoia ran high among them at the moment, especially after Myre had seen to it that a particular rumor started.

That was a good touch, planting the story that Shana's ally Valyn was really a halfblood. If Dyran, who supposedly hated the halfblood worse than anyone, could have had a halfblood heir, where else might halfbloods be lurking?

Lorryn knew that something was up, though; he'd severely curtailed his visits to his friends, and had stopped attending official gatherings altogether. Myre had a pretty good idea that the fete this evening was going to be one of those times and places where the young males came under magical scrutiny. If Lorryn also knew or guessed this, it was probably the reason why he had an attack of *kryshein* at the very last minute.

Myre was calm again, contemplating the jaws of the trap that were closing around Lorryn with satisfaction. *He can't hide forever. Sooner or later, the High Lords are going to send someone to test him in person, here, and it will all be over for him. And I will be there to play savior.*

She had been filling Rena's head with stories about the dragons, as well as the wizards, painting idyllic pictures of life in the Lairs and in the new Citadel. Those stories were surely getting back to Lorryn. When the jaws of the trap closed, she would be there in the very nick of time, revealing—what?

I think I'll keep the fact that I'm a dragon to myself for a while, at least until I have him safely into the wilderness—

unless I need to shape-change in order to actually get him out of here. Right now, Rena has every reason to trust me. She'll probably believe me if I say I'm an agent of the wizards, when I offer to rescue Lorryn.

Lorryn would have no reason not to trust her, after all. Myre could spirit the halfblood out, get him into the desert, and *then* start working on him, once he was weakened by thirst and hunger. He'd be easy to manipulate.

I'll tell him that there are dragons who are against helping the halfbloods, and that I'm trying to get them out of power. It's even true. Once I have his help, I can depose the elders. Then I'll either have figured out how to keep him under control, or I'll just get rid of him.

The sun descended slowly, setting the thin clouds on the horizon aflame, as Myre contemplated her eventual triumph.

The first Portal transition left Rena shaking; the second left her partly stunned with confusion. She followed in her father's wake with her mind still spinning, too numb to really take much in. The reception chamber was about the size of her father's study; in fact, in other circumstances it might *be* Lord Ardeyn's study. They were ushered out immediately and into a dimly lit hallway, so she didn't get a good look at the room. She *did* notice an odd little tingling of magic along her skin as she passed the door, as if someone had cast a spell on her, but it didn't seem to mean anything and she dismissed it from her thoughts.

She hardly noticed her surroundings at first—the corridor her father led her through was very dark, which seemed odd, but that might just have been for effect. It was only when her foot brushed against something soft, something that hopped away, that she looked up, startled, and realized that the "corridor" she was walking through was formed by the trunks and interlaced branches of enormous trees, that the "carpet" beneath her feet was a thick, cushiony moss, and that the "room" they were entering was a huge glade, a sylvan paradise, a scene out of the days before the first Wizard War.

A perfect illusion of an evening sky, complete with full

moon and sparkling stars, stretched overhead. Rena only knew it was an illusion because the stars were scattered randomly across the heavens, and not set in the constellations she knew from her wanderings with Lorryn. Where the walls of the ballroom would have been, there were only tall trees, straight and perfect, their boughs holding the round globes of glass in which magically created, multihued light was held captive. The springy floor boasted flat white flowers, spread out on the surface of the moss, which opened their five moon-round petals to the false moon above and gave forth an intoxicating perfume when they were trod upon.

Lord Tylar and Lady Viridina were already lost in the crowd. Rena had the presence of mind to step aside into the shelter of the trees before stopping to gawk. She had never seen illusion or created-magic on a scale like this before in her life! Truly, Lord Ardeyn had spared no expense; a spectacle like this must have taken the talents of a dozen mages the equal of Lorryn, perhaps more!

An odd chirruping sound overhead made her jump; she looked up, and met the bright, shining eyes of a bird with plumage as fantastic as anything she had ever created in her garden. It chirped at her again, and before she could even think to call it to her hand, it flew down to her shoulder, and from there, to the hand she held automatically outstretched. She began to pet it, a smile coming to her lips without an effort. It had a long, sweeping tail, a high, upraised crest, and pale pink feathers as soft as thistledown. It leaned into her caress and closed its eyes with pleasure, crooning musically to itself.

A moment later, a young doe stepped out of the shadows and begged for a caress of its own. As Rena continued to look around, she spotted more tamed birds and animals wandering among the guests—mostly being ignored, which was a pity, for they seemed to crave attention and petting.

There must be a spell on them to keep them away from the refreshments, and to keep them from soiling someone's clothing, she thought, practicality intruding on the romance. And sure enough, just as that occurred to her, the bird took off and sought a perch a little distance away, making a discreet deposit before returning to her hand.

This was *exactly* the kind of fete Rena had read about, from the old days, when the elven lords were secure in their power and before they had begun to feud among themselves again. Was Lord Ardeyn trying to imply something by this?

Oh, probably not; he's probably just trying to impress the High Lords who remember what the old days were like.

"Would my lady care for wine?"

Rena controlled herself this time, and did not jump or let out a squeak when the voice came from behind her. The doe scampered away and the bird took off for the branches as she turned, to find herself confronted by a creature that did not in the least resemble the human slave she had expected.

Instead, the servant politely offering a tray of exquisitely fluted crystal goblets had the head of a stork, feather-covered hands and arms, and two definite claws instead of feet. But the feathers were brilliant blue and scarlet, the head boasted a crest never worn by any stork Rena had ever seen, and the body beneath the tunic in Hernalth colors seemed human enough.

"Yes," she said, as the bird-man cocked his head to one side and examined her with one bright eye. "I believe I would. Thank you."

The bird-man extended the tray, gracefully, and stalked, like a stork wading through water, off toward another guest. Rena blinked and watched him go.

After a moment, it occurred to her that her mouth felt terribly dry, and she sipped her wine. It didn't taste like anything she had ever drunk before, but that was no surprise; elven feasts and fetes were full of these little subtleties. The wine was faintly sweet, with a perfume like the flowers; it tingled on the tongue, and left a crisp, refreshing aftertaste behind.

As her eyes became accustomed to the light, and she began to distinguish the servers from the guests, it seemed that there *were* no openly human servants here tonight. They had all been transformed by illusion into half-bird or half-animal creatures. Or even half-insect; she caught sight of one with huge, faceted eyes, begemmed antennae, and gently waving butterfly wings. It seemed that Lord Ardeyn *was* making a deliberate attempt to conjure up the glory days of conquest, when human slaves were never allowed into the presence of their masters without some illusion or disguise to cloak their nature.

As long as she had the wineglass in her hand, none of the tamed birds or animals would approach her; when she gave the empty glass to another half-bird servant, a fox came out of the trees and rubbed against her legs like a cat. She bent down to pet it, and it arched its back against her outstretched hand.

She would have been perfectly happy to stay at the edge of the "woods" and play with the animals—

But if Father finds me here, instead of out there, he'll be angry with me.

Glumly she accepted another glass of wine, and tossed it off without pausing to admire the taste, hoping to drink down some courage with the sparkling vintage. Then, with much reluctance, she made her way toward the center of the glade, working her way through the strolling guests in their rainbow-hued costumes with some difficulty. No one seemed to even notice she was there; she might just as well have been one of the servants.

There was a cluster of multicolored lights there, illuminating a small number of musicians and a group of people whose understated elegance told her without words that they were *very* important indeed. Only a person of supreme importance could afford to look unimportant at a gathering like this one.

Lord Tylar was among them, managing to look dignified, although Rena knew from his very faint frown that he was vexed about something. *Maybe he's annoyed that he overdressed?* Whatever it was, the frown did not clear away when she appeared, standing uncertainly just within his line of sight, so it was either something she had nothing to do with, or she *was* the cause and her mere appearance had not set things straight.

Whatever it was that had brought that frown to his face, if it was her fault, she would probably find out about it when they arrived home—unless she did something else that was worse between then and now.

He gestured to her abruptly, and she managed to make her way through the crush to his side, still, as far as she could tell, without anyone noticing that she was there.

He took her arm as soon as she was near enough, and pulled her through a gap between two of the other guests. She found herself standing beside him, and facing two men, one young, one very old—she knew that the second was *very* old because he actually showed the signs of age. No elven lord ever did that until he was near his own end. No matter what the humans were led to believe, elves were not immortal—though to short-lived humans, they probably seemed that way. Both men were engrossed in conversation with three ladies, one of them the vivacious Katarina an Vittes, who was smiling raptly up into the younger man's face.

"Lord Ardeyn, Lord Edres, may I present my daughter, Sheyrena?" Lord Tylar said into the first break in the conversation.

The older man smiled into her eyes; the younger bowed over her hand without looking at her at all. Lord Ardeyn's attention was fixed entirely on Katarina to the point of ignoring everything else—not that Rena could blame him. Why would anyone even look at *her*, when Katarina was in the same room?

"Charmed," Lord Ardeyn said absently, then resumed his conversation with Katarina, who had no need of cosmetics or jewels to enhance *her* beauty.

"I'm very pleased to make your acquaintance, my dear," Lord Edres said, taking her hand as quickly as Lord Ardeyn had dropped it. The wrinkles around his eyes deepened as he smiled at her. "I hope you will enjoy our little fete." He actually *kissed* her hand, as Rena blushed with confusion, then released it and turned to her father.

"You have a most charming child, Tylar," the old man said, transferring his smile from the daughter to the father. "Sweet, modest, fresh and innocent. I am sure she will make a good match for you."

That was clearly a dismissal, and Lord Tylar was not too dense to know it.

"That is my hope, my lord," Lord Tylar replied, and with a tug on Rena's arm, took her out of the circle of Ardeyn's intimates.

She cringed inside, waiting to hear his immediate censure, but to her immense relief, Lord Tylar was not ready to take her head off for not captivating the guest of honor.

"That went better than I expected," he said quietly, as he continued to draw her along to some new destination. Fortunately for her neck, *he* was important enough that people noticed her trailing train, and did not step on it. "Lord Edres seems to like you. I suppose you must remind him of his daughter."

Oh, charming, I remind him of a half-wit, who can't even dress herself without help.

"I didn't really hope that Ardeyn would pay you any attention; it seems that other girl was one of the first to arrive, and he hasn't left her side all evening." Lord Tylar made a sound that for any other man might have been taken as a small sigh of regret. "Well, I can't fault his taste. You're hardly any competition for *that* beauty."

Even though she had thought that herself, it hurt to hear it from her father. Now she blushed again, but this time with shame.

"Never mind, there are plenty of other young lords here, and I haven't seen one of them that would make a bad alliance." He stopped, and gave her a brusque push in the direction of another group, this time of dancers. "Go on, get over there, let yourself be seen, talk to people. You know what you have to do, or you should by now."

With those gentle words, he left her, striding purposefully after another knot of men with that indefinable air of importance about them, leaving her standing stupidly at the edge of the group of dancers.

This time someone *did* step on her train. Fortunately, she wasn't moving.

"Oh, bother, I've gone and done something stupid again!" the young man said, a little thickly, and she immediately suspected he'd been drinking too much. He managed to get himself off the train without tangling his feet in it, and turned toward her, giving her a better look at him.

He wasn't very handsome, and his eyes had the sort of vagueness about them that she tended to associate with too much to drink.

In other words—he's the same version of Lord Ardeyn that I am of Katarina. A bad, blurred copy, and rather flawed.

"Excuse me awfully, would you? Terribly sorry and all that. I'm a clumsy brute, or so they all keep telling me." He laughed a little, a high titter, and she realized at that moment that it wasn't the wine that was making him silly—he was that way all on his own.

Correction. On his copy of Lord Ardeyn, they forgot to pour in the brains as well.

"I don't suppose you'd care to have a dance with a clumsy brute now, would you?" he asked hopefully, with another titter for his own "cleverness." "Perhaps if you'd loop up that tail thing, I wouldn't get tangled up in it again, and we could have a pleasant turn or two around the floor, eh?" He stared at her hopefully, and added, "They say I'm a silly ass, but they all admit I'm a good dancer."

Under other circumstances, she might have declined his awkward invitation, with an awkward refusal of her own. But she felt rather sorry for him—here he was, quite probably dragged here by *his* father as she had been dragged by hers, and for the same reason. He was supposed to be making the acquaintance of eligible females with good alliance potential.

In fact, it has to be harder for him! I just have to stand here, properly modest, and hope someone notices me. He has to make advances.

So she smiled kindly at him, and his dull eyes lit up with pathetic cheer as she nodded.

He must have been turned down an awful lot this evening to be so happy to dance with me. I'm not exactly a prize beauty.

His name, it transpired, was V'keln Gildor er-Lord Kyndreth; scion of one of the older and more powerful Houses. And he was probably quite a disappointment to his noble High Lord father. Everything he said to her about his "lord father" indicated that the patriarch of the family had more than once wished there were some way he could prove poor Gildor was someone else's offspring. She felt so sorry for him that she even danced with him again, several times, and let him bring her wine and a few refreshments.

He wasn't a really good dancer, although he wasn't a bad one, either. "Passable"; that was what her own dancing master would have called him. He didn't know anything but the most old-fashioned of dances, either, which left them standing on the sidelines watching, more often than not. He tried to make clever conversation, but he was, unfortunately, just as dull and stupid as she had feared he was. Still, he was company of a sort, and he seemed to like the tame animals— though he kept talking about how exciting it would be to hunt them instead of petting them. And as long as she was with a male, she was obeying Lord Tylar's orders, and he certainly couldn't take exception to *that*.

Finally, though, he spotted an older man making his way purposefully toward them, and said, with a trace of apprehension, "Oh, curse it. There's my lord father, and it looks as if he wants me. It's been grand—"

And he was off like a called dog, bumbling his way through the crowd as if summoned to his father's side by a whistle, without another word to her.

She sighed, and worked her way back through a thin crowd of onlookers toward the edge of the illusory "forest." Evidently her lack of charms—or perhaps, lack of status—was noticeable even to a dolt like Gildor. He hadn't even offered to introduce her to his father, which probably meant he didn't think she was worth introducing to him.

Well, the rabbits and birds didn't care if she looked like a wax doll in an absurd costume—and while she stood here, in the shadows of the overhanging boughs, there wasn't anyone treading on her train.

If this had been some other occasion, she might even have managed to enjoy herself. The birds and animals were very sweet. The expected headache did not manifest itself, due either to Myre's careful work with her hairdressing, or to the rather excessive amounts of wine she'd been drinking.

In fact, she felt very flushed, and not entirely steady, now that she came to think about it. Maybe all that wine had been a mistake.

I'm not used to drinking this much, but Gildor kept pressing wine on me. Rather desperately, actually. I think perhaps he'd been told to make sure whatever lady he was with always had a glass of wine in her hand when she wasn't dancing. That was probably a good idea, really; if he made sure his partners were tipsy enough, they might not notice he was such a dolt. Anything seems amusing when you're intoxicated.

She thought seriously about asking one of the servants to find something for her to sit on, and was just at the point of intercepting one, when her own father came striding through the crowd, clearly looking for *her.*

He spotted her, too, as the animals scattered into hiding, perhaps sensing her surge of apprehension. He made straight for her with an air of determination, as the crowd of young on-lookers parted respectfully for him.

He took her arm again, and this time she was grateful for his support and did not resist at all as he pulled her along, back toward the entrance to the ballroom-cum-glade.

"Are we leaving, Father?" she asked, hopefully.

He didn't notice the hope in her voice. "I won't be getting any more business done tonight," he said shortly. "And the wine's flowing a bit too freely for my liking. It's time we all went home."

Has he noticed that I'm tipsy? she thought, panic making her go cold.

"Ardeyn has some fairly wild friends—he's in thick with Lady Triana's crowd—and I don't want you around them if they start to get rowdy," he continued. "I've heard tales of *that* one—well, never mind. He'll be safe enough, shortly. The match with the House of Vittes is all but confirmed; I expect there'll be an announcement tomorrow."

Why am I not surprised?

She wondered if she ought to make some kind of comment, but he didn't seem to expect one.

"It's not the best match—*you* would be better, insofar as inherited power would go—but it's satisfactory, and the old man seems bent on indulging the boy by letting him make his own choice." The tone of his voice said what his words did not: *I'd never allow* my *son to be spoiled in such a fashion.*

"Yes, sir," she said automatically. He hardly noticed.

"Viridina has already gone ahead; I was just looking for you." Finally, as they broke through the edge of the crowd and entered the deserted corridor, he turned to look at her. "Did you do as I told you? Did you make yourself agreeable to some of the young men?"

Now she was more than grateful to Gildor the Dolt, and not just for his company; he had made it possible for her to tell the truth to her father.

"Yes, sir," she said, earnestly. "I was even asked to dance several times."

Lord Tylar did not smile, but there was some grudging approval in his nod. "Good."

That was the last thing he said to her; he simply towed her along like so much baggage, through the first Portal, across the floor of the Council Hall, and through the second. Once on the other side of the two Portals and back in the pink-marble hall of his own manor, he abandoned her, taking her escort of guards with him, and leaving her to make her own exhausted way back to her rooms and the sullen ministrations of the blond slave waiting there for her. Whether it was the wine or her own exhaustion, she hardly noticed the girl's surly manner; it barely intruded on her dazed thoughts.

And when her head touched the downy pillow of her own bed, she fell asleep immediately, and did not dream at all.

3

RENA WOKE BY herself, which was unusual; morning generally brought three slaves to wake her early, on her father's standing orders. He felt that no girl should be allowed to lie abed much past dawn; he said such practices encouraged indolence. She had no idea why he should feel that way—how could she or her mother possibly be *more* idle than they already were?

But idleness was not indolence, nor was it laziness. Being forced to sit with folded hands did not mean they were indulging themselves.

Probably it was just one more way to impose his will on them; it really hardly mattered, since if she happened to stay up late in bed reading, she could always dream in the garden once the servants were done dressing her.

Today was an exception, however. Either *she* had somehow awakened much earlier than usual, or—far more likely—he had left orders to allow her to sleep late to recover from her unusually long evening and the presumed "excitement" of the fete. At least he was treating her with the same consideration he would give one of his prize horses this morning.

She touched a carved flower on the headboard of her bed, and a dim pink mage-light (just enough to read by) appeared just over her head. It was impossible to tell exactly what time it was, since she couldn't see the water clock in the sitting room or the sun outside the manor, but she had the feeling that it was an hour or two past dawn, rather than before dawn.

There was a faint headache just behind her eyes, but otherwise she was none the worse for all the wine she had drunk last night. That was a pleasant surprise. *I know that Lorryn's complained about feeling* much *worse than this after a party. Either that wine wasn't as strong as I thought it was, or I didn't drink as much as I thought I had.*

Probably the latter. If Lord Ardeyn had invited the little circle of sybarites that hung around V'dann Triana Lady (or was it "Lord"?) Falcion, she would not be in the least surprised to find that his guardian had discreetly substituted a less intoxicating version of drink than the strong wine elven lords usually preferred, or at least had done so for the early part of the evening. Even Rena had heard stories about Triana—a particularly disreputable lady who had, shortly after the defeat of Lord Dyran, insisted and gotten the right to drop the title "er-Lord" from her name and claim the House of Falcion in her own right.

Triana was said to indulge in every excess known; Lorryn's friends were children playing kissing games by comparison. Most of her circle were the offspring of parents who were only a bare step up from being pensioners on some greater lord's favor—or were rare third or fourth children, useless to their parents, since no lord would ever divide his estate, and no lord would wed his child to a landless spouse unless he had no other choice. They could afford to debauch themselves; no one cared what they did, and no one would ever give them a scrap of responsibility. Most of them spent their time in endless parties, or traveling from city to city, staying at the town houses of friends or the friends of their parents.

They were generally granted just enough wealth to keep them busy in the spending of it, and not enough to get them into real trouble.

Which is a pity; surely one or two of them are brighter than poor Gildor, and would make a much better heir to his father's estate than Gildor would. For that matter, I can think of some girls that wold do better than he would.

She grimaced at the thought of Gildor. The salvation of his attention would probably be short-lived, knowing Lord Tylar. True, she *had* followed Lord Tylar's orders, the letter of them, anyway, but it had only been the merest chance that led even a nonentity like Gildor to pay any attention to her. For all the rest of the younger er-Lords, she might just as well have been one of the tame animals. The odds of anything at all to satisfy Lord Tylar's demands coming out of last night's fete were slim indeed.

If I'm lucky, Father will have enough on his mind that he'll just leave me to my own devices again. If I'm not—when no inquiries come about me, he'll blame me and Mother for it. He'll probably even forget the fact that Katarina completely captured Lord Ardeyn and blame us for not somehow en- thralling him! Then—I suppose I'll have to resign myself to a year of dancing lessons, music lessons, walking lessons, talking lessons, dressing-lessons....

At least it would be something to do.

But all those lessons would take away her precious free time. There would be no more rides with Lorryn, unless he could somehow spirit her away from her teachers. There would be no hours in the library, browsing through books col- lected, not only by the House of Treves, but by the House of Kaullis before them. There would be very little time for the garden and her birds....

And yet—it would be freedom of a sort, for there would be no time for *any* of that if she was no longer Sheyrena an Treves, but Lady Sheyrena, wife of—of someone else. Even- tually Lord Tylar would decide she'd had enough lessons, es- pecially once her teachers pronounced her proficient, and he would leave her alone again.

How can I not be proficient? she asked herself wryly. *I've had more lessons on being the perfect lady than any three other girls combined. If lessons could make me captivating, Katarina would never have stood a chance against me.*

And if it took lessons to earn her the tiny amount of freedom she enjoyed now, then she would endure the lessons as worth the reward.

Freedom always seems to come at a cost, and the more the freedom, the higher the cost, she thought, with a sigh. *And what would true freedom cost me, I wonder? Probably more than I would ever want to pay, I suppose. But—it would be nice to know it was available. . . .*

She reached under her pillow for the book she'd put there, one that was supposed to be a story of romance and treachery (did they always go hand in hand?) from the time when all the elves dwelled in Evelon.

If she could not read about dragons, this was the next best thing. And while she had a little free time to read, she would make the best use of it that she could.

A suntailed hawk soared high above the valley, on the watch for unwary rabbits in the meadows below. Lashana linked her mind loosely with his, enjoying the sensation of flight without the work. She had been doing quite enough of work lately, and it wasn't over yet. With power—or the appearance of power, anyway—came a *terrible* amount of responsibility.

This was a beautiful valley, and whether or not the rest would admit it, a site much superior to that of the original Citadel. Old habits died hard, and they would probably build their new fortress-home here with all the concealments of the old, but they wouldn't necessarily *have* to. The elven lords were far from here, and neither she nor any of the other scouts had seen any signs of habitation for several days' journey in any direction. The dragons were of the opinion that this site was blessed with a temperate climate; the forest that grew so thickly here was of mixed deciduous and coniferous trees, and was very, very old. Game was abundant, and would continue to be so if it was carefully husbanded and harvested. The one problem would be how to acquire foodstuffs other than meat; the wizards were so used to purloining what they needed from the stores of the elves that very few of them were woods-wise. She doubted that more than three or four knew what wild-growing forest plants were edible. They *could* clear some few acres and plant crops there—but that would be an open sign that they were living here, and she doubted most of the older wizards would even consider such a move.

Not to mention the fact that planting, tending, and harvesting a crop is hard, physical work, and very few of them would care to subject themselves to anything like manual labor.

Still, at the moment, all those decisions lay in the future. For once, she would not think about the future. For once, she would simply watch the land through the eyes of a hawk, and take in the beauty of the river below, the blue of the sky, the stately trees reaching up—

"Well, Elvenbane, how does the business of being a hero set with you?"

Shana released the hawk's mind, turned away from the hawk itself, and frowned at the great dragon Kalamadea, who was currently shifted into the form of a crinkle-faced old halfblood wizard. In this form, he had the bright green eyes and pointed ears of a presumed elven parent, but the coarser features, weathered skin, and gray hair that would have come from a human mother. "Father Dragon, I wish you wouldn't call me that," she said, crossly. "I don't like it."

"Why not?" Kalamadea replied, sitting down beside her, on the ridge of rock that crowned this hillside. "It suits you—or you suit it."

"What? Hero or 'Elvenbane'? I don't like either of them," she replied, turning her gaze back toward the sky, searching for that hawk again. "I don't like being called Elvenbane because I don't want people to—to look at me as if I was some sort of icon of destiny. I'm *me*, plain, ordinary, Lashana, and I can't help it if some people seem to think I match a crazy legend that you dragons made up in the first place! There are plenty of people who could be made to fit that particular legend, anyway! Why not call *Shadow* the Elvenbane? Or Zed, or even Denelor?"

"But you are the only one who actually instigated and led a revolt against the elven masters, to the betterment of at least a few fully human slaves," Kalamadea replied roguishly, tugging a lock of her long hair playfully. "And the only one who brought the dragons to help her!"

"Oh, *please*," she groaned, giving up the search. "If I hadn't done something, *you* would have found a way to interfere again, and *you* would have led the others to help the wizards, somehow. You know you would have!"

"Would I?" was Kalamadea's only reply. "But I am no hero, Shana."

"And neither am I," she said stubbornly. Then, with a heavy sigh, added, "And I'm no leader either. I wish I was. I wish I'd been trained for this, handling people. I hate to have to put all my trust in Parth Agon after the way he tried to use me, but at least *he* knows how to make people do what he wants them to do. People are used to thinking of him as the Senior Wizard anyway; often as not, they just obey him without thinking twice about it. They don't listen to me. Oh, they *say* I'm their leader, but I can't even get them to see sense when it's right in front of their noses. Look how I managed to find them the best site in the whole world, a *huge* cave complex, above a river in a rich valley, and *still* they have to argue about building the new Citadel here! And that Caellach Gwain is *not* helping matters at all."

"You do better than you think you do—" Kalamadea began, when he stopped in midsentence. Shana followed his gaze, catching sight of a dragon—in full, impressive draconic form—and his halfblood rider, kiting up the slope of the hill below where they sat, riding a rising thermal just above tree-top level. "Ah," he said, squinting into the bright sunlight. "Your foster brother and your young friend, I think. There must be word from the rest of the wizards."

A good guess, since the dragon was smallish by draconic

standards, and bright blue, and the rider no larger than Shana herself. They glided up the slope swiftly, and, with a thunder of wings and a wind that blew bits of grass into the air, landed beside Kalamadea and Shana in the clearing along the top of the ridge.

The slight, dark-haired rider tumbled off of the blue dragon's back quickly enough—dragon-riding, as Shana knew well from experience, was far from comfortable—and joined the two of them as the dragon shifted shape into wizard-form to take up less space. Shana averted her eyes while Keman took his new shape, that of a short, brown-haired, muscular young halfblood; the peculiar rippling and changing that accompanied the transformation always made her stomach queasy if she watched too closely.

"I have good news and bad news," Mero announced, as he got within easy conversational distance, close enough for the emerald eyes and barely pointed ears that marked him as a halfblood to be clearly visible. "The good news is that even Caellach has finally accepted the caves as the best site for the new Citadel; Keman found a spring at the back of the complex, and brought the water up through the floor. With a constant source of fresh water right in the heart of our holding, there's no reason to look anywhere else for a home."

"And the bad news?" Shana asked, knowing from the tiny quirk of Shadow's mouth as he tossed his long hair out of his eyes that it was likely to be more humorous than truly "bad."

"The bad news is that the only place he could bring it up into was that group of caves you wanted for your own lair," Mero told her, the quirk turning into a grin that displayed a strong set of fine, white teeth. "Sorry about that; it's now all underwater. Very *cold* water, I might add."

She groaned, but only halfheartedly. The complex of caves she and the other three had found here was vast enough that there were plenty of other choices for everyone, and *still* the caves would not be more than a tenth occupied, dragons, wizards, former human slaves, and all. And even though it was a great deal closer to the elves than Shana really liked, it was well outside the borders of any lands the elves actually held under control.

If it hadn't been for the dragons, though, the caves *would* have been a very poor choice for a new home. Wizards though the halfbloods were, they could not bring water where there was none, nor could they shape rock with anything other than physical tools and their hands. Their magics were of illusion, of attack and defense, of the ability to move objects or people, and very occasionally, of the ability to create something. If they had been searching for a new home without the dragons, they would have had to build everything on their own, and unmodified caves made for damp and often hazardous dwellings. And everyone agreed that the new Citadel should have an internal water source, for obvious reasons.

After centuries of living in the comfort of the Citadel the first wizards built, they were not prepared to use either their hands or tools, I expect, Shana reflected, and not for the first time. Before she turned their world upside down, the wizards had lived a life of relative luxury and indolence. Anything they needed, they had used their magic to steal from the elves. The Citadel was already built, and built to last—they had not even bothered to keep it repaired, and when something happened to make one room or suite of rooms uninhabitable, the wizard in question simply moved. There were dozens, hundreds, of rooms unused and unoccupied since the Wizard War. For those tedious little chores of cooking and cleaning, there were always the apprentices, halfblooded children spirited away by wizard-agents before they could be discovered and killed by their fathers and masters. That was the price of *becoming* a wizard: to pay for one's apprenticeship by being the servant of an acknowledged wizard until the rest of the brotherhood accepted that you had mastered your powers. There were always plenty of apprentices; Denelor, Shana's own master, hadn't lifted a finger to clean his own quarters, even, for decades.

It hadn't always been that way; when the wizards first banded together, there had only been the "experienced" and the "inexperienced"—there were no apprentices in service to masters. They had all worked side by side to create the Citadel in the first place, and then to engineer the revolt against the elven lords and free themselves and the human slaves.

Well, I certainly took care of that. Shana could not help but feel a certain grim satisfaction; for all that she really liked old Denelor, she had not much cared for playing servant to him, and there were plenty of other wizards who had taken shameless advantage of their situation. Now they would all be working side by side again, like it or not. The few humans— former slaves—that were with them now were mostly children, and even the hardest-hearted wizard would not put a child to that kind of work. Only an elven lord would be that cruel, to force little ones less than ten years old into the hard manual labor of an adult.

No, the caves would have been fit only for use as temporary shelter at best, if it hadn't been for the dragons.

The dragons not only *could* shape rock with their magic, they *enjoyed* it. Keman had appointed himself to the search for water as soon as one of the older wizards had objected to that lack; the others would mold and shape the place to the liking of each individual and to their own uses now. The wizards themselves could devote their efforts to finding supplies of food, to furnishing their own quarters, and to working out a way to acquire the things they used to steal from the elves. In a few months, they would have a new headquarters that was *better* than the old Citadel. Certainly it would be more defensible.

"I like this place," Keman said simply, as he dropped down beside the other three. Shana followed his gaze, over the rolling hills covered with mixed grasslands and forest, and nodded. So far as she or any of the others had been able to tell, there were no signs that anyone had ever lived here before. If there were any of the monsters that lurked near elven-held lands, they were few, and kept in hiding. The elves were probably operating under the assumption that the wizards had found a place to build a settlement by now, but they couldn't know *where* it was, exactly, and with luck, the wizards would be able to keep it that way. Hadn't they kept the existence of the Citadel a secret for centuries? The Citadel had been surrounded by elven holdings, too! Surely they would be able to keep *this* place from being found out, at least for a while.

"I like this place, too," Mero said unexpectedly. "I just wish we could get rid of about half the blockheads we had to drag along with us. A little less complaining and a little more work would get things done a *lot* faster."

Shana made a sour face. "I know what you mean," she replied. "If I hear one more graybeard whine about the old days and how much better everything was, I may pack up and leave again. *I* can do just fine in the woods; I'd like to see any of them manage to find me, too!"

Then let them do without their "leader" for a while and see where it gets them. See if any of them can figure out how to keep everyone fed and all, when they don't even know how to hunt!

"Don't tempt me to join you," Mero replied. "I may not be used to dragging around in the wilderness, but camping out in snow and rain is preferable to listening to them complain about the tiniest inconvenience! They could be *dead* instead of building a new home, and that would be a whole lot more *inconvenient* than anything they're having to do without right now!" He shook his head. "I'll never understand them, I guess. Look at everything you've done—you broke the siege, you made it possible for them to fight the elves to a standstill, you helped drive the bargain that kept the fullbloods from following us—we all four scouted for months and *months* to find this place—so what's their problem? Can't they be content?"

Shana shrugged; she didn't understand it either. She was used to living in far more primitive circumstances than this would be—in fact, for the first fourteen years of her life, she hadn't once had *cooked* food, for the dragons that cared for her ate everything raw, and she had done the same. But Mero, poor Valyn's halfblood cousin, had been used to the soft life of the special servant of an elven lord, and had adapted to scouting and roughing it just fine. Why couldn't those whining wizards do the same? For Fire's sake, if they were so deprived, why didn't they just use their magic to re-create everything they'd left behind?

Because they'd have to cooperate, pool their power together, and *use the trick I learned with gemstones to concentrate it, that's why. They will never cooperate with each other as long as each is so jealous of his own power, and they'll never admit I might have learned something useful.*

It was Kalamadea that answered them both. "I believe the source of their discontent may only be because we are no longer in immediate peril," he said thoughtfully, scratching his chin with one finger. "Once the danger was past, the old, inflexible ones stopped recalling that it was Shana who was their chief aid against the elves, started to recall that it was Shana who brought the elves down on them in the first place, and remembered all the comforts that she has therefore deprived them of. It seems logical for them to think of Shana as the author of their misery, rather than the elven overlords."

Mero snorted. "All the more reason for you to take me with you if you decide to leave these complainers behind. They might decide that if you're not around, they should blame me!"

Shana laughed, and patted her friend on the shoulder. "It's a bargain," she told him lightly. "If I bolt, I'll take you with me."

Keman rolled his eyes upwards. "If you bolt, you'd better not forget to tell *us*!" he exclaimed. "We dragons are only here because of you, little two-legger, and there's no reason to stay if you leave! You think *we* want to have to listen to them whining without you to keep them off our backs?"

"I can't imagine why anyone would," Shana told her foster brother. "Not for more than a heartbeat, anyway."

Caellach Gwain surveyed the cave that would be his home for what was left of his life, and seethed with resentment. The dragon that had "prepared" it for him *had* smoothed the floor and walls, it was true, had drilled a ventilating shaft right to the surface, and it was no longer as dank as it had been. He'd been promised that later another dragon would return, and shape a little cubicle into a bath and "necessary," and another into a fireplace and chimney. The dragons swore that there would be no trouble in creating a real sanitation arrangement, nor a good heat source.

But it was still a cave, with his few belongings heaped pathetically in one corner, and nothing was going to make it into anything but a cave. It was *not* his comfortable suite of four real rooms with real walls, floor, and ceiling of warm wood, in the old Citadel. There was no furniture, and there would be none until someone learned how to make it. No bed, no tables, no chairs—no rugs, no fireplace, no cushions, no blankets. . . .

No one to clean for me or cook for me, and everything topsy-turvy, with brats that should still be apprentices playing at being our leaders, and people who should be leaders forced to take their orders. Caellach grimaced angrily. *And if it hadn't been for those same brats, I would be sitting in my favorite chair with a nice cup of tea right now, or perhaps a glass of mulled, spiced wine.* His mouth watered with longing.

He had not forgotten that this Shana creature was the reason they had all been forced to flee the Citadel in the first place, and he was not about to let anyone else forget it, either. If she hadn't rashly used the old transportation spell to bring her and her three idiot friends straight *to* the Citadel the moment she thought they *might* be in a trifle of danger, the elves would never have known that it and the wizards in it even existed. Things would still be the way they always had been, the way they *should* be.

Comfortable, safe, and secure.

They kept telling him, whenever he tried to insist on his rights and get his apprentices back to their appropriate work, that "things were different now" and he would have to see to himself. *He* didn't see why things should be any different, especially not now. Wasn't it the duty of the young to see to the welfare of their elders? Hadn't it always been that way? And the elders paid for that with their wisdom and experience, which was only right.

But apparently that wasn't the way this new order operated. "Anyone who is able-bodied will have to take care of himself," he'd been told, rudely. "We'll get you started, but you'll have to make your own quarters after they're roughed in, and you'll have to see to your own needs."

The nerve of them, he seethed. That had to have been on that Shana's orders! She had never liked him, because he'd put her in her proper place more than once. He'd be willing to bet that her own master Denelor wasn't doing without the services of his apprentices!

And just what was he supposed to do to make this into something livable, anyway? He couldn't steal what he wanted from the elves, the way he had in the old days; *that* was part of the bad bargain that Shana had made to get the elves to agree to leave them alone. *Anyway, the moment I did, they'd know where we are now. That would be stupid, even by that brat's standards.* Was he supposed to go cut down trees and build his own bed, chests, chairs? Was he supposed to weave his own blankets? Were they all mad?

Of course, they're all mad, he told himself, grinding his teeth. *They wouldn't have done this if they weren't mad. They wouldn't have fought the elves in the first place, they'd have rendered that Shana creature unconscious and left her for the elves to find. They had no reason to suppose there was more than one halfblood, after all. She should have willingly sacrificed herself to save the rest of us! It was her duty! Not dragging us into a war we didn't plan on and never wanted! Not turning our whole way of life upside down just because she thinks she's better than her elders!*

He felt a flush of anger crawling up his face, and forced himself to calm down.

It won't be this way forever, he promised himself. *It may not even stay this way for long. The other senior wizards have been listening, lately, when I've tried to show them reason. There are probably a lot of them looking at holes in the stone and thinking now that I was right. Shana brought all*

*this on us; there's no reason for us to listen and obey when
Shana and those dragons start upsetting the proper order.*

There was every reason for the older and wiser wizards *to*
start returning things *to* the proper order. They were no
longer under a state of siege, nor were they trudging through
the wilderness. It was time to set things right again.

And if Parth Agon would not take care of the task,
Caellach Gwain was just the man to see that things *did* get
back to normal.

But meanwhile—

He surveyed the hard stone floor with ill grace. Supposedly—provided that their so wise "leader" hadn't appro-
priated the children for some other "necessary" task—the
human children had been sent down to the river in the valley
to cut reeds for bedding. Supposedly they should have made
several trips by now, and there should be many bundles
stacked up on the riverbank, waiting for someone to come get
them. That floor was going to be cursed cold to sleep on
without something between him and it.

He started to call for one of his apprentices to start fetching
bundles of reed down here, recalled that he *had* no apprentices now, and stopped himself with a growl.

Well, at least she can't forbid me to do this the logical way,
he thought hotly. *Cursed if I'll carry all those bundles down
here by hand!*

He didn't need a scrying crystal to locate the bundles of
reed; that was for mere apprentices. *He* was a senior wizard
and above such crude necessities. He simply concentrated and
called upon his powers—

A glowing, ball-shaped haze of light appeared in the center
of the cave, and within a heartbeat or two, the unmistakable
shapes of reed bundles formed within it.

He wondered for a moment, as the power drained from him
a bit, how many he should take.

As many as I can fetch! he decided. *And we'll just let them
see who the senior wizards are!*

He made a mental "grab" for his target, and with an audible thud, a dozen bundles dropped to the stone floor, bringing with them the scent of fresh air and river water.

He surveyed his prizes with smug satisfaction. He had really only needed three bundles of that size for an adequate bed, but—

But they can cut more. They're not even apprentices. And for once, I'm going to have the comfort I deserve.

After all, it was only what was rightfully due him.

"So now we have water," Denelor told Shana, gesturing at the filling pool of spring water with a smile of tired satisfaction on his round, good-humored face. He was thinner than he had been; months of hiking across the wilderness had trimmed off the excess pounds he'd carried, and had tanned his skin to a warm brown, against which his thinning hair seemed whiter than ever. "I think I can even replicate some of the old magics with help, eventually, and we'll have real running water all over the Citadel, hot and cold, in a few years. When I was an apprentice, I used to have to work on the plumbing, so I'm partly familiar with it." A look of determination replaced the smile. "What the first wizards learned to do, surely we, too, can rediscover."

Shana smiled back; her old mentor Denelor had done an amazing job of adapting to this new life. She would have expected him to throw in his lot with the "old whiners," but instead he had turned into one of the first to try and work out a solution to problems as they arose.

"In the meantime," he was saying, "I can get water to a kitchen area and a bathing area next to it; tomorrow the dragons will be sculpting tubs with drains for baths, laundry, washing things, and the means to actually drain the dirty water away without contaminating our fresh water. They're already putting in chimneys and fireplaces today—for now, to heat the water, all we have to do is heat stones and drop them into a filled tub. We won't be able to cook a stew or a soup, or brew more than a cupful of tea, though, until we find a way to get big pots."

"Food won't be a problem," she assured him. "There's

plenty of game in the forest, plenty of edible plants down there, too, I suspect. You won't even have to actually *hunt*, just bring in the game magically, the way we used to steal supplies, and you know it'll arrive dead."

Denelor chuckled; obviously he still remembered the way Shana had casually magicked in a huge buck elk when she first arrived, easily ten times the weight he, her master, had *thought* she would be able to handle. Shana had known better, of course, but he didn't believe her until she demonstrated her ability.

"At least it won't be mutton," he replied comfortably. "That is one aspect of the old Citadel that I will not miss; it was convenient to have that flock of sheep there, but one grew very tired of everlasting mutton."

He turned to go back up to the next level above this, the one where living quarters would now actually start, since this lowest level had been usurped by the water. The other two followed, their footsteps echoing up the slanting tunnel. "Does anyone here actually know how to *make* anything?" Mero asked. "You know, make pots, build things with their hands? You're going to need a lot of *things*, from bed frames to clothing, and you won't be able to get them from the elves anymore. Can you make things magically that will last? The elven lords can, some of them."

Denelor shrugged, and eyed his rather worn tunic ruefully. "I don't know," he admitted. "I must admit that I had an idea that was very, very tempting, though. We're forbidden to steal from the elves—but is there any reason why we can't steal from ourselves?"

Shana frowned. "I'm not sure I follow you," she said doubtfully, as they reached the place where the tunnel flattened out, and other cave mouths opened up on it.

"Well, we don't think the elves looted the Citadel after we left it, correct?" her former master said. "We don't even know for certain if they actually found it, since they were really looking for us, and not our hiding place."

Shana nodded. "They could have destroyed everything in

sight just out of spite, though, if they did find it," she warned. "They're like that."

"Yes, but I don't think they actually *found* it, and I'm sure they never had time to really do much but superficial damage," Denelor persisted. "I'm sure that they have some kind of magical guard placed around the forest, and I'm sure they have regular patrols there now, but I rather doubt they have a mage-shield about it—and even if they did, Shana, I am sure you can break it."

She flushed. "I wouldn't be *too* sure about that," she demurred, "but I think I see where your reasoning is going. And honestly—I can't think of any reason why we shouldn't start systematically bringing things out. I know it's a long way from here to there, but with several of us younger wizards combining our powers and using gemstones, I think we can do it. It would make our lives a great deal easier."

"Especially if we start by bringing out furnishings and whatnot for the whiners," Mero put in sourly, shoving his hands in his breeches pockets and grimacing. "Then maybe they'd shut up for a while."

Denelor sighed; Shana knew he had been hearing nearly as many complaints as she had. "The thought *had* occurred to me, too. The talk about how Shana has 'deprived' them of their 'rights' might die down a little. *Could* you get your little circle of friends together, Shana, the ones that know how to work with stones? I think you're right; they will be the only ones with a long enough range to successfully scry out the place and bring things back."

She grinned. "And they're also the only ones who've crawled all over the Citadel, down all the unused passages. I think you're right; even if the elves got in there and did some destruction, they won't have gotten into the older sections, and there are still furnished rooms and the like back there. Old Caellach may not get *his* bed, but we'll get him *a* bed, and whatever other gear he thinks he needs, too."

"Kitchen things first, please," Denelor admonished. "Objects that we *all* need, that will benefit all of us together. Then I'll tell the others that they can bring you their lists and they can ask you politely if you can fill them when you aren't too tired."

She caught the twinkle in his eye as he said that. "And if they don't ask politely, we can decide we're too tired, hmm? Oh, Denelor, if you weren't on my side, I'd be worried!"

Denelor shrugged, but he had a wry grin.

"We dragons have a solution, too," Keman said shyly. "There are minerals, gems in these hills. Gold, we think. We can bring those things up, shape-shift into elven form, and go into one of the elven cities to trade for things we all need, if you cannot bring them from the Citadel. Cloth and tools would be the best, we thought—foodstuffs, seeds for planting perhaps."

Denelor brightened at that. "Oh, now, that would be excellent!" he exclaimed, his voice echoing a little in the stone of the kitchen-chamber-to-be. "That solves a problem of continuing supply. Much as I hate to admit it, Shana, I don't think that there are many of us who would know an edible forest plant from an inedible one, and one cannot live on nothing but meat without getting sick."

"I was afraid you'd say that," she replied with resignation. "Oh well." She took a moment to order her thoughts. "In the short term, the best I can do is get my circle together and start bringing things over from the old Citadel, then," she decided aloud. "If the elves didn't loot the place, there was a lot of stored food there that was too bulky to take with us in the evacuation. That would be flour, tubers, other vegetables—"

"Don't forget blankets," Denelor reminded her. "You will gain a great number of friends if you bring blankets in quickly. Stone is cold to sleep on."

"What about the sheep?" she asked slyly. "That's wool for future blankets, mutton for future meals—I *can* bring them in alive now, you know, and there are a couple of the human children that can perfectly well tend a flock of sheep. They do reproduce themselves, you know."

He grimaced involuntarily and she giggled. "Oh," he sighed, "I suppose you must, after all. But—"

"Don't worry, Master Denelor," she told him with a

chuckle. "They'll be much too valuable in this situation to start slaughtering. You won't be forced to eat mutton any time soon."

"Thank goodness for that," he muttered as she moved off down a side corridor, trailed by Keman, to find Zed, the first of her "circle" of young wizards. "Now—may the powers grant that we do not find ourselves in a position where even old mutton would be a feast."

Working together, the young wizards were able to find and fetch a fair number of articles that very day—and as Denelor had requested, the first object brought by magic from the old Citadel was a huge kitchen kettle, and the last, a pile of blankets from the storeroom. The latter were snatched up greedily by the "old whiners," Caellach Gwain predictably among the first. Shana noted that there wasn't a single word of thanks from any of them, but she kept silent about it, in part because she was too tired to make an issue of the slight.

And the next day, fortified by a good breakfast of oat porridge made in the very same kettle they had brought in first, from the oats they had brought in as the last task, she and her group started in all over again. Those who were the very best at scrying examined rooms they were familiar with, in order to identify what was there and whether or not it might be useful.

They confined their attempts, at first, to objects that would not be harmed too much if they were clumsy with their magic, and which were not too heavy. That had been Shana's plan. She reasoned that until they knew their limits, it was better to bring in a few things at a time than to overstrain themselves trying to "lift" too much. Their first targets were therefore the kitchen and the storerooms, and they systematically looted both of everything that was still there, unbroken, or unspoiled by vermin.

The elves, it seemed, *hadn't* found the old Citadel after all—although they certainly would have if the wizards had remained there rather than fleeing. That was a cheerful discovery; it meant that virtually everything was still there, intact, and that eventually everyone in this new Citadel would have his belongings back.

Although she still didn't understand this preoccupation with possessions that the older wizards showed, Keman and the other dragons seemed to understand. They couldn't explain it to her, though, and after several tries, gave up.

"Let me just put it this way," Kalamadea told her, finally, with surprising patience. "The older the wizard, the more likely he is to *want*, desperately, all his familiar things—and the more likely he is to be less troublesome if he has them around him. He's like an old dragon curled up with his hoard. Don't try to understand why, just accept it, and use the fact."

She nodded, with a wry shrug. It would be a small price to pay for peace, she supposed, even though this "price" represented quite a bit of effort on the part of her and her friends, effort for which they would probably not even receive thanks. And it was very, very tempting to put the "whiners" on the very end of the list—

But if she did that, they could and would accuse her of playing favorites, and while they were waiting, they would be whining even more, and probably causing more trouble.

"Storerooms first, though," she told the dragon fiercely. "Things we can *all* use before personal possessions! Denelor agrees with me on that."

Kalamadea just shrugged. "It is your magic and that of your friends," he replied, and backed out of the bare little cave she had taken for her home. Kalamadea's and Keman's were both nearby, and she suspected that Kalamadea had been the one who had smoothed the walls and the ceiling, built in the sanitary facilities and the fireplace. It looked vaguely familiar—very near to the room *he* had once occupied in the warren of caves in the old Citadel, in fact.

But at the moment it held only a bundle of reeds and the two blankets she was using as a bed, and her scant pack.

A bed would have been nice . . . and she had to admit that the old wizards weren't entirely wrong about longing for some of the old comforts of their previous lives.

Extra clothing would be nice, too, she reflected wistfully.

All that she had now had served her over rough country for the better part of two seasons, and it was much the worse for wear. She had often thought about piecing together another dragonskin tunic from skin the others had shed; such a tunic would have held up to briars and rainstorms with equal ease. She'd never had time enough, though. Maybe now she would.

Still, first things first. There were plenty of storerooms to empty, as they honed their skills at magically transporting a variety of objects longer distances than any of them had ever dared to try before this.

None of them would even have dreamed of trying, if Shana, in her apprentice days, had not made an experiment with a tiny cache of gemstones, to see if any of them could be used to increase her power and range. She had discovered that, yes, they *could*, and had begun teaching the use of stones to her peers, when a group of human children with the human wizard-powers on one of the elven estates was about to be eliminated. She had insisted on leading a rescue to save them—thus being the one to meet with Valyn and his halfblood cousin, Mero, as they made their *own* escape from Valyn's father. And that fateful meeting had carried with it the seeds of the destruction of the old ways of hide-and-conceal of the wizards of the Citadel.

Within two weeks, Denelor had the kitchen, bath, and laundry functioning, with human children employed in all three, as well as some of the older wizards—none of whom qualified as "whiners"—who were not fit for heavy labor. By that time, Shana and her crew had begun looting the private quarters of the senior wizards themselves.

Favoritism or not—the first ones they ransacked were their own and Denelor's, though they kept very quiet about it, transporting the belongings directly to the appropriate rooms rather than bringing them into the central chamber they were all starting to call the "Great Hall." After that, though, they stifled their irritation and started on the whiners' things, beginning with Caellach Gwain.

And he did *not* thank them. In fact, he was rather irritated with them for bringing his property to the Great Hall, forcing him to use his own powers to take it to his rooms.

Shana was so annoyed with him that she ground her teeth until she had a headache. That brought the whole circle to a halt; she was, after all, the strongest power in it, and without her, the others couldn't move much more than a single pillow or so at a time. That irritated her even more, until Zed, as the oldest, called for a break so that they could all soothe roused tempers and perhaps get something to eat and drink.

It took more than bowl of soup and a cup of willow tea to soothe Shana's temper, but at least she managed to get rid of her headache, if not her irritation. "I'm sorry," she apologized, as she came back to the circle and took her place on a cushion with the rest, in the exact middle of the huge room. Her voice echoed quite a bit, since the roof was quite high, and had been left exactly as nature had carved it. "I shouldn't let my temper get the best of me around him."

Zed only snorted contemptuously, but said nothing. Shadow patted her hand, and shrugged. The rest grimaced or smiled as their natures dictated. There was really nothing to be said, after all. Caellach had been unbearably rude, but someone with the kind of power that Shana controlled *had* to have better control over her emotions than she actually did—at least where Caellach was concerned. She knew that, and so did they. What if Caellach had annoyed her while she was in the middle of—say—creating a defense against attackers? That would be a poor time for a headache!

"Well, we fetched the old buzzard's things and we *won't* have to deal with him anymore," Daene, one of the older girls, said at last. She winked openly at Shana, and wrinkled up her snub nose. "He's good for three or four days at least, fussing with his furniture and all, like some old hen with her nest and a new load of straw to put in it. We won't see *him* for all that time, I'll wager!"

The comparison, apt as it was, for Caellach cackled exactly like an irritable and irritated old hen, made even Shana smile at last as the rest chuckled. "You're right, and we'd better be grateful for the peace while it lasts!" she replied. "Well, let's get to work on someone who's likely to at least thank us. Parth Agon, do you think? Do any of you remember what his rooms look like to scry for them?"

"I—" Zed began.

"Shana!" The shout from the doorway echoed across the entire room. The shouter followed, scrambling in the door and across the stone floor of the Great Hall, all out of breath. "Shana!" the little human boy gasped again, forcing his words around his panting. "Shana, Denelor and the big dragon want you! Down by the river! There's a stranger!"

At first she didn't quite understand what he meant. Then—

There's a stranger? Here? Oh no—

Here, in the wilderness, where there should be no one but the wizards and the few humans that had fled with them? Who was it? And more important—*how had he found them?*

:Kalamadea!: she called to Father Dragon with her mind. *:Is there danger? Should I bring weapons?:*

:No danger yet, I do not believe,: he replied the same way. *:But I want you to see him and speak with him. You have more experience than Denelor or me with full humans.:*

A full *human?* But how had he gotten here? Was he an escaped slave? Before the others could react, she had vaulted to her feet and was running out the door.

The Great Hall was the very first real "room" in the Citadel; from there, a long and winding trail led up to the surface, leading through caverns that had been left, more or less, in their natural state. The only concessions to habitation at this end of the Citadel were the mage-lights at intervals, and the smoothing of the path. This place was like the limestone and alabaster caves that she had lived in with her foster mother and the rest of the dragons; there were hundreds of fascinating formations she had promised herself that she would examine properly one day. But not while she had so much work to do.

Not while there were strangers showing up out of nowhere!

She burst out into the pool of sunlight directly in front of the cave mouth, and flung herself down the path that led to the river, a path they had cut carefully so that it was screened and protected by the trees and bushes—hoping to avoid detection from the air. Unfortunately, this plan made it impossible for her to see Denelor and the others down at the riverside.

*I wish I knew what to expect. I wish I knew how he got so close to us without any of us seeing him. I wish—*No point in wishing. *Just get down there, now!* She pounded down the path at her fastest run, feet thudding into the dirt, breath coming hard even though she was running downhill.

When she made the last turn the river came into view, a patch of brilliant sunlight reflecting off the water, at the end of a tunnel of trees. There were several figures down there, dark against the bright light—and something, low and long and dark, in the water itself, or at the very edge of it.

As she ran closer, the shape resolved itself into a hollow object, pointed at each end, with a place to sit. She had never seen a canoe herself, but she did recognize what it was from descriptions in some of the old chronicles.

A boat? But of course—we weren't looking for anyone on the river! She could have flogged herself in vexation for not taking the precaution of putting at least one sentry above the river. Too late now.

There were only three people standing beside the canoe, which had been tied to a stake driven into the riverbank. Denelor, Kalamadea in his wizard-form, and the stranger. They were all obviously waiting for her, and neither Denelor nor Kalamadea looked at all tense—

As she took in that, she slowed to a walk, so that she would not be completely out of breath when she reached them, and so that she could get a good look at the stranger before she had to speak to him.

She got her first surprise when she realized that although he was fully human, his neck bore no slave-collar and no signs he had ever worn one. For the rest, he looked like a field hand or a caravan trader; his eyes were an ordinary enough brown, his hair black, and his hair had been pulled back into a tight braid, to show that his ears were not in the least pointed. He was moderately tall, very wiry and muscular, dressed in a rather tattered linen tunic and trews of cloth so old and faded, it wasn't possible to tell what the original color had been. He had a bow slung across his back, a long knife in a leather sheath at his rope-belt, and what appeared to be clumsy boots made of rawhide on his feet. He hadn't shaved in several days, but despite his scruffy appearance, her first impression was that he was not dangerous.

At least, not at the moment. But what was his purpose here? Could he be a spy?

"Ah, Shana—" Denelor said genially, waving at her to come closer, and then turned back to the stranger. "Collen, this is Lashana."

The stranger nodded, his eyes narrowing. "Not much t'look at, ye be," he said to her in the elven tongue, strongly accented. "Wouldn' hev figgered little bit lak ye woulda caused s'much trouble. Bin a mort uv tales abaht ye, though."

"I take it you've heard about me, then," she replied dryly, concealing her agitation from him. She still had no idea what he was doing on the river—or who, if anyone, he served.

He nodded, and his thin lips curved in a reluctant smile. "Hardly thought, when I seen smoke on th' ridge, I'd be passin' greetin's wit' sech troublesome an' savage rebels, lak."

"Collen is a scout for a trading party, Shana," Denelor said easily, and her eyebrows rose with alarm as she stepped back an involuntary pace. "Oh, not a *bondling* party," the wizard amended hastily, as Collen's grin turned into a chuckle. "Can't you see? He's got no collar, no elf-stones about him."

Shana flushed with chagrin. As she had seen for herself, the neck of the man's tunic was open to his breastbone, and he wore absolutely *nothing* else that could have served in place of the collar that could have bound him to an elven overlord. His belt was rope, the sheath of his knife was leather, the knife itself had a plain, wrapped handle with none of the dangerous spellcarrying beryls set into it. And in any case, if he'd been a bondling, she, Denelor, or Kalamadea would surely have sensed the blankness that meant there was a spell on him that blocked all the purely human powers of magic. They *all* knew the "shape" of that particular blankness.

"Oh, aye," Collen said agreeably. "No collars, no leashes. We be jest as dangerous a lot of savages as ye, I 'spect, an' the cat-eyes knew we was here."

Her eyes widened. This was the one thing she simply had not expected. "You mean—you're *wild*?" she exclaimed, her voice shadowed with disbelief. Oh, she'd heard that so-called "wild" humans existed, but after tasting the efficiency and ruthlessness of elven rule for herself, she hadn't believed they were capable of anything more than scrabbling out a bare and brutish existence. And *that* was only allowed so that the elven lords would have something to hunt, now and again, that ran on two legs rather than four.

Then again, she chided herself, as Collen's grin widened at her reaction, *the wizards existed for hundreds of years without the elves knowing. There are wild humans beyond their lands; we already knew that. Why not wild human traders to serve them?*

"Oh, aye," Collen repeated. "It's none so bad a life, lak. Call oursel's outlaws, though. Has a better soun' t'it." He shrugged. "Some on' us be 'scaped, some born free, lak. Got no land, no set home, an' we figger we hev't' move about a bit, but got no overlor' neither."

"Collen would like to talk trade with us. I think we should invite these people to come talk to us, Shana," Kalamadea said gently, breaking into her daze. "I think we might have something we can offer each other."

:And since he already knows we're here, there's no point in trying to hide the Citadel,: the dragon added, deep inside her mind. *:The more we show them, the more impressed they are likely to be, and the less likely to betray us.:*

"Ah, of course, Kalamadea," she said, to both statements. "How far away are the rest of you?"

"Not far. Be here 'fore sundown, lak," he replied with a nod. "Lemme put out flag, they'll pull in here."

Without waiting for their consent, he pulled a faded red rag out of the canoe and tied it to a branch where it would be seen by anyone passing on the river itself. "There she be," he said with satisfaction. "Now—we jes' wait, lak."

She itched to touch his thoughts, to see for herself if he was telling the truth. Did she dare? If she did, would he know, and how would he take it?

"Fine," Denelor said, easily. "I'll just go up and tell the others to fix a meal for our new—allies?" He raised an eyebrow on the last word.

Collen shrugged. "Canna speak fer the lot," he replied laconically. "Could be. For sure, an' ye got stuffs t' trade, we'll be 'greeable t' tradin' for 'em."

That, apparently, was enough for Denelor, who strode back up the path at a much brisker pace than he would have been able to set a year ago. Collen folded his arms and leaned back against the trunk of a willow, watching both Shana and Kalamadea.

"Bloods," he said finally. "Heard on ye, heard on the troubles ye set, last summer, but never saw none."

"I could say the same about outlaws," Shana retorted mildly. *Can I test him out? Should I ask him if I can?*

He grinned, as if he found the retort amusing.

Kalamadea simply examined him calmly, as calmly as he regarded nearly everything, from impetuous young dragons to elven mage-craft. "Why the river?" he asked, finally.

"Mun leave no tracks on water," came the easy reply.

"Ah," Kalamadea said. "But—there are no elves here, nor bondlings, either."

Collen nodded. "Aye. But we *trade* wit' th' collared. Mun leave no tracks, no way fer collared t' follow, lak. They can' follow, they got no hold on us. They got no hold, they gots t' trade fair."

Shana nodded, too, for Collen's reasoning made excellent sense—and it made her a bit more inclined to trust him, if *he* did not trust the collared bondlings he traded with. It showed a good, strong sense of self-preservation, and a disinclination to place any possible power in the hands of those controlled by elves.

"So why should you trust us?" she asked. "After all, you don't know us—we *might* be elves in disguise."

He laughed aloud at that, throwing his head back and closing his eyes. "Oh, aye, ye mot," he chortled. "'Cept there be a reason I be scout."

"And what's that?" Shana asked, since he was obviously waiting for her to do so.

:I got the human-magery, little Blood,: he said, deep in her mind, grinning as she started. *:That's how I tell Niki, back wit' th' rest, t' come on, lak. An' I know ye be Blood, 'cause I heered ye when ye made talk wi' the old one, there. So ye got the human-magery, an' ye got no guise-spell 'bout ye.:*

She blinked—and so did Kalamadea, taken quite aback by the voice that resonated in *his* mind as well. A remarkably strong and controlled "voice"—as indeed it must have been controlled, for him to have called to the absent "Niki" without either of *them* "overhearing" him.

"So—ye want t' be seein' inta my head?" he asked genially. "Go on. Got nothin' t' hide."

Given the invitation, she did not hesitate, but reached out with her own thoughts to touch his before he could withdraw the invitation.

Perhaps because it was so strongly on both their minds, she touched a memory rather than a thought—a recent memory by the power and "newness" of it. So powerful was it, so charged with emotion, that she found herself actually caught up in it, as if she were living the moment with him, looking out of his eyes.

The tension was just short of unbearable, and Collen's heart pounded, his chest was tight, and he was a little short of breath as he crouched in his shelter. He waited and watched from behind the concealing bushes for his bondling contact with the traders. Their trade goods, mostly furs, spices, a few very odd precious gems, were all hidden beneath a brush pile nearby. The rest of the group was hidden down by the water's edge; he alone would take the risk of immediate capture.

That risk was always there, every time he met the traders.

Not even his powers of human-magery could warn him if this time they planned to betray him, for he could not "hear" their thoughts past the blankness imposed on their minds by their spellbound collars. Other traders had been captured in years past, by other groups of bondlings. The particular furs he and his clan brought to trade were very valuable to the bondlings, and he didn't think they would risk the loss of their source—but you never knew. Especially not since the Elvenbane and her wizards had sent everything so topsy-turvy, and given the cat-eyes their comeuppance. There might be enough profit in "capturing" wild humans this time that the loss of the supply of furs would be no great problem.

Especially if one of those wild humans was also a wizard.

His stomach knotted as he heard the sound of cautious footsteps coming toward him. His contact had arrived, and with him, the moment of truth.

He stood up, slowly, and stepped forward, out of the concealing branches of his bushes—

With a wrench, she pulled her mind out of the memory and back to the real world. Collen looked into her eyes, and nodded knowingly, as she shook her head to try to rid it of the last clinging vestiges of that terrible tension.

"It's death fer ye Bloods wi' th' cat-eyes, lak wi' us wi' th' human-magery," he said. "*Ye* seen, what's lak fer us. So ye got here, or nowheres. An' no point in us gettin' up t' games wi' ye; I reckon since ye messed wit' yon cat-eyes, me an' Niki'd be no match fer ye," he continued, eyes twinkling. "Still, we be *traders*, lak. I reckon we mot do some business. Eh?"

"How many of you have the human magics?" Kalamadea asked, slowly.

"Don' see no reason t' giv' ye th' lie," Collen told him candidly. "Ony me an' Niki. There be four hands on' th' rest uv th' boats, an' no more wit' human-magery than us. Give boats, lak."

Twenty, twenty-two. That's a good-sized group; big enough to protect themselves, but not too big to hide, Shana reflected, and smiled. "Well, I hope they aren't too far away," she told him. "My curiosity is about to drive me to distraction!"

For answer, Collen gestured at the river, and just at that moment the first of the canoes came into view.

The remaining five canoes were much bigger than Collen's little boat; big enough to hold six people and a fair amount of baggage. The person in the prow of the first spotted Collen's rag and directed the rest with silent gestures, to row their boats into the shelter of the willow branches there. The first boat in held five people, including "Niki," who greeted Collen with restrained enthusiasm. Niki proved to be a woman, and from the family resemblance, she could well have been Collen's sister. The rest of the canoes held four people each, with one child in three of the boats and two in the last. That also surprised Shana; she wouldn't have thought "outlaw" traders would bring their children with them.

On the other hand, it might not have been safe to leave them anywhere.

The boats were wood, each carved from a single tree trunk, and from the size of the boats, the original trees must have been quite large. The rest of the "outlaws" were just as scruffy as Collen, but although their clothing was shabby, it, and they, were immaculately clean.

Shana and Kalamadea waited with no signs of impatience while the traders beached their canoes on the riverbank and took great pains to conceal them, using branches and netting. They worked in silence for the most part—probably out of habit. Shana had noticed that voices tended to carry across the water disconcertingly well, and these were people who clearly were used to concealing themselves and their movements as a matter of course.

When they were finished, they dusted their hands off and stood up, and Kalamadea indicated that they should follow him, which they did without a backward glance.

But they know that we had to flee the elves, so they know that we're in danger, too, if we're discovered. I would think, though, that they might worry about us getting rid of them—no, maybe not. I doubt if they have anything we want at the moment, so what would be the point of us attacking them?

Or so Shana reasoned. There would be no point in the outlaws attacking the wizards—they were patently outnumbered, and they probably knew it.

Collen dropped back to walk beside her. "It's I'm hopin' we can do a bit uv' trade, ye an' we, lak I said," he told her, quietly. "We trade furs an' oddities t' th' collared; I'm hopin' ye mot hev' summut a bit better nor furs?"

Shana thought about that. "We might," she said cautiously. "And—there *is* something we have that might be useful just for you and your people—we've got a kind of arrow-tip that's as fatal to elves as elf-shot is to you and me."

Collen's eyes widened at that, the first time he had shown any kind of surprise. "No lie?"

"No lie," she confirmed. "One scratch, and they're down; a good hit, and they are *dead*. We both know, I think, that it takes a lot to kill an elven lord."

She was not going to tell him *where* the wizards got their arrow-tips—which were actually formed from the tips of dragon-claws. If he asked about the dragons, well, she would let Kalamadea decide what he should hear or see. But there was no harm in trading him some of their special weaponry. It had no particular efficacy against halfbloods, whose constitution and lifespan were nearer the human than the elven, anyway. And if he ever *needed* such a weapon, it would be criminal not to have put in his hands.

And one more dead elven lord is all to the good. That was how Shana felt about it, anyway. She'd only seen one of the elves, ever, that had been worth anything at all—and it was all too apparent from everything she had learned, then and since, that Valyn had been an anomaly among his kind, an elven lord with a conscience and a heart.

"I be *damn* glad t' hev that, lady," Collen breathed, fervently. "An' that be a fact."

She nodded, pleased. At that point, they reached the mouth of the cavern-complex; the entrance was quite impressive, being about three stories tall, opening into the side of the hill and surrounded by heavy woods. Neither the wizards nor the dragons had done anything to alter the entrance, and from here, there was no sign of the mage-lights or the smooth path deep within. Kalamadea conjured a hand-light, and continued to lead the way; Shana called up a light of her own and brought up the tail.

The ground was a bit uneven here, and the traders stumbled now and again. Their footsteps echoed in the vast darkness as they descended, and a couple of the children whispered nervously to their parents as they paced nervously into the cool and gloom. Shana smiled to herself: they were in for a surprise.

The pathway down made an abrupt curve, doubling back on itself, and *that* was where the mage-lights began, out of sight of the entrance.

The dragons had placed their lights with care, illuminating not only the pathway, but the most impressive of the cave formations as well. For the first time, Shana heard the voice of someone other than Collen in this group, as first the children, then the adults, began to talk quietly to one another, pointing out this or that formation in tones of awe and wonder.

But the best was yet to come, as the cave narrowed, and finally widened out again into the Great Hall. Mage-lights were everywhere, in globes along the walls, and even in the cluster at the top of the ceiling. The humans blinked as they emerged into the spacious Hall, and stared about with as much shock as surprise.

Denelor had been as good as his word; he had arranged for tables and benches, lights and plenty of food—and a good number of the wizards to share the meal, including Parth Agon. The eyes of the children and adults alike went wide at the sight of all the people, but Collen seemed to take it all in stride. He left Shana and went to the head of the group, made a nice little speech of gratitude to Denelor, and then ushered all of his people to the seats awaiting them. Very clearly, no matter what he had claimed earlier, he was not "just" the scout for the traders, he was their real leader.

Well, that tallied with the glimpse she'd had into his memory.

With customary tact, Denelor had seen to it that not only was Parth Agon seated with himself, Shana, and Kalamadea at the strangers' table, but so were several of the human children Shana had rescued and brought to the old Citadel. The sight of other full humans seemed to reassure Collen's folk; they relaxed, and so did Collen.

They were hungry, but not starving; they ate well, but did not bolt the food nor stuff themselves—except at the sweet course, when their greed was frankly shared by the wizards as well. The trader children and the former slaves began eyeing each other halfway through the meal, shyly, and there were signs of tentative overtures on the part of the strangers' children as well as Shana's brood. She didn't get much of a chance to watch the children, however, for as soon as Collen's appetite was satisfied, he cleared his throat in a significant manner, and got the attention of all of the Citadel adults at his table.

"I tol' these three, down by river, we be outlaws, traders," he began, taking it on himself to repeat what the others might not yet have heard. Clearly, he was not assuming that they all had the same ability as Shana to speak mind to mind. "Some on us be freeborn, some on us be 'scaped. We trade, lak, wit' collared that be workin' fer th' cat-eyed."

Parth Agon, the only one at this table other than the children for whom this really was new information, considered it and nodded. "So long as you keep them from following you—which, presumably, is not difficult if you travel by water—you should be safe enough. So—I take it that you trade whatever odd things happen to come your way, and they in turn take the goods back to their overlords?"

"Summat lak that," Collen agreed. "We got an unnerstandin', lak. We—we're willin' t' chance risks they ain't. We bring in thin's th' cat-eyed don' see much. Furs, mostly, but now an' agin' it's summat odd. *They* tell th' cat-eyed 'twas *they* went an' fetched the things, an' they keep quiet 'bout us.

We get what we can' make, can' grow, lak. Now, we ain't 'tonly freeborn out here—"

"You're not?" Parth Agon's eyebrows rose, though it was obvious to Shana. How could you be a trader with no one to trade things to?

Collen shrugged. "'Tothers, 'tis th' odd clan, family, all farm folk, lak; couple herders, couple hunters, trappers, an' we trade wi' 'em all. They bin here since there was dirt. Got nothin' th' cat-eyed want t' go huntin' after, not no kinda threat, wouldn' know one end uv a spear from 'tother, so they ain't gonna fight. Them cat-eyed pointy-ears, they got to figger us traders is bad, since we got runaways 'mongst us, so we don' let 'em know we's here. But them—nay, they ain't no threat, an' cat-eyes don' care if they be out here. So figger we make same deal wi' ye as we got wi' them. An' ye can find summat t'trade, we take it downriver, an' get what ye canna make nor grow. Tell us what ye need. We get some, ye get some."

"Fairly standard offer, fairly made," Parth Agon said at last. "Denelor?"

"Oh, I've been in favor all along," Denelor replied quickly. "The—ah—storerooms won't stay full forever." He said nothing about the complete lack of crafting or farming ability among the wizards; he didn't have to. Parth Agon knew that lack as well as he. Eventually the wizards were going to have to learn to work with their hands, but the longer it took to come to that eventuality, the better off they would all be.

The more time we have, the more time we have to get some practice in. I'd really rather not trust my soup to a wizard's first pot.

"A very good point." Parth Agon actually turned to Shana before he checked with Kalamadea. "Shana?"

"You could—if you want—ask him mind to mind," she said forthrightly. "Collen has the human mage-craft, and you know he won't be able to lie mind to mind. But I don't think that will be necessary. He has a great deal to gain by dealing fairly with us, and a lot to lose if he doesn't."

"The only question is—what have we got at the moment

that we can trade that *wouldn't* be traced back to wizards?" Parth Agon mused aloud.

Shana's mind ran to the metals and gems that Keman said lay in these mountains—would the dragons be able to get enough out at this short a notice to make it worth the traders' while? And would it be wise to divert them from the important work of shaping the Citadel? It took a long time to bring up gold, and longer to extract gems; that much she recalled from her years of living among them. How much of the dragons' precious time could they all spare?

Keman coughed shyly, and they all turned to look at him. "You know," he said, ducking his head a little, "you could say that our troubles started over that bit of—of hide that the elves called 'dragon-skin,' the stuff Shana's tunic was made from when she was taken captive. The elves *wanted* that stuff, they sent out all sorts of expeditions looking for the source of it—and we have more of it right here."

"Dragon skin?" Collen looked very puzzled. "Can ye show me what 'tis ye be callin' 'dragon skin'?"

"Just a moment—" Keman slid out of his seat and ran off, returning in a few moments with a strip of his own shed skin, wide as a human's palm and about as long as a man's arm. Since it was Keman's, it was a brilliant blue, overlaid with a shimmer of rainbow hues. Collen bit off an exclamation, and reached out involuntarily to touch it, then pulled back.

"Go ahead," Keman urged, handing it to him. "It's pretty tough."

Collen took the strip of skin gingerly, testing the strength and suppleness, and running his hands down the smooth scales. "Where ye get this?" he asked, his eyes filled with wonder.

Evidently, although he had heard of the second Wizard War, he had *not* heard of the existence of real dragons. Had the elves decided they were illusions? Or had they made up their minds that the dragons had been constructs, artificial creatures made by some of the strongest wizards?

If they had, that certainly eased some of Shana's guilt about the situation. She still felt bad that the dragons had been forced to abandon their long-held secret to help her and her friends. She hadn't *wanted* the elves to know about the dragons, any more than the dragons had, and for good reason. The elves would never tolerate a race as powerful as the dragons or allow them to continue to exist in the same world—and as Keman had said, they *wanted* the dragons' skins. They would quite happily kill every dragon alive for the sake of the skins.

:He can't know about you, Keman,: she told him. *:Make something up, quick.:*

"It's from a lizard, and we use magic to make it prettier," Keman lied blithely. "We can make a lot of it, and we have quite a bit on hand now. It's very useful." He glanced over at Kalamadea, who nodded agreement. "It's tough, besides being pretty."

"If that be so—then ye' got th' bargain!" Collen exclaimed, his hands closing possessively on the piece of skin when Keman showed no interest in reclaiming it. "We kin get 'bout all ye mot need wi' *this* as the trade goods."

"What about our settling here?" Denelor asked. "Is that going to be a problem? We didn't see any signs of habitation in this valley, and we plan to be as discreet as *you* would, in our place. I think we can make sure the elves don't find us."

Collen shrugged, as if it was a matter of complete indifference to him. Maybe it was. "I think ye got yersel's a fair home. Sure, an' we won' be disputin' it wi' ye, an' there's none *I* know of that hev a claim here. 'Tis all yours fer the claimin', lak. Be nice t' know that his part 'o th' river's safe from cat-eyed spies, eh?"

'So we could say that—this is a kind of welcoming, then?" Parth Agon said, mildly.

"Oh, aye!" the human trader laughed, as if Parth had told him a joke. "Oh, aye, an' well-come indeed!"

4

SHEYRENA COULD HARDLY believe her luck when, the day after the fete, absolutely nothing happened. She had spent the day in a state of dulled dread, expecting—at the least—to be called into her father's presence and interrogated about just whom she had spoken and danced with, and what they had said. Worse were the fears that Lord Tylar would somehow discover her lack of "conquests," and call her to account for that.

Instead, there was no summons, not even a note. She was, as usual, ignored. With the sole exception of the fact that she was permitted to sleep late, her day passed precisely as any other day. She walked in the garden and tended her birds, had her lessons in music and etiquette, and made her daily call upon her mother in her mother's bower. Only there did she have any reminders that this was not quite an ordinary day. She and Lady Viridina discussed nothing but the gowns the other elven ladies had been wearing—speculating on how they had been made and of what materials, deciding whether or not the particular style would be suited to Rena or the

Lady herself. In other bowers, with a collection of elven ladies, there *would* have been other comments, too, of course—
comments on how poorly suited the gowns of certain ladies
(absent from the current group, of course) had been, either in
terms of style or in terms of the wearer's endowments. Lady
Viridina did not encourage gossip, however, so none of that
entered the discussion in *her* bower.

Nor were there any discussions of which young lords
seemed to have paired off with young ladies. That, in Lady
Viridina's opinion, was also gossip, and of no one's concern
except the parties involved.

The truth of the matter in the bower today was that Lady
Viridina discussed the gowns, and her slaves-of-the-wardrobe
murmured appropriate comments. Rena simply listened, and
not very attentively. Oh, normally she enjoyed the topic as
much as anything except riding with Lorryn, but today she
had rather not be reminded how wonderful the other ladies
looked—not when she had suffered in all ways by comparison. She had thought until last night that she had no pride left
to bruise, but that was simply not true. It had hurt to look into
the mirror and see a laughingstock. It still hurt this morning.

I wish there were a way to destroy that horrid gown, she
thought resentfully. *I don't ever want to see it again!*

Viridina didn't seem to notice her silence, though, which
was just as well. As she rattled off details of trains and trim-
ming, it occurred to Rena that her mother was oddly distracted, as if Lady Viridina also had something weighing
heavily on her mind, and was trying to disguise the fact with
idle chat.

*She's probably worried about Lorryn, I suppose. I rather
doubt it has anything to do with me.*

After what seemed like half the day, Viridina finally dismissed her daughter, and Rena was free to return to her garden and her books. There, with two of her birds sitting on her
shoulders, she carefully worked out the spell that had been
used on the birds at the fete, the one that made them fly off
to make their droppings, then return. That was the most use-

ful spell she had ever seen, and it was *definitely* going to come in handy here!

She set it on only one of the birds, at first—she didn't want to hurt them by getting the spell wrong, after all—but when it worked perfectly, she quickly made it part of every flying thing in her garden. Now she could pet and play with them to her heart's content, and never have to worry about the results!

One of the prettiest, an especially gentle little thing with bright red feathers and a hooked bill, loved to sit on her shoulder and press his face and body against her neck for hours at a time. She'd been reluctant to let him do that for very long, and especially reluctant to allow him to sit there when she was reading, since she tended to forget where she was—with the result that Visyr would usually do something unfortunate before she noticed, and she would have to run and change her gown before either her mother or her father saw it. There were days when she'd had to change her gown no less than three times! So that afternoon was an occasion of perfect enjoyment for both of them—for Rena could sit in the garden with her book, and Visyr could sit on her shoulder and be petted for as long as he liked. She discovered that his capacity for being petted was a great deal greater than she had ever suspected. He was the perfect tranquilizer, and she ended the day in a calm and cheerful mood.

She woke with the same apprehension as before, though, for her dreams had been filled with images of Lord Tylar and the punishments he was creating for her, for not having caught a husband.

But once again, her fears were all for no cause—nothing happened that was out of the ordinary during the entire day.

The next day, and the day following, were repetitions of the same. Most important, there were *no* expressions of disapproval from Lord Tylar. Rena began to relax, slowly, as she attempted to puzzle out just what was occupying her father. At a guess, the political connections that her father had made at the fete were proving to be so engrossing that he had forgotten his original intention—that of ensuring she found an advantageous alliance. That would, indeed, be typical for his thinking. Anything having to do with her and her future (or lack of it) would always take a poor second place to Lord Tylar's personal aspirations, and that was precisely how she wanted things at the moment. The more he thought of himself, the less he would think of her.

The only cloud on her cautious happiness was that Lorryn was still recovering from his illness, and had not come to visit her. Normally he would find an excuse to stop by her garden at least once during the day, and more often if he planned to include her in a surreptitious excursion. Indeed, the word from the slaves was that he had not even left his suite since before the fete. There was no hint that his case was more serious than she had been told, only that he had exhausted himself more completely than anyone had initially thought.

She would really have been worried sick about him if there had been any indication that something was wrong with him. As it was, she missed him; not only because she truly loved and admired him, but for his conversation. The slaves were hardly up to much clever repartee, and he was the only person besides Myre who didn't treat her as if she had the same mental capacity as a child. Even her mother spoke to her as if she were *always* as dazed and absentminded as she had been over the past few days.

Still, he shouldn't have been sick for this long; attacks had never laid him low for more than a day before. She fretted over him as she walked in her garden, and stared in the direction of his suite. What had he done to himself? Was this why her mother was upset, and covering her concern with false cheer?

She went to bed on the evening of the third day following the fete in a state of anxiety herself, when repeated messages to him brought only the reply that he was a little ill, but would be all right eventually. Eventually? Just how long could "eventually" be? She even forgot most of her worries for herself in worries over her brother.

But the morning of the fourth day brought an end to her peace of mind, in the form of a message from Lord Tylar.

It arrived with her breakfast, an elegantly written note, folded and inserted beneath her plate—Lord Tylar never delivered messages in person if he could avoid it. She picked it up, and unfolded it, expecting the worst.

You will come to Lady Viridina's bower at the hour of the Skylark to discuss a matter of some importance. That was all it said, but that was enough to completely shatter her illusions of peace.

She stared at the note, her hand shaking only a little, and carefully put it down, her appetite quite gone. Discuss? Oh no, that was hardly what would happen—given that the note was in her father's handwriting and with his personal sigil impressed into the paper. No, Lord Tylar had *orders* for her, and her mother was the one, as bound by his will as any of his slaves, who would deliver them. Having Lady Viridina deliver these orders only proved that they were going to be unpleasant. He always had his wife handle domestic orders that were going to bring trouble. He felt it was her job to ensure *his* domestic peace, even if it was *his* orders that were about to destroy that peace.

Her stomach churned and knotted, as she tried to guess just what the "matter of some importance" was. Had he finally noticed that there were no suitors clamoring for her? Had he gotten back reports from some of his underlings that showed she had spent more time with the tame animals than with any male? She would not have put it past him to have set spies on her, or questioned his associates about her movements.

Unreasoning dread blossomed in her heart, an evil flower of darkness and foreboding. Was he going to order a whole new round of lessons for her, designed to mold her into something more desirable than she was—or—

And one of her nightmares of the first night returned to make her "unreasonable" dread only too reasonable.

There was something worse, much worse, that he could do to her—or have done. The nightmares she had been enduring had been about a possibility that she had not even considered, had not even remembered, until her own evil dreams brought it back to her.

If he was not happy with her, and saw no possibility of voluntary improvement, there was one other step he might take. It was drastic, but he was ruthless enough to take it, if he could find a mage powerful enough to oblige him. She had dismissed the possibility because she could not imagine him ever devoting that *much* of his profit and resources to *her.* But if he was angry enough, economic considerations might vanish before the prospect of having his will thwarted by his ill-mannered, unsatisfactory daughter.

He could have me Changed.

The Change was something only whispered about in the bowers. No maiden of Rena's acquaintance had actually *known* a girl who had been Changed, but everyone had a cousin or a friend who did. If a maiden just was not *satisfactory* to her father—or, more rarely, a wife was not satisfactory to her husband, and the husband could get her father to agree to the Change—there was a remedy. Great elven mages had created beasts like the alicorns in the past, after all, creating them out of common beasts of the fields. And hadn't she herself changed the drab sparrows and pigeons into charming companions? Changing a maiden—making her more beautiful, more graceful—was just a bit more subtle than creating an alicorn.

Especially if one is not terribly worried about damaging her, so long as it doesn't show. A maiden would never have to gallop across a battlefield, after all, and if, afterwards, she was just a bit delicate, a bit sickly, so long as she could bring forth *one* heir, that was really all that mattered. Once the heir had been produced, another wife could be found—or done without, as the case might be.

A maiden was taken away, so the whispers went, and when she returned, she would no longer be merely attractive, she would be a beauty, a living work of art. She would be incapable of a clumsy movement, of a missung note, of a social mistake. She would always be graceful and gracious. She would never lose her temper, never weep, never complain, but show the same smiling face of peace and contentment wherever she went, in public or in private, to her peers or to her slaves. She would obey her father's or her husband's every wish, willingly and immediately. She would become the perfect wife, the perfect lady, in every possible way.

The trouble was, the Change worked in the mind as well as the body, and maidens who underwent the Change were rumored to lose some vital spark of themselves. They had no ambitions, no interest outside their own bowers, and no creativity. If given a work to play or a piece of embroidery already designed and ready to sew, they would go about playing the piece or embroidering the design with mechanical perfection. But they could not design a piece of embroidery for themselves, or compose their own music, even if they had been superb artists or musicians before the Change.

Nor was that all. Their pleasures turned to simpler things; they lost interest in anything that was an intellectual challenge. They generally stopped reading or writing, left the household accounts to underlings, often left anything vaguely creative in the hands of their slaves, and saw no reason to leave their own bowers except at the insistence of their husbands. Their lives became centered on three things: their appearance, pleasing their husbands, and childbearing. They became obsessive about jewels and gowns, often changing four and five times in a day, they would throw themselves off a cliff if that would make their lords happy, and they longed for nothing more than to bear as many children as they could, and as quickly.

In short, they were as controlled as the human concubines, and just as compliant. It was no accident that while the Change was worked on a maiden's body, her ruler saw to it that it was worked on her mind as well. Why alter the body only, when with an exercise of magic, discontent, improper ambitions, and inconvenient interests could be wiped away as cleanly as if they had never existed in the first place? One could completely remold a maiden or a wife to suit one's own needs.

How convenient for their lords.

She'd had that nightmare about being Changed, enduring the pain of the Change itself and the horror of feeling her mind, her *self*, drain away, and had done her best to forget the dream and how vivid it had been. Now it came back to her with redoubled clarity, as if it had been, not a dream, but a premonition.

Her hands and heart went cold as ice.

She fought her fear down. No, Lord Tylar wouldn't have her Changed, surely! It was *very* difficult, and very expensive, either in terms of strict recompense or in terms of the demands the mage would later make on the "customer." Only the greatest of mages dared to meddle in such ways, and the greater a mage, the more power and prestige he *already* had. Surely there was nothing Lord Tylar could offer that would tempt one of the High Lords to help him in such an undertaking!

But her body would not respond to her desperate reasoning. Her body and her heart were afraid, deeply, deathly afraid. Her throat closed so tightly that she could not even swallow; her face felt like a mask of wood, stiff and unmoving, and her mouth went dry.

Her breath came in short, frightened gasps, as if she were a rabbit at the end of a chase; her heart pounded as she again reached for the piece of paper. She reread the note, searching for a clue and finding nothing. But—there was no indication that he *was* going to have her Changed, and surely he'd have let *something* slip if that was his intention. Wouldn't he have told her to dismiss her slaves, or insisted she *not* speak to Lorryn? For that matter, if he intended to have her Changed, why send her to her mother to be *told* about it in the first place? Why not simply have a pair of burly guards come and take her away without any warning? By letting her know in advance that he had planned something for her, he actually increased the chance that she would cause a scene when she learned what it was.

Perhaps, she told herself frantically, it was something simpler—an ordinary scolding for not living up to the standards her father had set for her, for not carrying out the orders he had given her.

Gradually her breath eased. That made more sense; that was logical. Lord Tylar always took the easiest route to anything, and he always left the scoldings to Lady Viridina. Her throat opened a little, as she forced calm on herself.

Yes, that *must* be it. Lady Viridina was going to deliver a lecture on duty and how she had failed in that duty. Then, perhaps, would come another round of the lessons she had foreseen; unpleasant and time-consuming, but not a disaster, just something to be endured until Lord Tylar forgot about her again. And he would forget about her, especially if she kept herself out of sight, as long as there were no choice matrimonial prospects in view. She was no real drain on his resources, and she was ornamental enough in a plain, quiet way. She occupied Lorryn, and kept him from getting into trouble by doing so. She could even be trusted to oversee some of the household on the occasions when he needed his wife at his side.

Surely that is all that this note means. If it were something that would be as expensive for him as having me Changed, wouldn't he want to deliver the orders in person, and see to it that I was conveyed away with a minimum of fuss and damage? Wouldn't he want to oversee every tiny detail, from telling me what was to happen, to seeing the end result for himself? He would be here to make certain he got his money's worth.

So she tried to convince herself, although her heart was not so easy to calm. It was hard to get her fear down to even a manageable level. It took every bit of will to rise from her uneaten breakfast and pretend that she was calm and collected. She ordered her dress with extra care, her voice so subdued with dread that it was hardly more than a whisper. She allowed the slaves to tend to everything; she was afraid that her hands would begin to tremble, so that even the simplest task would be impossible. In a haze of fear and depression, she took herself to her mother's bower at the appointed hour—which was directly after the breakfast that she could not force herself to eat. At least she would not have to wait to hear her fate. . . .

She walked down hallways in a state of tension that made every tiny detail stand out. Her mother's bower was not entered by a conventional door, but through one of the magical curtains of sheeting energy that also protected the harem from intrusion. A slave was there to meet her, and steered her away from the sitting room to another part of the bower entirely, and Lady Viridina received her daughter in her own study, though the room bore very little resemblance to Lord Tylar's study. This was a stark room, small, with only a desk and two chairs of the simplest design; the floor, walls, and ceiling were a uniform cream, the desk and chairs a slightly darker shade of the same color. Viridina was reading something as Rena came in; she gestured to the single empty chair without speaking, and Rena took it, obediently, without a word of her own. She sat there, stiffly upright, with her hands folded in her lap, her whole body so taut with tension that she felt as if she vibrated with every heartbeat.

Finally Lady Viridina put the paper down, and looked up at her daughter, her face and eyes completely inscrutable. "My Lord Tylar wishes me to tell you that he is very pleased with you," she said—words so surprising that it was only by force of will that Rena kept her mouth from dropping open with shock.

He's pleased with me? With me? How? Why? What did I do? What does he think I did?

"It seems that you spent a great deal of time with V'keln Gildor er-Lord Kyndreth at the fete," her mouther continued, and waited for an answer.

Rena nodded, numbly. Was that all it was? Just that she was kind to a bumbling idiot? A handsome bumbling idiot, granted, but then there were no such things as uncomely elves—

—except maybe me.

"The House of Kyndreth is an ancient and powerful House," Lady Viridina continued. "Not quite as powerful as that of Hernalth, but older. There is a great deal to be said for their lineage, and Lord Lyon is accounted a power in the Council. His favor is eagerly sought after."

Again Rena nodded, unable to imagine where this was going. Had Gildor's father been grateful that she had spent any time at all with his son—grateful enough to have complimented her to Lord Tylar? Perhaps even grateful enough to be willing to support Lord Tylar in the Council?

"Well, you seem to have impressed Lord Gildor in many ways," her mother said, without so much as a lifted eyebrow. "And it is difficult to impress Lord Gildor enough to cause him to remember *any* experience for more than a few hours. Or so it is said, according to your lord father."

There was no hint of irony in her mother's voice, and nothing in her expression to suggest humor. Rena hardly knew what to think. She certainly had not expected either candor or irony from either Lady Viridina or her father.

Lady Viridina regarded her with a penetrating gaze, as if looking for any hint that Rena found her comment amusing. "At any rate, you did impress the er-Lord, and as a consequence, you have impressed his *father*, which is much more important."

Again she waited for a reply.

"Yes, my lady," Rena managed to say. "Naturally, it would be more important to impress Lord Lyon. Poor Gildor—must be very difficult to deal with for his own lord father. He seems a—" she sought for a word to describe him that would have at least a hint of flattery amid the terrible truth that the young er-Lord was a fool "—an *amiable* young lord, and he certainly seems eager to please his lord father. As is only right, of course. But I would say that he has very little ambition."

Or wit. Or intelligence.

Her mother nodded, and now she smiled, thinly. "Good. You understand the situation, then. V'denn Lyon Lord Kyndreth made your father an offer for your hand last night, on behalf of his son. Naturally, Lord Tylar has accepted on your behalf. He is very pleased; what is more, Lord Lyon seems to believe that this acceptance puts *him* in your lord father's debt."

She took the words as if they were blows to her face and body, and with nearly the same shock.

Offer? For me—from Gildor? Accepted?

Shock turned to horror, and Rena was paralyzed, quite unable to speak, move, or even think past the reality of her mother's words. She had been sold away, all in an instant, without any warning—given to—to—

Gildor! A—an idiot who can't even remember what he did a few hours ago! A dolt completely controlled by his father! A booby who—who has barely more sense than a child still in the nursery, whose only interest is hunting, and who hasn't a single clever thought in his head! A fool who is cruel without even knowing that he has hurt someone!

She was too stunned even to tremble, and evidently her mother took her silence as a sign of agreement. She smiled, more with relief than with pleasure. "I am pleased to see that you are properly grateful to your lord father and to Lord Gildor. Your good sense does you credit, and is a testimony to your training." She stood, and handed Rena another folded piece of paper, this one sealed with Lord Tylar's formal seal. "The formalities must be observed, of course, and with someone of Lord Gildor's lineage, that is more important than usual. Everything must be done properly, with the appropriate care, on our part. Go to your quarters, and have your slaves gown you for a formal dinner," she ordered, as Rena stood in automatic response to her mother's movement. "You will be leaving by means of the Portals to go straight to Lord Lyon and Lord Gildor yourself, bearing the acceptance, as is right and proper. Your escort will come to take you there in an hour."

That was clearly a dismissal, and Rena walked blindly out of the study, out of her mother's bower, and down the hallway to her own suite, still wrapped in a cocoon of stunned numbness.

* * *

The next few hours were a blur, lost in a haze of shock. She kept thinking that this was just another nightmare, that in a moment she would awaken in her own bed. *This* wasn't what was supposed to happen! It was like some horrible twist on a romantic tale, wherein the High Lord falls in love with the daughter of one of his underlings and petitions to wed her. Why, oh why had Lord Gildor chosen *her* train to tread on? Why couldn't he have blundered into someone else's unwanted daughter?

She must have given her slaves orders, and they must have been sensible, for the next thing she knew, she was gowned, coiffed, and bejeweled, and standing next to her escort in front of the Portal. *Someone* must have seen to it that she had the most flattering of her formal gowns brought out—perhaps one of the slaves had taken pity on her. This time there were no cosmetics, her hair had been done in simple braids twined with strands of pearls and fastened at her neck in a complicated knot, and her dress was of heavy pink silk, with a high neck and long sleeves that swept the floor. A belt of pearls held it close in at her waist, and more pearls circled her throat. She faded into the walls of her chamber, but at least she didn't look like a clown.

She thought she recalled Myre issuing orders and being obeyed, while she stood, sat, and turned in a state of mental blankness; she simply could not remember exiting her chamber, and now she stood on the threshold of the Portal. There was a sealed scroll-tube in her hand, an elaborately decorated, ivory-inlaid, gold scroll-tube. She didn't remember picking it up; someone must have put it in her hand without her being aware of it. And as she raised her hand to touch her temple, dazedly, there was a new ring on her finger; this one of white gold, set with a beryl engraved with a winged stag.

Lord Lyon's seal—?

It must be. How else would she be able to use the Portals to cross from here to Lord Lyon's estate? It must have arrived with Lord Lyon's messenger.

She had no time to muster any other thoughts; her escort

moved, carrying her with them, and she was through the Portal—

There was no intermediate pause in the Council Chamber this time; perhaps that was the reason for the signet ring, to enable her to go directly to her destination. She emerged into a reception room—

It was like no other room she had ever seen, though it was not one that had been altered by magic. This was a chamber with leather furnishings and hunting trophies everywhere. The blank-eyed heads of dead animals stared down at her from walls paneled in dark woods; whole dead animals and petrified birds had been made into lamp holders, table supports, or grisly display pieces. Hides with the heads intact carpeted the floor, and the whole of one wall was taken up with a mounted pair of stud alicorns locked in combat— one with a coat the black of ebony, and one white as a cloud. Both had mad, orange eyes that glittered with malice, and there was blood—or something made to resemble blood—on their twisting, spiraling single horns.

She shuddered, and looked away.

Anything that could possibly be hunted was here in some form and had been made into a trophy of some kind. Alicorn horns made a rack holding boar-spears, ivory and horn inlay covered every inch of the furniture that was not already upholstered with hides, some finished as smooth leather, and some with the hair or fur left on. Teeth snarled at her from all corners. Stuffed snakes twined around the bases of quivers mounted beside their bows. Racks for knives and swords had been fashioned of antlers.

Everywhere, glassy eyes stared at her, and she fancied that their stares held anger, bewilderment, or accusation. The place felt haunted by silent rage.

A silent human servant appeared, bowed deeply, and gestured for her to follow. She did so, glad only to be free of that room of accusing eyes.

Was this Lord Lyon's way of impressing his visitors? Or did he truly take pleasure in having victims of his hunting expeditions displayed in a place where he could view them frequently?

Was she to become just another such trophy?

The servant led the way down a corridor paneled in more of the dark wood, lit by globes of mage-light caught in sconces made of yet more antlers, and carpeted with bloodred plush. She gave up trying to reckon how many deer and elk the sconces represented; Lord Lyon was one of the older High Lords, and he had many long years of hunting behind him. He might even be displaying only a fraction of his trophies here, given how long he had been alive.

What a horrid thought!

What was he trying to say, with this room of death? It was the first thing any visitor arriving by Portal would see, after all. Was he showing them, wordlessly, just how ruthless a foe he was? Did he mean for them to be impressed with his physical skill, or with the mental ability it took to stalk and kill so many creatures?

The corridor seemed to go on forever; the lights brightened as she reached them and dimmed behind her, so that she could not tell where the real end of it was. It said something for the dazed state of her mind that somewhere along it she lost her escort of guards, and she did not even notice that they were gone until the human servant stopped at a doorway and waited for her to join him. This was no ordinary door, of course; as soon as she stepped in front of it, she saw that it was an inlaid geometric mosaic of thousands of tiny bones, all of them vertebrae, fitted together with exacting skill to cover the entire face of the door with bone ivory. The design was probably supposed to signify something, but what that was, she had no notion.

The servant opened the door smoothly and bowed for her to enter. She stepped hesitantly through, into the half-dark beyond.

Once again, she found herself at the edge of a sylvan glade beneath a full moon. There were no tame animals here, though, and the moon and stars overhead were all too clearly magelights. Most of this was illusion, and it was not as perfect an illusion as the fete had boasted. In fact, given Lord Lyon's power and prestige, it was probably not as perfect an illusion as he *could* create, if he cared to. An unseen musician played quietly on a dulcimer, and the branches of the trees moved to a breeze that did not stir even a hair of Rena's coiffure.

The door closed behind her.

In the center of the glade was a table, set for three. Magelight caught in a candelabra of antlers centered on the table, though it did not appear that the occupants had been served yet. There were two people there already; the dim light made it impossible for her to identify either of them, but she assumed they were Gildor and his father.

She stepped forward a few paces and the light at the table brightened. The two occupants of the table turned toward her—and she saw that one of them was really a female.

A *human* female.

Sharing the board at what was supposed to be *her* intimate betrothal dinner with her Lord-to-be.

She froze where she stood, unable to go on, or to turn and leave.

The light was bright enough now to show humiliating details. The human was very beautiful, exquisitely and expensively gowned and jeweled in crimson satin the color of blood, with rubies and gold circling her throat, and her wrists—and from her posture and Gildor's, obviously his favorite concubine.

A concubine? At what was *supposed* to be her betrothal dinner?

For a moment, she wondered wildly if her mother had gotten the time of the invitation wrong, or if she had somehow misheard her orders.

But—no, that was not possible. The escort had been waiting for her, the acceptance ready for her to take with her, the ring that allowed her to come here readied for her hand. There was no mistake here.

Far from suffering from the paralysis and fear that had held her until this moment, her mind suddenly leapt free of its bonds of dazed indecision. She saw everything with heightened clarity, and her thoughts raced as if she had been playing the games of intrigue for decades. Perhaps it was only that for the first time in this awful day, she had confronted something she could act upon, rather than being in a position in which she had no control whatsoever.

This was no accident, nor had Gildor thought of this arrangement on his own. He could not simply have "invited" his concubine; his father would never have permitted such a thing, and the servants would have reported such a social gaffe immediately, long before Sheyrena arrived. Lord Lyon had orchestrated everything so thoroughly thus far that this insult to her dignity and pride could only be due to some plan of his—or of him and Lord Tylar combined. It could not be designed as an affront as such—Lord Lyon would not go through all that he had just to insult a nonentity like her, and if he wished to insult Lord Tylar, he would do so directly and not through her. He was the more powerful of the two, and it would be a social gaffe on *his* part to insult her House through a female.

It's a test. And Father must have had a hand in it. Only he would think of using a human concubine as the tool and weapon.

She was being presented with a situation designed to test precisely how biddable, how obedient to her Lord's wishes, she would be in the future. Gildor was clearly not capable of making any kind of decent decision; to present him with a bride who had a mind of her own and a will of her own was to concoct a recipe for disaster. A willful wife could show him to be the fool that he truly was, and with no difficulty at all. Almost as bad, a willful wife might learn to manipulate him.

If I make a fuss, if I take insult with this and walk out, what would that mean?

Probably that she was going to be too much for Gildor to cope with.

She was tempted to do just that—

But if I do—

If anything would tempt Lord Tylar into having her Changed, it would be just such a reaction. She *had* her orders, after all; she was not supposed to have any pride that could suffer insult. If she dared to think for herself, she was a danger to her father's ambitions as well as to Gildor. And with Lord Lyon's help and influence backing him, her father would be able, monetarily and politically, to afford having her Changed so that she would no longer cause problems for her betrothed. Lord Lyon clearly needed, with some desperation, a bride who would not challenge Gildor or attempt to usurp his own power through Gildor. And if he could find a maiden whose father countenanced sending her away for the Change, wouldn't he seize such a chance with both hands? A Changed bride would be a bride who also would be unable to manipulate Gildor and use him against his father—and one who would make Gildor completely happy. A perfect bride, in other words, insofar as Lord Lyon's purposes went.

On the other hand, she could prove at this very moment that she was as pliant and meek as her father and Lord Lyon demanded. *If I just walk right up there as if there were nothing at all out of the ordinary with my being asked to share my betrothal feast with my betrothed's favorite lover, I'll be just as good as a Changed bride.* If she acted as if she simply didn't notice the insult, as if this was a cheerful little dinner party, it would mean that she was "safe"; she would obey her Lord in the future, and not embarrass him in public. She *might* be clever enough to try to manipulate Gildor—but Lord Lyon was probably operating under the assumption that if she had been kind to him without knowing who he was, she was doubtlessly too stupid to be *that* clever.

Her cold had given way to the heat of humiliation as she stood there, however. Not even Lady Viridina had ever been forced into a position like this!

If I go—if I walk out of here and go straight home again—

She would be forced to wed Gildor anyway. *But there won't be enough left of the real me to care.*

For one short moment, that almost seemed preferable to her current situation.

Then she shook herself mentally. This was only a betrothal. Hundreds of things could happen between now and the actual marriage. Gildor might die; if he spent most of his time in hunting, he stood a reasonable chance of discovering that he was not as good a hunter as he thought. Her father might die, which would leave Lorryn head of the household, and *he* would never force her to wed this lout. *She* might die. She and Lorryn together might find some way of getting Lord Tylar to break the betrothal. She might find a way to make Gildor disenchanted with her. Lord Lyon might make some disastrous move that would reduce his power, and make Gildor a less-than-desirable husband for her, in regard to Lord Tylar's ambitions.

At the very worst, she would be wed to the dolt, and if the marriage proved childless, Lorryn might be able to free her from it sometime in the future. Or Gildor could die.

And meanwhile, Lord Tylar looked upon her with grim favor. She might win a few freedoms out of this.

It was hard, hard, but she forced her feet to move forward, one slow step at a time. She forced a fatuous, false smile onto her lips. Gildor rose as she approached; the concubine did not. This did not escape Rena, and her cheeks burned with further humiliation.

"Sheyrena!" Gildor said, with childish enthusiasm. "Welcome! Please, come join us—"

The empty chair moved back of its own accord for her, and she took her place in it, moving stiffly. The concubine, a stunning raven-haired beauty with the healthiest set of pectoral endowments that Rena had ever seen in her life, smiled maliciously at her, and did not even incline her head in a token bow. *She* knew who the real power was here. She was the favorite; Sheyrena was the convenience.

"This is Jaene, the chief of my household; Jaene, this is Sheyrena." He grinned foolishly at them both; without a doubt, he was completely unaware that there was anything wrong with the situation. "I hope you'll come to be very good friends. You'll be seeing a lot of each other from now on."

Jaene smiled, the same cruel smile Rena had seen on her father's face as he assigned yet another of his castoffs to Lady Viridina's household. "I'm sure," she purred. "I'm sure we will."

Oh, surely. The chief of his household. As if the household of an er-Lord ever could consist of more than his harem, his personal servants, and his hunting-master! Did his father tell him to tell me that? Probably. And if I pretend to believe it, I'll prove that I'm as stupid as he is.

Sheyrena could not bring herself to say anything, nor could she bring herself to actually hand the sealed scroll-tube to Gildor. Cheeks hot, she simply placed it on the table between them, avoiding Jaene's eyes altogether.

Another invisible servant made it vanish before she could snatch it back.

Gildor settled back into his chair, a smug expression of blissfully ignorant happiness suffusing his features, making him look particularly handsome if one didn't gaze too closely at the vacant eyes. "We'll have to do this often," he said to no one in particular. "Just one happy little family!"

Jaene's smile widened just a little. "Whatever you wish, my lord," she replied, with mock submission, ignoring Sheyrena altogether.

Sheyrena nearly choked.

Fortunately, a plate settled in front of her, saving her from having to look anywhere else. That was just as well; she found it hard enough just to look at the plate.

She did not say more than two words during the entire painful meal—nor did she eat more than a single bite before her throat closed in rebellion. Jaene continued to smile poisonously and eat slowly, deliberately making each bite a display of sensuality. Gildor inhaled vast amounts of food, oblivious to the tension at the table. Invisible servants came and went with multiple courses, all of which were probably succulent; they certainly smelled inviting, and they looked beautiful. They might just as well have been straw for all that Rena could taste of them. She tried a bite or two, but gave up when her throat refused to unclench enough to allow her to swallow, and thereafter simply pushed the foot around on her plate with her fork until the servant came to take it away.

She did drink the wine, feverishly, and a servant kept her glasses full, a different wine for every course. She probably drank too much of it, for it made her a bit dizzy, but it did not impair her enough to make her lose control of her tongue. She only wanted it as a kind of anesthetic, to keep the pain of the moment at bay.

She said nothing, kept her eyes on her plate, and endured. The invisible musician played on, supplemented by a harpist. The trees swayed in the breeze that was not there. The unseen servants whisked full plates from under her nose, replacing them with more full plates. Jaene continued to smile, looking more and more catlike with every passing moment as she turned her posture into a lazy, seductive lounge. She had allowed the neckline of her gown to slip, and Gildor was staring at her cleavage with a rapt attention that nearly matched that which he had given the food. *She* might just as well not have been there by the time the unendurable meal was half-over.

Only the wine gave her the strength to sit there and endure—the wine, and the certainty that, no matter what she did, she (or her body, at any rate) *would* be wedding Gildor if her father had any say in the matter. She had only the choice that would permit her to keep her mind intact; the choice that proved she was obedient. Her father wanted this wedding; she might get a little of what she longed for only if she earned it with her silence.

And of course, except for Lord Lyon, her father had the only say in the matter.

Finally, as she gulped yet another glass of wine and her feeling of dizziness increased, the dessert course arrived. The invisible servant whisked away the last plate, and replaced it with a tiny white sugar alicorn, romantically idealized, a ring balanced delicately on the end of its single horn. The ring was made of heavy white gold, and was engraved with winged stags and moonbirds. She knew what it was: the betrothal ring, of course. If she accepted it and put it on, it sealed her fate.

She hesitated for just a moment, holding back her fate for an illusory heartbeat. As long as this thing was not on her finger, she could pretend that she was free.

But I'm not. I never was. I never will be.

Numb and dizzy, she took the ring and fumbled it onto her finger.

Then, with her fork, she slowly and deliberately crushed the alicorn to tiny, sugary crumbs.

She had thought that her ordeal was over, but Gildor showed no signs of rising, and neither did Jaene. In fact, Gildor showed no signs of noticing that she had even *accepted* his ring. She was forced to sit there, crushing the dessert into smaller and smaller bits, while Gildor stared at his concubine's bosom and ignored her. *She* could not leave until Gildor produced a written and signed betrothal contract for her to deliver to her father, and he didn't seem to be prepared to do that while Jaene sat there and fluttered her eyelashes at him.

Finally, with the alicorn reduced to powder, and her temper smoldering under the influence of the wine, she decided she'd had enough. Let Gildor explain why he hadn't presented her with the contract. *She* had gone out of her way to observe the formalities; she had obeyed far more than the mere letter of her orders.

She stood up abruptly, and the chair she had been sitting in fell over as she shoved it violently back. Gildor and Jaene suddenly turned to stare at her as if they had only just noticed that she was there.

"It is very late," she said, rather thickly, as the wine made speech a bit difficult. "I beg your pardon, my lord, but I am not often abroad from my father's house and am unused to such late hours. I must go."

The moment the last word left her lips, the room changed.

The glade, the sky, and Jaene all vanished, leaving only the table in the middle of a room paneled with dark wood, floored with black marble. The table had not been set for three, but for two—Jaene's place setting and chair vanished with the human. Two servants stood to one side. Gildor blinked with confusion.

And a tall and powerful elven lord stepped out of the shadows.

"Lord F-father?" Gildor stuttered. "Where's Jaene gone? Where's the glade?"

Lord Lyon ignored his son's questions, turning to regard Rena with a slight bow of amusement. "Forgive the deception, child. Gildor insisted upon the slave's presence, but of course, I would not have inflicted such an insult upon you. It would have been unacceptably rude."

Oh no, of course. Not while you could create an illusion instead, one good enough to fool Gildor. I thought you were a better mage than this silly setting showed.

But she bowed her head, meekly, and clasped her hands in front of her. She was afraid to speak, lest her own mouth betray her, but the effect of the wine was swiftly burning away with her anger at such a double-deception. She had been used. She had to endure it, but she didn't have to like it.

Now Lord Lyon turned to his son. "Let this be a lesson to *you*, Gildor. No slave must be permitted to eat with her masters, *ever*," he said sternly. "And no slave should be given the kinds of liberties you would have given this Jaene, and have given her in the past; it makes them proud and insubordinate. I had her sent away while you were eating; once you learn how to keep your females in line, you may have her back."

Once you learn to curb your hounds, you may have them back. And apologize to the Lady who just had her dress drenched with piddle.

Out of the corner of her eye she saw Gildor flush and bow his head. "Yes, Father," he murmured submissively. But he did not apologize to Rena. Not that she expected him to.

"My apologies, if your feelings were abused, dear child," Lord Lyon said smoothly. "But you have displayed a proper maidenly modesty and forbearance that do you credit. Here."

He held a scroll-tube out to her; this one just as elaborately decorated as the one she had brought, but with designs of moonbirds and winged stags together. She took it automatically, and although it was cool, it felt as if it burned her hand as she clenched her fingers on it.

"Please convey the contract to your noble father, with my thanks," Lord Lyon said, as Gildor stood dumb. The older man took her free hand, and kissed the back of it, a mere brushing of lips across the skin. "Tell him for me that he has just such a daughter as both of us hoped, and I am pleased to welcome you to my family."

That *was* the signal that she could escape; she murmured something appropriate, and took her chance to flee.

Her escort met her outside the door, and ushered her toward the Portal with what would have been unseemly haste if she had not wanted to be out of there as quickly as possible. She wanted to fling the horrid tube away from her, but before she even entered the Portal, the chief of her guards took it from her nerveless fingers, then sent her through with a none-too-gentle shove.

Attendants swarmed her on the other side, a display of special attentions she had never been granted before, and which was probably due entirely to a message from Lord Lyon that she had been a good and obedient little girl, doing precisely as she had been told. They hurried her off to her rooms, and once there, fussed over her as if she were some kind of prize object.

She let them; exhausted by the tension and the need to keep her own emotions in check, she was too tired to think clearly.

It's over. That was all that was important, for now.

They bathed her, not permitting her to do anything for herself, in a bath foaming with perfumed oils. They dressed her in a silken nightgown she had never seen before, a gown luxurious enough to wear as a dress. They combed out her hair, shining each strand with soft cloths lightly moistened with scent. They rubbed scented creams into her hands, her feet, and her legs. They gave her tiny dainties to eat—just as well, since she hadn't had more than two bites of dinner to hold off the effects of all that wine. They handed her an exotic drink to soothe her throat and her nerves, foaming, sweet, and warm. That was the only thought in her mind, as they pampered and preened her, and finally put her to bed. *It's over.*

She fell asleep immediately, before the lights went out, while they were still crowding the room, putting things away.

But when she woke, with dawn still an hour away, alone in her room, it was with cold dread. It *wasn't* over. She had been sealed to Lord Gildor, and last night signaled the preparation of the sacrifice. *That* was why all the pampering. There would be more such, an attempt to make her into as comely a creature as possible without an actual Change. There would be less in the way of freedom, not more.

She had been maneuvered into precisely the position she was most afraid of.

And this was only the beginning; after the wedding it would be worse. She had deceived herself, with her thoughts of greater freedom as the er-Lord's lady.

If living under her father's roof had been difficult, living under Lord Lyon's would be harder still. There would be no Lorryn to whisk her away on occasional escapes. Lord Lyon would have her watched, every moment, to make certain that she was the obedient little fool he thought she was. Every book she read would be scrutinized, every exercise of her powers weighed and measured. Every hour of her day would be spied upon. She would have no secrets, for Lord Lyon would be certain that a secret meant a secret plot against himself. There was only one ruler in that House, and Lord Lyon would permit no other.

If she wanted to survive, she had only one choice: She must conform completely. She must become a copy of her mother; serene, obedient, and dead inside.

There was only one person who could possibly help her— *Lorryn! He's clever, he'll think of something!*

Just as she thought that, there came a faint tapping on her door. Three taps, a pause, then two, then one.

She flung herself out of bed and ran to let her brother in. For one joyful moment she was certain he had heard of what had happened and had come to tell her how to extricate herself from her plight. But as he slipped inside and shut the door quickly behind him, he turned toward her with a face as pale and as fearful as her own.

"Rena, you *have* to help me," he whispered hoarsely, his voice choked with tension, his eyes huge and dark-circled in his white face. "I don't have anyone else to turn to!"

The shock was worse than being plunged into ice-cold water. Lorryn? *Helpless?* With no one to turn to?

And I do? she thought, and shook her head. "I was— Lorryn, what on earth could *I* do to help you? What's happened to you?" Possibilities swarmed her mind. Had he been indiscreet with someone who had a powerful father? Had he gambled disastrously and lost? Had he gotten into a quarrel with another er-Lord—oh, dear Ancestors, had he quarreled, fought, and the fight ended fatally? She blurted the first words that came to her lips. "Did you get in trouble with—"

He shook his head violently. "It isn't anything you can guess," he replied, and seized both her hands to pull her over to a seat on the couch opposite the bed. "Trust me, it isn't anything you can even imagine. I'm in terrible danger—I'm—"

He swallowed audibly, and passed the back of his hand across his forehead. "Something was supposed to happen at Lord Ardeyn's fete. The High Lords of the Council were testing everyone under a certain age as they arrived to see if they were halfbloods in a disguise of illusion."

She nodded, remembering that tingle of spell-casting she had felt as she arrived, and remembering, too, that she had wondered why her father had ordered cosmetics for her instead of an illusion of better looks.

"Well, I didn't go to the fete, and late last night three members of the Council arrived *here* with orders to test me for illusion," he went on, beads of sweat starting out on his forehead.

She shook her head. "I don't understand," she said, bewildered. "What could be so bad about that?"

She couldn't help thinking about her own plight—how

could *anything* Lorryn faced in the way of some kind of test be worse than the trap she was in?

"They *can't* test me!" he said hoarsely, his hands clenching on hers until she made a sound of pain in protest and he released his hold. "Rena, they *can't* test me! If they do, they'll find out I *am* halfblood!"

She stared at him, the words refusing to make sense. "How can you be a halfblood?" she asked stupidly. "Mother—"

"Lady Viridina is my mother," he said woodenly. "But Lord Tylar is not my father. My father was a human slave, master of her household. She kept the illusion on me until I was old enough to hold it on myself. I am a halfblood, a wizard, and when the Council finds that out—"

Once again, shock—and the fact that this time she *might* be able to do something—gave her mind speed and clarity.

"They'll kill you," she breathed. "Oh, Ancestors! Lorryn, how—we have to do something! Can't Mother help you?"

He took her hands in that crushing grip again, but this time she hardly noticed. Despair had turned his features into a mask of pain. "Mother can't save me this time; Father locked her in the bower until the testing is over. You are the only person I can turn to. Can't you hide me among your servants or something? Can you—"

"I have a better idea," she replied quickly, as she made, then discarded, a dozen plans in a heartbeat. He couldn't hide here; he *had* to run away. And if he ran—

He had to take her with him.

She calculated, quickly. "At least, I think I do. One of my maids always seems to have all kinds of information about the dragons and wizards—it's reliable, too; I've checked it against all the things you've found out."

"What has that—" he began, then blinked. "Oh. Oh, of course! If she has a way of getting information, she may have a way back to the source!" A glint of hope entered his eyes. "Do you think she's an agent of the wizards?"

Rena shrugged; the idea had never occurred to her before, but it certainly made complete sense. "What else could she be? She's terribly forward, not much like any slave I've ever seen. She's not one of Father's castoffs, and anyway, they have a different kind of insolence. The wizards *must* have spies among the slaves, right? Or how else would they know what we were doing? And how else would they know who the halfbloods among the slaves were, to rescue them? She told me that the wizards were always rescuing halfblood children from the slave pens. Didn't they rescue the Elvenbane that way?"

He nodded, and his face took on a grave intensity. "They couldn't have known about me, because I wasn't a slave—unless this Myre of yours was sent here because they *thought* that either you or me might have had human blood."

"It makes sense," she agreed. "It makes even more sense when you think about all the stories she's told me about the dragons and the wizards, all the news she brought me about what they were doing. She says they're building a new stronghold right now, in fact, and that the dragons are helping them." It was her turn to clutch his hands. "We should run away, both of us, Lorryn! We should go to the dragons!"

"Both of us?" he said, sudden doubt in his voice. "But you aren't—"

"If you disappear, what do you think will happen to me?" she countered fiercely, before he could object. "Father would *never* believe that I didn't know something."

"He wouldn't use a coercion on his own—" Lorryn began.

"Oh yes he would," she said, with a savagery that took him aback. "He wouldn't hesitate, not for a moment, and especially not with three members of the Council breathing down his neck." Years of resentment at Lorryn's preferential treatment came to a boil, and she gave him truth after bitter, angry truth. "He was ready to wed me to the first drooling dotard or prize idiot that made an offer. He was willing to use coercions to get me to the fete. And he was quite prepared to have me sent away to be Changed if I didn't please Lord Lyon last night. You've never seen him fling his used concubines at Mother and expect her to smile and take them into her service! You've never listened to him insult both of us and expect us to nod and agree with him that we are useless,

worthless, empty-headed idiots. You've never had to sit at dinner while he told his friends that you were hardly satisfactory, but if any of them were willing to take you off his hands, he'd be grateful! And you've never sat there in silence because if you *dared* to look insolent, he'd mage-lash you as soon as you were all in private. Mage-lashing," she added bitterly, "leaves no marks, after all; no scars that might disfigure a potential bride."

Lorryn looked stunned and shocked. "I didn't know—" he began in a whisper.

"It didn't matter," she replied, with bleak forgiveness. "You couldn't have done anything except get yourself in trouble. I learned quickly enough to be meek, silent, obedient, and invisible. Just the way he wanted, and something he didn't have to think about. Then he left me alone."

"But—"

"It doesn't matter," she repeated. "All that matters is that I have to escape with you, because he will use coercion to find out what I know if you leave me behind. So take me with you! I still have those boy's clothes that you gave me; we can find Myre and find out what she knows—"

He nodded, slowly. "If she can help us—if she knows how to find the wizards—"

"She must," Rena replied, "or where would she be getting all her news? I'll ring for her—"

"Don't bring the others!" he said in alarm, as she reached for a bell-cord. "If you call servants to come boiling in here, there's no way we'll keep this silent!"

She shook her head, exasperated. Didn't he know anything about the way a bower was served? There were times when a lady did not want *anyone* except the personal servant of her body to come anywhere near her. "Don't worry, Myre's bell goes only to her room; that's the price of her privacy and her status as my personal maid. They won't have changed that much yet."

It occurred to her that the timing of this crisis was nothing short of a miracle, so far as their escape possibilities went. One more day, and Myre would likely *not* be her personal maid anymore. Lord Lyon would surely send over slaves of his own to assure her continued obedience and docility. There had been something in that drink last night that had made her sleep like a stone; surely there would be more such drinks to ensure she had no second thoughts on the betrothal.

And in another week, she would be so busy with wedding preparations that Lorryn would have been unable to come anywhere near her during the day—and at night, there would be real guards mounted on all entrances to her rooms. Nothing was ever left to chance in a situation in which the bride might become—awkward.

And after that, she would not even *be* here; she would begin a round of visits to her own female kin, then to Lord Lyon's. There would be fetes in honor of the betrothal, and long talks with each chosen female on the duty of wives to their husbands. That round of visits would end, not here, but at Lord Lyon's estate, where the wedding would finally take place.

No, the timing on this could not have been better—

And here was the escape she had longed for, dreamed of— even prayed for, although the elves had no deities to entreat, and felt such superstitions were the product of inferior minds. Perhaps the humans were right after all—something *did* listen to prayers!

Myre appeared within moments of her sounding the bell, looking a bit out-of-sorts, but not at all disheveled; it had never occurred to her before, but Myre always looked like that, no matter how odd the hour when Rena summoned her. Did she never sleep? Or was she something other than what she seemed?

Did wizards sleep, for instance?

Myre's eyes widened just a trifle to see Lorryn sitting on the couch, but she nodded as Rena motioned for silence.

"There's no one listening, not even with magic," Lorryn said wearily. "Believe me, I would know."

Myre stared at him—then slowly smiled. "So, wizard," she said softly. "I heard about the three Council members arriving last night, but I had thought it was because of Sheyrena's betrothal."

"Sheyrena's—what?" Lorryn said, taken aback.

"Never mind, it doesn't matter," Rena told him fiercely, then turned to Myre. "Please," she pleaded. "You seem to know so much about the free wizards—we have to get away from here! We need your help!"

Myre's smile broadened, as if none of this surprised her in the least. "Indeed," she said calmly. "I would say that's an understatement."

The slave sat down on the edge of the bed as if she were the master, and not the other way around.

Then again—right now, she is. Her posture certainly seemed to confirm every speculation Rena had just made about her. No slave ever unlearned discipline to look the way Myre did now.

"So, I do believe I can help," the slave said, leaning back on her hands and regarding them both with an amused eye, as relief made Rena feel faint. "The first thing we'll need is a weapon or two. And after that—" She smiled, as if at a secret only she knew. "Just how good a swimmer are you?"

5

THE DISCOVERY OF a few wild humans out here was startling in its way, although Shana had assumed ever since they began their search through the wilderness for a new home that sooner or later the wizards would come across humans that had never been subjugated by the elves. This world was simply too big, and the elves too few, for them to have either conquered or destroyed all humans in it.

Now that they all knew the facts, though, this discovery was very intimidating; from everything they learned from Collen's clan, there were *many* more humans out beyond the lands she knew than Shana had thought; here was a group—one of many—that existed simply to *trade* with the other wild ones.

Collen's family of traders had been unable to tell the wizards anything about the grasslands to the south of the Citadel, or who might be living there now. He and his kin stuck to the river, seldom venturing beyond it. He could only tell her that there were many groups of nomadic herdsmen that roamed the plains, and that once in a great while some of these sent representatives to the river to trade with *his* people.

Shana had taken that lack of information as a reason to escape the Citadel on a scouting expedition, and Mero, Keman, and Kalamadea had not been much behind in volunteering as well. The retrieval of personal belongings was proceeding at what Shana considered to be a reasonable rate, but it was not satisfying Caellach Gwain and his cronies, who seemed to see no reason why they could not come barging into any given session with demands that the circle of young wizards bring back a particular object *right now.* Nor, despite much urging both polite and brusque, would they stoop to the use of stones to amplify their powers, or to work in a circle to combine their abilities as the younger set had learned. *They* had much more important work to do; "fetching things was a job for apprentices," or so Shana was told at least once a day.

What that "important work" was, Shana had yet to learn. To give them the benefit of the doubt, they might be working on ways to defend the Citadel or keep the magics practiced within it cloaked. She herself had seen no evidence of that, however, nor had anyone else she'd spoken to. Unfortunately for all, it was most likely that the "important work" consisted of arranging their personal quarters to their liking, and trying to bully the dragons into making changes and additions before those changes were scheduled.

Caellach himself had treated Shana to a lecture on the duty of an apprentice to her masters, and a tirade on how an apprentice who had single-handedly brought about the wreckage of her masters' lives should be grateful they still permitted her to walk among them. Shana decided then and there that *she* had much more important work to do than fetching things as well—seeing if there were any more wild humans to the south. After all, it stood to reason that the plains could support any number of groups of "nomadic herdsmen," and one of those groups *might* retain knowledge of human magic from the times before the elves arrived. The elves didn't own the world, though they might think they did, and what they knew about it was probably only a fraction of what there was to know.

Shana had another reason for her expedition, though it was one she kept to herself. Realistically speaking, even though Collen's traders had been friendly, there was no law saying that the next batch of humans that stumbled on the Citadel might not be hostile. According to the old chronicles, humans had warred with other humans long before the elves came here. Fullblood humans might consider the halfblood wizards to be as bad or worse than the elves themselves.

Her absence would give the circle a clever excuse not to accede to Caellach Gwain's more unreasonable demands if they didn't feel like it. If she—the most powerful of the lot—wasn't there, they would "naturally" be very limited in what they could bring. Caellach had already gotten far more than his share of their time and effort. If they told him that getting the particular trinket he had his heart set on would mean that he and the rest of the wizards would be enjoying a dinner of oat porridge instead of nice fresh game—and that they would be certain to let everyone know *why* there was oat porridge on the table that night—he would probably go away.

And if the old whiners didn't like that answer, there was no way they could refute it, since they hadn't bothered to learn the limitations of the new ways of using magic. What was even more delightful, it was not a situation they could win by addressing that ignorance; if they learned the new ways, they would *obviously* be capable of doing their own retrievals. Denelor had promised that was how he would deal with the situation, and even Parth Agon, who had grown heartily tired of their demands, had agreed to back him up. The Chief Wizard had changed a great deal in the days past, and in Shana's opinion, it was all for the better. She frankly had not expected it; she had really thought he would become more like Caellach and not more like Denelor. Having him on her side instead of opposing her had made her situation marginally more comfortable.

"I will tell them that since they have proven that they are ready to learn new magics, they must, of course, practice them diligently," Parth had said without cracking a smile. "As the Chief and most senior, of course, I have the obligation to set such an assignment on those who are my junior. And how better to practice than by retrieving their own gear?"

The rest of the circle had greeted the solution with sighs of relief, and everyone, even old Denelor, had been amused by the thought of Caellach Gwain begging one of them to teach him the use of stones.

The most important of the supplies had been brought to the Citadel, and certainly by winter their stocks would be adequate to hold them for a while. Collen would be returning with the fruits of his trading in a few weeks, and that would further supplement their stores. Some judicious experimentation was going on in the way of finding edible forest plants, by following the tracks of wild boar and bringing back samples of everything the boar ate. Shana was not particularly needed as leader or as figurehead for any of that, and if she was out there looking for allies or possible danger, no one could say she was shirking her duties. Shana left the new Citadel with something of the sense that she was fleeing into freedom; she had been all too aware of the oppressive weight of responsibility on her shoulders, responsibility she had never wanted and was only too glad to leave behind her in the caves.

So now the four of them were far from the stronghold, past the point where the forests faded into prairie, in the grass-covered foothills with nary a tree for miles. Keman and Kalamadea, rather than assuming their halfblood forms, were in their own skins; though riding dragon-back was uncomfortable, it was easier than walking for leagues and leagues under a hot sun—and it was much easier to spot things from the air. Terrain like this was ideal for aerial scouting, for nothing escaped the sharp eyes of the dragons, and there was nothing in the way of cover to hide beneath in the land below them. Game was plentiful enough here: herds of wild horses, of other grazing animals, even of alicorns. The dragons had no trouble feeding themselves, and resolved to tell the others from their Lair about the abundance of game here.

Their search thus far, however, had turned up nothing other than those herds of grazers. There hadn't been so much as a single human herdsman or signs of one since they left the hills.

They were all four lounging next to a tiny spring-fed pool at midday, taking a rest. Shana and Mero were disinclined to fly in the heat of the day; there was no way to keep a hat on one's head while flying, and the sun's rays reached a punishing strength by about noon. The dragons loved the heat, and were only too happy to provide shade for the two halfbloods while they spread their wings and soaked up sun, basking contentedly.

The pool watered a small stand of scrub willow; judging from the number of tracks in the mud, it played host to a vast array of animal life in the course of a day and night. A tiny stream threaded away from the pool, into the grass, its path marked by more scrub brush as it snaked off in the general direction of the far-distant river. The waist-high grass all around them was full of insects that chirped and droned, and thronged with tiny birds that flitted from stem to stem and happily ate those insects. Shana watched one of them, balanced on a long stem of something that bent and waved beneath his light weight, singing his declaration of territory to any invading males.

A hot breeze rose up, making the grass stems bend, carrying the scent of drying grass and the damp-earth smell from the pool toward Shana. "You know, there is one thing I've wondered ever since I found that one horrid, heavy old chronicle about the elven invasion," Shana said—not to Mero, but to Kalamadea. "The one that was about as thick as your leg, Kalamadea. I'm sure you probably saw it; reading it was the best cure for insomnia I ever encountered."

"Hmm? The one by Laranz the Insufferable?" Father Dragon said lazily, his eyes closed to mere slits as he absorbed the sun and heat. He kept his size close to that of Keman for this trip, but his natural size was far larger, and if he had taken it now, he could have provided shade for a small army. Dragons grew as they aged, and Father Dragon was the oldest dragon Shana had ever seen or heard of. He had meddled, shifted into halfblood form, in the first Wizard War, and he had not been young then. Shana had found his personal journals in the old Citadel after the wizards rescued her from an elven auction block and guaranteed discovery of her elven breeding. They formed part of the reason why she was here right now.

"Who *were* the grel-riders? And how in the world did they manage to keep the elves from conquering them when they had no trouble eliminating just about everyone else?"

"You've seen grels, of course," Kalamadea said, after a long pause. "At least, you've seen the desert-grels, the ones that the traders ride."

Shana nodded; the caravan of traders that had captured her when she was first exiled from the Lairs had ridden grels, and used them as pack-beasts.

"Well, the originals of *those* grels are about as different as—as an alicorn and a goat," Kalamadea told her. "The elves took some liberties with them. The original grels are just as ugly, but not as tall, and can't go without water for quite as long. The grel-riders used them as mounts for controlling their herds; they started out as nomadic cattle herders, but when the elves began their conquests, they withdrew from the civilized lands altogether. They didn't even trade with other humans in or around elven territories anymore. They just went away, as far away as they could."

"That makes sense," Shana said, after thinking about that. "In their place, I'd have done the same. The way those elves use illusion, you'd never know if the trader you were dealing with was human or one of them, spying on you. The best way to eliminate spies from outside is to eliminate all contact from the outside."

Kalamadea gave her a lazy grin, full of teeth. "You're thinking," he said with approval. "Well, the grel-riders originally used only their grels for herd-riding and for packing, but when the grels turned out to be useless for fighting, they developed a special kind of cattle they used for warfare. They called them war-bulls; roughly twice the size of a horse, with long, wicked horns. The grel-riders taught them to use those horns in combat, and even an alicorn couldn't kill a war-bull."

"But that can't be the reason why the elves couldn't conquer them," Shana persisted.

Kalamadea nodded slightly. "The real reason was probably fairly simple, but Laranz would hardly have wanted to admit that. They were nomadic, after all, which meant they had no cities for the elves to attack. The elven lords didn't fare well when they lacked a large, specific target, and as far as I know, the grel-riders simply rode away when they got tired of fighting the elves. General consensus is that they went south. That is all I know about them."

"Huh." Shana plucked a grass stem to nibble on, and settled herself a little more comfortably in Kalamadea's shade, leaning up against the dragon's scaly flank. His hide felt cool under her hand, probably because he was absorbing the energy of the sun and storing it deep inside. Dragons could do that; it supplemented the energy they got from their food, which was probably the only reason they didn't eat the countryside bare of game.

The grel-riders intrigued her. The chronicle had hinted that the grel-riders had some sort of protection against elven magic, but hadn't offered any details. Given the writer's pomposity, that was possibly because he didn't *know* any details, and would never have admitted that. Still, no matter what Kalamadea thought, it seemed to her that anyone who pretended to the title of "Truth-Seeker" (as the chronicler had) would not have mentioned arcane protection unless he had some reason to.

"You don't think we're likely to meet up with these grel-riders, do you?" Mero asked, slowly, as if he were following Shana's thought.

Shana favored him with a lifted eyebrow. "Why do you think I chose this direction in the first place?" she replied. "Collen knows the river, and the people who live near it, and he didn't know about any grel-riders, so that left south." She waved her stem at the rolling plains. "It would take people who were nomadic *riders* to live here, I think. It's a bit difficult to hide out here, and if there were any numbers of settled people, the elves would find them and eliminate them. I *want* to find the grel-riders. Kalamadea, I hate to contradict you, but I think you might be wrong about why the elves couldn't conquer them. I really think they know something we don't."

Mero sat up, suddenly, looking at something on the southern horizon, a view that was blocked for Shana by Kalamadea's bulk.

"I don't know if we're about to find grel-riders, Shana," the young wizard said, slowly. "But there is certainly *something* on the way towards us."

She scrambled to her feet, and moved around Kalamadea to where she could see what Mero was looking at.

It was a cloud of yellow dust rising up against the empty blue of the sky—a huge cloud of dust. And although it was fairly dry out on these plains, nothing would produce a dust cloud of that size except an enormous herd of thousands and thousands of beasts.

She shaded her eyes with her hand, and tried to see if she could come up with any clues—either visually, or with other senses. Was there anyone with magic out there? Or were there any humans with the mind-powers only human magicians had? She ought to be able at least to catch a stray thought or two from whoever or whatever was kicking up all that dust.

She came up against a curious blankness beneath that cloud. That, in itself, was odd. She couldn't detect even a single thought—and in the past, she hadn't had any trouble reading the shape-thoughts of creatures as small as a ground-dwelling rodent.

"Are you not-sensing what I'm not-sensing?" she said quietly to Mero, who nodded.

"Neither of us can sense anything either," Kalamadea said, speaking for himself and Keman.

"There *are* animals that can make themselves blank to the sense of magic power," he reminded her. "And there are

beasts whose thoughts—such as they are—can't be detected
either. Remember that leaping thing in the forest? The one
that almost ate Valyn and me?"

She nodded. "But those were created, either by accident or
deliberately, using magic. And if there is a *herd* of creatures
like that out there, we need to know about it." She raised an
eyebrow. "I think we need to go take a look."

This prairie land was not entirely flat; that was just as well,
because Shana didn't want to get any closer to the strangers
than she was right now. The ridge they'd hidden themselves
on to wait for the makers of the dust cloud to arrive was just
high enough to afford a bit of a prospect.

The four of them—now all in halfblood form, since it was
rather hard to hide something the size of a dragon—lay on
their stomachs in the scant cover of some scraggly bushes
growing at the top of the ridge. From this vantage, they
waited with mounting impatience while flies buzzed around
their ears, and ants explored the regions inside their clothing.

The objects of their study might well be the fabled "grel-
riders," but if that was so, they had abandoned the grels entirely in favor of their cattle. There wasn't a grel in sight,
only shaggy cattle; bulls, cows, calves, and oxen.

And there were thousands of them.

In the lead of the group, and riding guard along the side,
were men and women with skins of the deepest brown Shana
had ever seen, a brown that was a scant shade lighter than
black. They all wore armor: tight scale-metal corselets that
covered their torsos, metal gorgets, and arm guards on the
lower and upper arms. Most wore wide-brimmed hats against
the sun, but the few without head coverings had their hair
cropped to scarcely more than a dark fuzz, and none of the
men had even a trace of a beard or a mustache.

The beasts they rode were bulls with huge, wickedly
pointed horns, as wide as Shana could reach with both hands
outstretched as far as they could go. The tip of each horn had
been sheathed with metal; the point on the end looked needle-
sharp. The cattle were of many colors, from a solid brownish-

black like the skins of the riders, to pied in red and white, to
a few who were probably pure white under the coating of yellow dust.

In the middle of the riders was an enormous cattle herd of
cows and calves; all of the beasts were very hairy and not
very tame-looking. Between the herd and the riders were the
wagons, wide platforms supporting square felt tents with
peaked roofs, and pulled by teams of four and six oxen
hitched abreast.

The herd, the riders, and the wagons filled the plain for as
far as Shana could see.

"No matter what your chronicle said, these people aren't
barbarians, Shana," Mero whispered to her. "Take a look at
their metalwork, at the fittings on that tent-wagon!"

She had to agree with that assessment. The work on the armor was some of the finest she'd ever seen, and the wagon-
tent was of a very sophisticated design. Both the armor and
the tents boasted refined abstract decorations, showing not a
hint of crudity, either in pattern or execution.

"Well, look how the guard-riders are organized," she
countered. "They're not riding randomly; each one has a
place, and an assignment. No, I agree with you, that writer
was just being pompous again. These people are quite civilized."

"These people are behind us," Kalamadea said, in a tone of
strain.

She turned, to find herself staring at the point of a spear,
held by one of the half-dozen warriors who had crept up behind her little party while they watched the group below. The
warriors were all quite alert, quite competent-looking.

And she could not touch the minds of a single one of them.
When she tried, she touched that curious blankness she had
met before.

Behind the spear-carriers, the bulls stood patiently, watching them and their masters. She had the feeling that they
wouldn't *stay* patient if she and her crew charged, however.

On the other hand, they didn't have much choice. If they
didn't make an escape attempt now, they probably would

never get another chance, assuming they weren't killed out-of-hand.

Mero launched the attack before she could say anything; he flung a levin-bolt at the nearest fighter. It crackled through the air between him and the warrior, blue-white as lightning, and just as powerful.

The levin-bolt touched his armor, and was deflected off into the grass, leaving a scorched mark there—despite the fact that the warrior made no move to counter it himself. Worse, he didn't seem at all startled by the attack. He hadn't moved, not even to step back involuntarily. It was as if he had known he was safe from magic attacks.

Blast! Mero had taken care of any chance to parley—and it was obvious these people weren't going to be spooked off by a display of power.

I'd better try something quick! Shana flung an attack of pain and blindness at the mind of the one holding the spear on her at the same time that Mero flung a second magical levin-bolt. This was a combination of the elf-shot magic that the elven lords used, and a mental attack of the sort the human wizards chose. It *should* have worked, felling her attacker. Even if he was protected against elven magic, he shouldn't have been proof against the combination of elven and human magics.

He didn't even blink. The attack went into that curious blankness that surrounded his mind, and was absorbed, effortlessly.

She stared back into the deep brown eyes of the warrior facing her, and took a deep breath.

"I think we're in trouble," Keman said quietly, getting slowly to his feet as the warrior nearest him gestured he should do so with his spear.

Shana did not bother to thank him for the observation.

"I think we should surrender," Kalamadea added, as yet more riders thundered up on their shaggy mounts, spears at the ready. "I really do think we should surrender."

"Fine," Shana snapped, without taking her attention from the spear pointed at her throat. "Now—just how do you propose we do that? These are strangers; they don't know our language, and we don't know theirs! One wrong move—"

She didn't bother to finish the sentence.

Myre had led her two charges down into places that Rena had never dreamed existed in the estate cellars—not all of them very nice, most of them very dirty. The maid hadn't really wanted to take Rena along at all, even when Rena used the argument she'd used on Lorryn, but she had finally agreed when Lorryn told her flatly that *he* was not leaving without Rena. The maid had changed what had always been a faintly superior attitude to one that was faintly insolent. Yet Rena could not find it in her to object; they were, after all, at her mercy. She didn't *have* to help them.

They threw together what supplies and weapons they could as Myre led them to rummage through the storerooms; their short time before the household woke stretched considerably by Lorryn, and a magic he used to keep the inhabitants of the house sleeping soundly and a lot longer than they normally did. They didn't dare go out of the house itself, for there was no way of extending the magic to the stables and slave pens and beyond, so all of the useful weapons and gear (not to mention horses) that lay outside the house walls might just as well have been on the moon for all that they could reach it.

They fled into the cellars carrying crude packs made up of bedding, with straps improvised from belts. Rena carried the food they filched from the kitchen, knives, a firestriker, and a single metal water bottle she'd found in the cellars. Lorryn carried his bow and his arrows, knives and sword, his own clothing and bedding, and things Myre had found for them: rope, a small axe, a huge square of waterproofed silk, and their heavy cloaks, which were too bulky for Rena to take.

There were exits to the outside from the cellars, doors through which barrels and boxes were delivered without having to take them through the kitchen or any other door. Myre tried all of them until she found one that was unlocked. They scrambled up over a pile of roots tumbled down through a hatchway from above, when she tried *that* and found it open.

The roots were filthy and hard as rocks, and Rena could hardly imagine how they could be made edible.

They popped out of the hatchway into the dim gray of false dawn, scuttled across the yard into the relative shelter of the kitchen gardens, and from there followed Myre across the paddocks and fenced-in home-fields toward the edge of the estate. Each field was bounded by hedges and ditches bringing irrigation water, ideal cover for someone who was escaping.

Except that they were going in the opposite direction from the gate and the road. Rena hadn't seen the point of that; the estate was completely walled in, and the only entrance was at the front of the manor. But she was afraid to say anything; Myre could decide to leave her behind "accidentally," and in this half-light, it wouldn't be difficult to do so. Then what would she do? It would be rather difficult to explain what she was doing, dressed in the clothing of a male slave, carrying a pack, with her hair hacked off at chin length. Even if she made her way back to her own quarters undetected, the hair would *still* be difficult to explain, and taken with Lorryn's absence, would be bound to get her into immediate trouble.

Finally they came to the wall; made of smooth stone, it was many feet thick at the bottom to prevent anyone digging under it. It towered above them, and as Rena already knew, the top was well protected by shards of glass set into mortar. There was no way to climb it, and no way around it.

But Myre didn't seem dismayed; instead, she led the way along the fence as the false dawn gave way to the true blue-gray light of early morning. Rena was getting more and more nervous; in a little while the supervisors would be bringing the slaves out here to work the fields, and they would be seen. What was Myre up to?

But Myre clearly knew exactly what she was doing; she led them to something Rena hadn't even dreamed existed, a place where a small, deep ditch or aqueduct led under the wall. The tunnel itself was as black as a starless night, and seemed to be very long. It probably led underground as well as under the wall—a clever deterrent to escape attempts. Water came up to within a half a foot or so of the ceiling.

"I see now why you asked if we could swim," Rena said, staring at it. The water looked very cold. "Won't there be bars or something across the mouth of this, though? I can't imagine Father not barring this somehow."

"Leave that to me," the slave replied, then looked over her shoulder at Rena with a sardonic expression on her face. "Last chance to go back."

Rena shook her head, wordlessly. Now that she was in this, she was hardly going to turn back, no matter how difficult it got.

Myre snorted. "Don't say I never gave you a chance." And with that, lithe as an otter, she dove into the water and disappeared.

A moment later her whisper echoed through the half-flooded tunnel under the wall. "Are you coming, or not?"

Lorryn took off his pack and lowered himself into the water, letting the pack float behind him as he towed it by one of the straps. It occurred to Rena that his bow was going to be useless for a while after this, at least until the bow itself and the bowstring dried out.

Oh well. What use would a bow be against Father's magic, anyway?

The water came up to Lorryn's chin, which meant it would be over Rena's head. Not a good sign. He let the current carry him into the tunnel, and was quickly lost in the shadows.

Rena hesitated only a moment longer; it was growing light, and it wouldn't be long before someone came along here. She followed Lorryn's example and took off her pack, tying one strap to her own belt. Then, clutching the side of the aqueduct, she lowered herself into the water.

It was colder than it looked, and quickly soaked through her clothing. She couldn't feel the bottom at all, and suppressed the urge to panic. But she could not make herself let go of the side of the aqueduct. Her teeth chattered as she clung to the brickwork of the side, and worked her way hand over hand into the darkness of the tunnel.

That was where she discovered that the ceiling quickly dropped much closer to the water than it appeared from outside, and she found it was impossible to hold on to the side and still have room to breathe. With a shudder, she let go of her last handhold and let the sluggish current take her, hoping she'd be able to stay afloat.

She looked back over her shoulder. The light at the end of the tunnel receded slowly, though when she looked ahead, no new light showed where the other end might be. She was so cold now that her feet and hands were numb, and behind her, the pack was soaking up water and acting like an anchor, slowing her down. She tried to paddle forward without churning up the water too much—thinking that too much splashing might echo out of the tunnel and alert a supervisor to something irregular. With the pack dragging at her, it was hard work to keep her head above water; she paddled more vigorously, gasping for breath as the cold water lapped around her chin and lips.

Finally a hand came out of the darkness and seized her shoulder; she stifled a yelp, knowing it had to be either Lorryn or Myre.

It was the former, clinging to a metal grate that blocked the tunnel. "There's a door in the grate," Lorryn said, spitting water, his own teeth chattering. "It's just under the surface. It's usually locked, but Myre opened it. Follow me."

By now there was enough light coming from the end of the tunnel for Rena to see, dimly. Lorryn patted her shoulder encouragingly, then ducked under the water. She felt his legs thrashing past her, then his head reappeared on the other side of the metal grate.

She hung on to the grate and felt cautiously under the water with her free hand and the toe of her boot, until she encountered the open space down there where the door must be. By then Lorryn was gone, floating away out of sight. She took several deep breaths, and told herself that if Lorryn— who was a worse swimmer than she—could manage this, it should be easy for her. Then she ducked her head under, eyes tightly closed, grabbed for the edge of the opening, and hauled herself through, head-first.

She had a moment of panic when her pack caught; it pulled her back under before she managed to get a good breath. Fear chilled her more than the water; she fought the pack strap mindlessly, thrashing and getting pulled under again and again, breathing in more water than air each time she reached the surface for a breath.

She couldn't even cry out for help; she kept choking on the water.

Finally her gyrations freed it quite by accident, and she bobbed to the surface as it dragged downward on her belt. She clung to the grate then, panting, until she recovered enough to follow her brother.

Fortunately, the end of the tunnel was not far away; now she was able to make out another dim half-circle of light up ahead of her, and a pair of dark blots that must be the heads of Myre and Lorryn side by side in the middle of the light. Now she actually swam, rather than letting the current take her or simply paddling like a child, and in spite of the drag of her soaked pack, she reached their side in a very few moments.

Lorryn heard her coming, and held out a hand to catch her. As she peered past him, she saw that the aqueduct gave directly out on a river; the bank here was overgrown, and the weeds hung down into the water, forming a screen between them and the open water.

The sun was up, but the day was overcast, and it looked like rain. Heavy, black clouds rolled sullenly across the small patch of sky visible from the tunnel, and Rena thought she heard the growl of thunder in the distance.

"If you had to pick a day to run, this was a good one," Myre said, her whisper echoing down the tunnel. "We should wait here until the rain starts. Once there's a downpour going, even patrols will stay inside until it's over—and a good strong rain will wash away tracks and scent if they try to follow us with hounds."

Rena was already soaked and cold; the prospect of traveling through the punishing rain of a thunderstorm wasn't a pleasant one.

But we're running for our lives! she chided herself immediately. *Be sensible! What's a little water, if it will help keep Father from following us?*

The only trouble was—if the rain kept people inside, it would follow that she and Lorryn might be missed sooner.

I can probably count on Father letting me sleep late this morning, too, after my little "betrothal dinner," but what about Lorryn? How soon would his servants come to wake him? And would he actually be missed if he wasn't in his bed? Would they assume he was at a gathering and hadn't yet come home?

Thunder *did* rumble in the near distance, making her jump. Of all the things she had imagined she would do to find the dragons, this situation had never entered her mind. The girl dreaming in the garden, surrounded by birds, seemed another person entirely.

Lightning arced across the sky overhead; thunder exploded above them as Rena shrieked involuntarily, and the skies opened up.

"Now!" Myre said fiercely, and thrust herself through the weeds, out into the pouring rain.

Lorryn followed; Rena, gasping and clutching at handfuls of clay and tough weed stems, followed him. Myre was already halfway up the bank; Lorryn stopped only long enough to give her a hand out of the river before taking to his heels himself.

She scrambled up the bank behind him, pausing only long enough to wrestle her pack back on. She slipped and fell along the slippery clay bank so many times, she lost count; her hands stung and burned from weed cuts and nettle strings, and they were the only parts of her that felt warm.

Her sides ached, and she was panting for breath by the time she reached the top of the steep bank, and dove into the dubious shelter of a tangle of wet bushes beside Lorryn. Myre was already peering through the rain, looking for something. Rena was glad, now, that she had cut off her hair when she'd put on the slave's old clothing; at least she wasn't fighting masses of wet, tangled hair.

"We need something faster than our legs," Myre muttered. "Horses, maybe, if we can steal them."

"What about a boat?" Lorryn countered. "There are usually small boats just downriver from here. Father keeps them there for pleasure-angling and dallying on the river."

Myre finally turned to look at him, her dripping hair straggling over one eye. "Just how ornamental are these boats?" she asked skeptically. "We don't want to float off in something that screams 'elven lord.' And *I* don't know the first thing about boats, anyway."

"I've used them," Lorryn assured her, "and it doesn't matter how ornamental they are. I *know* how to use my magic, remember? I can make it look like—"

Then he stopped, and Myre smiled sardonically. "Exactly. And have your *magic* scream to anyone that can sense it that you're right down here."

He winced, shamefaced. "Well, they aren't that ornamental," he muttered.

Rena remembered the boats; Lorryn had taken her out in one, a very long time ago, for a long, lazy afternoon on the water. Like every moment she had spent outside the bower, every detail was etched into her memory.

"There may be some heavier boats that the slaves use on the other side of the dock," she said, closing her eyes to call the memories up. "And if there aren't—well, pick the plainest, and I can make it plainer. I can fade the paint with *my* magic; that's so weak, I don't think anyone will sense it. And we can use the axe to pry off any ornamental woodwork; it's all just tacked onto the original boat, anyway."

Myre turned to look at her with surprise; she obviously hadn't anticipated Rena being anything but a tagalong and a burden. "We can try that," she said shortly. "We aren't that far from the dragons, anyway. The dragons will be happy to see you and shelter you, and once we're away from Lord Tylar's estate, it won't be hard to get to them."

She peered out into the rain once more. "Come on," she

said, gesturing to them to follow, and darted back out into the downpour.

The docks were there, and so were the boats, including those used by the slaves to catch fresh fish for their master's table. Lorryn and Rena untied the stiff, water-soaked ropes that held one of the boats to the dock at stern and prow; Myre stood in the middle of the boat and pushed it away from the dock with a long pole at Lorryn's direction. There were oars, but with this storm sending so much water into the river, they didn't need them. The current caught the light boat right away; with Lorryn at the rudder, it moved out into the center of the river with ever-increasing swiftness. It was left to Myre and Rena to bail out the bottom while Lorryn steered.

How long until we're off Father's land? Rena wondered fretfully, as she scooped water out of the bottom with a canvas bucket and tossed it over the side. Not only was rain continuing to pour down on them, the boat itself leaked at every seam; it was all she and Myre could do to keep the water level from rising dangerously. *How long until the Council members are told that Lorryn is missing? What will they do when they know? Will they go back to the Council and report him or—* She could not think of an alternative. She could not think of anything at the moment—

"There they are!"

The shout rang across the water from the bank; Rena looked up, startled, through a short swath of dripping, rainsoaked hair.

On the bank were riders, all elves, in full armor. One of them was pointing directly at *them*. Rena felt a tingle along her nerves, a shiver along her skin that had nothing to do with the cold.

Lorryn swore. "They know it's us," he said, shortly. "They're using magic to identify us."

And was their magic strong enough to seize the runaways—or even kill them here and now?

Myre looked around frantically, as if for a weapon or a means of escape. "Can't you make this thing go any faster?" she shrieked over the pouring rain and the thunder.

Of course he can! He has the power—"Do it!" Rena urged. "It can't matter; they already know it's us and where we are! Hurry!"

Lorryn dashed his hair out of his eyes with an impatient hand and let go of the rudder. He raised both hands over his head, as the riders on the bank milled, then retreated, obviously expecting an attack.

They must be some of Father's underlings, or they'd attack us now—

"Hold on!" Lorryn shouted. Rena obeyed instantly, knowing from experience that Lorryn never issued a warning unless it was necessary.

Myre didn't respond immediately, however; she was still looking around fruitlessly for a weapon or a means of protection.

With a *crack* and a flash of light, the boat suddenly lurched forward, throwing Rena into the bottom. If she hadn't been holding on to the side with both hands, she'd have been thrown overboard.

Just as Myre was.

Rena let go with one hand and snatched for the slave's clothing as the girl tumbled past her and over the side; too late. The last she saw of Myre was the girl's face floating above the water, vanishing behind the curtain of rain, as the boat accelerated with twice the speed of a running horse.

"Stop!" Rena shouted to her brother. "We've lost Myre!"

He shook his head regretfully, hands still held over his head, face creased with concentration. "I can't!" he shouted back. "Once I let this thing loose, it goes until it runs out by itself!"

Rena looked back; Myre was out of sight, and the elven riders mere dots on the riverbank—a moment later, they vanished, too, in the gray sheets of water pouring from the heavens. The boat was still picking up speed.

They were on their own, and her heart contracted with fear.

The boat didn't slacken speed until they had passed out of the storm and were well into some of the untamed lands held by no elven overlord. By then, Lorryn's face was gray with exhaustion, and Rena's hands ached with the effort of holding on to the sides. The river was full of debris, and Lorryn had been forced to make several abrupt corrections to their course to avoid hitting any of it, corrections that would have thrown *her* out of the boat to be left behind like Myre.

Finally, when the spell at last ran out, Lorryn used the slackening momentum, took the rudder and brought them in to the southern bank of the river; they both pitched their packs into the underbrush and clambered clumsily over the side onto the low bank. Lorryn pushed the boat away with a branch and let the river take it again; they stared after it until it disappeared.

"With any luck, they won't be able to guess where we put ashore even when they find it," Lorryn said, shouldering his pack. "That should give us some time, I hope."

Rena shrugged into her own pack, wishing it held something dry and warm to wear. She was so cold now that she had stopped shivering; the cold went all the way down to her bones. She couldn't have shivered now if she wanted to; fear and chill held her in a kind of choked silence and stillness. "Now where do we go?" she asked timidly, trying *not* to sound as if she was accusing Lorryn of anything. "We lost Myre."

He sighed, and stared off into the forest. "Well, she *said* the dragons weren't far. Didn't she say they were south of here?"

Rena didn't remember anything of the kind, but it hardly mattered. One direction was as good as another, as long as they went *away* from those who were hunting them. She made a gesture of hopeless bafflement. "Can you—do you know if there's anyone around here? Anyone who might come after us?"

She was so afraid—so very afraid. Enemies behind them, the unknown all about them, and their guide lost beyond hope of finding again—what could they do?

"Any elves, you mean? I don't think it's safe to use elven magic, but there's that human trick of listening for thoughts that I can try." He closed his eyes, and his face took on that "listening" look. "I can't sense anything but the minds of animals. We should be safe enough for a while. Maybe safe enough to find some shelter, build a fire, get dry."

Dry and warm. Dared she hope that they might escape after all? Right now, simply being dry and warm sounded like paradise. "You had better lead," she told him. "You've hunted, you know what to look out for. And you're the one with the weapons."

At that reminder, he checked his bow, found it useless, and drew his knife instead. He looked as if he was about to say something else, frowned as if he thought better of it, and led the way into the underbrush.

There's no one within range of Lorryn's mind. For now, we're safe, she told her pounding heart, her sinking spirit. *We can escape. We can!*

Rena followed behind him, wishing she weren't carrying a huge weight of water along with the pack, wishing this were all a nightmare. As fear ebbed, other discomforts began. Her stomach ached with hunger, and her shoulders hurt where the pack-straps cut into them. Right now, marriage to Lord Gildor didn't seem like such a bad thing after all. . . .

They might have come out of the storm, but the day was still overcast, and every tree dripped water down onto the deer path Lorryn had found. She had thought she couldn't be any colder or more miserable, but every time another branch sent a load of cold drops down the back of her neck, she discovered she was only beginning to learn what misery meant. Her boots didn't quite fit, despite all the stockings she wore, and she was getting a blister on one heel. She could hardly feel her fingers.

She kept her eyes on her feet and the path in front of her, as her legs began to ache, joining her aching shoulders. And a headache began as well.

She was so wet, so cold. If only she dared use a little magic—

Well, why not?

*My magics are so small ... I can at least make myself a
little warmer, a little drier. Surely no one will notice that.*

She narrowed her concentration, and insinuated her magics
into her clothing, working from the skin out, and the feet up,
driving the water out of the fabric, fiber by fiber. It was
something like flower-sculpting, after all; just shoving the
water away from where she didn't want it, slowly and patiently. When it reached the surface of her clothing, she let it
bead up and run off.

At least while she was concentrating on that, it was easier
to ignore her aching legs and shoulders.

And it was working! First her feet inside her boots, then
her legs, then her torso, and finally her arms, were dry,
warm—she turned her attention to her pack, shoving the
water ahead of a kind of barrier she created at her back. The
pack got lighter and lighter as she squeezed the water out,
and before too long, it was actually bearable to carry the
lightened weight of it!

"Rena? Are you working magic?" Lorryn said, breaking
her concentration.

She hesitated a moment. "Just a little," she replied, meekly.
"I was so cold and wet—I haven't done anything wrong,
have I?" Her eyes opened wide with alarm. "They haven't
felt it, have they? I—"

"It's all right," Lorryn said quickly, pushing aside a heavy
branch with his free hand. "I wasn't sure you were working
magic, it was that faint; I just felt it, and thought it might be
them, looking for us. It stopped when I asked you about it."

"You broke my concentration, so it must have been me you
sensed," she said with relief. "Oh, good. I was just so cold
and wet, and I didn't think it would do any harm to drive the
water out of my clothes. You ought to do the same."

"I can't," he said, in a very small voice.

She wasn't certain she heard him right. "You can't?" she
replied, with astonishment. "But—you made the boat practically fly! And I've seen you do so many other things! How
can you—"

"They don't teach boys to do small magics—or the ones

they *call* 'small' magics," he told her ruefully. "I'll tell you what, though—when you're soaking wet, those magics don't *seem* small. I'd give anything for a pair of dry socks."

She laughed; and was astonished to hear her own laughter. "Well, in that case, you can give me something to eat and find a place to rest, and I'll see you get dry socks and dry everything else!"

He turned back to look at her, surprise warring in his face with amusement. "In that case, let me say that you are the most *useful* escape companion that anyone could ever ask for. Better even than a fully armed warrior—who would be just as helpless as me, and probably a lot more cross!"

Unspoken were other thoughts, which she knew he had even though he was too tactful to say anything. Like Myre, he'd been certain that she would be more of a hindrance than a help; a rock tied about his neck and slowing him down.

She didn't mind now, though that would have hurt earlier. Now he knew better.

And so do I. And at that realization, her heart and spirits began to rise, just a little.

Lorryn found shelter under the wreck of a huge fallen tree. Tiny magics dried his clothing and pack, his bow and bowstring. Tiny magics dried the heaps of sodden leaves she piled up, so that they formed a warming cushion against the damp air and earth. Tiny magics kept the insects away, while Lorryn concentrated on searching the woods for hunters, both elven and animal.

Every exercise of her magics made her feel better. She was *not* as useless as Father had always claimed she was! She *could* think of solutions to some of their problems! Maybe she couldn't make a boat speed down the river at a breakneck pace, but she *could* keep Lorryn from catching cold and maybe getting so sick, he wouldn't be able to move! Elves didn't get ill, at least not very often, but humans did all the time, so Lorryn probably would.

She held a bit of bread in her hand and nibbled it slowly. This was slave-bread, heavy and dark, and not the white bread eaten by the masters. Myre had said that was all to the good; she claimed that the slave-bread would make better field rations, that it was more nourishing, and that it would fill the stomach better. Maybe she was right; it certainly hadn't taken much of it to satisfy the ache in Rena's stomach, and she was finishing the piece Lorryn had broken off for her more out of sense of duty than out of hunger.

The thought of her former slave made her wince with guilt. *Oh, Ancestors. Poor Myre. I hope they didn't catch her. I hope if they did, she has the wit to claim we coerced her into following him.* Surely Myre, so clever, so resourceful, could come up with a way to explain herself! Hadn't she gotten herself out of every other predicament?

And surely, with two renegades to chase, her father's men would never bother with a mere slave ... surely, surely....

Lorryn opened his eyes. "I can't find anything out here except a pair of alicorns," he said, finally. "They're young ones, so they shouldn't give us any trouble as long as we stay downwind of them."

"Alicorns?" she replied, her spirit shrinking a little again, despite her earlier burst of confidence. The stories she'd heard about how fierce the one-horned creatures were had given her nightmares, and the little tableau in the Portal-room in Lord Lyon's manor had only reinforced those stories. "Aren't they supposed to be able to pick up the least little bit of scent?"

"But they're downwind of us," he assured her, and yawned hugely. "And I—"

He yawned again, and Rena saw with concern how exhausted and strained he looked. Had he slept any more than she had? Probably not.

Probably not for days.

"Lorryn, we're safe enough here for the moment, aren't we?" she asked, and at his cautious nod, continued. "Well, why don't you rest? You did all that magic—then we've been walking for leagues."

He looked as if he would have liked to object, but a third yawn overcame him. "I can't argue. We're warm and dry, and there's no place better to shelter than what we've got at the moment."

"So rest," she urged. "I can watch for trouble. I'll wake you at the least little hint of it."

"I'll just lean back and relax for a little," he said, putting his pack behind him and suiting his actions to his words. "I won't sleep, I'll just rest a little."

He closed his eyes, and as Rena had suspected, in a moment he was sound asleep.

She smiled, and shook her head. How could he have thought he could go on without a rest?

Well, it doesn't matter. He's getting one now.

She looked over their primitive shelter and took a mental inventory of the materials at hand. If he slept right up until nightfall, could she improvise a better shelter out of sticks and leaves? She'd done things with flowers before—why not with leaves?

Experimentally, she took a leaf and sculpted it, retaining its water-resistant qualities while she spun it out into something a bit flatter and bigger. She took a second leaf, did the same, then tried to see if she could make the two join together.

To her delight, she *could*!

I can make a whole canopy of this leaf stuff, then get ordinary leaves to stick to the outside so that this will look like a place that's been covered with vines! she decided, enthusiastically. *It will probably all wilt in a day or two, but by then, we'll be gone!*

She gathered more leaves and began making her green fabric of them, fitting leaf to leaf to make a waterproof seal, keeping her concentration narrowed in a way she had never been able to achieve when she was just flower-sculpting. She had so much of her mind fixed to the task in her hands, in fact, that she ignored everything else.

Right up until the moment that a twig snapped and she looked up into the mad orange eyes of a white alicorn.

It snorted at her, close enough for her to smell its hot breath. She froze, holding her own breath.

The long, spiral horn rising from the middle of its forehead kept catching her attention as the alicorn watched her. It gleamed softly, a mother-of-pearl shaft that started out as thick as her own slender wrist and tapered to a wickedly sharp point. The eyes, an odd burnt-orange color, like bittersweet berries, were huge, the pupils dilated. The head was fundamentally the same shape as that of a graceful, dainty horse, but the eyes took up most of the space where brains should have been. An overlong, supple neck led down to muscular shoulders; the forelegs ended in something that was part cloven hoof, and part claw. The hindquarters were as powerful as the forequarters, with feet that were more hoof-like. A long, flowing mane, tiny chin-tuft, and tufted tail completed the beast, with one small detail—

Which the alicorn displayed as it lifted its lip to sniff her scent. Inch-long fangs graced that dainty mouth, giving the true picture of the beast's nature.

It was a killer. They all were. That was why the elves had given up the task of making them into beasts of burden or war-steeds.

In a moment it would charge her, unless she thought of some way of preventing it.

A crackling of brush made the first alicorn raise its head, but not with any alarm. In a moment, she saw why, as the alicorn was joined by its—her—mate.

Now there was more than double the danger. A mated pair tolerated nothing that might be a threat within their territory.

She couldn't move to wake Lorryn. She dared not move to take up a weapon herself. She had none of the greater magics—

—but perhaps,. . . the lesser?

It was the only "weapon" in her pitiful arsenal, that knack with birds and animals. Tentatively she reached out to the alicorn with her power, using only the gentlest of touches.

I am your friend. I would never harm you. I have good things to eat, and I know where to scratch.

The alicorn flicked her ears, and her mate raised his head a little to peer more closely at her.

I am your friend. You want to be my friend.

The alicorn's hide shuddered, and Rena watched in hope and fear as a wave of relaxation made all of its muscles go a bit slack.

Come be my friends, both of you.

Her magic drifted into their minds, subtle, like a whisper, changing *just* a tiny thing—that killer instinct, the urge to destroy anything that might prove dangerous. Their minds weren't any smaller than a pigeon's or a sparrow's. There was something there to work on. She half-closed her eyes, watching both of them, as her magic wove its way into what they were, soothing the too sensitive nerves, calming the wash of instant and hot emotions.

The mare took a tentative step toward her; the stallion followed. Carefully Rena reached into the pack beside her, and took out another piece of bread, breaking it in half. They didn't react to her movement, except for a slightly nervous flicking of their ears.

I have good things to eat. She held out both hands, each with a piece of bread in the palm, invitingly. She'd never yet seen a horse that could resist bread.

The stallion's nostrils flared as he took in the scent of the bread, and he shouldered the mare aside, coming to the fore. His eyes fixed first on her, then on the bread in her outstretched hand.

I will make you more good things to eat. While she worked her magic in their minds to tame them, she could not work another spell, but if this actually succeeded, she *would* be able to turn plain grass and leaves into alicorn treats. That would be a reasonable recompense for what she wanted out of them.

Come to me, come help me, and I will give you sweet treats to eat. I will keep you warm and dry, and I know all the right places to scratch. Flies will never bite you again. She wasn't actually sending thoughts into its mind, nor could she sense its thoughts the way Lorryn could, but her magic carried the promises she made to it, and somehow made it understand.

That, and the tiny gentling changes she wrought, were all that was needed.

The alicorn stallion made up his mind—now that *she* had made it up for him. He stepped forward, briskly, the mare right at his heels, and walked calmly right up to the edge of the shelter. He bent his long neck, and accepted the morsel of bread from her hand, his nose soft and velvety against her palm, and only the barest hint of the sharpness of his fangs touching her skin. A moment later, his mate did the same.

They both stood staring at her for a heartbeat or two longer, after the bread was gone. She could still lose them. They wouldn't attack her now, but she could still lose them. When she turned her magic loose, they could flee. Well, for that matter, they could simply *walk* away and she wouldn't be able to do a thing about it. Her magic just wasn't coercive; either they would serve her, or they would not.

She let go of their minds. She had done all that she could. If they were going to flee, they would do it now.

With a sigh, the stallion folded his long legs and lay down at her feet. The mare did the same, placing her head in Rena's lap. She looked up at Rena with eyes that were more brown now than orange, and she waited for Rena to make good on her promise of scratches.

Rena stretched out her hand and tentatively began to scratch the area at the base of the horn, reckoning that it was one place the alicorn couldn't reach for herself. The alicorn's coat was just as soft as it looked, much silkier than horsehair, though a bit longer as well. After a moment, the stallion stretched his head forward to get his own share of caresses.

When they both tired of having their horns, the area under their chins, and their ears scratched, Rena took leaves and began sculpting them, making them tender and enhancing the sugars in them. The alicorns accepted these new dainties with greed, eating until the area around the shelter had been denuded and their bellies were stuffed full.

Then they both laid their heads in Rena's lap again, and slept, one on either side of her, for all the world like a pair of huge horned pet hounds.

And when Lorryn woke, that was the sight that met his astonished eyes.

* * *

"You're sure they'll bear us?" Lorryn asked, dubiously. It was hard for him to even think of trusting an alicorn; their reputation was such that if he hadn't been too stunned to move, he'd have tried to kill both of these the moment he saw them. Only Rena's assurance that she had "changed" them made him—warily—trust them. After all, elven lords had tried for centuries to "change" the alicorns and make them useful, so how could Rena have done what they could not?

Then again, they didn't ask a female to help, did they? Of course not. Their magics are all weak, useless. As useless as keeping me from dying of pneumonia. Rena was a fount and a wellspring of surprises today.

They were certainly acting tame enough at the moment. He'd petted and scratched them at Rena's direction, and they had actually behaved as nicely as any horse he'd ever owned. Their coats were extraordinary; softer and silkier than any horse. And for once in his life, he'd gotten the chance to touch a still-living horn; it had been warm beneath his tentative caress, very much a part of the creature.

Rena shrugged. "As sure as I can be of anything. I wouldn't ask them to behave like a trained horse, though. They won't take a bit or a bridle, and we'll have to go in the direction *they* want, but they'll take our weight on their backs easily enough. I tried with my pack, and it didn't bother either of them." She patted the mare on the shoulder; the beast didn't even move. There was a certainty in her words and her actions that hadn't been there before today.

Lorryn thought that over; Rena had blossomed in the last day into someone he hardly recognized. Not all that long ago he had wished that she would somehow grow some spine and stop being such a burden—well, perhaps this was a manifestation of the old admonition to be careful what one wished for. It had taken *this* to bring her into her own.

But to trust her to tame an alicorn? Was the risk worth the benefits?

"Well—they're faster than we are, and they won't leave boot-prints," he said, thinking out loud. "That alone, I think, is worth the risk—even if we have to go where they want to. And since I've never, ever heard of an alicorn trying to invade settled lands, at least we won't have to worry about them heading for someone *else's* estate. If you're sure they won't turn on us, that is—"

He couldn't help it; those orange eyes seemed gentle, but could he trust that they would stay that way? That horn was as long as his arm, and sharp as any spear, and he'd heard even the foals knew how to use their horns as weapons almost from birth. Add in the fangs and the foreclaws . . .

"I'm sure," she said firmly. "I tamed a shrike once, and it was more vicious and had less mind than these do. I can *do* it, Lorryn; it's one thing I am completely sure of."

She had certainly done wonders with her garden full of birds. "Good enough." He walked over to the stallion, the bigger of the two, and cautiously laid a hand on its shoulder. It didn't even look up from the pile of grass that Rena had pulled and changed for it to eat. He hefted his pack in his free hand; would it really bear the weight of him and the pack as well?

"Put your pack on him first," she said, "just over the shoulders. Then get on slowly. Just don't make any moves that might startle him."

That wasn't going to be easy, not without a saddle. Still. He followed her instructions, as she draped her own pack over the mare's shoulders; her pack, like his, was now arranged so that it was a tube with her gear in equal parts at each end and a flat place in the middle. That had been his idea, to make it as much like saddlebags as possible. Staying on bareback would be hard enough; they'd never be able to stay on with packs strapped to their backs.

The stallion looked up, craned his long neck around so that he could peer at the pack, then resumed eating.

Lorryn put both hands on the stallion's warm back, just behind the pack. This would be something like one of the exercises he'd trained in, just slower. He only hoped his arms were up to it; it was going to be a real strain on his muscles.

He hoisted himself up with his arms alone, moving slowly and leaning his weight onto the alicorn's back, and slid his leg up over the alicorn's rump at the same time. He had a bad moment when the stallion jumped slightly, and fidgeted as it felt his weight. But then the beast settled again, and he got his seat, thankful he'd learned to ride bareback.

Rena was already in place, looking uncommonly cheerful, considering their current condition. She also looked far more alive than he'd ever seen her; there was a faint rosy flush on her cheeks, her green eyes sparkled, and even her hacked-off hair looked better fluffed in untidy curls around her face than it had when it was beaded and braided and beribboned. It was too bad all those so-called friends of his couldn't see her now; they'd never call her "plain" again. She was definitely in her element. Freedom suited her.

"We'll have to wait until they finish eating," she told him. "Then they'll go wherever it was they were heading in the first place when we caught them." She tilted her head to one side. "Are you wearing an illusion?" she added, changing the subject so completely, she took him by surprise.

With a start, he realized that he was; it had become second nature. He nodded. "I can't remember a moment that I've had it off," he told her. "Except very rare times when Mother and I were checking to see that it was solid. I even have it up, sleeping."

"Can I see what you look like without it?"

He considered her request, and shrugged. "I don't see why not." It took an effort of will to cancel the illusion on himself, and he saw from her face that she was disappointed in the result.

He grinned at her reaction, in part because he had expected it. "Sorry, little sister. No fangs, no bulging muscles, no horns. The best and easiest illusions are always simply enhancements or slight changes in what was already there, you know."

She tilted her head to the other side, birdlike, and considered him from all angles before she answered him. "Your hair is yellower than any boy's I've ever seen, except the humans," she said at last. "Your ears are blunter and smaller. And you're just a *bit* more muscular. But you're still Lorryn. I'd still know you anywhere."

He bowed, mockingly. "Exactly so, and precisely the point. I suspect Mother may have worked some of those *weak* little magics on me as a baby to make the illusion easier to carry—lightening my hair, for instance, and seeing to it I didn't turn into a muscle-bound gladiator. But—"

At just that moment, the stallion finished the last scrap of grass, and without any warning, went from a standstill to a fast walk, heading south, the mare behind him. He lurched onto a deer path with a half-turn, as Lorryn fought for balance.

Lorryn clung to the slick back, wishing the alicorn would at least tolerate some kind of bellyband to give him something to hold on to! Especially if it was going to move off without warning like that!

"They're going the way we wanted to!" Rena exclaimed behind him, pleased.

At least she had a little warning!

"They're also going a lot faster than I thought they would!" he exclaimed, as the stallion moved from a fast walk into an even faster pace—it *wasn't* a trot, but it was just as fast as a trot. Fortunately, whatever this gait was, the alicorn moved more smoothly than any horse he'd ever ridden, and from the way it had its ears perked forward, its head up, and its tail flagged, it could probably carry on like this all day. If so—nothing short of magic would have served as well to get them out of danger. Magic—or maybe a dragon.

"This is amazing," he said after a while, full of awe. No *wonder* the alicorns were so hard to track and hunt! *No one* had ever described them moving like this! Why, they would be long out of reach before a hound picked up their scent, even though the trail itself seemed fresh! "I've never ridden a beast like this in my life!"

"They are lovely, aren't they?" Rena agreed. Her voice sounded wistful. "I wish we could stay with them—but I don't think the changes I made run deep enough to hold if they ever begin to hunt. Once they taste blood—I have the feeling nothing would keep them tame. There's a feeling about that under the surface of them. Their instincts are very powerful, and instincts are the hardest things to change."

"Well, we'll have to make certain they don't *get* any blood," he said firmly. But that observation set his own thoughts running; no matter how grave a situation, there was always a stray part of his mind that would analyze everything. His ancestors had bred the alicorns as war-beasts; it might be that if *that* part of their nature could be expunged, and the taste of flesh eliminated, they'd revert to a gentler nature.

Well, gentle enough that girls like Rena could tame them, anyway.

It would certainly be a fine thing to have a mount like this, with its great beauty and easy pace—

And total lack of any way to control it! he reminded himself, as the stallion made an abrupt leap over an obstacle across the path, jarring him and making him lose his balance and fight to regain it. *No, maybe not.*

He realized a bit later, as he ducked a little to avoid a low-hanging branch, that the only reason the alicorns didn't absentmindedly scrape them off was purely because of the way *they* were built. Their necks were so long that their heads were very nearly even with the rider's—and the horn more than made up for the difference. Anything Lorryn would have had to duck under, the stallion did, too, giving him a moment of warning so that he didn't brain himself on a branch. If they ever got tired of carrying a rider, they would have no problem getting rid of that rider. Perhaps Rena's bribery was the only thing keeping them "tame."

Ah. Another good reason to put off domestication.

They had set off in midafternoon. By the time night fell, between the mad boat ride and the alicorn trek, they would have gotten far beyond where even the wildest estimation of their abilities would have placed them. And they *were* going south, into the lands no elven lord had ever set foot on. The lands where the dragons and the wizards had supposedly gone. *That* came from more reliable sources than Myre; it was part of the treaty between the elves and the wizards.

And in the space of a few hours, thanks to Rena, he was a great deal more optimistic about their chances than he had been this morning. He no longer needed to worry where they would find food; Rena had already proven she could change the leaves of the trees into treats for the alicorns; presumably she could make them as nourishing for the riders as well. *A little bland, not at all fete fare, but I don't think I'm going to complain to the cook.* He could still hunt—though on the whole it would probably be better to wait until the alicorns went on their own way before doing so. He could sense the minds of even animals, which meant he *should* be able to sense dangerous beasts or pursuit before it got too close.

Even if they didn't find the wizards immediately, they were *not* doing badly!

For now, he reminded himself, before he got caught up in unreasoning optimism. *It's barely summer. When winter arrives, we'd better have found the wizards. We haven't got real shelter, and it's going to be hard to magic that up out of the wilderness without someone noticing and coming after us. I'm not certain Rena can make dead grass or pine needles into anything edible, and we don't have warm clothing except for our cloaks.*

He noted something with half of his mind, while the rest worried over the problems to come. The alicorns had the same effect on forest life that a human or elven hunter would; where they passed, silence fell. Evidently they were just as fierce a predator as their reputation made them out to be. Off in the far, far distance, he heard birdsong, and the occasional animal call, but right here, along this deer path, there was nothing but the dull thudding of hooves on the bare earth and damp leaves.

"We really did it, didn't we?" Rena said, wonderingly, into the silence. The stallion flicked its ears at the sound of her voice, but did not slacken pace. Wherever it *was* going, it wanted to get there in a hurry. He only hoped that his muscles and Rena's would be up to a pace like this.

"We really did," he called back, softly. "We got away, both of us, and I couldn't have done it without you. I'm glad you came."

He hadn't been, at the time. He hadn't been until the moment she dried his clothing for him. Cynically he admitted to himself that once she became a benefit to *his* comfort, his attitude had changed.

But how was he to know that she would be anything other than a burden and something to be protected every step of the way?

She giggled. "It was almost *me* bursting into *your* room to beg for help last night, you know," she said unexpectedly.

He turned his head just enough so that he could look back at her while keeping an eye out for those pesky branches. "Why?" he asked. "I—I knew there was something besides the fete that had everyone in a state, but I didn't know it had anything to do with you!"

"They didn't tell you?" she said, astonishment writ large in her wide eyes. "How could they not tell you? Father was even letting me sleep late!"

He grimaced. "Lord Tylar has never confided anything to me, and he has always forbidden the servants to tell me anything he thinks I might object to. I assume I would have objected to this?"

"I don't know," she said hesitantly. "I—I was betrothed to Lord Gildor last night."

He almost lost his seat over that. "Gildor?" he spluttered. "Gildor, the brainless wonder? Gildor, who couldn't find his—his behind with both hands and a map? Gildor the dullard, the dolt, the incredibly, impossibly boring?" Was there another Gildor he didn't know about?

"That certainly describes the Gildor I saw," she agreed, and her eyes twinkled. "Now you see why I was so insistent on coming with you, and why I told you Father would use coercion on me to find out where you'd gone! I'd rather face wild alicorns than go into Gildor's bower!"

He shook his head. "I'm not certain *this* is preferable to marriage to Gildor," he retorted, wondering if his anger at her deception was valid, even as the heat rose in him. After all, *he* wasn't the one being told to wed Gildor.

"Please don't be angry with me," she pled, wilting before the accusation in his eyes. "It wasn't a lie; if he thought I *did* know, he *would* have used coercion on me—but—"

"But it's possible, given his *high* opinion of females, that it wouldn't even have entered his mind that you would be capable of such a clever deception." He thought it over, weighed Lord Tylar's well-known fear in the face of halfbloods with his well-known contempt of women, and concluded she was right not to take the chance. "Ah, you were probably right to assume he *would*, anyway," he replied, and her face lightened. "He's not exactly rational about halfbloods. He'll probably be using coercion on every person on the estate. Thank the Ancestors that Mother is strong enough to resist him, and clever enough to have something to give him that will clear her of guilt. He won't dare offend her House by doing away with her as long as *she* can make it seem she went mad on being told I was halfblooded."

Rena's face went deathly pale. "What's going to happen to her?" she whispered, as if Lady Viridina's part in all of this had never occurred to her.

Lorryn wished he could be more reassuring, but that was difficult on the back of a moving alicorn. He tried to give her a smile that would convey the emotion. "It's all right, we've planned for this for some time. *She* is going to concoct a false and very clouded memory for Fa—Lord Tylar's benefit, of the midwife-slave substituting me for a stillborn child. You know, don't you, that he left her alone on the estate for the birth? She'll let him hear that under a coercive trance, let him hear the midwife supposedly using her wizard-powers to make her forget; then she'll 'go mad with grief' as soon as he wakes her and confronts her with it." It was a thin enough story, but Lady Viridina had never, ever been suspected of so much as an improper thought by her husband, and with the three Council members there, he would be forced to take it at face value. "The Council Lords will insist she be placed in protective isolation, of course, but that won't be so bad."

It would be better than death, anyway. And perhaps it would be better than being subject to her husband's every irrational whim and cruel trick.

But Rena shuddered. "That means being confined to her bower, with slaves watching her day and night," she replied. "I *would* go mad. But I suppose it's better than—"

Better than the alternative. "The Council will believe it," he told her, this time quite firm in his conviction. "Ever since the Elvenbane appeared, they've been seeing halfbloods under their beds, and behind *anything* that goes wrong. I'm sure they'll find a way to 'prove' that this switched-at-birth nonsense is how Dyran ended up with a halfblood as his own heir without ever being aware of the fact."

"Oh," Rena said, looking a bit less dubious. "I'd forgotten about that. Actually, they'll probably *want* to believe it, and when they get done with him, so will Father."

"Very likely," he agreed. "And Mother is clever enough to carry it all off." He sniffed. "It's just a good thing they *don't* have the wizard-powers to read thoughts."

"I hope they never get themselves some kind of tame halfblood then," Rena replied, soberly. "And oh, I hope Mother will be all right—"

"At least you *won't* have to marry Gildor-the-idiot!" he said quickly, and got a wan smile in answer.

"Yes—" She got spattered by a shower of drops from a branch above her, wiped them away, and got back a little more color and a real smile. "And before you ask, *believe* me, life eating leaves in a howling wilderness is much, *much* preferable to that!"

6

KALAMADEA AND KEMAN simply stood where they were, like a pair of perfectly ordinary halfbloods, and not a pair of extraordinary, shape-shifting dragons. What was wrong with them?

:Do something!: Shana thought furiously at Kalamadea. *:Shift! Fight them!:* He should already have been flinging himself into the sky!

Kalamadea did nothing except to look at her. *:Lashana, these people are not afraid of magic, and they are all carrying very sharp spears. Spears which, may I point out to you, will penetrate dragon-hide. I think shifting would be a very bad idea, just at the moment; they could certainly use those spears. Can you think of anything else constructive?:*

Try as she might, she couldn't. Even a dragon needed a storm to call lightning down out of the sky, and the weather wasn't obliging with one. Perhaps the dragons could use their powers with rock to turn the ground soft beneath their captors' feet, but an agile warrior could certainly leap free before he was trapped.

And as for flinging himself into the sky—well, even a dragon needed *time* to shift. These warriors would certainly react before then.

It looked as if giving up was their only option. At least the warriors had not retaliated for the magical attacks the two wizards had made.

She stood up slowly, and held her empty hands over her head in what she hoped was a universally accepted gesture of surrender. Mero and the two dragons followed her example.

It must have been the right thing to do, since the warriors relaxed, just a trifle, although they did not lower their guard or their spearpoints. They all stood staring at one another for several moments.

Their captors were a striking people; this close, it was quite obvious that the dark skin was natural and not a dye or cosmetic. Their armor was of extremely fine make; beautifully finished with first-rate craftsmanship. Beneath the armor corselets, they all wore loose trousers of light, brightly colored fabric, and half-boots of felt.

Shana wondered how she and her group looked to them.

Finally one of the warriors said something to Shana directly, very slowly, in a complex and musical tongue. It sounded from the inflection as if it was a question. She glanced over at Kalamadea, who shrugged. "It isn't a language I understand," he said softly.

She turned to the warrior who had spoken and made a cautious gesture of apology. "Sorry, I'm afraid we don't speak your language."

The warrior muttered something, his tone conveying his frustration, and after a brief conference with his fellows, gestured with his spearpoint, nodding at the wagons below. That was clear enough. He wanted them to go down to the wagons, presumably without making any more trouble.

:I think we'd better do as he wants, Shana,: Mero said uncomfortably. *:We might get a chance to explain ourselves later.:*

Since there didn't seem to be any choice in the matter, Shana nodded, then turned and headed down the slope of the ridge in the direction he'd indicated, leaving her gear on the ground where she'd left it. After a moment, the others followed. She glanced behind, briefly, and saw that two of the warriors had snatched up the discarded gear and slung it across the backs of their bulls before mounting up again.

All of the warriors took to their bulls before following the prisoners: Shana didn't think it would be a good idea to try and test the agility of the cattle by trying to escape. Cattle weren't horses, but she'd already seen how agile these beasts were, and over a short distance there was no way a human would outrun one.

Curious eyes followed them down the slope of the ridge, although no one stopped to question any of the warriors who'd captured them. The dark people had a very simple solution for the keeping of prisoners, it seemed. The warriors took them directly to a particular wagon; the driver stopped it briefly while someone produced a set of iron collars and chains from within, and they were all chained by the neck to the back of the wagon itself. That was all there was to it, but it proved to be very effective. The collars were too well made to break, the locks too intricate for either Shana or Mero to pick, and both of them discovered to their complete astonishment that elven magics would not work on the collars at all. They could still speak mind to mind, thank goodness, but at least as far as Shana and Mero were concerned, the collars themselves were impervious to tampering.

The oxen kept up a slow pace, but it was a very steady one; they simply never stopped. That, too, was an effective means of keeping them from causing trouble. It wasn't hard to keep up with the wagon, but that was *all* one could do. Even when Shana and her group had been scouting, they'd taken frequent breaks; she and Mero were not used to this. Kalamadea and Keman didn't have much problem with the steady walking, but Mero and Shana were tired and footsore by the end of the day, when the nomads finally made camp.

If circumstances had been otherwise, Shana would have admired the efficiency of the nomads' arrangements. The wagons were pulled into a formation of several concentric circles, and the wheels staked down. The oxen were un-hitched, and taken to the common herd. Fire pits were carved out of the sod and cleared out down to the bare earth, and that was all there was to it. This was all done with the ease of something that was more than habit, it was custom. Once camp was set up, people could get about with doing their chores: fetching water, starting fires, cooking, the lot.

As it was, Shana was too busy sitting in the grass and rub-bing her sore feet and calves to offer much in the way of ad-miration. *I hope someone remembers us and brings us food and water,* she thought forlornly. Not that she and Mero couldn't both fetch for themselves—or at least, she *hoped* they could. It would be pretty rotten if all of the magic they knew was no longer working. But she wasn't certain she wanted these people to know everything the four of them could do—not yet, anyway.

Sunset was approximately an hour or so away, and it was pretty clear that no one was going to even approach the pris-oners without permission from *some* authority. People would glance at them covertly, but without wasting time to gawk, and without interrupting whatever chore they were engaged in. Shana began to wonder if she and her group were going to be left all night, chained like dogs to the tail of the wagon. But it seemed that their original captors were not yet done with them; six of the warriors appeared from between two of the wagons, finally, and marched purposefully toward them. All four of them got to their feet warily as the six surrounded their prisoners, just as warily.

So at least they think we might *be dangerous. I wish I knew if that was good for us, or bad.*

One of the dark people—Shana thought it might have been the one who'd led the group that captured them—unfastened all four of the chains and marched off with the four prisoners, exactly as if they were his pets and he was taking them for a walk. The other five warriors, following with their spears at the ready, made certain of the captives' obedience. The one with the chains did not, however, try to pull them along too quickly, or torment them in any other ways. It was all very brisk and businesslike, quite impersonal, without malice.

The camp was full of all of the normal noise and activity of any large group of humans, although the language was nothing but sheerest babble to Shana. Children dressed in short tunics of the same brightly colored fabric as the warriors' trousers shrieked in shrill voices, and played incomprehensible games that involved a great deal of running and shouting. Women in loose, comfortable robes or wrapped skirts, and men in more of the loose trousers, walked by with burdens, pausing to stare at the captives with curious wide brown eyes. Women nursed babies, stirred pots suspended over fires, or laid out bedding and clothing to air in the last of the sunlight. Young men idled about, shoved each other, and laughed; young women pretended to ignore them and giggled together behind their hands. There were no animals in the camp at all, however, and no sign of any other beasts than the cattle. That seemed odd; Shana would have expected that they would at least have dogs.

The closer they got to the center of the encampment, the larger, more elaborate, and more decorated the tent-wagons became. Finally they reached the center, and a set of four wagons that were the fanciest of the lot. It must have taken teams of ten or twelve oxen to pull *these* monstrosities. Presumably these belonged to the leaders of this group of people.

Shana noted that the four tents were set at the precise compass points; they were taken to the eastern-point tent. There was a clever set of folding stairs at the side of the wagon, now unfolded, that gave access to the tent door. The man holding their chains climbed up it, leading them the same way; the other five stayed behind on the ground beside the wagon. There was an extension of the flat bed of the wagon that formed a kind of porch all around the tent, wide enough for them all to stand together on, with the warrior holding their chains about an arm's length away. He paused at the entrance and called something; from within, someone raised the flap of the tent, and they all paraded inside.

The tent was very dark after the bright sunlight outside. It took a little time for Shana's eyes to adjust. When they did, she saw that they had been brought before an older man, whose close-cropped hair showed a few threads of gray in it, and whose many scars attested to the fact that he was no stranger to combat. He had a rather square, stern face, and was as muscular as any gladiator, although, like many retired gladiators, he had gone just a trifle to fat around the midsection. He wore an iron torque, iron bracers, and a belt made of flat, round iron plates cleverly hinged together. All of this jewelry was elaborately engraved in abstract designs. His eye-searingly scarlet trousers rather clashed with the orange and green cushions he reclined on. There were two warriors standing on either side of him, faces as impassive as statues, and two more on either side of the tent entrance.

He studied all four of them for a very long time, giving Shana equal time to study their surroundings—which she did, making her study obvious, as if she were here by choice. The interior of the tent had been draped with appliquéd hangings; the floor covered with fine hand-woven rugs. Both echoed the same abstract designs Shana had seen in the rest of the camp. There were lamps hanging from the ceiling, too, although they were not yet lit. She had to wonder where these people got the metal, the fabric, and the wool for these things, since there obviously weren't any sheep around and nomads didn't normally operate mines. Surely they traded for it—perhaps with Collen? He hadn't said anything about black herders, but why should he? He had no reason to disclose all his secrets to her, especially not if he intended to trade wizard-goods to these folk and vice versa. If that was so—since Collen would be coming back down the river again after trading with the bondlings, might they be heading for a meeting with him?

She hoped so. He might be able to persuade these people to let the four of them go—or at least to negotiate for a ransom.

Their captor and the leader spoke at some length, with a great many gestures and hand signals. The leader went silent for a moment, then barked an abrupt command, and hangings behind him parted. Another warrior entered, with two more prisoners, similarly collared and leashed.

Shana's eyes nearly popped out of her head with surprise as soon as she saw them, and the other three had similar reactions.

Elves? They have elves as prisoners?

So it seemed, since there was no mistaking elves for anything else. Slender bodies, pale porcelain skin, white-gold hair, long, pointed ears, and those green, cat-pupiled eyes ... the new captives couldn't be anything else. Both of them wore the clothing of their captors, and neither of them seemed to be suffering any mistreatment, though Shana could not think if that was a good sign or a bad one.

But what were elves doing here—and more important, how had these people managed to capture them?

Like us, maybe? Could it be possible these two came out here without human fighters to protect and guard them?

One of the prisoners ignored them, but the other's eyes widened as he took in the sight of them. "Ancestors!" he exclaimed. "Tell me you aren't what I think you are!" Then he shook his head sardonically. "Never mind. You couldn't be anything but halfbreeds. To think I've fallen to this—"

The leader of their captors interrupted him with a barked command. He shut up immediately, bowed soberly and with every outward evidence of humility, and turned back to Shana.

"It seems we're to be your translators, wizard," he told her, with a sour twist to his mouth. "Count yourselves damned lucky; *we* didn't have anyone to translate for us, and we had to learn everything the hard way." His expression was a strange mixture of sardonic amusement and distaste. "Much as I hate to admit this to a wizard—you are at least half-civilized, and it has been so long since I have seen a civilized creature, I would be prepared to befriend even a bondling slave at this point. Now, bow nicely to Jamal. He's the Chief of these barbarians, and he is very important. They call themselves the Iron People, by the way."

Shana and the others bowed, as gracefully as they could,

encumbered as they were by their collars and chains. Their translator took a certain amount of amusement out of that; the silent one ignored it all.

"You might as well call me Kelyan. My titles, such as they were, hardly mattered a bean back home and they're nothing here. My sullen companion is Haldor." He poked the other with an elbow; Haldor looked up at them briefly and grunted.

"Shana, Keman, Mero, and Kalamadea," Shana introduced, pointing to each of them in turn, and watching Jamal out of the corner of her eye. He was listening, and she didn't think that much got past those sharp eyes without being noted.

"Jamal wants to know where you come from," Kelyan continued. "That's his first question."

Shana thought fast; she *didn't* want to inadvertently lead these warriors anywhere near the Citadel! "North," she said briefly, waving in that general direction. "The river." That was a lot of territory—vague enough to be useless as a direction, specific enough that if these Iron People *did* trade with Collen, the direction might ring a bell.

Kelyan translated; Jamal pondered the answer, and barked another question. "He wants to know why you were here." A sardonic smile. "He assumes that you are spies, of course. He's a War Chief; it's his job to be suspicious."

The truth would serve the best. "Looking for people to trade with," she said, trying to look clever and harmless. "We aren't warriors—well, look at our hands if you don't believe me; there're no scars or sword-calluses. We trade; that's how we get what we need, and we're always looking for new people to trade with."

:Laying it on a bit thick, aren't you?: Kalamadea asked.

Kelyan snorted disbelief, but translated anyway.

Jamal made a bark of equal disbelief and said something else, something long and complicated. Kelyan nearly choked; his companion Haldor looked completely disgusted. "He wants to know why you paleskin demons have taken to trade instead of warfare!" Kelyan said. "Unbelievable! He thinks you halfbreeds are really elves!"

Before Shana could say anything, Kelyan turned back to

Jamal, chattering at high speed, apparently just as eager to convince the Iron Chief that they were *not* elves as Shana was. Jamal, however, was not going to be convinced. He kept pointing at Shana's ears and eyes, and no matter what Kelyan told him, he clearly didn't believe it. Finally he shook his head and rattled out a series of orders.

"You're going to be imprisoned with us," Kelyan said with resignation, as Haldor looked even more disgusted than before. "He wants the Iron Priest to have a look at you—meanwhile you're going in with us. Ah well, at least you'll be someone to talk to—"

Before he could finish, two more warriors came from outside the tent and picked up the chains to lead them all away. Kelyan and Haldor were taken out first; the second warrior led out Shana and her group.

A spectacular sunset painted the western sky in colors as vivid as the colors of the clothing about them, as the warriors took them all to another wagon-tent, this one just outside the innermost circle, one that bore no decorations at all. At the entrance, the warriors suddenly dropped the chains and walked off, leaving the six of them alone.

Haldor turned his back on all of them and climbed into the tent; Kelyan seemed disposed to continue talking to them, at least.

"Pick up your chain," he directed, "and come on inside. We've got food and water, and the Chief's servants will be bringing more later. And don't even bother to think about using that as a weapon and making a run for it—" he added, as Shana hefted her chain experimentally. "These people all learn to fight with chain-weapons from the time they can crawl. They'll have you before you get more than two circles away. By leaving you here, they've signified that you are on your own recognizance and you have the freedom of the camp, but if you try to escape, believe me, you'll regret it."

"Sounds as if you learned from experience," Mero ventured, as Kelyan climbed the narrow stairs into the wagon. Kelyan waited until they were all inside before answering.

"Let's just say that I've seen what they can do," he said,

as Haldor flung himself down on a pallet with his back to them.

The inside of this wagon was furnished simply, but with surprising comfort: pallets, cushions, and piles of blankets and spare clothing in baskets, all arranged around the edge of the round tent. A lantern (iron, of course) hung from the center, and there was an iron brazier in a flat box of sand in the middle of the tent below it.

Kelyan helped himself to a cushion and sat down on it, inviting them with a gesture to do the same. Mero was the first to take the invitation, sitting himself down next to the elven lord with a defiant air. "You seem very friendly towards us," Mero said with heavy irony. "I have to wonder what your motive is. There's not a lot of love between your kind and mine. I'd give a great deal to know how you ended up out here."

Kelyan shrugged. "It hardly matters whether you lot are wizards or elves, does it? It doesn't matter what I am, either. We're not *home*, any of us. We're all prisoners—and if you have half the powers your type is supposed to, at least you can take some of the burden of entertaining these barbarians off the backs of myself and my companion."

Haldor grunted, but kept his back to them.

"Entertaining?" Keman asked, puzzled. "How? We aren't musicians or anything—"

"Follow us later and you'll see." Kelyan advised, and turned back toward Mero. "I'll tell you the truth, because I don't have a thing to gain by lying to you. We're both useless second sons of hangers-on. The most we can do is make pretty illusions. We went off looking for something to make our fortunes with, and this is what we found." He gestured at his collar and chain. "We've been prisoners here for decades. No one knows where we are, and if they knew, they wouldn't care."

"Speak for yourself," Haldor growled, the first time he'd actually said anything.

"*You* can live in a constant daydream of being rescued by an army, but I have better things to do," Kelyan snapped, and turned back to Mero. "Right now, I'm just happy to see someone with a veneer of civilization, someone who *might* be able to tell me what's been going on without me back home." He glanced over his shoulder at Haldor. "Someone who can speak my tongue—and is willing to do so." His expression took on an unmistakable air of hunger. "I want news. I'm starved for news of home."

"You won't like it," Shana warned.

Kelyan grimaced. "Probably not, but then, you never know. It's been a long time since I left. You might tell me that— overbearing brute Lord Dyran got skewered by an alicorn or something, and *that* would make me very happy. He's half the reason I ended up out here."

At the mention of Dyran's name, both Shana and Mero started, and Kelyan flashed an unexpected smile. "You know him! So something *did* happen to the boor? How pleasant! I hope it was nasty."

"It—was," Shana managed. "It's very complicated, though. It will take a while in the telling."

"Let me just savor the moment then, and give you some useful information while I do so." Kelyan smiled again, the satisfied smile of a child surprised with a sweetmeat. "You know, for my supposedly deadliest enemies, I'm beginning to like you four quite a bit! Now—to begin with, these people are the ones the oldest chronicles refer to as the 'grel-riders,' although *they* haven't seen a grel for a century or more."

"Ah." Kalamadea nodded, satisfied. "I thought they might be. They certainly match what was written."

"First, a piece of *really important* information. They have something, and I do not know what it is, that makes them immune to magic, so don't bother trying anything on them." At Shana's grimace, he nodded. "I see you already discovered that."

"The hard way," she agreed, rubbing her arms. "At least they didn't attack back, so I suppose we're lucky."

He laughed. "Oh, they're utterly contemptuous of our magic. They have legends of it, but meeting with us has convinced them that the legends of truly powerful mages are exaggerations. Illusions do not deceive them unless it is an illusion of something that they *expect* to see and don't pay too much attention to—ah—" He thought for a moment. "For instance, if one of them looked into this tent, I could spin an illusion of Jamal sitting here until I was blue, and they would still see me—but if I happened to manage to get into Jamal's tent and sit on his couch of state, they would believe it *was* Jamal there unless they looked at me very hard."

"Which means there's no point in trying to make them think we're oxen or invisible, and trying to escape that way," Keman finished for him.

He nodded. "Magical weapons—levin-bolts and the like— also do not work on them. Right now they are all very much on edge and nervous, because this is all foreign territory to them. They normally live hundreds of leagues south of here, but there has been a five-year drought in the South, and there's nothing for the cattle to graze on down there. They live by their herds; nearly everything they have or use comes from the cattle. They don't understand what's causing the drought, and that makes them nervous as well. They're afraid that their ancestor-spirits are angry with them, and nothing I can say seems to make any sense to them."

"May I assume you *do* know the cause of the drought?" Kalamadea hazarded gently.

"I can guess," Kelyan told him, with some evidence of interest. "That fool Dyran started meddling with the weather long before I was born, and convinced everyone else to give it a try—now there's no such thing as normal weather anymore. That was what ruined my family; what *used* to be a very nice little manor ended up flooded so often, it turned into a swamp, and now it's nothing but swamp and rain forest."

"And that was probably no accident, if someone in your family managed to get on Dyran's wrong side," Mero put in with a glower.

The flash of anger in Kelyan's eyes would have been answer enough, but he nodded to confirm Mero's guess. "Well, if too much rain has ended up there, it stands to reason the water had to come from somewhere else."

Kalamadea nodded, but said nothing.

"This arrangement of four tents in the center of the camp is very important," Kelyan went on. "The easternmost is Jamal's—he's the War Chief. The westernmost belongs to the Iron Priest. *Do not*, no matter what, go into the northern and southern tents, unless and until a priest takes you there. Those are sacred to the spirits, and they will beat you to within an inch of your life if you desecrate the tents. *Then* they'll make you go through a ritual of purification that will make you wish they *had* beaten you to death."

He looked so grim when he said that; Shana had to wonder if he'd learned that the hard way, too.

A woman appeared at the entrance to the tent with a flat basket of finely woven grass; Kelyan rose immediately and took it from her, bringing it back to the center of the group. "Are you eating?" he called over his shoulder to Haldor, as he sat down.

Haldor shook his head.

Kelyan shrugged. "Your loss." He waved a hand at the basket; it contained a pile of flat white rounds, strips of what appeared to be grilled meat, onions, a set of round cups and a skin, and a bowl with something white in it. "The flat things are bread, more or less; the strips are beef and they are tasty enough, but tough. There's butter in the bowl, and the skin is full of fresh milk. You'll get flatbread and cheese in the morning, and more milk." He reached for a round of bread, deftly wrapped it around a strip of meat and onion, and poured himself a cup of milk. "Down south they had beer made from barley, but the barley ran out a while ago; I don't know what they'll do up here. Before the drought, the food was better than this; there were farmers to trade with, more variety." He raised an eyebrow at Shana, who was juggling a hot strip of meat from hand to hand. "I don't suppose that drivel about wanting to trade happened to be true by any stretch of the imagination?"

"Well," she said, getting the meat into the bread, and blowing on her fingers to cool them, "as it happens, it was. We—the wizards, I mean—had another confrontation with the elven lords; this time the ending was a bit more on our side, and the truce-treaty specified we could come down here and settle unmolested. We have things we can trade, and it's easier to trade for things than use up magic creating them."

Not that too many of us can *create things, but let him think we can, like the greater elven lords.*

"Hmm." He said nothing more, but ate, quickly and neatly, and washed his meal down with the milk. Shana did the same, finding that the fare was not at all bad—although she could see that it would be very easy to tire of it quickly.

Kalamadea and Mero took more time with their meal, as she and Keman sketched in as much as they knew of the time that Kelyan and Haldor had missed. "I always figured that they couldn't possibly be getting rid of all of you halfbreeds," he commented, when they got to the second Wizard War. "There are just too many accidents, too many times that a concubine or a human field-slave happens to be fertile when her lord takes a fancy to her. And I figured that the results were being left out on the edge of the forest or something of the like. There's always been rumors of halfbreeds in the forest, living wild as wolves. I can't say it surprises me."

Since he was being so frank, Shana decided to return the favor. "Your entire attitude towards us surprises *me*," she told him. "I can't understand why you aren't—well—like Lord Dyran—"

"Because I'm *not* like Lord-Damned-Dyran," he replied fiercely. "Very few of those of us on the bare edges of society are at all like the High Lords! Have you any notion of what it's like to be elven and yet have next to no magic?"

She shook her head, dumbly.

"I have," Mero put in quietly. Both Shana and Kelyan turned to look at him. "After all, I spent most of my life in Dyran's manor. Shana, the elves base everything on how much magic a person commands. If you have a lot, you have everything. If you don't—well, I've seen slaves treated better than some of Dyran's pensioners."

Kelyan nodded, bitterly, and even Haldor seemed to be listening and not ignoring them.

"At least the slaves have set duties," Mero continued. "They aren't expected to perform miracles with nothing, and they aren't punished or ridiculed when they can't make those miracles happen. The slaves are ignored, which is better than being watched, when the watcher is someone like Dyran. I saw him set one of his overseers an impossible task, make him work to exhaustion, then accuse him of shirking and as punishment order an arranged marriage for the fellow's daughter with another of his underlings who was—well, just vile. I watched him drive another quite mad, then order his wife be taken away and given to someone else as a lady. And at least the slaves of someone like Dyran have mercifully short lives compared to the elven lords. A pensioner can look forward to *centuries* of that kind of treatment."

Kelyan nodded all through Mero's explanation. "Exactly right, halfbreed—" He paused, and tilted his head in inquiry. "Sorry, I've forgotten your name. You're very quiet—"

"Mero," the wizard supplied, and smiled. "They called me Shadow; I *am* very good at making myself ignored."

Kelyan gave him a nod of acknowledgment. "Mero, then. Yes, exactly right. There were plenty of Dyran's slaves who would look at *me* with pity in their eyes—and my father, too, before he worked himself into a premature senility." He sighed. "Well, needless to say, there are—or at least there were, when last I walked civilized lands—plenty of younger elves who would be only too happy to find a way to limit the High Lords' magic. And given enough time to think about it, there are probably any number of them who could find it in their hearts to sympathize with the wizards. And actually, now that I've had a taste of being a slave myself, I even find it in my heart to sympathize with the humans." He quirked another of his ironic smiles. "At least Dyran met a nasty end. I will sleep *very* peacefully tonight, knowing that."

He would have said more, but another of the warriors appeared at the door to the tent, pushing the flap aside and gesturing peremptorily. Kelyan made a face, and got to his feet, prodding Haldor with a toe. "Come on, old thing," he said with resignation. "Time for our performances. Our masters are awaiting us."

Haldor just grunted again, got to his feet, gathered up his chain, and followed Kelyan out.

"Want to watch?" Shana said to Mero in an undertone. "I really have got to see what it is they're doing. Especially if we're going to be expected to do the same."

He shook his head.

"I'll go with you," Keman offered.

"I'll stay with Mero," Kalamadea said. "You two go see what you can see; we'll see if we can come up with any plans."

Shana didn't need a second invitation; she gathered up her chain and followed the two elves, Keman on her heels.

Just as Kelyan had told her, no one tried to prevent either of them from following the two elves as long as it was obvious they were not trying to escape. The elves didn't go far; only to about the third circle. Their destination was a tent—a real tent and not a tent-wagon, the kind Shana remembered the caravan-traders using, only much, much bigger. She reflected that it must have taken a dozen people working together to put this up. As they neared it, colored lights played on the tent walls from inside, and music drifted through the quiet night air.

The elves went inside; Shana and Keman followed them.

They stopped just inside the tent flap, which was tied open. Inside, it had been furnished much like Jamal's tent; there were painted hangings decorating some of the walls, rugs forming a floor, and large piles of cushions for people to sit or recline on. At one end was a group of musicians; at the other, someone dispensing food and drink. Servers brought both to the men and women who were dispersed about the tent. Most of them had the look of fighters; most were relatively young. Some sat or reclined, eating, talking, or playing games of chance. Some danced to the tune the musicians played.

But most were drifting toward the musicians' end of the tent where the elves had just arranged themselves.

"What do you suppose they're up to?" Shana wondered aloud.

"I haven't a clue," Keman told her. "But we ought to see if we can't get nearer."

They worked their way through the crowd; carefully, trying to attract no attention to themselves. They managed to get into a corner where they had a good view, but were out of the way.

The musicians finished their current piece, and stopped, clearly waiting for the elves to settle themselves. There were six musicians: two drummers, two with string instruments, one with a horn, and one with something Shana couldn't identify. Kelyan took a comfortable position, and nodded to the head musician, the one with the horn, who started a new piece. He played the first phrase alone, and the others joined in after a few beats.

That was when Shana understood why the riders were so intent on keeping the elves as their captives.

Kelyan spun a complicated illusion of fantastic birds and creatures with the bodies of lithe young females and males, but with butterfly wings. He danced them around each other in time to the music, to the evident pleasure of the watching riders. It wasn't a very good illusion; the birds and butterfly-creatures were quite transparent, easy to see through, impossible to believe in. But as an artistic piece, and as entertainment, it was excellent.

Certainly it was something the riders would never have been able to produce for themselves.

When the piece ended, the illusion faded. Haldor sat up, face full of resignation, as the next piece began. His illusion, like Kelyan's, was a frail thing and quite transparent, but his tiny horses of flame, darting and rearing and galloping in the air, were quite mesmerizing to watch.

Shana tapped Keman on the elbow and inclined her head toward the less crowded part of the tent as Haldor's piece

ended. He nodded agreement, and they made their way to the
end nearer the open doorway.

"Before you ask—I can't work any magic on the collar itself, and I'm not certain I can shift," Keman said quietly.
"Kalamadea and I have tried; I think it may be something in
the collars."

She made a face of distaste. "Well, the elves manage it; I
don't see why these people couldn't, too. Oh, fire and blast
it! At least none of them know our tongue; it's easier talking
than thinking at you."

"We are going to *have* to convince this Jamal that we
aren't fullblood elves and we can't do illusions," Keman continued urgently. "Otherwise they'll have us sitting there making butterflies and flowers, for the rest of our lives—"

"Unless Collen runs into them and arranges a trade or a
ransom or—yes, well, that isn't very likely at the moment."
She chewed her lip. "Let's sit here and watch the people for
a while. Maybe we can find out more about them, something
useful."

They didn't learn much, except that the riders worked the
elves to sheer exhaustion—and that both Haldor and Kelyan
grew depleted of magic and weary a great deal faster than either Shana or Mero would have under the same conditions.

Even then, the riders didn't seem disposed to let the elves
go for the evening. Instead, they were plied with food and
drink, allowed to rest for a bit, then put back to work.

This did not bode well for the four of *them,* if ever the riders discovered their real abilities, Jamal would not want to let
them go, ever.

It was interesting, though, that although the warriors did
not wear their armor here, they did retain their iron neck-
pieces and armbands, and sometimes added a browband as
well. The women wore truly exquisite jewelry of black filigree, some of it faceted and polished in places until it sparkled like gemstones. All of the people here favored bright
costumes of light, flowing fabrics; oranges, reds, and golden
yellows, in more elaborate versions of the garments Shana
had already seen them wearing during the day.

"Who's that?" Keman whispered suddenly, as there was something of a stir at the entrance to the tent. She peered through the half-lit darkness and made out a familiar face among the crowd pushing in through the entrance.

"That's Jamal," she whispered back, as the War Chief and his entourage were offered a hastily vacated set of cushions by those who had scrambled to their feet. "But who's that beside him?"

An older man with the physique of a blacksmith, his short hair as white as sheep's wool, had entered at nearly the same time, with his own entourage. While Jamal's followers were all clearly warriors, though none of them actually carried weapons here, this man's followers were all of *his* type; they all wore an odd headdress of folded fabric, and all wore spotless leather aprons. They differed from Jamal's group in one other striking way: *They* all wore iron torques from which a stylized flame-shape was hung as a pendant, formed out of the same filigree as the women's jewelry.

"Don't know," Keman answered, "But he seems to be just as important as Jamal!"

Indeed, there were as many people waiting to talk to the older man or hastening to serve him. He and his entourage got the same deferential treatment. Shana didn't detect any open animosity between the two groups, but she thought there was a certain undercurrent of tension when the two men glanced at each other.

If she were to hazard a guess about it, she'd say that the Iron People had *two* leaders, not one, and that this older man was the second of them. And that it was just possible that neither of them was entirely happy about sharing power.

Well, that was interesting! It might be useful, too. If there was some rivalry there, it might just be possible to exploit it.

The first thing to do was to find out just what, exactly, the function of this older man was. Then she could see if there was some way to use one of them as leverage against the other.

She turned her attention back to Jamal, studying him further. He was the younger of the two, and might be the more flexible and forward-thinking. It might be best to appeal to him, rather than to the older man.

"He's watching us," Keman whispered urgently. "The old man, he's watching us."

She transferred her gaze, quickly. The old man *was* watching them both closely, eyes narrowed. Even as she looked, he turned his head slightly aside to talk to one of his followers, never taking that speculative regard off of them.

"I wish I knew what he was saying," Keman muttered to her.

She nodded; there was a great deal of intelligence in that man's face; something about the determined set of his mouth and chin told her he would be a bad man to cross. He would take his time about a solution to the problem you represented, and when he had his solution, he would methodically and thoroughly implement it. And she could not tell what she and Keman meant to him. Now, more than ever, she cursed the ability these people possessed that enabled them to keep her out of their minds.

"I wish," she replied fervently, "That I knew what he was *thinking*."

"Where did these new green-eyed demons spring from?" First Iron Priest Diric asked one of the acolytes in an aside. He took care to show none of his displeasure in his expression, but he made it very clear in his tone of voice. "And more to the point, why was I not informed of their capture?"

"Lord, as to the first, I was told that they were caught spying upon the wagons this afternoon," the acolyte replied, keeping his voice down and cultivating a pleasant tone, as if he spoke of nothing consequential at all. "As to the second, lord, I cannot tell you. I only heard of them this very evening."

Diric raised an eyebrow, both at the words and at the precautionary tone of voice, and took a sip of his beer, savoring it carefully. Only he and Jamal received beer; there wasn't a great deal of it left, and there was no more barley to brew more. Somewhere, somehow, the Forge Clan of the Iron People were going to have to find farmers to trade with. The People were running short of all manner of grain and grain products; in a month or so there would not even be flour for bread.

For that matter, they would have to find supplies of iron ore, or better yet, iron ingots. The last farmers they had found to trade with had been clustered in a village six months' travel behind them—the last miners, nearly a year in their wake. The forges had not been unpacked for far too long; the war-bulls would need horn-tips soon, surely. The women were already complaining that they needed new jewelry.

But Jamal did not seem particularly interested in finding miners or farmers with whom to trade. He seemed much more intent on finding someone to *fight*.

It was a good thing that the land itself had conspired against this particular plan. The People could not have sustained a war with supplies in their current state. The only creatures they had encountered on this endless grass-plain were alicorns and these new green-eyed demons.

Of which no one bothered to inform me until I saw them myself when I entered the gather-tent. He had a sour taste in his mouth that the beer could not remove, and a bitter taste in his mind when he considered his War Chief. Jamal was ambitious; he had known that from the start. The War Chief had made no attempt to cloak that ambition, and indeed, *most* War Chiefs were ambitious. Diric himself had outlived three of them—ambition was a good thing in a leader whose functions were all of aggression and defense. But Jamal was also *popular*, and that was beginning to worry Diric. The fact that he had been able to convince his followers to conceal the existence of these new green-eyed demons was very disturbing.

He cast a veiled glance at the War Chief, who reclined at his ease and watched with a paternal smile on his lips while the unmated danced and disported with one another. He had heard rumors that Jamal had greater ambitions than any other War Chief in Diric's memory. Those rumors spoke of Jamal's dream of returning to the homelands laden with booty, to unite all of the Iron Clans under his sole leadership. No one had ever done that before; the only body with any authority between the Iron Clans were the Priests, who oversaw disputes and made all needed arrangements whenever two or more Clans gathered together. Never had any two Clans agreed on a single leader before, much less all the Clans together. Had it been anyone else, Diric would have dismissed the ambition with a snort as idle dreaming. The trouble was, Jamal was just charismatic enough to carry the plan off. If he returned with the wagons groaning with foreign booty, his chances of success were very good.

And then what need would he have of the Iron Priests? Diric asked himself, knowing what the answer would be. None, of course. And if he coveted the power held by other War Chiefs, how much more must he covet that held by the Priests?

Diric had not realized how much power the War Chief already held until this very evening. It had happened before, of course, that he did not hear of something until it happened to suit his rival—but it had never happened with something as important as the capture of these green-eyed demons.

The original two demons had been caught in the days of Diric's father's father, and were the Forge Clan's treasured possessions. Until that time, the fearsome pointy-eared paleskins had been deemed only legends, the kind of creature one frightened a disobedient child with. Diric knew the legends better than anyone else; it was his job, after all, to remember them and recount them so that the Iron People never forgot them. The legends told of a great war with these demons, who entered the world through a door between this world and their own. The demons had coveted this world—how not, after all?—and had killed and harried the ancestors and their former allies, the Corn People, until the Iron People were forced to flee into the South with their herds, leaving their allies to hold the demons back so that they could escape. Only the cattle had survived that flight; there had been another sort of beast commonly ridden by the warriors and used as a pack animal, but these had not been able to bear up to the stresses of the flight or the hotter and wetter climate of the South. In time, the ancestors learned the twin secrets of the Magic-Metal and the Mind-Wall, and the few demons that followed after them were defeated and slaughtered.

The legends spoke of the contempt of the People and of the god, the First Smith, for these cowardly demons, who employed weapons that revealed that cowardice, weapons that killed at no risk to the wielder. But no one had believed in the legends of green-eyed demons except the Priests—until these two had appeared.

The War Chief of the time had made much of the fact that he had captured the terrible demons and enslaved them for the entertainment of the People, but Diric knew these two, Haldor and Kelyan, very well, and he knew they had been little or no threat to a well-armored warrior. They were children, youngsters on some kind of impulsive excursion, and as unprepared for the Iron People as the People were unprepared for them. The *accepted* story of the encounter was that the magics of Iron and the Mind-Wall discipline had protected War Chief Alaj, and had made it possible for him to overpower them. Diric had a rather different view of the encounter.

Those two, Haldor and Kelyan—they were not and are not as fearsome as their legended ancestors. Their powers are nothing like the powers those demons were said to call upon.

Now, either the legends greatly exaggerated those powers, or these *two* were simply weaker. Diric was inclined to think the latter. In general, the legends as he had studied them made very few mistakes—they had not exaggerated the danger of the one-horns, for instance, nor their suicidal ferocity. So why should the danger represented by the green-eyed demons be any less than the legends painted it?

By this point, most of the people took the former view, however; they were used to having Haldor and Kelyan running tame about the camp and making their pretty illusions whenever the gather-tent went up. Diric had not been particularly worried about that until now; he had assumed that the Iron People would never again encounter their old foes. Now he was not so sure, and he feared that complacency could be a danger in itself.

He studied the two new demons; they looked back at him boldly, making no pretense but that they in turn were studying *him*. There were two of them, a male and a female, and he was told by his whispering acolyte that there were two more males back in the prisoners' wagon.

Interesting that one was a female; even more interesting that they did not seem to be quite the same breed as the original two. They were darker for one thing; the skins of Haldor and Kelyan remained white as a dead fish's belly no matter how much sun beat down upon them. They were not nearly so frail-looking, for another; their hair was of colors, and not like hanks of bleached linen fibers. The female's, a brilliant scarlet, was clearly the envy of many of the unmated women in the gather-tent. The male's was a proper dark color, although it hung sadly straight and did not wind tightly in proper curls.

Then again, the Corn People were said to be as pale and colorless as the corn they grew. Could these new demons be only half-demon? Could the demons have mated with Corn People to produce these creatures?

"Odd, the female's hair," he muttered to Haja, the acolyte. "I have never seen hair of that color."

"They claim they are not demons at all, but creatures of another sort," Haja replied softly. "Our demons say that this is the truth; in fact, Kelyan was quite argumentative about it, and Haldor was clearly insulted by the very notion. I do not recall them ever reacting so strongly to anything before."

Diric raised an eyebrow. There would be no advantage that he could see for Kelyan to claim that these creatures were something other than his own kind. *Interesting*.

"Are they to be housed permanently with the others?" he asked, taking care that his voice did not carry beyond Haja's ears.

"So I have been told," the acolyte replied. "It seems logical. Two of them did not fare well, walking behind a wagon. There is no reason to kill them with exhaustion when they make such good trophies, but equally no reason to house them separately from the other two. Kelyan and Haldor have made not one successful attempt at escape, and Jamal does not think that the addition of four more demons will make escape any more likely."

Much as he hated to admit it, Jamal was probably right. If Magic-Metal and Mind-Wall had held the demons until now, it should keep holding them.

"I believe I will speak with them myself," he told his acolyte. "Tomorrow, while we are on the march. See to it."

Haja bowed slightly. "There should be no difficulty," he replied.

Diric smiled slightly. "And see to it that Jamal does not hear of it," he added. "At least not until after the fact."

Haja's eyes widened just a trifle, and so did his smile. The acolyte had been trying to warn Diric for many moons now that Jamal was *too* clever, *too* ambitious, and Diric had apparently dismissed his warnings. In actuality, Diric *had* given them some thought, but he had not yet been convinced that Jamal was a real hazard.

"Yes," he said softly, as Haja nodded imperceptibly in Jamal's direction. "I believe that our War Chief may be harboring other thoughts—thoughts that the First Smith might not approve of. The time may be coming when actions should be taken. I will meditate upon the subject."

Haja nodded.

"In the meantime," Diric concluded, sitting back on his own cushions with an air of relaxation he in no way felt, "you might go a-scouting yourself, and see if there are other demons where these sprung from—or perhaps a sign of our ancient allies, the Corn People. This would be Priestly business, of course. It would be better if the War Chief were not to hear of things wherein he has no lawful concern."

"Such as the questioning of demons?" Haja asked, with a smile. "And the scouting for Corn People? After all, demons are rightly the business of the Priests, and the Corn People are only legend, which is *also* the business of the Priests."

"Exactly so," Diric told him. "Exactly so."

* * *

Myre circled above the wooded hills, too high in the sky for anyone below to see her *real* shape, and fumed as she circled. No sign, not one single sign, of Lorryn and Rena—and she had only herself to blame that they had eluded her. She was the one who had suggested escaping by water.

When the boat lurched forward so unexpectedly and threw her out, she had been so stunned by the shock and the impact that she didn't even react to save herself until it was well out of sight. Then, and only then, did the shouts and arrows of the elves on the bank awaken her to the fact that she was in a certain amount of danger, as the current carried her downstream.

She reacted immediately; she took a deep breath, dove under the water to escape the arrows falling around her, and shifted once she was there into the form of a huge whisker-fish. Once safely in a form that could breathe water rather than air, she set out in hot pursuit with great, driving thrusts of her tail.

But that boat had been much faster than any fish that ever swam. She didn't catch up to it for more than a day, and by the time she found it, a bare hour ahead of an elven pursuit party, it was drifting and empty. There was no sign of where it might have gone ashore—if there ever had been, the rain had wiped such traces out completely.

She made a guess, then, and took to the skies. But that had not been a particularly clever move, either.

She was used to the barren, scrub-covered hills around the Lairs, not these hills with trees so thick, you could not see the ground beneath them! Why, even a dragon in his proper form could skulk for furlongs beneath these trees and never fear being spotted from above!

Still she circled, for days, hoping for a stroke of luck, the betraying smoke from a campfire, a single track of a shod foot in the mud of a stream bank. But every sign proved to be made either by lone hunters, or by more searchers sent to recapture Lorryn and his sister, and her temper frayed and snapped a dozen times over. She managed to assuage some of her rage in hunting—alicorns were particularly thick here, and it was *almost* as satisfactory to break their necks as it would have been to snap the neck of that fool, Lorryn—

In desperation, although she was certain that the two soft, pampered creatures could not possibly have gotten beyond the immediate vicinity of the river, she increased her range. She saw nothing, nothing whatsoever, except for a group of ragged humans making their way along the river in crude boats. Whatever they were, those humans were *not* wizards, and Myre doubted that either Rena or Lorryn would even have attempted contact with them.

Assuming the humans themselves permitted such contact. If they were wild humans, uncollared, then they certainly must fear the elves. Neither child was woods-wise enough to hide an approach from feral humans who were used to living in these forsaken forests. It was far more likely that these humans would evade the two runaways before Lorryn and his sister even guessed they were there.

Still, perhaps she should take a closer look at them. She circled again, noting those same humans putting in at a point along the bank. No sign of alarm there; not a chance they had encountered the fugitives.

She ground her teeth together in fruitless rage.

She might as well admit it. She had lost them. And with them had gone her chance for her own captive wizard. She had been so certain that she was in complete control of the escape that she had not anticipated that Lorryn might do something unexpected, and now, thanks to that carelessness, she had lost them.

She happened to look down at just that moment—and even to an idle eye, it was obvious that the little party of humans had suddenly and inexplicably doubled.

Now what was this?

Her rage evaporated, and she sharpened her gaze, focusing in on the group below. No—the humans had not multiplied. They had been joined by another group, much better clad—

Myre's wingbeats faltered for a moment, as she caught sight of forms much like Shana's. Pointed ears—but dark complexions and hair in more colors than pale blond. These were no humans—these were *wizards*! She had found the missing wizards!

And where the wizards were—so were the renegade dragons.

Quickly she spiraled up, until she reached a space above the clouds, so high that the air was thin and hard to breathe, and ice crystals formed on the tips of her wings.

Now what? She knew where the wizards were—surely, surely she could use that somehow, couldn't she?

She needed information. And she needed to get it without a chance that she might be caught by Keman or any of the others.

In short, she needed a plan.

And this time she had better not underestimate anyone or anything. This time her plan must be perfect. And for a perfect plan, she needed information.

But information was easy to gather, so long as she stayed away from her fellow dragons. She could shift into any one of hundreds of shapes to spy on the wizards, anything from a human child to a rock formation. So long as no *dragon* saw her, she should be safe from detection.

Well, her first shape should be something with a good nose—and inedible. All those creatures living together should be easy to scent, but she didn't want to find herself the target of some hunter's arrows while she searched for them!

Her mind made up, she folded her wings and dove for a secluded vale just out of sight of that riverside landing.

The alicorns reached the summit of yet another hill; they had phenomenal endurance, and even with Rena and Lorryn on their backs, they were able to make twice the speed of any horse she'd ever ridden. They had a kind of ground-devouring fast walk that they could keep up all day if they had to. They needed to stop two or three times each day for food and water, and then it was no more than the equivalent of an equine snack.

Of course, what they were eating was not grass alone, but

whatever they could catch that lived in the grass as well. They were *fast*; they caught and ate mice and voles as easily as any house cat.

At night they would disappear for several hours, coming back with traces of blood around their mouths. At least they came back—and didn't consider Lorryn and Rena to be good prey.

Rena had been revolted. Lorryn had been fascinated. He told her that it was very likely that the *reason* why the alicorns were able to keep up that fast pace was that they were eating meat. "Meat is a more concentrated food than grass," he told her. "If they weren't eating meat, I expect they wouldn't be able to go on any longer or faster than one of our horses."

Rena had already decided that she was no longer interested in having a tame alicorn.

Meanwhile, *she* was not possessed of the same level of endurance as Lorryn or the alicorns. They wanted to be off at sunrise—which meant rising before sunrise just so *they* could manage a bite to eat—and didn't stop for the night until sunset. Nothing in Rena's life had ever prepared her for this kind of endurance test. She fell asleep exhausted and sore, and woke very little rested. She had long since given up any interest in the passing countryside, even though they'd had more than one narrow escape from hostile animals and potentially hostile hunters. Now all she could do was cling to the back of her alicorn and use her own little magics to keep it tame. All she really wanted to do was find the wizards, so at last she could rest.

Rest! Oh, if only she could! Her entire world had narrowed to the need for rest. Every muscle ached, and her eyes burned with fatigue; there was a dull headache right behind her eyes, and if Lord Gildor had appeared at that moment with an offer of a bed and a warm meal in exchange for a wedding, she would probably have wedded him then and there.

Well, maybe not. But she would have been willing to entertain the notion.

"Interesting," Lorryn muttered out loud, as his beast reached the top of the ridge first.

"What's interesting?" Rena asked, dully. *She* couldn't imagine anything interesting out here. They'd traveled through a pass in the mountains to come out amid a range of forested hills several days ago. The hills were bisected by a wide river, which the alicorns had followed for a few days. She'd had hope that they were about to reach whatever goal their tiny minds had set—since she didn't see any way that they could cross a river that must have been wide enough to have swallowed Lord Tylar's manor, gardens, and all without a splash. But yesterday the alicorns had plunged into the stream without any warning at all and had swum across it while she clung on to her mount's mane with one hand and her bundle of belongings with the other, terrified that she would lose her grip on one or the other.

She'd swallowed water more than once, and her chest still hurt. She hadn't said anything to Lorryn, though, for fear he'd decide to abandon the alicorns and continue the trek on foot. *He* was thriving on the hard pace, and she didn't want him to think that she was holding him back. His surprise and approval of everything she'd done so far was so sweet—and she couldn't bear to do without it again. It was the one sliver of triumph in the midst of the grueling journey.

"Well, I think I know what the alicorns are doing, where they're going," he replied, as he studied the ground ahead of them. "We're headed down into a great plain, and I've been seeing what I think are alicorn tracks all along. When we topped this ridge, I *thought* I saw alicorns out there in the grass, all heading south. I think our mounts are migrating."

"What?" she said, surprise breaking her out of her weary apathy for a moment. "Like birds?"

"Exactly like birds," he replied. "I think I know what's going on in their tiny little minds. I've been *trying* to sense their thoughts, but I couldn't make anything of them until just now. You know that they're predators sometimes—"

"Yes," she replied, holding back a shudder.

"I think that they're predators during the winter when there isn't much to graze on, combined grazers and predators during this migration, and then become grazers all summer. I think that while they're grazers, they form up into big herds, but *only* then. That would be so they can find mates and protect their young." He sounded very pleased with himself. "That would be why our hunters scarcely ever see them in the summer and never with young—and why when we hunt them in the winter, they're solitary. They act like predators in the winter, then in the summer, act like grazers to choose mates and bear and raise young."

"Well," she replied, as she thought about that from the standpoint of the fact that she *knew* they'd been created from other animals by some long-ago High Lord, "the High Lords wanted something that could feed itself in all situations, so I suppose that makes sense. But what does that have to do with us?"

Lorryn turned back to look at her, bracing himself with one hand on the stallion's rump. "Not much, except that we're going to have to abandon these two before they reach a big herd. I don't think the herd would tolerate us, and I don't think you can gentle an entire herd of the beasts."

She thought once again of the blood on her mare's muzzle, and shivered. "No, I don't think I can either. But what about the wizards?"

"Well, I've been thinking about that," he replied. "Once we crossed that river, I daresay we're beyond *any* holding the elven lords ever claimed. If we don't find any sign of habitation, we can turn back to the river and follow it for a while. I can start listening for thoughts, which ought to give us a clue where they are. And we can both watch for dragons."

"I've been watching for dragons," she replied truthfully. "And I haven't seen any."

"I haven't sensed any thoughts but beasts' since the river either." He studied her from his seat on the alicorn's back. "I also think I ought to put an illusion of full humanity on both of us. Just in case."

She covertly stretched aching muscles, and gave him the

same close regard. "I think you might be right," she replied thoughtfully. "You look a little *too* elven."

"Plus, we're out where we might well run into free humans," he reminded her. "I've read a lot of history from the first Wizard War and before. I know of several groups who were supposed to be out here, at least back as far as the histories go—the grel-riders and the Corn People. The last thing I want to do is frighten anyone. Or—well, neither the riders or the Corn People have any reason to think of elves as anything but enemies. I would rather they didn't shoot at us before asking questions."

As if the alicorns themselves wouldn't encourage them to do that? But she nodded her agreement, and a few moments later, sensed that tingling that told her Lorryn was working magic on her.

I wonder if I could change my own shape, the ears and the eyes anyway, the way I changed my birds? she thought. *Better not try right now, though. It's probably a very bad idea, with all the other things I'm doing with my magics.* If she lost control over the alicorns—

Best not to add one more ball to the lot she already was juggling.

She looked off to her right, and saw with relief that the sun was near the horizon. It would be time to stop soon.

"We should talk about when we want to leave the alicorns," he called back to her. "Tonight."

"After I make supper," she replied. She would literally be "making" supper out of the plants they would gather—and she would make some sweet treats to ensure that the alicorns would come back after their hunt.

That was another reason she was so tired. The entire burden of their food supply rested on her slim shoulders, and she had never worked so much magic before this. She'd never realized it would tire her out so much, the more so the farther along they were.

"I wish the alicorns were enough like hounds that you could get them to bring us something back," he said wistfully.

He was probably as weary of grass-cake and stewed grass as she was.

But—

The recollection of the mare returning one night, with not only blood on her muzzle, but a shred of what could have been *cloth* stuck in her teeth, made her do more than shiver. There had been a hunter on their trail until then, and Rena *had* been wishing that the alicorns could drive him off. Had the mare somehow sensed her wishes and followed through on them in her own way? She didn't know, and probably never would know, but the hunter had certainly disappeared after that night.

"I don't," she said with a shiver. "I don't."

Caellach Gwain surveyed his audience with satisfaction. So far, he had most of the oldest and most senior of the wizards behind him—even those who had not cared to speak out before were more willing to show their true feelings now that Shana was gone.

Caellach only hoped she would stay away forever. Without her egging them on, the youngsters were not so sure of themselves or of their powers. Only her "inner circle" continued in their impudent defiance of authority, and *they* were kept so busy denuding the old Citadel that they had little time for mischief among the others.

"I'll tell you how I've been getting my proper help back," Caellach told the others. "I started with the humans. They're so used to taking orders from anyone that looks even vaguely like an authority that they never once question me, they just go and do what I tell them to." He frowned slightly. "Granted, they're bare children, but even children can pick up after me or fetch my dinner."

"Doesn't anyone ever come looking for them?" ventured one of the others.

Caellach shrugged. "Maybe, but they never come looking in my quarters. I suppose whoever's in charge of these brats must think they're sneaking off to play. I just tell them that they are to say that a wizard had important tasks for them, and that seems to take care of the matter."

He doubted, in the confusion that the new Citadel represented, that anyone had missed the children he borrowed from the work crews. There was a veritable swarm of human and wizard children, and children were of very little use at anything requiring strength or stamina. That left only what he would call "household chores," and why should they not be using their time properly in serving a single master rather than gathering reeds or some other such nonsense?

He said as much, and the other nodded sagely.

"Pick out the frightened ones," he advised, "the ones that try not to be seen, that shrink away into shadows and corners when they get the chance. They're the most tractable, and the least likely to be missed. And think—if they're that shy, we'll be doing them a favor, keeping them away from crowds! Without a doubt, those children need a firm hand, someone to give them specific orders so they don't have to think." He lifted a sardonic eyebrow at one of the others who looked a bit doubtful. "Children should not *think*, anyway. They aren't equipped to think. They should learn, listen, and obey."

"I suppose you're right," the wizard said, a bit doubtfully. "But still—"

"Oh, don't get sentimental over them, they're only *human*," snapped someone else, before the dissenter could come up with anything concrete to base his objections on. "It's not as if they're ever going to be of any real use to the Citadel except as servants! Better they learn that little fact now, while there's time to train them in their proper place!"

More heads nodded agreement, and the dissenter subsided. Caellach took control of the meeting again.

"That's not the only reason I asked you all here," he said, in a low and confidential tone. "We really need to do something about the state of things here."

"State of things?" one of the oldest quavered indignantly. "Travesty, you mean! Young brats carrying on as if they were senior—seniors being forced to fetch their own meals and sweep their own floors—" His unsteady voice rose, full of

unsteady wrath. "No respect! No proper conduct! No regard
for custom! *That's* what's wrong here! I was willing to put up
with nonsense while we were out there." He waved his hand
vaguely in the direction of the mouth of the caverns. "You
expect a certain amount of disorganization and slackness
when there's no real structure to living, so to speak. But now,
now we're living in proper quarters, and things should go
back to the way they were! It was good enough for our fore-
bears, by heaven, and it should be good enough for us!"

A rumble of ill-tempered agreement arose from the rest,
and Caellach rubbed his hands together with glee. Better and
better—the complaint *hadn't* come from him—and they all
agreed with it!

But he held up a cautionary hand as the rumble grew
louder. "I agree, I agree—but we mustn't be precipitous here!
We may realize this is what's best for the Citadel and all wizards, but those proud little brats of Lashana's think they know
better, and they have the dragons to back them up!"

At the mention of the dragons, the rumble faded into uncertain silence. He hastened to reassure them.

"It isn't impossible to put things right again," he told them
firmly. "It is simply going to take time. We must be cautious,
and lay our plans with care. Eventually the dragons will become bored with us and find other pastimes. Or—Lashana
might not return, and they will go out looking for her. A hundred things could happened to tilt the balance to our side, and
we must be ready to act when the time comes, act decisively
and quickly."

He had them again, leaning forward, listening to every
word he said. He allowed himself a slight smile.

"We must all go and think on these things," he told them.
"I will call another meeting in a few days, and I would like
to hear your ideas at that point." He met each of their eyes
in turn, and got nods, some thoughtful, some determined,
from all of them.

That was close enough to a dismissal that they soon drifted
out, by ones and twos, some talking and some silent. Caellach

waited until they were all gone, struggling to keep his feelings of triumph from showing too plainly on his face.

Now it was all just a matter of time. And when that young pest Lashana *did* return—*if* she did—she would find things changed, and not to her liking!

Two days later, they reached the plain itself; there was no sign of an alicorn herd, nor of the wizards. Lorryn elected to stay with their mounts as long as possible, and the alicorns themselves dropped abruptly from the fast pace they had set to the normal walking pace of a horse. They no longer hunted at night, and Rena found them eating nothing more sinister than grass and the treats she made for them. It was easier to keep them gentle, too, and between that and the easier pace, she began to recover from the grueling marathon of their escape.

Lorryn was certainly in his element. She didn't think she had ever seen him so happy. His hair was a wild mop, his clothing as threadbare as the lowest slave's, and he didn't look *anything* like the cultured elven lord he'd been—but there was a light in his eyes she didn't ever remember seeing before. "I'm not sure if I care whether we find the wizards now or not," he called back to her, on the third afternoon of riding through the waist-high grasses. "I could live like this forever. Think of it! As free as a hawk in the sky, no one telling us where to go or what to do—"

"That's all very well now," she said, a bit tartly, thinking about her uncomfortable couches on the cold ground, "but what about winter? It's going to get very cold down here, once winter comes, and I don't fancy huddling against an alicorn who's turned predator for warmth all night."

Lorryn laughed at her, and shook his head. "You're too practical, Rena. Too practical for romance, anyway."

"I can be romantic!" she protested, stung. "I just like my romance with comfort attached to it!"

"But would it be romance then?" he countered. "What's romance without—" He suddenly sat straight up, choking off his words, as they mounted their ridge and saw what was on the next one.

In the next moment, Rena saw what had alarmed him.

Sitting on what *looked* like very fierce cattle, ranged along the top of the next ridge, were a dozen people. Humans, she thought, but not like any other she had ever seen. They were so dark of skin as to be black, wearing brightly colored head-cloths and loose trousers, and they were armed with long, iron-tipped spears.

"Ancestors!" Lorryn breathed. "Grel-riders? It must be! I don't know of any other race with skin that color!"

"You know who these people are?" she whispered, as the alicorns came to a dead halt and stood stock-still, looking across at the six bulls and snorting a challenge.

"I studied them, when I was trying to study the wizards and the human cultures that used to be here," he muttered back, his face betraying only excitement. "I even learned the language; there was a spell of tongues on one of the books that gave me nine different human languages. I never thought I'd get a chance to use one, though—"

He broke off, and waved solemnly at the riders above them, calling to them in a peculiar liquid tongue.

"I just told them that we're from one of the extinct tribes that *used* to be allies of theirs," he said in a hasty aside to Rena. "I hope that works—according to the histories, they're notoriously—"

One of the figures above them rode his mount a little ahead of the line and called something back. Lorryn's face lit up. "It worked!" he exclaimed. "He just gave us the safe conduct to ride up to meet them!"

"Are you sure that's a good idea?" she asked, shivering with fear, and trying not to show it.

"We don't exactly have a choice," he countered. "They've already seen us, and if we turned and ran, they'd be after us in no time. They *have* to be better trackers than we are, so sooner or later they'd find us. No, we need to present our-selves as being too strong to harass." He reached out as she rode her mare up beside him and patted her hand. "I know how you feel; it's a good thing I'm mounted or I don't think my legs would hold me up. But we have to act as if we belong here, that we're their equals in strength." He gave her a quick smile. "Come on. Look brave. Think of Gildor."

That made her smile weakly, and he gave her hand another quick pat. "You can tame alicorns, remember? You have been the one keeping us fed and warm. You're clever and brave and I wouldn't want anyone else at my side in this. Let's go."

As they rode up the ridge toward the waiting riders, the bulls began to sidle sideways and back up, rolling their eyes with fear. The alicorns raised their heads and stared straight at the bulls, lifting their lips to show their fangs, and stepping like dressage-trained horses as they walked up the slope. The nearer she and Lorryn got to the dark people, the more the bulls reacted with fear, until all the riders had to dismount and hold the heads of their animals to keep them from bolting.

Lorryn stopped at that, and called out again to the rider who was apparently the leader.

"I've told him that I don't want to frighten his mounts anymore," he translated for Rena, as the leader of the group nodded, and replied. "He thanks me, and tells me that the Corn People—that's who we're supposed to be from—are wise. He says that they have heard of alicorns in legend, and that they have seen enough of them since they began their search for grazing and sweet water to know that they are terrible enemies. He wants to know how we tamed them." He laughed, softly. "We've impressed him, I think, little sister!"

Indeed, the man looked impressed, holding tightly to the halter of his bull, which tossed its head and tried to fight him. Lorryn called something back, and the man transferred his admiring gaze from Lorryn to Rena.

"Smile and wave, Rena," he whispered. "I told him you were the one who tamed them."

She smiled, a little woodenly, and waved.

"Can you hold both beasts here?" he asked her, after the man spoke several more sentences. "I think we have a rare opportunity here.

She wasn't certain what he meant by that, but she knew that if she dismounted and stood with a hand on the shoulder of each of the beasts, they wouldn't move. "I can," she told him. "But I wish you'd give me their language. *You* are the one with the spell of tongues."

"Later," he promised, and slid off the back of his alicorn to approach the leader of the dark people. She dismounted before the stallion could react to his absence, and steadied both beasts while Lorryn and the dark man spoke together. She began to lose her fear, and then her nervousness, when she realized that the man's posture and tone of voice were both not only friendly, but respectful. And whenever he looked in her direction, or indicated her, that respect only deepened.

Lorryn returned to her. "I'll tell you more later, but I made out as if we were the last of our tribe, and we've been looking for our ancient allies—them—to let them know how things stand in the lands the elves hold. They are *very* impressed by tame alicorns, and we have been invited to exercise the rights of our ancient alliance and join them. These people are associated with their head Priest, a fellow called Diric, and they want us to meet him at least." He paused, and looked gravely into her eyes. "Rena, if this is not something you are comfortable with, we'll go on—but with these people we'll have shelter and food, and I think from my reading that we'll be safe with them. It's up to you."

She looked from him to the leader of the dark people and back again. They were human—and alien—but at least they were *people*.

It would be better than riding across endless seas of grass on the backs of animals they might have to abandon at any moment.

At the moment, it seemed the best choice.

"What do I do with the alicorns?" she asked.

"Can you send them away?" he replied. "The bulls won't tolerate them. That's what Haja asked me to do, anyway."

She nodded after a moment of concentration. "Go tell him we'll come with them, and give me a little time."

She waited until he walked off and joined the man he'd called Haja, then turned her magic on the alicorns for the last time, concentrating on increasing their urge to find others of their kind until it overrode everything else, including the urge to challenge the bulls. Then she lifted her hands from their shoulders.

They half-reared, startling the bulls and their riders, and pivoted on their hind feet to point their heads west. As soon as their forefeet hit the ground, they were off, not at a fast walk or a lope, but at a run, claw-hooves flashing in the sun, manes flying, tails flagged. They looked beautiful. She watched them go with a little regret. There had been things about them that she would miss—

—but not enough that she wanted them back.

With her head as high as theirs, she walked toward Lorryn and his new "ally," and realized with a flush of pleasure that the murmurs she heard from the riders were sounds of admiration.

Now, if they could just hold their illusions—this might have been the best thing to happen to them since they escaped!

7

THE IRON PEOPLE had not moved their encampment for days, which was just fine with Shana. She'd been afraid that when they resumed their wanderings, the trek might take her little group even farther from the Citadel than they already were. But there was good grazing at this spot, and water, and as long as the grass lasted, the Iron People were not inclined to move on.

All to the good. Now they had time to make plans to get away. Shana was increasingly uneasy about being gone for so long. Not that she didn't think that Denelor and the others couldn't handle everything on their own—but—

But—things happen, sometimes. . . .

Their felt-walled tent was surprisingly cool in the heat of midday; the sides rolled up to let in a cool breeze at floor level, and heated air rose to escape through the smoke hole. With no real duties to perform, they spent most of the time that they were not being questioned in the relative comfort of the tent. After all, where was there to go? How much interest was there in watching cattle graze? Kalamadea was marginally interested in seeing how the young warriors fought in their practices, but those were always held in the cool of the morning. And whatever the magic was that held their own powers in abeyance, no one was practicing anything that looked or felt like magic near enough for any of them to detect it.

"Are you sure we should be talking with *them* around?" Mero whispered, nodding at the two elves drowsing on their side of the tent. Within two days of their capture, a peaceful accord had been reached between the newcomers and the original prisoners. The tent was divided down the middle by arranging the rugs to conform to that pattern. The elves stayed on their side, the wizards on the other. Haldor continued to ignore them; Kelyan, after questioning all of them about the particulars of the Wizard War and Lord Dyran's demise, fell into a kind of apathetic stupor. He *said* he was meditating, but it looked to Shana like he was staring off into space just like Haldor.

She had to wonder if either of them was quite sane anymore, after being held like this for several decades. There was really nothing for them to do or to think about—and if boredom was a real problem for elves in their own lands and in control of their own lives, how much more so was it a problem for these two? As she had studied them, she had come to the tentative conclusion that they were hardly more than the shadow of real elves; Haldor in particular had retreated into himself until there was nothing showing of his personality anymore. It was rather horrible, really. Was this how *they* would act after being held captive for too long?

"I don't think it matters," she told Mero truthfully. "Neither of them seem particularly interested in getting free, and it isn't as if we're planning an *escape*. We are trying to figure out how we can get the Iron People to let us go with honor all the way around, and that isn't going to get anyone in trouble. We're not doing anything to violate our parole, so to speak."

Mero shrugged then. "All right, I see your point. Even if

either of them told tales on us, all the Iron People would hear would be—"

"What they already know," Shana finished for him. "That we want to go back to our people, that we were here to find trade, and that we are *not* elves."

Mero nodded. "Well, then, if we're going to approach any-one, I think we ought to go with Jamal," he told them. "He's young, he's in the process of changing their customs—if any-one can be persuaded that it would be better to turn us loose against the custom of holding captives, I think it's likely him. And he's very popular, popular enough that people won't question it if he orders something that seems odd or unusual."

But Kalamadea shook his head at that, emphatically. "He is also grasping, that one, and he will *not* let go of anything, once he has possession of it. We are *his*, so to speak, and he will not release a piece of booty on the promise of trade to come. And—I do not think he is interested in peace with any-one. I think if he learns of the existence of the Citadel, he will seek to conquer it, not to trade with it. I have seen noth-ing that makes me think otherwise." He frowned. "And I do not like *who* he has garnered as his followers. They are war-riors all, and when was a warrior interested in anything but war? No, I am for the Priest, Diric. He is one who thinks long and deeply, and he does not ponder war without also ponder-ing the losses that war entails."

It was Keman's turn, and he shrugged, and looked con-fused. "I don't know," he confessed. "Except that I don't know how we're going to convince either of them that we aren't elves." He looked back at Shana. "Diric spent more time with you than with the rest of us, and so did Jamal, es-pecially after they let the elves give you their language. They've asked you more questions than they have all of the rest of us combined. So what do you think of them?"

She chewed her lip thoughtfully. "Initially I thought we should try to concentrate on Jamal, mostly because of Jamal's popularity, but also because I thought Diric would be like the old whiners. I thought that Diric would be very prejudiced against us just because we're 'green-eyed demons,' and he'd be more in favor of loading us down with more chains than with setting us free. But—I don't know if it was because I'm a female, or some other cause, but Jamal has been incredibly arrogant with me, and Diric has never been less than courteous. I think Diric already believes we are something other than elves. And I *know* he is far more interested in setting up trade with others than in going to war with them; he's asked me any number of times about what, exactly, our people have to offer in trade. He was very specific in what he was interested in—grain and metals, for the most part, though he'll take raw wool, linen, and ready-made goods. When Jamal wasn't trying to browbeat me, he wanted to know about terrain, and *where* I was from, precisely—and what our people *possess*. That sounds like someone looking for booty and an easy target to conquer to me, too, Kalamadea. So, on the whole, I am inclined to concentrate on Diric myself."

Kalamadea looked from her to Mero and back again. "Two for Diric, one for Jamal, and one undecided." He turned to Mero. "Would you like to make further arguments to convince us, or have we convinced you?"

Mero rubbed the side of his nose with his finger. "I'm not really strongly in support of going to Jamal," he said, finally. "If the two of you are strongly in favor of Diric, I'm willing to go along with that." He made a disparaging face. "After all, even though I know more about life on an elven lord's estate than either of you, both of *you* know more about how to read a person's intentions from what he says and does—and doesn't say."

"I am quite strongly in favor of approaching Diric," Shana replied firmly, as Kalamadea nodded agreement.

"Diric it is, then," Mero agreed. "At least he isn't as scary as Jamal. I always have the feeling Jamal is a hair away from doing something I hadn't expected—and whatever it would be, it would probably be unpleasant."

"That may be another sign he is not a man of peace," Kalamadea observed.

Shana didn't have anything to add to that—she would have said that Jamal didn't feel "safe"; as if he could and would change his moods with lightning swiftness, even though *she* had never seen such a mood change. "Now, to change the subject, have any of you figured why neither elven magics nor human magics work on these folk?"

Kalamadea threw up his hands in despair. "I am *baffled*," he replied in disgust. "I have never encountered anything like this, and I am older than the oldest elven lord on this world! I can speak mind to mind with you and Shadow, Shana, but I cannot touch the minds of *any* of the Iron People. I can mold a bit of rock to my will, but the collar remains stubbornly immutable. And I cannot shift. Now, speaking mind to mind if enough like human wizardry that I can see how, perhaps, they could block my ability to do the same—but not the purely draconic abilities of rock-shaping and shape-shifting! It is most vexing!"

Shana nodded ruefully; her own experiments had come to nothing as well, and so had Mero's. "Kelyan has no clue how they do this, and I haven't caught anyone actually working whatever magic they do that blocks ours. I'm baffled, too."

"These collars are very old," Keman said, softly.

Shana turned to him in surprise. "Why do you say that?" she asked.

He shrugged. "They can't be *very* new," he said. "They're iron, and I've overheard people complaining that they haven't had fuel or metal for the forges for months. If you look at these collars, though, you can see that there is a great deal of wear on them, enough that they could have been around for hundreds of *years*. In fact, I don't think they were ever intended for humans or elves at all. I think they were meant for animals; huge hounds, most likely. There may be some protection against control or against magic being used against the wearer in them, but I don't think there's much more than that. After all, we can speak mind to mind with each other, we just can't read *them*. We haven't tried anything else except shape-shifting and rock-shaping, and the rock-shaping works."

Shana nodded, slowly. "So the reason our magic is blocked might be something that they are each doing for themselves, and not the effect of the collar at all?"

"Except in that our magic can't be used *on* the collar, yes," Keman told her. "That is my best guess, at any rate."

"Which would be the reason why the elves can continue to cast their illusions, even though they wear similar collars," Kalamadea mused aloud. "That is logical. But why can we not *shift*?"

"Have you tried shifting to a form the same size as a halfblood?" Mero asked, suddenly intent. "Or did you try something larger or smaller?"

"This is the smallest form we can shift to," Kalamadea told him. "And—no, the only thing I have tried is to shift to one of the oxen, and I did not actually try to shift back to my draconic form until last night."

"Which is bigger, much bigger. So is the ox." Mero's eyes narrowed. "It *could* be that the reason you can't shift is because your body knows very well that you won't break the collar before it strangles you in a larger form. It isn't magic that stops you at all, it's instinct, to keep you from choking to death."

Kalamadea and Keman looked at one another, startled. After a moment, Kalamadea nodded.

"That makes even more sense," he said, slowly. "No matter *what* new form I shifted to, if the 'neck' is even a hair larger than my neck in this form, that is precisely what will happen. I will have to think about this, and perhaps between us, Keman and I can arrive at a form wherein this will not be a problem." He frowned. "The trouble is, we have never learned to shift into anything that we did not have the pattern for in nature. I am not certain that we could learn *how* to do so now."

"I wish I could pry more out of Diric," Shana said after a long silence. "I have the feeling that I would be able to figure this out, if only I knew the right questions to ask." She toyed with a lock of her hair. "I think he's feeling me out—trying to decide if *he* can trust *us*. There is something going on here that none of us are privy to between him and Jamal, but it's something that is *going* to cause us trouble. I think they're in the middle of a very subtle and covert struggle for power."

"Huh," Mero said. "That actually makes sense, and matches what I've been seeing and hearing."

"It matches what I know also," Kalamadea added. "I would not call Jamal 'rash,' precisely, but he would much rather control something directly, and that means conquering it if he can, whether it is the power over his own Clan, or the means of obtaining grain and metals, both of which are in short supply among these Iron People."

Keman groaned, and massaged his temple as if he had a headache. "This is not fair! I *hate* being stuck in the middle of a power struggle at any time, but why must I be stuck in the middle of one that hasn't got anything to do with me?"

"How do you think I feel?" Shana retorted. "I've been in the center of power struggles since before I was born! No one ever asked me if I wanted any part of this!"

"You have great *hamenleai*, Lashana," Kalamadea said, with one of his inscrutable smiles. "I said so when Alara brought you to the Kin. Since you are such a center of great change, you can hardly be anything but the focus of power struggles."

"Oh, thank you," she replied sarcastically. *Sometimes I wish Father Dragon would take his position as Chief Shaman and—ah, never mind. Foster mother is like that too; she just doesn't get quite so pompous about it.*

"Oh, you are welcome," he replied, with equal irony, but more humor. "I merely point out the facts, Lashana; I am not responsible for them."

She only snorted. "Fact or not, we *are* here and I would like to do something to get us *out* of here. So has anyone got any ideas about approaching Diric?"

There had been some disturbance outside; Shana had been ignoring it. There were often disturbances outside the tent: quarrels between young warriors, noisy games by mobs of children, the occasional cow taking it into her head to charge through the center of camp. Such disturbances usually faded after a while.

This one did not. In fact, the crowd noise had increased over the past few moments.

"What is going on out there?" she wondered aloud, getting to her feet. She coiled the loose end of her chain around her waist and walked over to the entrance, followed by the other three and the two elves.

They emerged into the bright light and heat of midafternoon; the sun struck her like a blow to the head, and she shaded her eyes with her hand as she peered in the direction of all the noise.

Now, now that Haldor had been coaxed to work something the elves called a "spell of tongues" upon them all, and had imparted to all four of them all of the knowledge of the language of the Iron People that either he or Kelyan had, she could understand the shouting.

"Are they saying something about 'Corn People'?" she asked Kalamadea in puzzlement.

He nodded, frowning furiously. "They are," he replied, "and that is an impossibility. They were a tribe that allied with the grel-riders in their struggle against the elves, but unfortunately, they were handicapped by being farmers rather than nomads. They would not leave their land, and they had not really acquired the skills of war—they had always relied on their allies to protect them. The Corn People were slaughtered long before the first Wizard War, and their children made into slaves. There *are* no more Corn People."

He seemed so certain of it that she could not doubt him, but that was certainly the gist of what the shouting was all about. So if there were no Corn People, then what—

The shouting neared; clearly the crowd was headed in this direction.

A moment later the chaotic mob surged through the gap between the tent-wagons. In the middle of it all was a group of Iron Priests, escorting a pair of golden-haired, pale-skinned humans, who stood out among the dark Iron People like daisies blooming in a freshly turned field. The two newcomers clearly *were* being escorted and were not prisoners; the Priests gave them all the deference of honored guests, the folk crowding around them were excited at the sight of them, and most telling of all, they were *not* wearing collars and chains.

The entire crowd pushed and shoved their way past without anyone paying the slightest bit of attention to the prisoners.

Except for one of the newcomers.

The male of the pair looked up, catching first Shana's eyes, then Mero's—and *his* eyes widened in shock. His mouth opened, as if he meant to shout something.

But it was too late, he was already past, carried by the crowd heading for Diric's tent.

Lorryn could not have been more surprised if he had seen Lord Tylar disporting himself among these nomads. There had been two *elves* back there, with collars on their necks and chains around their waists—and beside them, what could only have been four wizards in like condition!

How had *that* come about? And why?

I don't have time to worry about that now, he reminded himself, casting a nervous glance around the crowd. He prided himself on being able to read people, and he did not like what he sensed. While he and Rena in their guise of "allies" might be an exciting new novelty, it was obvious from some of the subtler signals that the Corn People had been considered somewhat inferior to the Iron Clans. There was an air of amused superiority about the Priests, for instance, now that they had gotten over the initial shock of the discovery. And Lorryn thought he knew *why*; the Corn People had been farmers and not nomadic herdsmen. They had not been particularly good fighters, though they had held their ground valiantly to protect the retreat of their allies into the South. In the histories *he* had read, the Corn People had always relied on the Iron People to protect them from enemies, paying for the protection in the grain and goods only a settled population could produce.

That meant it was all the more imperative that he hold his illusion of full humanity over himself and Rena. It also meant that once everyone got over the novelty of seeing the blond

Corn People in their midst, he and Rena would be here on
bare and wary sufferance. After all, what did they bring with
them? Nothing. No grain, no hope of grain, no skills of war.
Only the ability to tame alicorns, animals the bulls would not
tolerate. That wasn't exactly useful—and a demonstration of
any *other* talents might well get them in more trouble than it
got them out of.

The Priests that had "welcomed" the two of them wanted
to take them directly to their Chief Priest—and Lorryn
agreed, even though he sensed there was something that they
were not telling him about that request. It was somewhat unnerving to realize that he could not touch their minds, no
matter how hard he tried; he was so used to being able to
read people's thoughts as well as their expressions that he felt
curiously half-deaf or half-blind. Was this how Rena felt? Or
the more ordinary human slaves without wizard-powers? If
so, he felt terribly sorry for them.

They were ushered into a large tent-wagon, redolent with
fragrant smoke, and once the flap dropped behind them,
seemingly empty. As Lorryn's eyes adjusted to the darkness,
something moved at the far end of the tent.

"I think you are not what you seem, tamer of one-horns,"
a deep and amused voice said, quietly, from out of the shadows there.

Lorryn started. "I?" he replied innocently. "How can I be
something other than what you see?" Rena clutched at his
hand, bewildered by the strange tongue and clearly ill at ease.
He peered into the shadows, trying to make out the form of
the speaker; it was hardly fair that these people were so *dark*;
that made it hard to see them in this half-light.

Someone stood up; a human form detached itself from the
shadowy form of a chair and moved forward. "I say you are
not what you seem," the deep voice continued, "because what
you *seem* to be is one of the Corn People—yet beneath that
seeming I see something else. Something I would have been
tempted to name a green-eyed demon, had I not had four
creatures like unto you brought to me within the fortnight."

A tall, powerfully built man with closely cropped, tightly

curling gray-white hair stepped into the shaft of light from the smoke hole in the tent roof above, and stood before Lorryn, arms crossed over his chest. He leveled a challenging gaze at Lorryn, who froze.

"So tell me what it is that you *are*, tamer of one-horns," he demanded. "Tell me why it is that you and four of my captives share a semblance, while this you call your sister looks all too clearly like the other twain I hold in chains."

He knows what we are! He can see through the illusions! Lorryn thought in panic. *Oh, Ancestors, now what do I do?*

Well, there was no real choice. *Tell the truth? It seems the only way out.*

"It's a very long story," he began, tentatively.

For the first time, the man who must be the Chief Priest cracked a slow, cautious smile.

"There is always the time for a long story," he responded.

So Lorryn began at the beginning; the priest interrupted him often to ask very pointed questions, and by the time he reached the end of his narrative, the light from the smoke hole had crawled halfway up the wall of the tent, and he was hoarse.

"I can't think of anything else to tell you," he concluded. "Two of the people you have *are* elves, what you call green-eyed demons; the other four are obviously halfbloods like me. It seems to me that the wizards *would* be very interested in opening up trade with you, just as they claim. They probably need all the allies they can get against the elves."

"Interesting." The man stroked his chin and stared quite through Lorryn. "I am inclined to believe you. I must think on all of this you have told me; clearly things have greatly changed since my people fled into the South." His eyes focused again, and he gave Lorryn a look that made the halfblood quiver inside; in all of his life he had never met someone with so powerful a personality. "Hold to your illusion; I think perhaps I am the only one to have seen through it, since I was consciously disposing myself to doubt it as soon as word of your coming reached my ears. The rest will see you both for Corn People. You will be on sufferance until I say otherwise."

Oh, just what I wanted to hear, Lorryn thought, suppressing a shiver.

"The War Chief will find you of no interest," the Chief Priest continued. "The Corn People were never of any use in warfare, and it is logical that he will dismiss you to my care. Be glad; if he penetrated your illusion, you would fare much worse than with me. And I think your illusion would not last beyond his desire to taste the strangeness of your sister."

The Priest's arched eyebrows left no doubt in Lorryn's mind about what *that* had meant. He fought down mingled fear and anger at the very idea; the Priest chuckled at his expression.

"Have no fear that she shall be subject to my whims, boy; my taste is for my life partner and wife, which is just as well. Had she not chosen me, she would have become a Man-Hearted Woman, I think, and gone running with the warriors—and she does not brook that I should look elsewhere than her." He chuckled again, as if the idea amused him. "Stay you in the dwelling to which I shall send you while I ponder upon the problem you have presented, and speak with the spirits of our fathers and with the First Smith."

Since they really didn't have any other choice, Lorryn nodded his agreement. The Priest went to the door of the tent and called out a soft summons; another, younger Priest came at his call, and ushered them out into the fading sunset, taking them to a small tent-wagon in the midst of many such. All of the people here were attired like the Priest, with the same iron torque with the flame-filigree pendant.

The tent itself was plain enough, just a few cushions and some colorful blankets, with a cold brazier set under the smoke hole. As soon as they were alone, Lorryn quickly explained to Rena everything that had happened. He halfway expected her to react badly to the news that they had been unmasked, but she heard him out without making a single comment until the end.

"It could be worse," she pointed out. "If he's a Priest, he

could have gotten quite a bit of prestige out of revealing us for what we are. He didn't; I don't think he will. *I* think there's some kind of power-playing going on between him and the War Chief. I think he might be holding us in reserve, to be used against this man."

Lorryn blinked in surprise; where had she come up with *that*? Not that it wasn't logical; in fact, it made altogether too much sense. But how had *she* seen it so quickly?

She might not be able to read thoughts, but she could certainly read his expressions like one of her romances. "Mother and I were subject to every shift in politics that Lord Tylar made," she commented ironically. "We learned to read the state of things very quickly and from very small hints. We had to; we had no choice. We had to be certain that if we said something complimentary about last week's ally, he was *still* an ally and not an enemy."

"Ah," he replied, at a loss for an answer.

Then he was saved from having to give one by the arrival of a woman with a basket of food: a soft white cheese and strips of dried meat the consistency of leather, together with fresh water. Rena frowned as she surveyed their limited meal.

"I could get very tired of that, very quickly," she said, gingerly picking up a meat strip and nibbling on it. "I think perhaps I'd better work a bit of magic on a handful of grass or two every day."

"I wouldn't argue with that," Lorryn agreed—although to his mind, the meat and cheese made a wonderful change from handfuls of grass. He'd begun to feel rather like a goat these past few days. He yawned hugely, only now becoming aware of how tired he was. "Meanwhile, maybe we ought to rest while we've been given the chance?"

Rena echoed his yawn as if she couldn't help herself. "I—I would have thought I'd never be able to sleep under a circumstance like this one—but—"

"But we might as well; the circumstance isn't going to change, whether we sleep or not." He took up a meat strip and began to work his way through it, valiantly. "The same goes for making the most of these meals—"

Rena took the strip away from him, before he'd even managed to worry a bit off. Before he could object, she'd handed it back. "Try that now," she suggested.

He did—and to his surprise, it was tender. It still *tasted* like unflavored dried meat, but now one could eat it without getting sore jaws.

"I didn't know you could do that with anything other than plants," he said in surprise.

She shrugged. "Neither did I until just a moment ago."

He felt his eyebrows rising. With every day that passed, she offered yet another surprise. Now she was trying her magic on something that was no longer alive—and making it work. What would she be able to do in a month?

Enough, perhaps, for them to win free of these people?

It could be. After all that they had been through so far, he was not willing to put *any* limitations on her potential abilities anymore.

He managed to muster up the energy to work the spell of tongues on Rena after a short nap, before anyone looked in on them. That was just as well, for immediately after they broke their fast, another young Priest arrived to bring them to the Chief Priest for another round of intense questioning. This time he concentrated as much of his attention on Rena as he did on Lorryn, pretty much dividing his questions equally between the two of them.

Not that this proved to make things any easier, at least for Lorryn. He was constantly worrying that Rena would say something wrong—not that *he* would know what was wrong or right! But the Priest—who finally introduced himself, belatedly, as "Diric"—was far more intent on learning what she knew about the wizards than about anything else.

Finally, after hours and hours of this interrogation, Diric dismissed them into the cool of the early evening. "Do not speak to anyone else, particularly not the prisoners," he cautioned sternly. "Be polite to any of my folk who speak to you, but answer to questions only that Diric has not given you leave to speak. Otherwise you may go about the camp and observe whatever you choose."

He did not insult their intelligence by ordering them not to try to escape; that was obvious. It was equally obvious, at least to Lorryn, that any attempt to use magic against the Iron People would be as futile as his own attempts at reading their thoughts. Obviously if magic could have gotten anyone free around here, neither the two elves nor the four wizards would still be captives.

He and Rena wandered about the camp, simply observing things, for the rest of the evening. No one stopped them or gave them orders to go elsewhere, and people seemed quite willing to talk to them and answer their questions. Lorryn found himself fascinated in spite of their obvious danger; he had never seen anyone who lived as these people did.

Their entire way of life revolved around their cattle. Fully half their food came from the cattle themselves; what Lorryn had thought was *wool* felt that made the tents proved to come from the carefully husbanded winter hair the cattle shed in the spring. While they might call themselves the "Iron People," they could with justification have referred to themselves as the "Leather People"; Lorryn had never seen anyone use leather in so many ways and for so many purposes. Often what he had taken for woven fabric turned out to be supple leather, thin and fluid as any woven goods, and cleverly dyed and embroidered to resemble cloth.

They had cloth as well, but Rena learned by asking a woman who was busy redyeing a faded shirt over a pot on the fire that it was all obtained by trade. "We have had no trade, and no new cloth, for many moons," the woman said sadly, stirring the dye-pot with a stick. "We are not poor, but we must husband our cloth as if we were the poorest Clan among the People! It is a sad thing."

They walked on through the warm evening breeze, the sharp scent of the dye following them.

Their next campfire proved to belong to some of the warriors—and there was a single woman among them, a woman who wore virtually the same garments and armor as a man, and who was treated exactly as another man. There he learned what the "Man-Hearted Women" were that Diric had obliquely referred to, for she was one of them—women who took vows to forgo marriage and children in order to join the warriors' society. There were not many of them, and it was often difficult to pick them out from the young men, so hardened were they by their intense training. The term seemed to refer, not to their courage, but to the fact that their hearts chose a way otherwise reserved for men.

Were there such things as "Woman-Hearted Men"? When he asked that question, the answer was a matter-of-fact "Of course—but I doubt you could tell them from maidens."

He also learned that the smiths were as honored among these people as the warriors—although there had been no metal for the smiths to forge for some time, a fact that made all the people restless and a bit uneasy. Their god was the First Smith, after all, who had given to humans fire and the knowledge of metalcraft. To be unable to worship this god by working in metal was unsettling to everyone in the encampment. So the Iron People were suffering many deprivations besides that of new cloth.

Although women could be smiths as readily as men, there were again differences in *what* they wrought, based on their sex. Men tended to concentrate on arms and armor—women on the iron jewelry that both sexes wore. Men's jewelry was utilitarian and based on armor—wrist cuffs, torques, headbands, belts, and ankle cuffs. Women's jewelry, however, though also of iron, was the most amazing stuff Lorryn had ever seen. As delicate as black lace, the filigree-work done by the women smiths would have attracted the envy of any elven crafter. It was sophisticated and lovely, and it would not have been at all difficult to start a fad for the jewelry among not only the elven ladies, but among their lords as well.

The sound of distant music caught both his attention and Rena's; they followed their ears to the tent where the music originated, and *that* was where they discovered why the Iron People had kept a pair of elven captives in the first place.

After the initial shock wore off, and the initial feeling of smug self-satisfaction at the fate of two who would in another time and place have been his enemies, he was reduced to feeling an odd sort of pity for them. Both of them were hardly more than caricatures of what they must have been when they'd first been captured. Neither could survive in his own society anymore, even if they somehow won free. It was impossible to feel anything *but* pity for them.

But as he and Rena returned to the relative security of their own tent, he wondered how long he would have for the luxury of pity for anyone but himself.

For Keman, the arrival of the new humans that their captors called "the Corn People" was only the second surprise of the day. The first was something he had not even told Kalamadea about, because he was not certain what it meant, nor what he was going to do about it.

One of the pack-beasts, oxen trained to carry enormous loads on their backs, had a dragon-shadow.

Back in the long-ago time before he and Shana had any notion that elves *or* humans existed, Shana had showed him how he could look for a dragon shape-shifted into something else by a kind of "shadow" it had, a wisp of form that showed its true nature. The more of its mass a dragon had shifted into the Out, the stronger the "shadow" would be, although as far as he knew, only he, his mother, Alara, and Shana knew how to spot those shadows. You had to know what you were looking for, then be looking at the right time to see it. It wasn't like breaking an illusion, which only needed disbelief.

He was rather fascinated with the variety of livestock the Iron People had bred for their uses, taking the place of beef and milk cattle, horses, donkeys, and grels. He had taken to watching the herds, idly trying to spot something new. This morning he had been looking over the pack-beasts, a variety of short-horned, broad-backed cattle with stout legs and placid tempers, when one of them caught his attention, perhaps because it moved just a little differently from the rest.

That was when he spotted the other difference; a dragon-shadow.

Certain that he was somehow mistaken—or that the circumstances of their captivity were doing something to his mind—he watched that particular animal all morning, right up until Shana called him after her session with Diric for their little meeting.

He returned to that herd, looking for it, as soon as the meeting was over. It was still there, and it still had a dragon-shadow.

He sat down to watch it while the afternoon sun crawled across the sky and headed for the horizon, oblivious to the heat, to the flies that came to drink his sweat and went away disappointed. He watched it from the best vantage points he could manage, moving with the herd until he was certain it did not act like the others.

Or rather, it *acted* like the others; its actions and movements were a little stilted, a bit of a caricature. After studying the beast for some time, he realized that it had selected one particular ox and was copying everything *that* ox did, acting a heartbeat or so behind it. When it bent its head to graze, so did the cow. When the ox turned to look at something, so did the cow. When it ambled down to the river for a drink, the cow followed, and when it lay down in the afternoon to chew its cud, the cow did the same a few feet away. The cow never once took its eyes off the ox, which was very peculiar behavior for a herd-beast, and a female at that.

Which meant that he wasn't delusional; that dragon-shadow *was* there. The pack-beast was a shape-shifted dragon.

But since it hadn't made itself known to him, it wasn't one of the rebels who had cast their lot in with Shana and the wizards; they all knew what his halfblood-form looked like, and one of them would have signaled to him as soon as they saw him. So what Lair was it from? That was important; if it was from his old Lair, it was likely to be an enemy, and might cause trouble for him and for Shana if it knew they were here. If it was from another Lair, there was no telling how it would feel about them, and it still might cause trouble for them.

So just at the moment, it didn't look as if it would be a

good thing to just stroll up to it and greet it in the dragons'-tongue, or speak to it mind to mind. Best to keep quiet and study the situation, perhaps.

So he continued to watch the beast as the sun sank and twilight turned the sky a deep blue, adjusting his eyes to compensate for the growing darkness. Insects called from the grass around him, and the herds settled for the night.

His secret weapon was Kalamadea; if this was a stranger, the presence of Kalamadea, the oldest dragon in any of the Lairs he knew, could be enough to make it simply go away if it came to a conflict. Unless, of course, it was from his old Lair; in that case, it *might* go away peacefully, unless it happened to be one of a handful of dragons who would be only too happy to discover that Kalamadea was as helpless as he and Shana, and who would take immediate advantage of the situation.

He debated the question with himself as twilight turned to true night, and as the moon rose to gild the backs of the cattle with a soft dusting of light, without coming to any kind of a conclusion. He started to head back to the tent and the others, but found himself drifting back toward the herd to stare at the not-cow and ponder his options.

I wonder; she—if it is a "she" and the sex as well as the form hasn't been shifted—is just as vulnerable as we are right at this moment. As Kalamadea pointed out when we were caught, shifting takes time, and if I raised a fuss about her, she wouldn't be able to get away quietly.

The not-cow was watching him as warily as he was watching her, as a soft evening breeze ruffled his hair. Had she noticed his regard? Could *she* see dragon-shadows too?

If she can—then she knows. And if she knows, she could get away as soon as I leave and she can work her way beyond the edge of the herds, out of sight of the herdsmen.

That decided him; he had no options now, and there was no time to get Kalamadea. He was going to have to do something, and he'd better figure out what it was, and quickly!

The dragon-cow moved uneasily, and he *knew* that she realized he was watching her. She had just forced him to act.

He could only hope that what he was about to do would be the right action for all of them.

Rhiadorana had chosen to follow this clan of the Iron People mostly because they happened to be passing through her Lair's territory during the season she had chosen to undergo her Adult Trial. Her Lair had the custom of sending the adolescents out one at a time to spend at least a season shifted into a single form—generally one in which they could spy on the doings of humans. *Humans*, not elven lords; the elves were too far away, quite out of the Lair's territory, and too dull and predictable to prove to be any danger or even challenge to the Lair. There had been some rumors a few seasons ago to the effect that the situation among the elves had changed drastically, but they were still too far away to bother with. Life in the mountains and plains of the South and West was quite exciting enough without going that far afield only to be disappointed.

It had been a real trial to control her shape for such an extended period of time, but that was the point of the exercise, after all. It had turned out that she had made a good choice of subjects, too, for this clan, driven out of their old range by an extended drought, was doing some entirely new things for the tradition-bound Iron People. If Dora was any judge, there was going to be a revolution here, and the War Chief was going to try to become the *only* leader of the clan. She'd shifted into a beast of burden that bore his brand upon her precisely so she could hear rumors about him, and even some of his own intriguing, and what she had learned was going to be very valuable to the Lair. He had ambitions, did Jamal. He wanted to be the ruler of *all* the Iron People. And the way things were going, he just might be able to achieve that goal, especially if old Diric underestimated his ambition or his guile. This was an unusual Clan even without Jamal; they were the only Clan Dora had ever seen that had ever taken elven slaves. They could turn out to be unusual in other ways as well, perhaps enough to be a threat to the Folk.

That had been quite enough to keep her here, many weeks

past when she might otherwise have gone home. The Folk needed someone here, at least to see whether Diric or Jamal won in the imminent power struggle. So she stayed, and was pretending to graze at the edge of the herd when the *new* prisoners were brought in.

They looked like elves—but they weren't elves. No elven lord or lady had ever boasted tanned skin, or hair of any color other than palest blond. Their ears were gently pointed, not the lance-headed shape of the aristocratic elves. She had stared in bovine astonishment as they were chained to the tail of a wagon pending their disposition—and then as she stared at them more closely, she got another shock.

Two of them had dragon-shadows.

She hadn't known *what* to think or do then. Immediate instinct urged her to come to their rescue, but prudence dictated a more cautious course. They might not *want* to be rescued. They might be here on purpose; this might be part of a plan of their own, and by rescuing them, she might spoil it.

They might also be on their own Adult Trials, and to interfere would be to cast disgrace on them. A dragon who encountered difficulties during her Adult Trial was supposed to get *herself* out of them. That was the point of it being a trial, after all. How could it be a trial if someone else rescued you? She didn't *think* any of the others had been planning to follow her to this Clan of Iron People, but it was always possible that they had.

One of the two dragons had been watching her all day, and she began to suspect that he had spotted her for what she was. So since all the Lair knew that she was making her own trial here, he would recognize her. This was not necessarily a bad thing—

Unless he was not an adult, this was not part of a clever scheme on his part, and he planned to get himself out of his own troubles by making trouble for her!

She eyed him dubiously, aware of a growing hunger that no amount of grass was going to cure. She needed to kill and feast on real meat at least once every two or three days, even in this form, and she was overdue. Ordinarily she would simply drift to the edge of the herd, work her way into the darkness, shift, and fly off. She'd be back before the herdsman noticed she was gone, good for another two or three days of acting like a cow. But with this stranger here—if she started to "stray," he *could* call attention to her before she could get away, shouting to the herdsman. As long as he was here, she didn't dare move!

She cursed him mentally, and wished she could call a thunderstorm out of the sky the way the shaman could—under cover of a good downpour, she could slip away with no trouble at all. Better yet, with enough lightning hitting the ground, even the best-trained cattle would stampede, and she could pound away with them!

But she was not a shaman, and there were no thunderclouds overhead. The sky was horribly clear, every star shining cheerfully, and the only scent that the breeze carried was the scent of grass torn by thousands of busily chewing mouths.

Her stomach growled, cramping with hunger and revolting against the grass she had sent it. The situation was getting desperate!

If he keeps standing there, she thought frantically, *the only recourse I'm going to have is to shift into a one-horn and stampede the herd myself!* No matter if she would have to leave her post, and perhaps fail her trial—that hardly mattered, given that if he exposed her, she'd fail anyway!

Wait a moment—the dragon was walking toward her! He was going to accost her directly!

:Well, my friend,: a voice said cautiously into her mind. *:What are the two of us to make of this situation? I can't escape—but neither can you, while I watch you.:*

The voice was male—and it sounded older than she had thought. But more than that—it was no voice she recognized!

How could that be?

Where would a *strange* dragon have come from? The very idea of a dragon she did not know was—impossible!

:Who are you?: she asked, before she thought, her mind full of stunned amazement.

:Kemanorel, formerly of Lelanola'a's Lair,: he replied promptly. *:And now of the Wizards' Lair. Who are you? What Lair is yours?:*

She could not reply at first; her knees locked, and her mouth gaped as she looked up at him in his strange not-human, not-elven form. Lelanola'a's Lair? What was *that*? She had never heard of any Lair of the Kin but her own! And what in the name of Fire and Rain was a *Wizards'* Lair?

More than one Lair of dragons? Did that mean there had been more than one Gate that brought dragons into this world? Could there be *other* Lairs that her Kin had never even dreamed existed?

:Rhiadorana,: she replied weakly, after a long silence. *:Of—of the only Lair I ever heard of. It doesn't even have a name. And—I believe that we need to speak!:*

A long silence, just as stunned as her own, followed.

:I—believe we do,: came the slow reply, after an agonizing wait. *:And perhaps the best time is now.:*

Shana was not expecting another summons from the Iron Priest so late at night, so when one of the under-Priests came to fetch her, her immediate response was fear. Keman was *not* in his sleeping place; she saw that with a glance. Had he tried to escape, and been stopped—or worse, killed or hurt? Why else would Diric want to see her in the middle of the night?

Kalamadea and Shadow started up at the same time, but were sternly sent back to their places by the Priest—who, besides carrying a lantern, was armed, and could enforce his will, and probably had a half-dozen fellows waiting outside that he could call with a single word. They both watched helplessly as Shana crawled out of her bed and got slowly to her feet, their eyes mirroring the same fear that clenched her stomach tight against her backbone.

The Priest motioned her to follow; she glanced back at the others, shrugged, and pushed aside the tent flap, emerging into the darkness. It was late; very late. The camp was entirely quiet except for the sounds of the herds in the distance and the insects in the grass. The night air held that peculiar heaviness it only attained after the midpoint of the night; damp and still, and quite cold. She shivered, not just from fear and cold, but with reaction at being wakened out of a sound sleep; she felt unsettled, nerves jumping as she walked at the direction of the Priest and the expected half-dozen other guards. The moon was gone, and most fires were out; the only light came from the Priest's lantern. She yawned and wrapped her arms across her chest, trying to regain some of the warmth of her bed, and studied the Priest's face to see if she could learn anything from his expression.

He looked solemn, but not angry, not even terribly concerned. Perhaps this had nothing to do with Keman, then?

The Priest brought her to Diric's tent, but for the first time, he did not climb the steps to follow her inside—he simply motioned to her to make the climb herself, watching to see that she did so. The wood creaked under her slow footsteps; she reached for the heavy felt of the tent flap and pushed it aside, slipping into the incense-scented warmth within.

Diric was there, sitting on a cushion and wearing a loose robe, rumpled as if he himself had arisen from a restless sleep. A lantern burned above his head. He was not alone; there was someone else standing near the entrance in a posture of waiting.

But the person with him was not, as she first feared, Keman.

But it *was* a wizard, not a human, nor an elven lord. The shape of the ears and gleam of emerald eyes as he turned toward her was unmistakable. There was only one problem.

She and Mero were the only two wizards in this camp, and Mero was back in the tent.

"Shana," Diric said softly into the darkness. "This is Lorryn. I requested that he drop the illusion he held over himself for now. I believe that you know what he is, though you do not know him personally."

After a stunned moment, she saw past the ears and the eyes to the shape of the features, and realized *who* he was. "You—

you're one of those barbarians that came in with the Priest's scouts!" she blurted.

He nodded, his mouth twisted in a wry smile. "And my illusion of full human blood was not good enough to persuade Priest Diric," he replied ruefully. "I *was* looking for you, but I didn't expect to find you like this!"

"Me specifically, or wizards in general?" she asked, distractedly, as Diric watched them both with a certain amusement.

"Wizards in general—" he began, then peered at her more closely until his shock mirrored and echoed her own. "No—" he said then, shaking his head in utter stark disbelief. "No, you can't be—there must be more than one female—red-haired—"

So he's heard the description of me.

"Can't I?" she replied, grimacing a little at her own plight, and the embarrassment of being caught in it. "Why not? Because the Elvenbane couldn't be so stupid as to get caught on a simple scouting expedition? Well, maybe the 'Elvenbane' couldn't, but Lashana is *quite* stupid enough to make any number of ridiculous blunders, I'm afraid. I'm just usually a lot more clever about getting out of them!"

Lorryn just stared at her, and Diric resumed control of the situation and the conversation with the aplomb of one used to control.

"Now I am convinced," he said at last. "Neither of you children are old or crafty enough to have feigned any of your reactions just now—and the tales I have heard from both of you are a match for one another. You are *not* green-eyed demons; you are something else entirely." He motioned to a set of cushions near his own. "Sit," he ordered. "I spent most of this night sleepless, pondering the difficulties that you present. We must talk."

Shana yawned, unable to help herself, as she dropped heavily down onto a cushion. *Couldn't this have waited until morning?* she thought, a bit resentfully.

"I could not wait until morning," Diric said, as if divining her thoughts. "In part because in the morning Jamal's eyes will be watching, and his ears stretched to hear what I say. By rousing you both from your dreams, I can, if I choose, claim convincingly that the First Smith sent a night-portent into my sleep that forced me to interrogate you both, here and now."

Shana nodded reluctantly. Lorryn waited to hear more.

"I do not have the power here that I once held," Diric continued, with a candor that shocked her. "And more of my power ebbs with every passing day. If it were my choice, my decision, you would all walk free of this place at dawn, to return to your own peoples, and bring to us an alliance and a new trading partner. But Jamal rules here, particularly where prisoners are concerned, and it is his will that you remain forever, visible signs of his power and prowess as War Chief. He has convinced himself that all green-eyed demons are of the ilk of the two we hold; he is certain that this clan can conquer them all and take the riches of their lands from them."

Lorryn shook his head violently at that. "Sir, forgive me, but you have *no idea* what the really powerful elven lords can do!" he exclaimed urgently. "Please, believe me, if your people come up against them directly, you might kill some of their *human* soldiers, but you'll never get near one of them! Even without being able to use magic against you directly, there is plenty they can do! They can open chasms up under your feet to swallow your warriors, they can—"

Diric held up a hand, forestalling him. "You speak to one who is already convinced, young one," he said softly. "I know this, as well as one can who has never actually seen such things with his own eyes. It is Jamal who must be convinced, and it is Jamal who never will be convinced save by a slaughter of our clan."

"Then what are we supposed to do?" Shana asked, only too well aware of how helpless *they* were. "You didn't bring the two of us here in the middle of the night to tell us that you can't let us escape and you know Jamal is leading your people into a war they can't win."

Diric gave her an approving glance. "No, indeed, I did not," he said easily. "I brought you here to include you in my—conspiracy, if you will. Or to be included in your own.

I wish to see you free. I wish to have a trade alliance with your people. I wish to avoid a conflict with the demons. Each springs from the other—so I believe we need to begin our discussion with thoughts on how we may engineer your escape."

For the second time in the past few moments, Shana felt faint with relief. She concentrated on the spicy scent of the incense-laden air, of the texture of the soft fabric under her hands, of her own weight resting on the cushion to steady herself.

"We'll need to work this out in such a way that no blame falls on you, obviously," Lorryn said, while she was still recovering.

She snapped herself out of her dizziness at that. "More importantly—if we want to throw some immediate doubt on the wisdom of Jamal's war plans, shouldn't we make it look as if the escape was *easy* for us?" she added. "Shouldn't we make it look as if we could have gotten up and walked out of here any time we pleased, and we chose not to?"

Diric blinked, as if her words surprised him, and he nodded. "That would be a very good thing to have happen," he replied solemnly. "A very, very good thing indeed. It would discredit Jamal's assumptions of our superior powers; discredit anything so fundamental to the heart of his power and we might begin to weaken it."

Lorryn's brows knitted. "Can I assume you can't offer us much in the way of overt help?" he hazarded.

Diric nodded, which didn't surprise Shana particularly.

"Covert help, then," she suggested. "The key to these damned collars, for instance? They *are* interfering with some of our powers, and if we want to make it look as if they have no effect on us, you'd better give us a way to get rid of them so we can act."

Diric considered that for a moment. "I do not *have* the key," he said, after a moment, then smiled. "But I *am* a smith, after all. I believe I can either make a key, or pick the locks and jam them, so that the collars look functional but can be removed at your will. Is that sufficient?"

"That will do," she said with satisfaction. "We'll also need to get Lorryn to us covertly, so that he can learn to use wizard magics to their fullest. Mero and I know some tricks I'm sure he never picked up on his own."

To her pleasure, Lorryn gave her a half-bow. "I never doubted that," he replied. "The best I can manage is elven magic, and thought-reading. I may have some elven-learning that may prove new to you, however. I have been well schooled in those powers. I lived as Lord Tylar's acknowledged son and heir until a few short weeks ago, after all, and I have all the training of an elven son."

Shana felt her eyebrows shooting so high, her forehead cramped. "Now, *that* is a story I'd like to hear!" she exclaimed.

"And so you shall, but no more this night," Diric interrupted. Now he yawned. "These words of yours have stilled some of my anxieties, and now my own body is demanding the rest I denied it."

Shana tried to hold back her own yawn, and failed; when Lorryn added his, it was obvious that none of them were going to be able to work or speak with unclouded minds.

"I shall devise a meeting for you and yours, Shana, and Lorryn and his sister," Diric promised. "And I think—I think I shall facilitate that by granting the Corn People a great honor in the morning."

He arched a brow at Lorryn, who smiled, and asked the expected question. "And what honor will that be, Iron Priest?"

"Why, I shall invite you to be of my household and share my tent," Diric replied. "And you, of course, will agree immediately, conscious of the enormity of the honor and the protection my rank will give you."

"Of course," Lorryn said, with an ironic bow. "And being as we are only Corn People, not warriors, with nothing of value to Jamal, he will see this as no more than your desperate scrambling for a success to equal his taking of four green-eyed demons as prisoners."

Diric grinned broadly, his white teeth shining in the darkness of his face. He motioned to them to rise, and did so himself. Shana heard his joints popping as he did so, and wondered, not for the first time, just how old he was. "Why, I could almost believe you to be as crafty as an Iron Priest yourself, oh wizard."

"And I," Lorryn said, with a chuckle that Shana echoed as they both stood to leave, "could almost believe you to be as crafty as a halfblood, oh Priest!"

Myre flew lazy circles in the sky above the encampment full of those strange, black-skinned people, and watched everything that was going on below her. It was no great task to sharpen her eyesight until an eagle would be myopic by comparison; though she flew so high that she was scarcely visible even as a dot to those below her, she could count the rings on a woman's fingers, the number of rattles on a baby's toy.

And after dark, there would be one more warrior prowling the pathways between the tents. It was easy enough to counterfeit the iron jewelry so long as it didn't need to bear close inspection or the light of day.

She had learned a great deal this way. Not as much as she had in the elven trade-cities, however.

She'd been dividing her time between the wizards' Citadel, generally disguised as a rock formation in Caellach Gwain's favorite cavern for meeting with his band of conspirators, and the trade-cities in several guises, all of them rather clever. But the best and most entertaining spying she'd done had come when she chose another shape and another household to infiltrate: that of a male slave in the house of Rena's would-be husband.

She stayed there longer than she would have liked—but what she learned made up for the danger.

From there she once again took wing and returned to the new Citadel of the wizards. It was easy enough to slip into the cave complex and hide herself among the rocks of the unfinished portions to eavesdrop. That, too, took longer than she wished, but was well rewarded.

She learned that Shana and Keman were not with the wizards; she learned what direction they had gone in. That was how she had found them; following *their* track to its logical conclusion.

And she learned firsthand that the wizards themselves were spending far too much time debating who should be in charge, and far too little time on their own defenses.

Nothing that she had learned was going to be pleasant news for her big brother, now that she had found him, but she intended to deliver that news at a particularly bad time for him. . . .

She was watching one tent in particular; there was someone in it that she wished to have a chat with.

There. Good. As she had hoped, Jamal strode out of his tent with a stiff-legged gait that bespoke a fair amount of temper held firmly in check. When he was in a temper, he always went out hunting, and he always went alone.

As she had seen before, he paused only long enough to collect his bow and arrows from the weapons rack in its shelter at the side of the wagon, and strode out of the encampment. No one ventured to stop him; everyone knew what he was like in this state, and no one wanted him to vent that temper on anything other than a few wild beasts.

Once Jamal reached the grasses at the edge of the encampment, he broke into the ground-devouring lope typical of these people when they were not riding their cattle. They could cover as much ground as any wolf when they chose, and right now, Jamal seemed intent on bettering his record.

Excellent. She needed him to be well out of sight or sound of the encampment for what she planned next.

She continued to circle, but now the center of her orbit was Jamal, a tiny black figure flowing through the grass as a dolphin flowed through water.

Soon . . . soon . . .

Abruptly he changed direction, and as she saw which way he was going, she thrilled with pleasure. *I couldn't have planned this better.* He was heading for a shallow blind canyon, so remote from the camp, it might as well have been in elven lands. There was a spring at the back of it, and two-horns often came there to graze; that was probably why he was going there.

She waited, a falcon preparing to swoop, as he reached the mouth of the canyon, paused for a moment, then moved inside.

Yes!

She dove, wings flattened tightly to her body, falling from the sky, a dark stone out of heaven. Wind rushed against her nostrils, against her eyes, forcing her to pull her second lid over them to protect them, forcing the corners of her mouth back.

At the last possible moment she flipped and opened her wings, back-winging in a thunder of wingbeats, breaking her fall and turning it into a true and graceful landing at the entrance to the valley.

And Jamal whipped around, mouth falling open in surprise, bow and arrows dropping from nerveless fingers, as he gaped at the creature that had suddenly appeared to block his way.

He froze for just a moment; then, eyes narrowing, he snatched up his weapons again and prepared to sell his life dearly.

Myre laughed.

"Put your toys away, my friend," she rumbled at him in his own tongue. "And I call you *friend* most deliberately. It is said among your people that 'the enemy of my enemy is my friend,' is it not?"

Jamal nodded cautiously, clearly taken aback again, as much by her ability to speak his language as by the speech itself.

"Well, then," Myre chuckled, "I am your friend. My enemies are yours. Shall I name them?"

At his second nod, she did so, and watched as his own eyes narrowed in satisfaction at each name.

"Iron Priest Diric. The two Corn People. And—" She paused significantly. "The so-called demons, Shana and Keman. Who are *not* demons, but something else."

"Like you?" Jamal said, quickly, and she gave him a mental accolade for his quickness.

"One of them," she told him. "Which—I will tell you later. But for now, you and I have plans to lay. Between them, we will both have our revenge, and you—*you* will have the leadership of the Iron People to share with no one."

Jamal smiled, and stood up, now completely relaxed. He saluted her, recognizing a kindred spirit in a strange body. She returned his salute, and smiled her own smile. Things were going precisely as she had planned.

Life—was very, very good.

8

DIRIC ISSUED THE promised "invitation" in the morning, and Lorryn and his sister arrived promptly on the heels of his messenger, with all their belongings. Not that they had any real possessions to pack up and move! Even by the standards of a nomad, they had been traveling lightly burdened. When they presented themselves so promptly, with shy smiles and their feet in boots that were wet with dew, he wondered what Shana was going to think when she learned that Lorryn's sister was not another wizard. . . .

He welcomed them himself, as was proper for people he had taken into his household, and then left their disposition among his tents to Kala, his wife. He would not usurp even a particle of *her* authority, and where the management of tents and living arrangements was concerned, tradition declared that the wife's word was the only word.

"You are certain you do not wish to see them disposed?" she replied, with a quizzical lift of her eyebrow.

"So long as you do not put them in *our* bed, I shall be content with your wise judgment," he told her.

She kept that eyebrow raised. "Many men do not see it that way" was her comment.

Diric snorted. "And that is both a shame and a disgrace; what, must they prove themselves men by giving no responsibility whatsoever to the women in their lives? Can their pride not bear it, that their woman would dictate even the disposition of a pot or a rug?"

"The young warriors must needs be the masters in their tents," was all she said, as she left with the youngsters in tow. "Before long, I fear they must be such masters that they will admit no woman to their ranks."

Diric could only shake his head, but it occurred to him that this was just another symptom of how Jamal was undermining even the traditions of Forge Clan. *Even the First Smith had beside Him the First Wife, who gave Him the fire for His forges from the hearth that She guarded, and taught Him every secret that flame and coals held! Had She not constructed the bellows Herself, and tended them while He forged out the world? While He created the sky, the sun, and the moon, She caught the sparks of the forge and set them in the night sky as stars, the smoke from the fire and placed it there as clouds. While He forged the earth and the seas, She created the delicate filigree of plants to clothe it. When He turned His attention to filling it with life, She added the ornamental touches of Her own—song and bright feathers for the birds, horns and antlers for the grazing beasts, scales and fur and hair in all the colors of water, earth, and sky.*

The man who forgot all that was not only impious, but a fool, depriving himself of good counsel and a good friend. . . .

Whoever fails to honor his help and mate by honoring all her due authority has no sense and little judgment.

And besides—why would anyone *want* to take on more work, when there was someone there to share it?

Hmm. Well, it is not the work *such fools are taking on, but the power. The women still must do the work, handicapped by the fact that it is a fool who ordered it.*

Well, that was but one more place where he differed from

Jamal, and it was small wonder that the War Chief could not find a single maiden willing to enter his tent as a wife, given his well-known feelings on the subject of "a woman's place." Perhaps that accounted for his preoccupation with conflict—

He scolded himself for allowing his mind to wander as Kala led them away, smiling. Their children were all grown, and she often found time hanging heavily on her hands with only the tasks for two to occupy her. She was never happier than when they had guests, and this long trek so far from other clans had made the possibility of guests unlikely. Kala knew everything that was in his mind, and he could not have trusted the security of these two pale-skinned strangers into more certain and capable hands. Before long, she would have seduced their trust out of them, and it would be trust well placed. Kala could answer every question they had, and surely they had many.

Kala will also gleefully take it upon herself to clothe the maiden properly, and it is just as well that she seems pliant and cooperative, for Kala will not be denied!

Now he had another facet of his plot to think on: how to manufacture an excuse to see the captives frequently. They were, technically, under the jurisdiction of Jamal, and Jamal would take it askance if he called on them too many more times. The First Smith did not send portents that often that Diric would be able to use a portent as an excuse, either.

There were no inquiries about my late-night summons, though, so that excuse does remain fresh to be used again. Next time, however, he must make certain to have some physical evidence of a portent.

"Priest Diric!"

The voice at his tent flap startled him, the more so since it was an unfamiliar one. He composed himself quickly; perhaps he had been hasty in thinking his portent-ruse would not be needed. "Enter," he said, in a deep, even tone, putting on all of the dignity of his office.

The young man who entered was arrayed as a warrior, but his torque bore the crossed spears of the War Chief, which meant that he *was* one of Jamal's men, and not, say, a herdsman seeking divine consultation. He gave the full bow of respect, however, if a fraction belatedly, when Diric bent a stern gaze on him.

So in that much, at least, I still have some power among the tents.

"Priest Diric, I am come from the War Chief," he said, as he rose from his bow.

Diric waited for the man to speak his piece, but he seemed to be struggling with the words. Odd. If this was a challenge from Jamal, would he be so reticent? Surely Jamal would have sent a bolder man.

"The War Chief begs a favor of you, a gift of your time," the man said at last.

Diric raised one eyebrow. "A gift of my time? My time is always at the service of my people; the War Chief knows that. What is it that required a *favor*?"

The man shifted his weight uncomfortably. "It is—the slaves, Priest Diric, the new captives. He wishes you to assume the questioning of the new captives as to their origin and the disposition of their people."

Now both eyebrows rose, and Diric's surprise was unfeigned. "I?" he replied incredulously. "*I?* Are not such questions the proper realm of the War Chief?"

The man's discomfort grew. "This is true, yet he requests that you assume this questioning, and send him word of what you learn."

Diric assumed a stern expression. "What possible reason can he have for this? My time is as valuable as his—and dedicated to the well-being of *all* the clan, not only the warriors! He had best have a compelling reason for asking me to devote my time to the questioning of demons for the purpose of making war upon them! There is nothing in all of the edicts of the First Smith that demands we make war upon demons, for gain or for good."

Now, this was something of an about-face for Diric, who had been trying to get *more* access to the prisoners, not less, but he hoped that the man would forget this and blurt something out under the pressure of the moment. And besides, there was a tale of the First Smith and the clever Sandfox—

If I protest, like the Fox, that "I do not want that rich, red meat, I truly hate that rich, red meat, and none but fools eat rich, red meat," perhaps the meat will be left unguarded. . . .

He was not disappointed.

"They—they will no longer speak to him, Priest Diric," the man got out under the pressure of his disapproving glare. "The female has told the males with her to refuse to speak to him. Jamal is reluctant to put them to the question, for they could and would say anything to end it, and he would have no way of telling truth from falsehood." He gulped, and sweat stood out on his forehead. "The female says that she will speak only to *you* from henceforth."

Diric did not ease his glare in the slightest. "Oh? And for what reason does the female demon say she will speak only to me? I do not think I care for this—it is altogether too suspicious. Perhaps the demons wish *me* some harm! Perhaps they fear the power of the First Smith and seek to rid themselves of the First Priest so that they can act without hindrance!"

I do not want that rich, red meat!

Whatever Shana had done, it had embarrassed and angered Jamal—but she had done it in such a way that losing his temper would have only brought further shame upon him. Oh, she was clever, that maiden! Mentally he applauded her while giving no outward indication of his glee.

"She says—" The man's voice was a whisper now, as shame for his Chief became shame he shared. "She says she has given him repeated proofs that she and hers are no demons, and that she is the War Chief of her own people. She says that he refused to treat her with the respect of leader for leader. He treated her with scorn, and she returns scorn for scorn. She says that *you* gave her the proper respect of a warcaptive, and that as a consequence, she will speak only with you from henceforth. She made this declaration this morning, before many witnesses."

Oh, my! How quickly she learns, this clever maiden! She

has used custom against him in a way he cannot refute! He wanted to laugh aloud, but he kept his demeanor grave. "Very well," he replied, after a moment's pause, as if he were considering the request. "I will speak with the prisoners on Jamal's behalf. It could be that these are not demons, and even if they are, I will trust in the power of the First Smith to protect me from their ill wishing. Perhaps courtesy will win from them what contempt would not."

He could not keep himself from adding that last; the temptation was too great to overcome. The warrior only ducked his head a little between his shoulders, as if he could hide his shame by imitating a tortoise.

"You may bring the female to me as I break my fast," Diric added, and waved a dismissing hand. The warrior seemed only too pleased to escape.

Kala returned from settling their two guests, burdened with his morning meal. "They are charming children, and the girl looks well in that jabba of pale cream," she said, settling the tray beside him. "The one that I made for Besheba, but which she outgrew ere I finished the embroidery?"

He nodded, even though he hadn't the faintest idea what she was talking about. Most clothing looked alike to him, except that it was new or old, this color or that, but Kala's one failing was that she never could believe that. "I think she will be more comfortable properly clothed, and it was kind of you to think on," he said, his voice warm with approval. "Now—here is a sudden change in things, and I have need of your thoughts! Jamal sent to me a man but a few moments ago—"

He described Jamal's messenger and the message, while Kala sat completely still, absorbing all of it. Her dark eyes flashed with pleasure at Shana's cleverness, and she nodded her round head vigorously.

"Ah, that was well done, husband!" she exclaimed, but not so loudly that her voice would carry past the walls of the tent, or past the floor beneath. "Now we may put forth your own scheme the easier!"

"I wish you to remain with me for this little while," he said, making his wish a request. "If you can spare the time, that is. You are better with locks than I; perhaps you can determine a way in which to unlock the collars, and make it possible to remove them without revealing that they are no longer locked."

"Gladly," she told him, her smile widening, making a white crescent across her face like a sliver of moon in the night sky. "I would like to meet this so-clever maiden; perhaps I should instruct her on the ways of a Man-Hearted Woman, so that she can claim that distinction as well! It would force Jamal to acknowledge her as a war-captive, and not as a slave, if she did."

"That is well thought," he chuckled. "Very well thought! It had not occurred to me. Jamal will be most discomfited; you know he is not in comfort when he must speak even to our own Man-Hearted Women, and this will vex him greatly!"

He chuckled again, thinking of Jamal's extreme discomfort if Shana were to successfully claim that she was Man-Hearted. She would then officially be a war-captive, and Jamal would be *forbidden* by law and custom to put her or her underlings to the question; he would be completely unable to question her effectively, and her mere presence would make him uneasy. Oh, Kala was a clever one!

"You remind me yet again why I sought your hand," he told her, capturing her plump hand in his and squeezing it, "though I still cannot comprehend why it was my suit that you favored."

"That is why I keep to your tent, silly boy," she teased, returning the caress. "You value wisdom, which lasts, over a slim-hipped and lissome figure, which does not! Ah—I hear them coming!"

Regretfully he released her hand, and put on his "Priest face." As he had expected, Shana arrived with a full contingent of Jamal's guards. Well, that would be changed. Henceforth, he would have his own men fetch her.

Trusted men. I believe I know who Jamal's eyes and ears are among the Priests, but I shall keep risks to a minimum.

"So." He regarded Shana with a stern gaze. "I understand that you wish to impart knowledge to me."

She nodded, and cast scornful glances to either side of her, as if to make it plain that she was not going to speak even in the presence of Jamal's underlings. "You know the ways of courtesy to a war-captive and a leader, Priest Diric. I will give you my word not to cause trouble nor escape; to you, and no other," she replied shortly, and shut her mouth firmly.

He wondered if her phrasing was accidental or deliberate, for she had implied that Jamal was *ignorant* of proper behavior. He caught grimaces from one or two of her guards, and hidden grins from others. *Hmm. And perhaps those last agree with her? Interesting. I wonder how many of his own people Jamal has offended with his high-handed ways.* He glanced aside at Kala, remembering their conversation. *All of the Man-Hearted Women, I would think. Perhaps I should begin offering them the counsel of the First Smith, and remind them that the First Daughter had a Manly Heart and fought beside her brother to great honor. . . .*

"I do," he told the girl gravely. "And I shall offer that courtesy to you now, as I have in the past." He looked to the guards. "You may go. The war-captive has given her word and her parole to me."

They were not slow to leave, making him wonder the more. Were they that eager to return to Jamal with word that they had completed their mission—or was the embarrassment of the mission so distasteful that they could not have it done with quickly enough?

As soon as they were out of the tent and gone, Kala clapped both hands over her mouth, stifling a giggle, and Shana relaxed, grinning at them both.

"Did you see how they scurried away?" Kala gasped around her laughter. "Oh, the shame! They will not make themselves prominent to Jamal's eyes any time soon! I think *they* will see to it that they volunteer for night watch and far scouting, and nothing near to Jamal's tent or his regard!"

"You think so?" Diric felt immensely cheered; Kala was better at reading the subtle signals of body and expression than he. "All to the good. Shana, this is Kala, my wife. Kala, this is our 'demon.' "

"I am very pleased to meet you," Shana replied gravely, and half-bowed. Kala waved an impatient hand at her.

"None of that!" she exclaimed, though Diric could tell that she was pleased. "I am no demon lady to be bowed to!"

"Nevertheless," Shana replied, "respect where it is due— and speaking of respect, what did you think of my play? We all matched wits after I got back, and this was the one notion we thought would give us unlimited access to you."

Diric nodded with approval. "It was a risk, but no more than we already have undertaken, and since you made your declaration public, Jamal could not do anything other than he did without incurring more shame or declaring open warfare between the two of us. That would tear the clan apart, and even Jamal is not prepared to do that."

Yet.

Shana shifted her weight uncomfortably from one foot to the other, precisely as the messenger had done earlier. "I knew it was a greater risk than you're saying," she admitted. "I *hoped* that your people didn't have a tradition of torturing captives . . . but I knew that was a possibility if Jamal was so angry with me that his anger overcame his sense."

She was wiser than he thought, and much older than her years. Then again, she had been, according to her own words, a captive of the real green-eyed demons, and perhaps she had seen cruelties among them that gave her that hard-won wisdom.

"Come, sit," he said instead, neither confirming nor denying her statement. "Kala is something of an expert in locks; let her look at your collar." As Shana obeyed, taking a seat on one of the fat pillows with no sign of reluctance, he added, "We first unearthed them from the coffers of the First Smith when we captured the two males. They are very old, and I had not seen the like before, but it was in the orders of the Priests that a store of them was to be kept intact to hold demons, and that they were not to be melted down nor reused in any other ways."

Shana tilted her chin to the side as Kala examined the lock of the collar. His wife made some soft sounds, as she always did when she was looking closely at anything, and in a moment she made a *tch*ing noise that signified her satisfaction.

"Simplicity," she said in quiet triumph. "Let me get my tools."

She rose and whisked off into the private quarters, returning in no time with a leather pouch of the fine tools that all women-smiths used in making their jewels. "This lock is very fine, very old," she said, settling herself beside Shana, and opening up the pouch to remove a set of probes. "It has the look of something made by a woman, in fact. It is a trifle more complicated than some I have seen, but not as complicated as many I have made myself."

"How old do you think it is?" Shana asked with interest.

"Very; more than that I cannot say." Kala probed at the lock with her probes held firmly in her plump, clever fingers. "I suspect that it is old enough that when it was made, it *was* the most complicated lock anyone of the Clans had ever seen. Something like this would not wear out readily, so it is hard to judge age by wear, or lack of it." The tip of her tongue protruded from the corner of her mouth as she concentrated, and Diric had to restrain a chuckle. She always did that, it always amused him, and that amusement always annoyed her. "It does bear out a tradition among the women, that it was the women who found the means to stop the green-eyed demons from exercising their power when captive."

"Oh?" Shana said, her tone very neutral. Kala looked up into her eyes and smiled slyly.

"So you have tried some of your lesser magics and they worked, hmm? It is well you did not try the greater, such as lightning. It would have been a painful lesson." Kala grinned broadly as Shana started. "It is the Iron, young maiden. Magic heats it when the wearer attempts to exercise it. Lesser magics only so much that you might think it no more than the doing of the sun. But greater, like calling lightnings down from the heavens—*aiee!*—you would be *most* unhappy, if it did not kill you altogether." She raised both eyebrows at the younger woman. "As my husband can tell you, that, as well as the Mind-Wall, came to all the First Priests in a dream one night, straight from the heart of the First Smith and His Wife. But it was the women, so the tale says, that first thought of using collars on their captives."

"Oh." This time Shana looked chagrined, and a little alarmed. "But what about the way that your warriors were immune to the magic we used against them?"

"Ah," Diric spoke up. "That, I know the answer to. Magic coming from outside is reflected from it, so that the wearer takes no harm. So you see, between the collars and the armor and jewelry, we are well protected. Unless—"

"Unless magic is not directed against you, but against what is around you," Shana supplied grimly. "Believe me, it would not take long at all for the greater elven lords to figure that out! They have the advantage of having waged war successfully against your ancestors, the ones who fled into the South with their cattle. *Personally,* I mean. It is not tradition that guides them, but memory."

"Eh?" Diric said, sure he had not heard her correctly.

"If your legends say that the demons live forever, they are not far wrong," Shana told him, so earnestly he could not doubt her. "Many of the same elven lords who fought your ancestors are still alive and hale today. I would not like to see what would happen if your warriors went into a charge on their bulls, and a great fissure opened up in the earth in front of them."

Since Diric had, in his time, seen the tragic results of many stampedes in uncertain terrain, he could and did know what would happen—with the addition of human bodies to the bovine ones. He shuddered, and welcomed the distracting *click* as Kala forced the lock of the collar open. She took it from Shana's neck with another smile.

"See how I trust you because my husband trusts you," she remarked, bending now over the collar in her lap. "You know all our secrets, and if you were a true demon, you would have us at your mercy."

Shana only laughed, and felt of her neck. "I would never have believed how heavy a simple iron band could be."

"It is not the weight of the metal, but the bondage that it

represents," Diric said solemnly, and she nodded. "But you have not all of our secrets. There remains one. Do you wish to know it?"

"How you can keep me from knowing your thoughts?" she asked. "I wonder that you have that secret at all, since the elven lords don't have that magic. Only humans do."

"But humans can be enslaved by demons," he reminded her. "They can even serve them willingly. So we learned, when we fought beside the Corn People and were forced to flee. But the discipline of the Mind-Wall is easy for one to learn who does not possess even the least and littlest bit of that magic himself. Our children all are taught it as they are taught to speak, until it is as unconscious as breathing."

"So how *do* you do this?" she persisted.

He laughed. "I think—very hard, and in the front of my mind—of just that. A wall, a simple, blank wall. So—"

He demonstrated for her. "Thus—it is down. Thus—I create it, slowly. Do you see? We call this being 'double-minded,' hiding our thoughts behind the Mind-Wall."

She frowned as he did it twice more, and shook her head. "I see how you do it, but to do it myself—"

"It takes much practice, when you come to it late," he assured her. "The Priests who have the thought-magic test all the people at intervals, and those who seem weak are given some personal attention to strengthen their wills. Now you know all."

Shana sighed. "I knew it had to be something simple, both the blankness and the problems with true magic. I knew that the elven lords didn't like having iron or steel around them, I just never knew why. I always assumed that it had something to do with the fact that if they are hurt with the metal, they can sicken."

"Possibly because bits of the metal too small to be seen poison the wound," Diric hazarded, "and then any magic they cast would turn upon the flesh that was wounded—well, it does not matter. Now, have you anything to offer me? Jamal will be expecting great amounts of information about your lands and people—what am I to give him?"

She grinned so hugely, he wondered what the jest was. "I couldn't take the chance that you people might have a way to tell if I was telling the truth or not, so I phrased that declaration very carefully. *My* people would be very, very pleased to see trouble come to the elves, so what I really *said* was that I would tell you everything I knew about the green-eyed demons."

Now Diric saw the jest, and stifled his own bellow of laughter behind his wrist. "Oh, most excellent! And let us be most pedantic and thorough, so that we have occasion for many, many meetings."

"I'll tell you right down to the number of blankets in their storehouses, if I know it," she promised. "So where shall we start?"

"With the property of the demon closest to our current line of march who is also farthest from *your* people," he said promptly. "If we must give him a target, let us give him a true and tempting one."

"Diric," she replied, after studying him for a moment, "I come to like you more and more with every passing moment."

"And I, you, oh crafty maiden," he told her truthfully. "And I, you."

Keman got his turn later that afternoon; he was looking forward to it with an anticipation that made his teeth ache. He wanted out of that cursed collar so badly, he could hardly stand it. Not only because he wanted to go hunt—in this form, it was easier to live on the kinds of foods available to him than it was for Dora in her bovine form, but he still needed fresh, raw meat in quantity every so often—but because he wanted to meet Dora tonight face-to-draconic-face.

What he had learned of her last night had been something of a trauma to both of them; she had no idea there were any other dragons in the world at all, and he had no idea there were any Lairs as far south as hers was. Without talking to one of her elders, he was not able to determine if her people had discovered their *own* Gate, if they were a late-arriving group from the peaceful haven that his Kin had left because it proved boring, or if she was even a dragon as *he* knew them. After all, dragons and elves were both immigrants to this place from elsewhere. There might be yet another group of creatures that had found its way here.

But the time spent in her company had been far too short, and despite all the momentous occurrences since sunset yesterday, the meeting she had promised with him for this evening was still the thing that preoccupied his thoughts. He begged Shana to let him be the second one to have his collar removed, using persuasion and some truth, so that he *could* go fly with Dora in his true form. She had not been able to shift where he could see it last night, because that would have been well within sight of both the herds and the herdsmen, so he still had no idea what she really looked like.

The truth was that he had traveled over more of the elven lords' lands than any of the four of them, when he had made his search for Shana after she had been captured by slavers. He had not confined his travels to being in elven form, either; he had made plenty of trips in the air. Draconic memory for territory was excellent and very precise; he would be able to draw maps that should send Jamal into paroxysms of delight.

Mero, Lorryn, and Kalamadea would be able to add their information that would send Jamal into fits of greed as well. All of them knew something about the properties that various elven lords held, and what they didn't know, they were equipped to make up. It should be interesting.

It would be even more interesting if Jamal actually got as far as attacking the elves.

One thing at a time. For now it was most important that he get this *cursed* collar off!

Diric was waiting, with stylus and a set of smoothed slabs of clay. So was his wife, with her little pouch of tools. Both were smiling as he entered the tent.

"Make your rough maps on the clay," Diric told him without preamble. "This way you can erase or change things; when you are certain of your map, I will give it to one of my Priests to be burned onto leather."

He nodded, and sat down beside Kala, Diric's wife. After several days of living with these people, he had begun to accustom himself to their idea of beauty, and he could see that she had been a great beauty when she was young, and was still quite attractive now. She still moved with a precise and studied grace, and when she smiled, she glowed. If her figure had spread with age, if gray had crept into her coarse black curls, it hardly mattered. Her eyes were the loveliest that Keman had ever seen on a human or even an elven lord; a beautiful, deep brown, as wide and guileless as a doe's.

"This will not take long, now that I have the trick of it," she told him—and a few moments later, after skillful probing with her tools, the lock gave a *click* and the collar came off in her hands.

He rubbed his neck reflexively with one hand, and picked up the stylus in the other, grateful now that his mother had taught him reading and writing as the elves practiced it. These Iron People still had no idea what he was—and he was not about to give that particular secret away!

And the sooner he got some maps into this clay, the sooner he would be out of here, free to meet Dora for a flight and a hunt.

It took a little longer than he had really wanted—it proved to be much more difficult than he had thought it would be to translate what he remembered from the air and the roads into scratches of the right relative length in the clay. By the time he had filled the four clay tablets with maps of the territory between here and Lord Tylar's estate, it was fully dark.

"This is very rough," he warned, as Diric placed the last of the tablets into the hands of one of his under-Priests. "There was a lot of detail I had to leave out because of the scale we were working in."

"Then you will have to return to give me that detail, will you not?" Diric replied, logically. "Indeed, you and Shana and the other two should all be here to give me that detail. It will mean many, many meetings, I would think."

"Oh," he replied, feeling very, very stupid for not seeing

that very thing. "Of course. We want to have many, many more meetings, right?"

"As many as it takes," Kala replied, and held out the hated collar. "Here you are, slip this on and push it closed; you will hear it click as if it has locked, but it cannot lock now, it can only latch." She showed him a tiny stud on the underside of the collar. "You push this, and it will release, and you can take it off."

"Thank you," he said, fervently, and slipped the collar back on. He tested her work by closing it, then opening it again, immediately, and smiled with relief when it came open exactly as she had promised.

She only raised an eyebrow at that, but made no comment other than, "You must promise to take those with you; I would not want faulty collars in among the rest. If all you say is true, and if Jamal has his way with his dreams of conquest, we may well need true collars in the future."

"Thank you again," he replied to both of them, and slipped out of the tent door, onto the platform, into the cool breeze that always followed the setting of the sun.

He scampered down the stairs, then stopped by the tent to see Shana, but Kalamadea reported that she and Mero were with Lorryn. "I shall join them shortly," the elder dragon added. "And what of you?"

"Ah—I want to hunt," he said truthfully. Kalamadea nodded.

"See to it that you go well beyond the herds before you shift, then," he only said, "and take the collar with you. We do not want it to be found without you inside it. Not yet, anyway."

Keman promised, and escaped while he still could.

Dora was waiting for him where *she* had promised, at the edge of the herds. He was both pleased and relieved at that; she could so easily have taken the chance of the day to make her own escape and he would never have seen her again.

:Something happened,: he told her as soon as he was near enough to recognize her among the other cattle. *:Diric is on*

our side, and his wife is fixing our collars so that we can take them off!:

Surprise and delight colored her thoughts. :*But—that means we can fly together! You can escape!*:

:*Not without my friends,*: he replied immediately, and perhaps a touch more sternly than he had intended.

She ducked her head in shamefaced apology. :*I am sorry, Keman. I—I forgot about them. It is hard to think of them when I do not know them.*:

The shame in her thoughts made him feel bad. :*I'm sorry I snapped at you; it's been a very hard day,*: he apologized. :*And I haven't hunted since we were caught; I suspect I'm pretty sharp-set by now! My temper is none too certain when I'm hungry.*:

:*Then let's go, quickly—*: she urged, and he was happy enough to slip his collar, shift into the form of a young bull, pick up the despised circlet of iron in his mouth, and join her in making her way to the edge of the herds. She had done this before; he hadn't, so he followed her lead, moving when she moved, stopping when she stopped.

She waited at the edge of the herd for a very long time, or at least it seemed that way to him. The metallic taste of the collar in his mouth was distinctly unpleasant, and he had to keep his head down as if he were grazing to keep it from showing. It was very heavy, too; it made his jaws ache to hold it this way. Finally she moved out into the grasses, slipping like a huge shadow as clouds crossed over the face of the moon. He followed, his body knowing how to keep his bulky form from making any noise as they moved away from the herd at a rapidly increasing pace.

Soon they were running, but they were too far from the herd for the herdsmen to see, and if a scout or a herdsman heard them, he would probably assume they were some other beast running free, and not two of the cattle. Cattle and other herd beasts *wanted* to stay together, most of the time. They were uneasy when they were separated from others. Only a cow about to calve would wander off by herself, and no cow about to calve would be running at a bovine gallop.

Finally Dora stopped, in a small valley cut by a meandering stream. *:Here,:* she said, her flanks heaving with exertion, and the sweat of her run thick in his nostrils. If he'd been in draconic form, he wouldn't have been able to resist that scent—she'd have been his dinner, not his dinner companion!

:Here, it's safe enough to shift,: she repeated, and he dropped the heavy iron ring, only glad that he'd been able to keep hold of it all this time. His intention had been to watch her as she shifted, then to shift himself; hunger overcame his intentions as soon as the ring left his mouth, and he shifted into his real shape more swiftly than he ever remembered doing before.

When his sight cleared and sharpened, the first thing he saw was a young and delicately made female of his own kind, looking up at him with awe and delight. He returned the look with interest, elated that she *was* a dragon of his own kind, if not his own Kin.

Easy enough to sharpen his night-sight, now that he could shift without even thinking about it. There was enough moonlight for him to make out colors, and Dora was particularly beautiful in that regard. Her main color was a soft violet, with a dusting of gold over every scale; her crest and her neck and spine ridges were that same gold over a deep purple. Most females were larger than males, but Dora was exactly the same size that he was, and if she hadn't been holding her head and long, graceful neck lower than his, she'd be looking him straight in the eyes.

The eyes were beautiful, too, a sparkling gold that matched her crest. She was stunning—and he felt altogether stunned. He knew he had never seen a female as lovely as she, never in all of his life!

"My goodness," she blurted, still looking up at him. "You didn't tell me you were *handsome*."

"Well, you didn't tell me that you were beautiful," he replied, as gallantly as he could while still feeling stunned.

She giggled, and coyly bobbed her head, glancing at him out of one eye in the most charming manner imaginable.

"You must be faint with hunger to say something like that," she replied, breathlessly. "Come on, we'll hunt together."

She turned and launched herself into the air, as graceful as she was beautiful, and what could he do but quickly clasp the iron ring around his wrist and follow?

It didn't take them long to find game—the plains near the Iron People were virtually empty, but that meant that the game that was usually roaming there had been driven out of its usual pastures, into territory where the displaced animals were interlopers. The newcomers didn't know where cover was, where it was safe to rest, and they were under constant threat from the animals whose territory *was* "rightfully" here. In time, they'd settle down, but just now they were easy prey. The carnivores of the plains were taking ruthless advantage of their vulnerability, and so would Keman and Dora.

They each managed to bring down some sort of plains deer; showing off, he lifted his into the air to set it down next to hers so that they could feast together.

Once the edge was off his hunger, he kept giving her sidelong glances as he ate. More than once he caught her doing the same. Every time he looked at her, he got a strange, fluttery feeling in the pit of his stomach; like hitting a pocket of air turbulence, but more pleasurable. Every time she looked at him, he felt as if he'd called lightning to chase him.

She had eaten last night; she was quickly sated, and nudged the remains of her deer over to him when she was through. He accepted the gift with gratitude; he was starving, and no "fluttery feelings" were going to interfere with his hunger.

"So what exactly happened?" she asked, preening the blood from her claws delicately. "You said that last night Diric suddenly came over to your side."

Between bites he explained it all to her, right up until the moment that he'd left Diric with the maps. She listened carefully, nodding from time to time, and occasionally asking a question. Those questions showed that she knew more about these people than even Kalamadea, and that she'd personally observed quite a bit more about the important individuals among them in the time she'd been spying on them.

"Jamal is dangerous," she said flatly when he was done. "The problem is, he is also clever, intelligent, and very charismatic. If he is clever and charismatic enough, he could very well convince his people to attack these elves of yours. If he is even *more* clever, he will find someone or something to attack that will allow him a victory and some impressive booty, then before anyone can react properly, he'll turn the Clan around and take them back down to the Homelands."

"Then what?" Keman asked, a little bewildered. "What would that gain him except for a few trinkets? Even if he looted all of Lord Tylar's estate, the gain would be next to nothing divided up among all these people."

"But if he didn't divide it?" she countered. "If he kept it all in one big pile? It would look very impressive. It would awaken hunger for more in not only this Clan, but every other Clan he showed it to."

"O-o-oh," Keman said then, seeing exactly what she was getting at. "Then, once everyone wants some of the loot, he makes himself the leader of all the Clans, and comes right back up here."

She nodded. "I don't know if these elves of yours could beat him; if they are clever, they probably could. But I do know that with that many people coming up here looking for loot, the Clans are *going* to run into *your* friends unless they can pull themselves into that mountain of theirs and shut all entrances for a year."

He considered that. "They might be able to. The rest of my Lair could certainly make it very unpleasant for Iron People trespassing near the mountain."

"But here is the other thing," she continued. "Even if Jamal suffers enough defeats that he decides to put the Clans in retreat, he'll *still* be their leader. Once he reaches the Homelands again, he'll start looking for something else to conquer—and sooner or later, he'll find my Folk."

Keman shivered. He remembered Kalamadea telling Shana, quite calmly, that the iron weapons the warriors carried could and would kill both dragons before they could shift. And magic or no magic, dragons in the sky were still vulnerable to powerful bows. "We have to stop him."

"You have to escape first," she pointed out, and paused for a moment. "I'll help you," she finished, as if with the words she had finally made up her mind.

"You will?" His head reeled with delight. "You'll come with me?"

"Don't tell anyone about me yet!" she amended hastily. "Please! I have to think about all this first—I have to decide how to tell my Folk that there are others—I—"

"I promise," he pledged, before she could go on. "You can stay secret as long as you like. As long—as long as I can see you every night," he added shyly.

"You would? You want to?" she stammered. "Of course! But—"

There was no more talk of plans or escaping for the rest of the night.

Lorryn was not entirely sure how Shana was going to react to his sister. For that matter, he was not certain how the young halfblood that was with her was going to react. There was certainly nothing in Rena's true appearance to make anyone think of her as a threat, but still—

Well, there was no hope for it. The sooner they got the confrontation over with, the better.

This section of the huge tent that Kala shared with her husband that had been assigned to him and his sister was a far cry from the little tent they'd been given on their arrival. He'd always been under the impression that a tent was a tent—that there wasn't a great deal you could do to make one luxurious, or even all that comfortable.

He knew now that he was wrong. If he hadn't known they were in a tent and not, say, a pleasure-pavilion, he wouldn't have been able to tell the difference. Rugs softened the wooden floor of the wagon, lying six or seven deep; around the curve of the tent wall a finely woven mesh was fastened to ornamental wickerwork that came up to about his knee.

This was so that when the walls of the tent were raised to let in fresh air around the base of the tent, insects were kept out.

The walls themselves were hung with tapestries that extended down to the top of the wickerwork, hiding the rough felt of the tent walls and providing extra insulation against heat or cold. Beautifully made lanterns hung from the ceiling, burning what Kala said was scented butter; whatever it was, it gave a clear light and the scent in it perfumed the air with a faint but pleasant musk. The ubiquitous cushions were piled everywhere; their bed-pads were soft and stuffed with dried grasses and herbs, covered with finely woven blankets and furs he could not identify. The tent itself was divided by felt partitions, also covered with tapestries; the walls moved slowly in the breeze blowing through the mesh on the exterior wall.

Kala had provided Rena with garments she said had belonged to one of her daughters—a daughter who'd had a distressing tendency to outgrow clothing before it could be finished. Rena had changed into it gratefully; the clothing she'd brought with her was hardly suited to the summer heat of the plains. Lorryn thought she looked charming in it—and as unlike a typical elven maiden as possible. It only remained to see if the other two thought the same.

Kala ushered the two halfbloods in, leaving with a nod. Lorryn waved at the cushions and took one himself.

"Lorryn, this is Mero, Valyn's half cousin," Shana said by way of introduction. "I expect you know about him."

"Some." Lorryn tilted his head to the side, and studied the thin, dark young man with the startlingly bright emerald eyes, even as the young man studied him. "They're saying now in the Councils that Valyn himself was a halfblood; that he wouldn't have revolted against his own kind if he'd been truly of elven blood."

Mero snorted. "Oh, as if having Dyran for a father wasn't enough to make anyone with half a conscience and any amount of compassion revolt!"

"Both of those qualities are in short supply on the Council," Lorryn reminded him. "Well—I told Shana very little about the two of us, so now that I have both of you here, I should give you the tale in greater detail."

He did so, omitting nothing about their escape except the fact that Rena was *not* a halfblood. It was a deliberate omission; he wanted all this fresh in their minds when he did bring Rena in. Logically, since Mero was cousin to a fullblooded elven er-Lord who had risked and lost all to save *him*, they shouldn't be prejudiced against her.

On the other hand, logic had very little to do with prejudice.

When he finished, Shana let out the breath she'd been holding. "It sounds like quite an escape," she told him. "A lot more exciting than my personal escape after the auction, if it comes to that."

"More exciting than the one Valyn and I had, too," Mero admitted. "We never actually saw our pursuers, you know, we just knew they were there."

"I would have been just as pleased to have made a quiet escape, personally," Lorryn told them both, shrugging. "Although if we manage to come through this all right, I will admit to being glad things worked out this way. I wish I knew what happened to my sister's maid, though," he added with a frown.

"She doesn't sound like anyone we know," Shana said, after a sidelong glance at Mero. "On the other hand, there are ways that some of us can disguise ourselves that don't qualify as 'illusions,' so she could have been. If she was—trust me, she'll be all right. Not even falling into a river would harm one of our people with that sort of power."

Well, that was something of a relief! "You just took one burden of guilt off my back," he replied gratefully. "Now— I'll discharge myself of another." He raised his voice a little. "Rena?"

Rena pushed aside the partition to her segment of the tent on the cue she'd been waiting for, and came into the light. She looked worried, hesitant, and very vulnerable.

She also looked unmistakably elven.

Shana only raised one eyebrow, though Mero sucked in a

breath of surprise. "I wondered what you were hiding about her," the wizard told him, with a hint of smile. "It's nice to see that Valyn wasn't the only decent person of his blood around."

She stood up, and extended her hand to Rena with no sign of hesitation. "It is very good to meet you without illusions," she said, as Rena took the hand gingerly. "And any sheltered maiden who could partner her brother through the wilderness as cleverly as you did is something more than she appears to be. I'd like to hear your ideas."

"So would I," Mero said, and indicated a cushion between himself and Lorryn. "Would you join us?"

"Yes, thank you," Rena replied, smiling and relaxing visibly. "I hope I can help, at least a little."

"You can help a lot," Lorryn said forcefully as she took the indicated seat with a sidelong glance at Mero. Shana sat down again, and he turned instinctively toward her. "The one thing that neither of you know, and neither do I, is the kind of magic that only the females are taught. It's very subtle; it works on the level of the very small. For instance, where you or I would—say—collapse this tent by crushing it outright, Rena would do something entirely different."

"I'd weaken all the supporting poles and ropes," she offered diffidently. "As soon as the breeze came up the way it does every evening, it would collapse."

"Now, if the object was to trap people inside for a crucial few moments, obviously her way would be better," Lorryn continued.

"Well, only if you wanted to trap them at that particular time, but I see your point," Shana replied, then suddenly turned toward Rena and stared at her.

"What's the matter?" Lorryn asked quickly.

But Shana only shook her head. "Nothing really," she replied. "I just—something about your sister seemed familiar for a moment, that's all."

Lorryn had the feeling that there was a lot more to it than that, given the measuring glances Shana kept casting on Rena, but since she didn't seem hostile, only thoughtful, he finally decided that it was probably some mysterious female thing that no male would ever understand, and dismissed it from his concern.

"Anyway, if what Diric wants is some way for us all to disappear that makes it appear as if we could have done so at any time, Rena may be able to leave some signs that will confuse them no end," he pointed out. "For that matter, she could make changes in the food that will put Jamal's warriors to sleep, she *could* collapse the tent after we've gone—"

"Don't make too many promises, Lorryn," Rena interrupted, blushing. "I'll do what I can, but I'm not a great wizard like La—the Elvenbane is," she said, clearly unable to force herself to call Shana by anything other than her title.

But Shana only laughed. "Believe me, *I* am not the great wizard that the Elvenbane is," she replied warmly, with a friendly smile that brought another blush to Rena's cheeks and an answering smile to Lorryn's lips. "If I were, do you think we'd have been caught in the first place? No, the best thing we can do is to assess all of our abilities and use them to advantage. There is a real value in being able to work subtle magics; taming the alicorns the way you did, for instance. Or—say—stopping a heart."

Shana cast that last out carelessly, or so it seemed, but Lorryn caught a gleam in her eyes as she waited for Rena's response. And to his surprise, his sister went just a little pale.

But her reply was steady enough. "I—that had occurred to me," she said softly. "I did try it, once, with a bird that was already dying. Never again, though."

She had? *That* surprised him more than almost anything else today!

"It's not a power to use lightly" was all Shana said, but she said it so soberly that he knew, deep within his heart, that the burden of all of the dead of the second Wizard War lay heavily on her soul, and always would. "But sometimes—" Her eyes looked far away, into some bleak place where he could not go. "Sometimes, you aren't given a choice. If, by using a power like that, you could save an innocent life—"

Then she shook herself, and returned to the present. "Anyway, the last thing I'm going to ask you to do is use something like *that* on—say—Jamal. He hasn't actually hurt anyone yet. He might not. He might be so frightened and alarmed by discovering we're going that he might turn his people right back around and go home. He might get a late-night visitation from his god telling him that he's been a naughty boy. Anything could happen."

Rena nodded, but her relief at Shana's words was written clearly in her expression.

Mero reached out and patted her hand, comfortingly. She smiled shyly at him, calling up a reassuring smile in return. He did not remove his hand from hers.

Oh, really? was Lorryn's startled thought. And for just an instant, all the instincts of the protective brother rose up in him—

But they subsided just as quickly. Why not, after all? When had she ever met *any* fullblood who'd treated her with a fraction of the courtesy that Mero had, even in the few moments since they'd met? He could simply be offering kindness to her—

Oh yes. And my Ancestors on both sides will rise up out of their graves and declare peace between the races.

—and what if something more did develop between them? Was it any of *his* business? The little he knew of Mero personally, he liked. Certainly no one could live around Shana for long and continue to harbor the usual elven prejudices about females.

But what was Shana going to do about this? Had she even noticed?

A quick glance in her direction told him that she *had* noticed. Her eyes were on the linked hands—and she was smiling, ever so slightly.

Well, well, well. If Shana didn't mind, if she approved, who was he to interfere?

And nothing at all may come of this anyway, he reminded himself, and turned his mind and attention back to the topic at hand. After all, nothing *could* come of this until they were all free and away from this place.

* * *

Myre was altogether pleased with the way things were going. At the Citadel, old Caellach Gwain was slowly undermining the authority of those that Shana had left in charge—and with every day that passed that did *not* bring Shana's return, even those loyal to her lost some of their confidence. Careful never to go where one of the dragons might spot her, she moved among them in the guise of a former human slave, dropping little hints, fragments of doubt. Perhaps Shana had deserted them. Perhaps she had been captured by the elven lords. Perhaps she had fallen victim to some horrid monster of the wilderness, something no one had ever encountered before.

With care and guile she spread the insidious doubts—that, no matter what the cause, Shana, the Elvenbane, was never coming back.

Caellach Gwain, bless his twisted old heart, was quick to pick up on the rumors and spread them further. Denelor and the Senior Wizard were hard put to keep their hold over the others at this point. Let them come up against the first real danger or hardship, and the unity of the wizards would shatter like shale.

And as for Jamal . . .

She waited for him in her dead-end canyon. He had not yet been ready to ally with her at their last meeting, but she sensed he was close. He was probably waiting to find out just what it was that she wanted, like any properly cautious creature.

The soft thud of hooves warned her he had arrived, and she settled herself for a nice, productive talk. She had decided, if he asked her what her "reward" would be for her aid, that she would tell him the truth. It was a truth that *he* would certainly understand.

The war-bull, with Jamal leading it afoot, plodded around a bend toward her. He stopped at a prudent distance from her.

"I am here," he said simply.

"As am I," she replied, with a nod of her head. "So. I have

offered alliance, War Chief. You said that you wished to think on it. Have you thought?"

"I have." His heavy brows drew together. "You have not said what it is that you will gain from this alliance. It is said, 'an ally who asks for nothing expects everything.' That is not a bargain I am prepared to make."

Myre hissed laughter. "And a wise man you are. But you, War Chief, will surely understand what it is that I want—for although to some it may seem insignificant, it is a reward beyond price for *me*."

He waited, silent, for her to name that reward.

"Revenge," she breathed, and saw his entire face light up with understanding and appreciation. "You have as captives my enemy and my brother. *That* is my reward; a free hand with each."

"Done," he said instantly, and grounded the butt of his spear in the earth. "I swear it by the red earth and the black, by the Forge and the Fire. Now—how are we to make use of this alliance?"

He cocked his head to one side, quizzically.

"You know, for I have shown you, that I can take any form I please," she replied. "So—first, I shall go among your people in a form that *none* would suspect, and I will listen and learn who is your friend, who is your foe, and who is undecided. Then, when the time is right, you declare for yourself the full power of the Clan leadership, with a dragon to ride as proof of your mastery! You select a few who most oppose you and—" She delicately examined her talons. "I think I need say no more."

He nodded, pleased. "I doubt that many will continue in opposition once the first lessons have been dispensed," he said with a bloodthirsty chuckle that would have sounded well in the throat of a dragon. "And after, if you continue to walk in that form-with-no-suspicion, we will continue to learn who opposes in silence. Hmm?"

"Precisely." Now it was her turn to cock her head to the side, quizzically. "I assume you do have a form in mind?"

"Oh, yes!" Now he laughed. "And that is the cream of the jest! So let me tell you. . . ."

If Shana had allowed herself any time to think of anything but their immediate problem, she knew she would have been baffled, bewildered, and entirely turned round about by now. She had *thought* that she was and would always be in love with Valyn, poor Valyn, who had sacrificed himself to save all of them from his father.

Her friendship with Mero had never turned to anything more than that, after all. Nor did her friendship with Zed or with any of the other wizards her own age. She had told herself that love only came once—and that it was her job to take the life that Valyn had given to her and make the best she could of it. After a year, she was even able to enjoy herself again. She had thought that would never be so heart-touched again.

Now—now she was not only no longer so sure of *that*, she was no longer so sure that she had ever been in love with Valyn at all! Infatuated, of course. Emotionally at a boiling point, certainly. But in love? Perhaps not.

Her first reaction when she saw Lorryn without any illusion cloaking his features was to compare him to Valyn, and in that comparison he came out a poor second. In a way it was inevitable that she should do so, since his elven blood was so clearly in his features, as opposed to Mero, who looked far more human.

Or even me, she reminded herself. Her hair had grown out enough that combing it out was a necessity and a chore, but the time needed to untangle it gave her time to think about something other than problems. And that flaming red hair coiling itself around her fingers was a stark reminder that there was very little of the elven maiden in *her*, either.

Lorryn, on the other hand—well, compared to Valyn, he was a copy of a masterpiece by an inexperienced student. His human blood coarsened and thickened his features just enough that it was very noticeable. So her first impression based on looks alone was not a favorable one.

Ah, but then he opened his mouth.

That was when she realized that appearance was the smallest part of Lorryn, and that he could have been as coarse as a mud-doll, and she would have paid attention to him.

He listens to me, which is more than Valyn ever did most of the time. He gives my ideas the same weight as his own. And his own are nothing to be ashamed of.

She took a bit of leather cord and began braiding her hair, working carefully to keep from making more knots than she'd taken out.

He was sensible, too; just because he really liked an idea, that didn't mean he wasn't prepared to give it up if someone came up with a reason why it wouldn't work.

He was willing to learn from all of them: from Shana, who was female; from Mero, who was younger than he; from his own sister, whom by all logic he should have held in the gentle contempt that all elven males held for their women.

Not that they hadn't had their share of fights—

Well, more like squabbles. Mostly because we were all tense. But he had been just as willing to patch things up and apologize as she had been, once their tempers had cooled, and after the events of the past two years, she had learned to apologize to just about anybody if it had to be done. Hadn't she learned to be polite to the old whiners? She hadn't expected the same out of him, however.

And now—now she was going out of her way to spend time with him she could have been spending alone. She was fussing with her clothing and hair, things she hadn't cared about in a year or more. She had confided things to him that she hadn't told *anyone* else—not facts, but feelings, the way she hated being "the Elvenbane," the horrible weight it put on her when people expected miracles of her, and the worse weight of rancor when they didn't. She had confessed how the burden of responsibility often felt as if it was going to crush her spirit—and precisely how poor a leader she really was, when it came down to cases.

She thought he understood. At least he listened. He didn't trivialize what she was feeling.

She shook her head a little, and tied off the end of her braid. She'd made a kind of appointment with him tonight, him and him alone, because there was something else going on with their little group of conspirators that could cause some difficulties if he disapproved. She didn't know if he'd noticed, but it seemed to her that she'd better talk to him about this business of Mero and his sister just in case he hadn't.

Although how he could *not* notice, when the two of them were taking long walks in the moonlight before bed at *precisely* the same time, she had no idea. Then again, males were sometimes a bit more oblivious to that than females were, or so she'd heard.

She slipped out of the tent, the *empty* tent. Mero had already gone off on his quest for "exercise"; Keman and Kalamadea were hunting. The two elves were entertaining their captors, and would not be back until after midnight at best. There was no one to notice her going.

Kala noticed her arrival, though, when she presented herself to the Priest-guard at the entrance to Diric's tent. That wise woman only smiled, assured the guard that Diric was expecting the demon, and waved her inside.

Diric, of course, was nowhere to be found; Kala went off to her side of the tent, chuckling at something under her breath. Shana was just as glad she hadn't insisted on playing escort. This was going to be difficult enough as it was.

Lorryn was waiting at the entrance to his slice of tent, holding the flap of the partition open for her, his golden hair shining with the sheen of the true metal in the lamplight. "I heard you outside," he said by way of explanation.

She slipped inside and he dropped the flap behind her, taking his favorite pillow and gesturing to hers. "So what was so important that you needed to talk to me late at night—" one eyebrow rose shrewdly "—without Rena? And without Mero? Both of whom seem to have pressing concerns elsewhere. Or can I guess?"

"I think you already have," she replied, both relieved and

a little deflated at the same time. After the way she'd been steeling herself to present the terrible revelation to him—

"So my precious sister is falling in love with a halfblood, if she hasn't done so already." He shook his head dolefully. "Aye me, what is this world coming to? It is the end of civilization as we know it! Unnatural! Depraved!" He pulled a long face and stroked an imaginary beard with feigned agitation in a clever imitation of a horrified elder of *any* race.

It was so clever that she broke into a fit of giggles; he grinned, and dropped the pretense.

"As long as you don't mind, how could I?" he countered. "Mero is *your* friend, after all, and I don't know what he could have meant to you before this. And I'm not asking," he added hastily, before she could say anything. "Rena is her own woman, and has the right to make up her own mind about who she ties herself to in any way. The Ancestors know she paid for that right."

He fell silent for a moment, but she sensed he had a bit more to say. "She was betrothed to a complete idiot, just before we ran away. It was Lord Tylar's idea, a marriage-alliance with a family that was older and more powerful than ours, and he would have had her mind altered before if he had to if that was what it would take to put the marriage through. She says that, and in retrospect, I believe her. How could I *not* wish her well?"

Shana shrugged. "Mero and I have never been more than friends, although his cousin tried to play matchmaker between us. It didn't work." And the least said about that, the better. "I know that he really likes Rena as a person, and I know he'll never treat her as less than a person. After that?" She shrugged again. "Who knows? Whatever happens, happens. When we get back to the Citadel, though, I don't think you need to worry about the wizards refusing to take her in. Not after what Valyn did for us."

He sighed. "I have to admit that I had been worried about that; if you wouldn't take her, I'd have to go with her. I couldn't abandon her *too*."

Too?

She was aching with curiosity, but she wouldn't ask; not with the pain in his eyes so stark, it matched any of her own burdens. But he looked up from his hands, and he offered her the answer, like a gift.

"Mother—Elven Lady Viridina—is my real mother; it was my father who was the human," he told her softly. "She sheltered me with illusion until I was old enough to understand, told me what I was, and taught me to protect myself. I told you why we had to run, that mages of the Council were coming to test me for illusion, to unmask me as a halfblood. Father *knows* that he is fullblooded; I couldn't stay to be discovered, but by running, I practically admitted I'm a halfblood. So that leaves—"

"Your mother as having taken a human lover," Shana breathed. "And it *would* have to have been a deliberate pregnancy, wouldn't it?"

"It means the end of everything for her," he acknowledged, bleakly. "She can feign insanity; she can create a false memory for the Council members of having her own child born dead and a halfblood substituted by the midwife. If they choose to press the subject, that won't explain why I looked like a fullblood from the beginning, but if she pretends to go insane, all they'll do is lock her up in Lord Tylar's keeping. But she'll live out all of her time in three small rooms, a prisoner in her own home, denied anything but the most basic necessities. Lord Tylar will never forgive her deception; more than that, he will never forgive the implication that *he* could not father a son."

He was more troubled and guilty than he appeared; Shana sensed that clearly. He felt as if everything that was happening to his mother now was somehow his fault. Unfortunately, there wasn't a great deal she could say, and none of it would be very comforting or ease his burden of guilt.

So rather than mouth platitudes, she kept her thoughts to herself, and simply let what comfort could come from her presence ease him. Finally he looked up from his clasped hands with a wan smile.

"I have one question for you, Shana—but I'm afraid it's

personal and entirely impertinent, and I have no right to ask it."

Oh? "Then you might as well," she told him. "I'm supposedly an expert in impertinence."

"Were you in love with Valyn?"

Since she had just been pondering that very question herself, it caught her unawares, and she answered before she could stop herself. "If you'd asked me that a month ago, I'd have said yes," she replied with an honesty that shocked her as she listened to the words coming from her own mouth. "Now—I'm not sure. I'm beginning to think—maybe not."

"Ah," he replied, and his smile became a bit less wan. "Good."

"Good?" she asked sharply. "Why good?"

"Because it means I have a chance," he said, his own candor shocking her further, as he unclasped his hands and captured one of hers. "I can do my best, and see if it's enough—but it wouldn't be enough if you'd been in love with Valyn. I can't compete with a ghost."

"Oh." That was all she could manage, as she stared at him with wide, round eyes. "I see."

"I think you do." He stared into her eyes for a moment longer, then got to his feet, tugging her gently to hers. "Meanwhile, I think Mero and Rena have the right idea. Shall we follow their example?"

Sheyrena thought that she had never been so happy in her life. As she and Mero walked slowly in the moonlight, soft breezes stirring scent out of the grass beneath their feet, insects and birds singing all around them, it was easy to forget that they were captives and simply hold to the moment.

She had spent her life grasping at moments of transitory happiness; she was well practiced at it.

Mero was completely unlike a hero out of a romance—not too surprising, really, since all those romances were written under the careful eye of elven *males*, and while they would portray the kind of male an elven maiden would find attractive, they would also portray the male other males would find *appropriate*. He had not come into her life, swept her off her feet, and proceeded to wrap her in a cloak of protection and make all her decisions for her. No, he had been supportive, but not precisely protective. When her own uncertainties surfaced, as they were all too prone to do, he would give her a look or a handclasp that said without words, "You can do this. You can contribute. You are clever enough."

That was more important to her than all of the words of protection in the universe. "You can hold your own. . . ."

His hand held out to her was not the hand of the master, but the hand to help her over a difficult spot; one that expected her to do the same in return for him.

"A pin for your thoughts," Mero said softly.

She laughed. "Oh—that I am very glad that you are yourself."

"If I weren't myself, who would I be?" he replied comically.

"Not that idiot I was betrothed to, anyway." She had told him all about that horrid betrothal dinner; he had grimaced in sympathy, but then he had pointed out how the concubine must be feeling in all this. That she must surely be afraid of losing her position, and when that happened, it was a long, long fall—

At the end of that long fall, there would probably be plenty of her fellow slaves who would be happy to see her brought down.

She had thought, then, of all her own father's former concubines, and had realized that much of their bitterness was due to that very thing. How could they *not* feel bitter? And what other recourse did they have to ease their broken pride but the kinds of subtle insubordination she had seen over and over?

Her mother must have known that—and it was why her mother had ignored it, showing sensitivity that Rena had not at the time imagined.

"Well, I'm glad I'm myself, too. And I am glad that you are becoming more of yourself." He squeezed her hand gently, and she moved a little closer to him. Cattle lowed somewhere in the distance. "You are stronger every day, you know. You remember, more and more often, not to be afraid."

"Oh, I'm a coward for all of that," she told him, but he shook his head.

"No. You only forget, now and again, that you're really very brave. That's all." He took the hand he held, turned it palm upward, and planted a kiss in it, closing all her fingers around it. "Keep that to help you remember."

She shivered with pleasure and happiness, and felt herself blushing. "I will," she whispered.

"I know," he replied.

And he did. That was the glorious part. He *did* know.

She held to the moment as she held to the kiss. Whatever else came, she had this.

She would always have this.

9

TODAY, WHILE JAMAL was watching his warriors in their practice games, the conspirators were meeting for the first time under blue skies rather than beneath the roof of a tent. Keman glanced around their little gathering uneasily; he didn't like the fact that they were meeting in the open, in a clear space between two of the tents belonging to the Priests, but he hadn't been able to voice his objections clearly.

He had been uneasy from the moment when Jamal capitulated to Shana's demand to speak only to Diric. There was something wrong; there had been for some time, but the "wrongness" lay only in the fact that things were going entirely too well. That made his unease all the more difficult to justify. Jamal was silent where they were concerned; he made no inquiries about them, accepted the maps and lists of properties and the means used to guard them with no comment, and didn't seem to care about anything else. There was something very wrong about that—given the fact that Jamal had been shamed before his own people by Shana's declarations, and Jamal was not a man to take such things lightly. He was a bad man to have as an enemy; he would never forget a slight, much less a wrong.

Shana told Keman that he was manufacturing trouble where there was none, and asked him with a touch of acidity if things were simply not perilous enough for him. But he could not get over the feeling that there was something they were all missing, and the clues were in Jamal's behavior, if they could only read them.

Today had begun warm, and was soon sweltering; muggy, without a hint of breeze. Heat shimmered the air above the grasses, and sweat did not dry, it only trickled down the body without cooling anything. The tents had collected so much heat that not even the Iron People could bear to remain within them; even Diric had agreed to Shana's suggestion that they conduct their business outside for a change. After all, Jamal and every warrior in the Clan were supposed to be engaging in contests today, to determine their fitness—though fitness for *what,* Jamal was not yet ready to reveal. Not to the majority of the Clan, anyway. It seemed safe enough for them all to meet in the open.

Yet Keman could not escape the feeling that they were all somehow following a plan of Jamal's devising.

"If we could arrange for the roof of the tent to part, as if we had all grown claws to rend it, then wings to fly away," Shana suggested, as Keman returned his attention to the group. "Or would it be better to look as if we had escaped into the earth instead?"

"That would be my preference," Kalamadea began. "Perhaps by—"

"Oh, what a touching little gathering," a slow, drawling voice interrupted loudly.

Kalamadea, Shana, and Keman all jerked upright as if their heads had been on strings pulled by a puppet-dancer, for the language of the speaker was *not* the Iron People's tongue.

It was that of the dragons, and the voice was someone Keman recognized only too well—

Myre?

A tall woman of the Iron People, lean and muscular and dressed as a warrior, leaned indolently against the side of a wagon. It was no form that Keman recognized, and yet the woman had all of the arrogant stance that he associated with his sister. And she had a dragon-shadow.

"You see, Lord Jamal," the woman continued in the tongue of their captors, a sly smile on her face, "it is as I told you. The Priest confers with the demons to aid in their escape, and as I claimed, the two Corn People are not Corn People at all, but yet more demons."

Even Lorryn's illusions were something the Iron People were able to see through, if they simply stopped believing in them. Jamal's eyes narrowed as he stared at Lorryn and his sister, and he nodded, slowly.

Keman's heart stopped.

"So I see." Jamal stepped forward a pace, and stood with his arms crossed over his chest, an angry smile on his face. "I see six enemies, and one traitor. Or—perhaps not. I shall give you a chance to save yourself, Diric. Perhaps you have grown senile with age, Diric, and these demons have deluded you. Perhaps it is time for the powers of the Priest to pass into the hands of the War Chief. Should you decide to come to your senses and grant me those powers, I might forget this meeting."

This all had the sound of something carefully rehearsed, as if Jamal was reciting words he knew by heart. But—why?

Diric stood up, slowly, his face as still as the iron of his forges. "You will have those powers only if you dare to challenge me for them, young fool," he replied, his own voice as cold as the snows in the mountains. "And remember, I can name a champion."

Diric had been "courting" the Man-Hearted Women, who were angry with Jamal's treatment of them—and who composed some of the best fighters in the Clan. He could name one of them as a champion, and not only would the fight likely go to her, since Jamal was somewhat out of practice, but Jamal's defeat would mean disgrace in his *own* eyes.

"As can I," came the lazy reply. "And I choose—her."

And, unexpectedly, he pointed to Myre.

"I think you have no champion her like," the War Chief continued gleefully, openly reveling in the shock of Diric's face. "If I were you, I should surrender your authority now. It will go easier on all of you."

And Myre smiled, the smile of someone who knows that the dice are loaded, that the game is already decided.

Of all of them, Keman was the swiftest to realize what the sly smile on Myre's face meant, and the smug one on Jamal's. *She's told him! Or she showed him! He knows that she's a dragon!*

And before Diric could make the fatal error that Jamal was probably expecting, of naming one of the other Man-Hearted Women as his own champion, Keman acted.

He pulled open his collar, threw the collar to the ground, and shifted as quickly as he had ever done in his life, forcing the others to spring to their feet and back away as his rapidly increasing bulk filled the space between the tents. He shifted so quickly that it made him dizzy, but he fought back his dizziness, as he towered over them all.

The surprise—but utter lack of *shock* on Jamal's face—told him that he had guessed right. Jamal knew that Myre was a dragon, and he had seen the shift from human to dragon before.

But maybe Myre had not told him there were two other dragons among the prisoners. Or else both of them had assumed that the collars were still functional.

"Diric chooses me!" he roared, as Myre belatedly followed suit, shock still visible on her rapidly changing face. *"I am the First Priest's champion!"*

Then, before Myre could end her shift, leap upon him, and end the conflict before it could begin, *he* took to the sky with a thunder of wings that half-collapsed the tent nearest him. A cloud of dust and dead grass billowed up around the place where he had stood, and those closest to him threw up their arms to protect their faces from a pelting.

Then the tents dwindled below him as he pumped his wings, rapidly gaining altitude, going from tents to toys to the merest mushrooms on the green-gold plain beneath him. Altitude was his friend and ally. Myre had defeated him before in a straight combat; she was bigger and heavier than he was even now. He dared not allow her to close with him, to take the fight to a point at which that weight and length could make a difference.

He would have to defeat her with brain, not brawn.

:Running away, little brother?: came the sneering voice in his mind. *:Running so soon?:*

:Leading the race, little *sister,:* he taunted back. *:Having trouble keeping up with me? Been eating a bit too well lately, haven't you? I thought that might be a bit of a paunch I saw. Perhaps a layer of fat around your hips?:*

He'd seen no such thing, of course, but if he was going to force her to do what *he* wanted, he was going to have to enrage her until she wasn't thinking anymore.

His best weapons were agility and speed; he had to keep her in the air. For that, he had to keep her following him.

:Better give in to me before it's too late, brat,: she answered back furiously. *:Or else keep running and leave your pets behind. I might let you go crawling back to those two-legger friends of yours while there's still something left to crawl back to.:*

Something to crawl back to? Had she information that he didn't have about the wizards? It certainly sounded like it. He didn't reply; no point in it. If she wanted him to know something, she'd tell him; she couldn't help herself. And if it was bad news, she would definitely want to tell him, to demoralize him and make *him* stop thinking.

She was sending her voice out to every mind capable of picking it up, too, and he knew why. She wanted Shana and Kalamadea to hear. The trouble was, she didn't know that Dora was out there as well. Dora was his hidden ally, the unknown factor that could defeat Myre's ultimate purposes even if Keman lost this fight; if the very worst happened, and he *was* defeated, even if Myre managed to destroy or imprison all of them, Dora would know what it was that Myre wanted to taunt Keman with. If it was information vital to the wizards, Dora would surely see that it got to them before it was too late.

Wouldn't she? He didn't want to call to her; Myre might overhear. He had to keep all of his attention on what he was doing.

He could only hope, and wait for anger to force the words out of his sister.

:*Your wizards are in revolt against each other, little brother,*: she spat, as below him, she pumped her wings furiously to try and catch up to him. :*The old ones want the old ways back again, the younger are refusing to serve them, and they are all so busy with their little internal grievances that they are not bothering to keep a watch on the elves. And they really should. Lorryn's escape has sent them all into a panic, and they are already planning to unite their magics for the first time in centuries to track you all down and destroy you! The Council is moving to reconcile every feud and grievance that has ever erupted. They are moving slowly, but they are moving. Soon, within a few moons, by spring at the latest, the third Wizard War will begin—and it will be the last Wizard War.*:

His heart went cold; she would not have said anything at all unless she was sure of her information, and the feeling of familiarity with the Council that permeated her thoughts made him certain that her information was as accurate as it was foreboding. The elven lords' refusal to reconcile their differences and work properly together was all that had saved the wizards from annihilation the last time. With that factor gone—

He took himself firmly in hand. This was no time for distractions. Never mind. It hadn't happened yet. And he had a fight to win before he could see that it didn't.

He continued to gain height, wings pumping strongly, heading straight up into the sun, which gave him the added advantage that Myre couldn't see him—

—which meant she couldn't see what he was doing!

He had a considerable height advantage on her now; would it be enough? Only one way to find out!

Abruptly he flipped over; folded his wings and plummeted, straight down, talons fisted in front of him like a falcon's fisted claws. Not for nothing had he been studying the way that hawks and falcons flew and fought. He would have to be the little peregrine here, who weighed far less than the ducks he pursued. More than that, he would have to be the peregrine defending his nestlings from a goshawk. He would have to outfly her to outfight her.

He dove at Myre with the wind of his passage whistling in his nostrils and pulling at the edges of his wings. He had to fight the pressure of the air to keep his wings tucked in tight to his body; had to strive with aching muscles to keep his rear legs pulled in hard against his stomach. Myre still had no idea what he was doing; she grew larger and larger in his sight, squinting against the light, wings pumping, lungs panting as she tried to catch him—

Then suddenly her eyes widened as she spotted him diving down at her out of the sun; abruptly she turned, her first instinctive action to turn tail and evade his attack.

Too late.

With a *thud* that surely reached down to the ground, he hit her in the back of the head with both fisted fore-claws, knocking her into an uncontrolled tumble and surely bringing stars to her eyes. But it would take more than one blow to the head to knock Myre out of a fight, and her instincts were sure. Before she could lash out with her claws and catch him, he snapped his wings open again, and turned the dive back into a climb. The sudden pressure of air against his wings was so much like hitting a solid object that it made him gasp, and his speed was so great at that point that he shot past her before he could begin climbing again. He lost sight of her for a moment as he fought to control his own headlong climb; when he found her again, she was far below him, but doggedly climbing to reach him once more.

She said nothing now, though, even when he taunted her about being "too fat to fly." Though his chest muscles were afire with exertion, and his wings aching with stress, he smiled. The only time Myre didn't talk was when she was so angry that she *couldn't* respond.

But he knew he couldn't expect his attack to work a second time—at least, not in the same way. She might be angry, but she was a good fighter, and had probably gotten better since the last time he'd dealt with her.

So—make her think he was going to try the same tactic again, feint to draw her out, and switch to something else at the last minute? That could work.

He turned head over heels again, and dove a second time, although this time he did not have the advantage of the sun behind him. He had intended, instead of thumping her in the back of the head, to rake her back with his hind-claws, perhaps even tearing the tender membranes of her wings. But Myre wasn't finished yet; as he feinted, then snapped his wings open an instant earlier than before, she turned on her back, risking all in a desperate attempt to grapple with him and carry him down!

He eluded her only by side-slipping violently, and he lost all the advantage of the speed his dive had given him in that panicked maneuver. She could have had him then—except that *she* had counted on being able to close, and she lost even more height trying to recover both from the flip and the uncontrolled tumble it sent her into.

Once again he raced for the sun—but slower this time. His breath burned in his throat and lungs as he panted; his wings felt as heavy as stones, and his body a burden too great for his wings to carry.

Now what? Now what? I can't keep running like this; she has more endurance than I do! I have to end this, and end it quickly! Running me out of endurance was how she won that last fight!

Finally it came to him. It was desperate—but right now, a desperate chance might be the only one he'd have.

Once again, he turned and dove. Once again, she flipped over to grapple with him, claw to claw.

This time he let her catch him.

Her fore-claws grabbed and locked with his, her hind-claws raked across his belly-skin, sending rivers of agony racing along his nerves. He screamed—but pulled her closer, pulling her head between his wings.

And he sent the lash of captured lightning that was a dragon's most feared weapon arcing between the tips of his wings, catching her head in the middle.

Her mouth snapped open in a silent scream; her head arched back on her long neck until the back of her head met her shoulders. Her claws convulsed closed once, as he maintained the arc—then, when he released the lightning, she went limp.

He was ready for that, or else she might have achieved a Pyrrhic victory by making them both tumble headlong out of the sky onto the hard and unforgiving earth. He pumped his wings furiously as her limp body dragged at his; holding both of them in the air in a controlled fall instead of an uncontrolled one. Instead of both of them tumbling and plummeting to earth, he achieved a hard landing, with her body still locked in his talons. Fortunately, he had *her* to cushion his fall. He was not feeling charitable enough not to take advantage of that.

Just as well, since she had started to come to just as they landed. Her head hit the ground, and the force of the blow knocked her out again.

Not for long; just long enough for him to pin her to the ground, helpless beneath his weight, as the wizards ran toward them from the tents. Behind the wizards, the humans of the Iron People approached them cautiously.

"Shift, Myre!" he growled. "Into a human. Do it *now*, or I swear I'll—"

"You'll what?" she taunted, although there was panic in her eyes as she tried to squirm away and couldn't. "You'll kill me? You haven't the stomach!"

"I'll break your wings," he spat. "I'll shred them, and I'll break every bone, so that no matter how well you heal, you'll never fly again! I'll do it, Myre! I will!"

He saw by the fear in her that she believed him—and of course, it never occurred to her that she could simply shift to heal any damage he did to her! Father Dragon knew that little ploy, and his mother—and of course, he had been the first dragon to try it, to his best knowledge. But evidently Myre assumed, like most dragons, that damage to her true self was *permanent* damage.

Just as well.

Beneath his talons, she dwindled down and shrank into a helpless human, trembling under his claws, but staring up at him with hate in her eyes. *Not* a human of the Iron People, but a pale-skinned slave of the elven lords.

"Now what?" she sneered up at him as he loomed over her. "Are you going to eat me?"

He closed his talons around her, none too gently. "You're going to wish I had, Myre," was all he said.

:Shana!: he sent out the thought, even as he spoke. *:Get a collar—a new one—and bring Kala and her tools!:*

By now the humans were encircling them where they both sat, near-motionless, in the dry, hot grass. Keman was not going to give up his draconic form until he *knew* that Myre was no longer a threat. The sun beat down on both of them without mercy, but full sun was a friend to a dragon, the hotter, the better; he felt the pain of his belly wounds aching with every tiny movement, but the heat of the sun revived him, even as it wilted Myre in the form he had forced her to assume.

Shana came running up with a collar in both hands; Kala followed at a slow and wary walk, with her pouch of tools at her side. The Priest's wife paid no attention to Myre—all of her attention was on Keman. She was afraid; he knew that by the sweat on her forehead and the trembling of her hands. But she approached him even though she was afraid, proving that she was as brave as any person, two-legger or dragon, that he had ever seen.

"Put the collar around her neck, Shana," he ordered aloud, forming his words in the tongue of the Iron People so that everyone could understand it. "Lock it there."

She did so; he dropped Myre like the distasteful object she was and backed away a pace. Before Myre could even think to try to make a break for it, Shana seized her and wrestled her to the ground, sitting on her to keep her there.

Keman shifted again, concentrating not only on taking his halfblood form, but on healing the wounds that Myre had caused at the same time. It made the shift harder, but that didn't matter; the freedom from pain as he took the final form made him faint with relief.

If anything, Kala's eyes were even wider as she stared at him in his wizard-form.

"You could break the locks on our collars to keep them open, Kala," he said, softly, so that only she could hear. "Can you jam them so that they can never open again, as well?"

She nodded, slowly; then, while Myre cursed and tried to throw Shana off, she turned and walked to Shana's side. Motioning Shana aside to hold Myre's legs, Kala solved the entire problem by sitting on Myre's back and holding her head by the hair. Kala was not a light person; Myre's face reflected that, as she suddenly turned very, very red.

"You will hold still, creature," Kala said, slowly, and carefully, shaking the hair she held so that Myre winced. "Demon or monster, it matters not to me, for while you are in the form of a woman, and wear the collar, you will *remain* in the form of a woman, and there is no woman born I cannot deal with. If you do not hold still, I will not be responsible for what happens as I work. Some of my tools are very sharp."

Myre froze, not daring to move a single muscle.

That was all that Kala needed, and she released her grip on Myre's hair. Within moments, she had inserted one of her probes into the lock of the collar—jammed it into the mechanism, and snapped the tip off flush with the surface of the collar. Only then did she stand up, and allow Myre to clamber slowly and clumsily to her feet.

"No one will ever open that collar again," Kala said quietly. "You will remove it only when you may find someone willing to cut it from your neck. That, too, will not be easy. You will not be able to remove it with magic, and it is tempered to resist the most determined cutter."

"And while you're wearing it, foolish one, you will find

you are unable to shift, or to work any but the smallest of magics." That was Kalamadea, coming up from the rear of the crowd. "I would not try, were I you. I am told that the effects are most unfortunate."

The crowd parted suddenly; Diric marched up the middle of the empty space, followed by four of the Man-Hearted Women who had Jamal surrounded. He was not in chains, but from his demeanor he might as well have been. His shoulders were hunched, and he would not look at anything but the ground.

But Keman saw the fury in his eyes, though he tried to hide it. He was defeated, but he would never forget this defeat, and if he ever got a chance at revenge, it would be terrible.

All the reason never to give him a chance, then.

"While you did battle in the air, my champion," Diric said to Keman, gravely, "I did battle on my own on the ground."

He raised his voice. "Hear, oh my people, of the foolishness and the pride of your War Chief, who would risk your lives and the lives of your families that he might achieve a fleeting glory for himself!"

He began a highly edited version of everything that had happened since the wizards had been captured; Keman didn't pay too much attention to his speech once he realized what the gist of it was going to be. Instead, he watched Myre, who, despite the warning, had evidently tried something a little more potent than anything he or Kalamadea had attempted while wearing their collars. She stifled a cry of pain, blanched a dead white, and the skin beneath the collar reddened and blistered.

He could have felt sorry for her, if he hadn't still been so angry with her.

Lorryn was staring at her, though, with his mouth hanging wide open.

"What's the matter?" Keman asked softly. "Why are you staring at my sister?"

"That—that's my sister's maid, the one that helped us escape," he managed to stammer as he continued to stare. "But—wasn't she a dragon a little bit ago?"

"She's also my sister, and she's been trying to kill Shana and anyone who was a friend of Shana since before the Wizard War," Keman replied grimly. As Lorryn turned toward him, eyes wide with a thousand questions in them, he just shook his head. A great deal was becoming clear now, but it would all have to wait. "I'll explain it all later; we have more important things to handle right now than her."

He ground his teeth together, as Diric's oration wound to its close, with the declaration that Jamal would be branded with the mark of a traitor and cast out from the Clan. "Right now," he continued, "we have a war to prevent. If we still can!"

By the time night fell, Rena's head was reeling; this was too much to take in, all at once! Her maid, her *friend*—or so she had thought—was really a dragon? That much she could accept, somehow, for Myre had known an awful lot about the dragons, more than she should have even if she were an agent of the wizards. But to discover that she was a bad dragon, one who'd meant mischief, not good, by helping them escape—

It shook her, and it hurt her. She'd had so few friends, and she'd thought that Myre was one of them, despite the differences between them. Hadn't she gone out of her way to be kind to the girl? Hadn't she told Myre all of her secrets? The stories and romances all talked about the pain of betrayal; well, now she knew what they meant! How could she trust anyone after this? For that matter, *whom* could she trust after this?

That was her initial reaction, as she tried to take in all of the changes and make some sense of them. But as the moments flew past and her mind began to work again, she had to admit to herself that in the larger scheme of things—her own hurt was a very little incident in light of the things that Myre had revealed. *She* had not heard the "voice in the mind" that her brother described, but Kalamadea, Shana,

Lorryn, Mero, and (oddly enough) Diric all had. The danger to the wizards in their new home was not on the horizon—*yet*—but it most certainly would be soon!

"You are free to go as soon as you want," Diric was saying; once again, they were in his tent, but this time for comfort rather than secrecy. Jamal was already beginning his exile—Diric had not thought it a good idea to leave him within the Clan where he might manage access to Myre. A new War Chief had been appointed with Diric's full approval. Myre languished in the prison tent with the two elves, for Keman had reckoned that leaving her in Diric's custody was better than letting her wander around on her own. With the collar locked around her neck, she would certainly never be able to shift again. She might be able to escape, but where would she go? In her human form, that of the slave from Lord Tylar's estates, she would be pathetically vulnerable. Without being able to work magic to defend herself, there were a hundred deaths she could meet with out in the wilderness; all of them unpleasant.

So for the moment at least, Myre was no longer a threat to anyone. Later? Well, Rena was not so sure. If it had been up to her, Myre would be locked away for the rest of her life in a very deep, dark place, with food and water lowered to her on a rope.

"You have won us as allies, according to all our traditions," Diric continued, speaking mostly to Shana and Lorryn. "You defeated Jamal's champion in the view of everyone in the Clan. I do not know what we can do to aid you—but if there is anything we can offer, you have but to ask!"

Shana started to shake her head; Rena couldn't help but see how her mood had darkened in the last few hours. She was tense, very tense, and although she wasn't fidgeting, Rena guessed that if she had her way, she would have been a-dragonback and gone right after the fight. "Right now it looks like what we need most is an army. I won't ask you to come up against the elves; I wouldn't ask that of anyone. We both know it would be a slaughter, and what would be the point, anyway? But—"

Lorryn interrupted her. "Shana, wait a moment. The elves are not prepared to attack *now*. They are still trying to reconcile all their old grievances! What if we interfered with that process?"

"How?" she asked, skeptically. "I won't ask the dragons to go into their lands shape-shifted as elves; it's too dangerous! Now every elven lord that appears is going to be under the tightest of scrutiny, and will have to be vouched for by a dozen others! And if they went as slaves—they couldn't do a thing besides watch. I can't ask the wizards to go in, either, not when the elves are watching for illusions! How can we do anything from a distance?"

"Lorryn and I can go," Rena offered shyly. "I'm not sure what he has in mind, but we can do it. He could be *any* young er-Lord, or even a third or fourth son—no one pays any attention to them, or to women, either. We could go a lot of places, without ever meeting anyone who would recognize us."

Mero reached out and caught her hand and squeezed it. "If they go in, I'll go with them," he volunteered bravely, as Shana's eyes widened with shock. "I know plenty about the High Lords and their estates. And I know some about the cities, too. I could always pass as Lorryn's slave, after all. I am used to that role."

Shana looked over at Lorryn, who was nodding. "You obviously have some plan," she said slowly. "There's something you know that we don't—"

"One small thing, yes," he agreed. "And, Lord Diric, there *is* something your people can give me that will help that plan along immensely. The jewelry that your women make."

Diric raised an inquisitive eyebrow. "This sounds more and more complicated," he said. "I hope it is not so complex as to forbid success."

But Lorryn shook his head. "Actually, it isn't all that complex at all," he replied. "There is an ancient rift among the elven lords that no amount of negotiation is ever going to cure," he told them all. "And that is the rift between the powerful and the weak."

Now Rena saw where he was going, and she knew why he wanted the jewelry too! "The difference between the powerful and the weak is a matter more of *magic* than of wealth or property," she said excitedly, rather than waiting for him to explain. "Those lords with a great deal of magic make virtual slaves of those with little. Worse than slaves, in fact! That is a chasm so wide that nothing could ever bridge it; the hurts have gone on too long and have been made too deeply to ever be healed!"

Mero nodded. "It's a rift that would never appear as long as the powerful lords can *use* their power against the weaker, so I don't imagine that a single one of those powerful magicians is bothering to make any kind of reconciliation with those they consider inferior. I doubt it would even occur to them."

"Among those who are oppressed by those with power are most of the *women*," Lorryn added. "Now—what if suddenly all the power in the world meant nothing against those who have none of their own? What if—for instance, there was a fad for filigree jewelry among the not so well-to-do? What if those same souls learned that magic would have no effect on them while they wore it?"

"What if you got some of it into the hands of human slaves?" Shana added, her eyes glowing with excitement. "Oh, Lorryn, do you really think that the lesser elves would rise up against their lords if they knew they had an immunity to their power?"

"Not only lesser elves, but think about all the discontented sons who have nothing to do but be their fathers' heirs, with no true prospect of inheriting?" Keman added. "They're bored, they are withering away with boredom and resentment. They are tired of being given stupid little tasks as if they were superior slaves! I was among those people when I was hunting you, Shana. Remember Dyran, and remember that if Dyran was the worst of the lot, there are at least a hundred Lord Tylars who are nearly as oppressive to their sons! If *they* had an immunity from their fathers' magics, there are at least a handful of them who'd make more than mischief!"

"While they deal with the revolt of their underlings, and the insubordination of their women and children, they can't do anything about the wizards," Lorryn concluded. "That's my plan, anyway. Rena and I go back home. I go into the cities and hunt up the disgruntled underlings, the discontented heirs. *She* goes back home, spins some tale of how I forced her to come with me, and inserts herself back into the social round—only wearing this new filigree jewelry. My idea is that we can silver-plate it to hide the fact that it is made of iron. That way no one but the owners will ever guess what its powers are. The construction of it is exotic enough she ought to start a fad. The women are mad for anything new."

Rena nodded ruefully, and he continued, turning toward her. "The only problem—it could be very dangerous to you, Rena. I won't risk that if you really don't want to go." His eyes were grave, and his face troubled. "The plan will go better if you are in it, but I can succeed at least in part alone."

"Until you're caught," Mero said grimly. "No, if you go in, I go too."

"And I." Rena lifted her chin defiantly. "I think you're right. Revolt from the women is the one thing that the lords will not be looking for." She thought for a moment, to that long-ago time when she had been staring into the darkness of her room, looking forward to a bleak future as the near-enslaved wife of a complete idiot. What would she have done if she had known that she had a way to shield herself from anything her father or his could do to her? What would she have said if she *knew* she could not have her mind taken away from her?

Oh, her father could still have used physical force—but there were answers to that as well. And if her *mother* could somehow have gotten an iron collar locked around his neck, perhaps as he slept . . .

Mother.

"If nothing else, I have to return to help Mother," she said suddenly. "I have to, Lorryn! Wait a moment, let me think."

She closed her eyes for a moment, and let her thoughts settle. "We can find out if the news got around that *I* escaped with you quickly enough," she said, finally. "If it didn't—I can start visiting some of my female 'friends,' the farther away from our estate, the better. I can show them my jewels—tell them that they were betrothal gifts—and let slip where they can purchase their own copies. I won't stay more than a day at a time. The men never bother with visitors in the bowers, and they never remember a woman's name. As long as I don't linger, I'll be safe enough."

Lorryn nodded, and so did Mero. Mero's look of approval and encouragement was what she really needed to get on with the next part of her plan.

"That gets the fad started, so it can go on with or without me. Then I go home." She raised her hand to stop Lorryn's protests. "I tell Father that you kidnapped me, just as you suggested. All he has to do is cast a simple spell and he'll know I'm fullblooded. Then I become *important*, Lorryn, I become the only true child of his blood! I can even tell them that's *why* you kidnapped me, so that you could use me as a bargaining chip against him. Then I can slip some of the jewelry to Mother, and we can escape together."

"The only question I can think of is—are we going to make an organized revolt over this?" Lorryn said, finally, turning to Shana.

"I don't see how we can afford not to," she told him frankly. "Once the secret of the jewelry leaks out, the more powerful lords are going to start looking for ways to get around it—and they can *do* that if they can ambush the wearers one at a time."

Rena closed her eyes, bit her tongue, and tried not to show her fear. This was no romance, no dream in her garden. This was real, as real as their trek into the hills, as real as the rug under her hand. When they left this place, and reentered the lands of the elven lords, she would be in real danger. She could die. So could Lorryn.

So could Mero, and he didn't hesitate.

There was an icy hand clutched around her heart, a ball of cold clay in her throat, and a frozen lump of lead in the pit of her stomach. Was it only a night or two ago that she had walked with Mero in the moonlight, and thought that for the first time in her life she was truly happy? And now—

Now we risk all of it.

But she couldn't do anything less, not without making everything she'd gone through meaningless.

There was, for a brief moment while she strove to conquer that fear, another force warring within her. Temptation—to act like a real coward, a selfish coward. After all, she was no fighter, no hero like Shana! She *could* run back to her father and tell everything she knew. He'd not only welcome her, he'd reward her. He'd give her everything she ever wanted. She could *have* all those things she daydreamed about, her own manor where she alone would rule, books, music, gowns and jewels, and freedom to do exactly what she wanted. These halfbloods, these dragons—they weren't her kind. Why should she give them her loyalty and service when simply aligning herself with her *real* people would grant her all the freedom she ever wanted?

But the temptation did not last for more than the time it took for the thought to be born, for it wouldn't be real freedom, would it? She would still be constrained; by custom, by law. She might not be forced to marry a dolt, but she still would not be free to follow her own heart.

But most of all, it would be *wrong*. She would have bought all of it with blood.

She would be as bad as the worst of her kind if she did that. Worse, maybe. They had built their estates on the blood and bodies of their slaves and underlings. She would not buy hers with the blood and bodies of people who called her "sister" and "friend."

She might be a coward and weak, but she could not be a traitor.

The talk had gone on without her, but she was well aware that she was of no particular help at this point. She closed her will around the fear settling in throat, heart, and soul, and listened with an outwardly calm face.

There would be several days of travel before they even

reached the edge of the wizards' lands. She had that much more time to try and find some courage.

Hopefully it would be time enough.

Keman grew impatient with them all long before the others talked themselves out. Perhaps it was the excitement—he'd noticed that humans had to run a thing to ground before they tired of it if they were excited. Finally they talked themselves into circles, repeating the same things over and over, and Diric declared that they were all too tired to even think properly. He sent them to Jamal's tent, which he had commandeered for them, since the new War Chief was happy with her own home and had no wish to change. Keman was pleased to see that each of them had his or her own little chamber, now cleared of all the personal possessions of the previous owner, and furnished with comfortable pallets and other niceties.

That's probably Kala's doing, he decided, after surveying his own little pie-slice of carpeted tent. *She must have been taking care of all of this while we were talking. What an amazing woman! She and Diric work so well together—*

It would be so wonderful if he could find someone like Kala. . . .

He lay down on his pallet and waited, listening with every fiber for the sounds of the other people in the tent to die away. He didn't think that Mero and Sheyrena were likely to wander off hand in hand under the moon; not tonight, anyway. If they were as exhausted as he was—

Well, maybe they weren't. They hadn't fought; he had. Unless, of course, they'd all pitched in to subdue Jamal while he and Myre fought in the skies.

Gradually, though, the murmurs of conversation and the sounds of people moving about, the little shifts in the floor and creak of wood as people walked, died away.

Finally.

He needed to get out. Dora must be frantic by now. And he was *starving.* He hadn't wanted to take the easy way out and ask for a cow or two; people were frightened enough of him, and he didn't want to frighten them further by eating in front of them.

He slipped out of the darkened tent, wound his way through the camp as silent as a cat, moving from shadow to shadow with all of the skill of any predator. There was no moon tonight, which was a help, and most people were so bewildered and agitated by the turn of events today that they were keeping to their own dwellings while they sorted things out.

In some ways, Keman felt rather sorry for them. The Iron People were so ruled by tradition—and yet today so many things had happened that didn't fit within that tradition that they must feel almost as confused as if they had awakened to find themselves camped in the midst of a glacier, floating on the ocean, or perched atop a mountain-peak.

It certainly wasn't every day that you found a pair of dragons fighting over your head—then saw them both turn into people afterwards—and one of them was someone you *knew*. *Then* you discovered that your War Chief had been consorting with the other one in order to get you into a war against demons, and your Priest had been consorting with the one you knew, in order to *trade* with the demons. Poor things. No wonder every tent buzzed with talk, and most of it sounded confused.

Still, Diric has them convinced, I think. He'd have had more trouble if Shana had asked him for direct help against the elves, but I think he can manage to get them calmed down under the current circumstances.

But now he was going to have to force a confrontation on Dora. He hadn't wanted to, not this early, but there wasn't going to be much choice.

She's going to have to choose between running back to her own Lair—and—

And what? And him?

But what choice did he have?

With her help we can all travel back to the Citadel in a few days. Sheyrena is light enough that Kalamadea can carry her double with Lorryn. But without Dora—we'll have to make double trips, because I can't carry two people for very long. That's going to take time that we just don't have.

Besides that, in the morning all six of them were *leaving* this place. Dora would have to reveal herself sooner or later, so why not sooner? She couldn't hide her presence forever.

He stopped at the edge of the herds, and sent out a questing tendril of thought.

:Here. At the edge of the herds.:

Well, he no longer needed to hide what he was—and he wasn't going to have to explain to any of the herdsmen what he was doing out here! He shifted—slowly, and with a bit of the pain that weariness always caused when he shifted—and lumbered into the air. Muscles ached and joints creaked as he flew.

I am going to have to stay in better shape from now on.

A moment later, Dora met him in the sky above the camp. They flew together, neither one saying a word, as she led him off into the low hills beyond the encampment.

To his surprise and delight, she led him to a cache of freshly killed plains deer, and she waited patiently while he sated his ravenous hunger.

"Oh," he said fervently, when hunger-rage had worn off enough for him to be able to think clearly, "I needed that. Thank you."

"I knew you would," she replied, gravely. "Keman—I didn't know *what* to think when I saw that strange female! And then when she spoke—and you fought—I was so afraid for you!"

The words came out of her reluctantly, as if she was as afraid to voice her feelings as he was.

"I wanted to help you," she continued, "but I didn't know how."

"You couldn't have done anything," he told her, bluntly. "Myre has resented me from the time she was born, I think. That resentment curdled into hate long before we met, you and I. Anything you could have done to help me would just have delayed things between Myre and me."

"Oh." Her head sagged, deflated. "All I could think of was that you'd be hungry."

"I was. Thank you." He sat down on his haunches, wondering what to say next. Well, better get it out of the way at once.

"We're leaving tomorrow."

Her head shot up, her eyes wide. "Is it because of what she said, your sister? About the elves, and your wizard friends?"

"She didn't have any reason to lie, and *plenty* of reasons to tell the truth. We have to assume that's what she did," he replied. "We have to get back—Shana has to settle things with the wizards in case the elves do mount an attack, and Lorryn and Rena both think they have a plan to disrupt the situation in the elven lords' ranks. But we haven't much time."

"So you're leaving." She looked as if she'd bitten into something bitter. "I promised to help you escape, but it doesn't look as if you need me now."

Was *that* all that was troubling her? "We need you more than ever," he told her. "With your help, if you let Shana ride you, we can fly at something close to our normal speed. Without you, Kalamadea and I will have to make double-trips."

She looked into his eyes. "You're asking me to—to show myself."

He nodded. "Dora, you have to, sooner or later, or else just go home. And what would be the point of that? I'll be telling *my* Lair about yours. Some of *our* dragons are going to go looking for yours. And you'll be telling your Lair about all the other Lairs up here! Eventually our Kin are going to meet, whether or not you show yourself to my friends."

But she looked troubled. "Our laws have always said never to show ourselves to two-leggers as we are."

He snorted. "My two-leggers already know what we are, and Myre certainly took the matter of the Iron People out of both of our hands! As my two-legger friends say, 'the horse has been stolen, so what's the point of locking the barn?' You won't be accomplishing anything."

She sighed. "I said I wanted to help you. . . ."

"But not necessarily my friends?" he asked shrewdly.

She nodded. "I can't help it," she confessed. "It's hard to think of them as people."

"You have to start somewhere," he told her softly, "or you end up like the elves, who don't count *anyone* who hasn't got full elven blood as 'people.' Or like Myre, who sees anything that isn't a dragon as rightful prey. Can't you see that?"

"I wouldn't want to be like them." Her skin shuddered, and she looked away. "Especially not your sister."

"Then help us, Dora," he said, weariness creeping into his voice. He wasn't as good at this persuasion thing as Shana. He *really* wished he had Lorryn's gift for it. "Not me, help us."

She still didn't look at him. "I have to think about it," she said slowly. "I don't know what else to tell you."

"All right." He sighed, but what else could he say? He certainly couldn't coerce her, and he didn't want to use a different kind of coercion on her by telling her how very, very much he liked her. . . .

So instead, he stretched weary and aching muscles, and prepared to take flight again, back to the tent, and some well-earned sleep. "Thank you for everything that you *have* done, Dora; I really appreciate it," he told her as he stretched out his wings. "Just remember; we take off a little past dawn tomorrow."

"I'll—remember," she said slowly, making no move to take to the air herself, keeping her wings furled against her sides. "Good night, Keman."

"Good night, Dora." He forced himself not to add anything. She had to make up her mind by herself. Instead, he launched himself into the dark, star-spangled sky, and made a slow, weary flight back to the tents of the clan. From this height, the lights from their lanterns looked as if stars had dropped down out of the sky to arrange themselves in concentric rings on the plain.

This might be the last time he'd see it, too. From here on, they moved into unknown territory. Lorryn, Mero, and Rena would not be the only ones going into elven lands. *Someone* would have to set up shops to "sell" the silver-plated iron jewelry. It would be very dangerous for wizards to even attempt such a thing.

But shifted dragons, now . . . there was a possibility.

There was another possibility as well, something he hadn't bothered telling to Shana, because he didn't want to get her hopes up. But with Myre out of the way, *his* way was clear to return to the old Lair and recruit more of the Kin. In fact, there was nothing stopping him from going to other Lairs. That would free the original rebels, as many of them as were willing, to shift into two-legger forms to run those "jewelry shops," because there would be other recruits to take their places at the Citadel to help the wizards defend themselves. It wouldn't matter if they shifted to the forms of human slaves; only slaves ran shops anyway. And certainly none of the elven lords would be looking for trouble among the fat and contented merchanter-slaves!

That, he had decided, would be his responsibility, as soon as he was free to pursue it—which would be as soon as they reached the Citadel.

Already he felt the stirrings of impatience. He wanted to be *at* the job; he had the sensation of time pressing in on them from all directions, the feeling that he was only now beginning a race that had started without him.

Perhaps he had. Perhaps they all had.

No matter. They were in it now. They had no choice but to run this race full-out, and hope that they could finish it.

Dawn came much, much too soon for Keman; despite eating to beyond satiation, and sleeping as only a thoroughly bloated dragon *could* sleep, no matter what form he took, Keman felt as if he would have been a lot happier with a great deal more sleep.

Two or three weeks' worth, as a start.

He politely refused breakfast, and went out to the cleared space that Diric had arranged for them so that they would not frighten the cattle as he and Myre had with their shifts and appearance yesterday. He'd been told they nearly started a stampede . . . and one was only prevented because all of the warriors were out near the herds playing their war games. Certainly Jamal had not anticipated that, and yet it had been the one action he had taken that had a positive outcome yesterday.

He had half-expected a circle of curious onlookers, but there was no one there, and it wasn't because the Iron People weren't used to getting up at dawn.

They're afraid. I can't really blame them.

That was probably just as well. He planned to take his shift slowly, and that could be very unnerving to two-leggers at the best of times. At the worst—well, he'd seen one or two of Shana's friends grow rather green, and sometimes lose whatever they had in their stomachs.

Queasiness was not generally a draconic problem, unless one was very ill. He still had a hard time understanding creatures that were so quick to lose what they'd eaten. It seemed a very counterproductive trait.

When he completed his shift, he began stretching his muscles, slowly, as his mother, Alara, had taught him to do before he undertook anything that was going to be physically taxing. And this flight *would* be physically taxing, there was no doubt of that. Besides his burden of Shana and Mero, he would be carrying bundles of heavy iron jewelry, gathered last night by Kala from all the women she could persuade to give it up. Kalamadea would be doing the same, though his riding-burden would be Lorryn and Rena, and he could carry far, far more than Keman.

It was just too bad that no one had ever learned the trick of shifting the mass of something other than himself into the Out, as a dragon did when he had to shift to a smaller, lighter form. Perhaps it simply couldn't be done. It would have been useful, though.

The rising sun gilded the grass, and a light breeze blew up out of the South. His shadow reached to the tents and mingled with their shadows. He stretched each limb separately, several times, warming up the muscles and making them more flexible with each stretch. As he began the series of integrated stretches that would finish his warm-up, some of the Iron People began bringing the bundles of jewelry and supplies he and Kalamadea would be carrying. He watched them out of the corner of his eye and tried not to chuckle. They were very funny, really. They eased up to the edge of the area with one eye on him and the other on where they were going. They *tried* to look comfortable, casual, but they generally failed utterly. They would always drop the bundle as soon as it was humanly possible, and scuttle away as if they had heard he'd refused breakfast and were afraid that he intended to break his fast with one of *them.*

The others arrived at about the same time as the bundles. Kalamadea, who had not been the one fighting and flying yesterday, shifted quickly into his draconic form of Father Dragon. He was huge, easily twice the size of Keman, perhaps larger, and Keman was large enough to easily carry one two-legger rider. Dragons grew for as long as they were alive, and Father Dragon was the oldest dragon Keman knew of. Not even Alara knew exactly how old he was. He had been alive at the time of the very first Gate-opening, when the dragons had lived in a world with far more perils in it than this one.

We've grown soft and lazy, Keman thought, contemplating Kalamadea's huge wings fanning the morning air. *If those old ones could see us, hiding in our Lairs from mere two-leggers, they'd laugh at us. They had to worry about things so deadly that they would burrow* into *Lairs to kill and eat the occupants!*

Kalamadea might have read his thoughts. *:The elven lords, given enough incentive, could be just as deadly to us as the perils our kind once escaped from, Keman,:* he said quietly, so that no one else would overhear. *:Don't think too badly of those who only want to hide. That was why we escaped here, after all. To hide. We* were *running away, technically speaking.:*

Well, maybe.

He was resolutely keeping his mind on anything and anyone *except* Dora. He awoke this morning resolved to assume that she would not be coming along. He had tried not to feel too disappointed or hurt.

Unfortunately, as he had learned all too often in the past, resolutions are usually not heeded by the emotions. All the resolve in the world did not help the feeling of disappointment and—yes—loss as the sun rose higher and Dora did not appear. He wasn't sure if it was his heart that was aching, but there was certainly something holding a core of dull pain, deep inside him.

He waited patiently while the others rigged him and Kalamadea with harnesses, both for the benefit of their passengers and to strap the bundles of supplies to.

"You aren't going to like this at all," Shana was telling Lorryn and his sister, as she explained how the harnesses worked. He sensed her tightly wound nerves, and guessed that she was chattering to relieve them. Poor Shana! It was not only the threat of the elven lords that disturbed her, it was, he knew, the threat of revolt from within the wizards' ranks. That was what had undone the wizards in the first war. He only hoped history was not about to repeat that tragedy. "And don't listen to Kalamadea or Keman—dragons don't get flying-sick. I mean, think about it; they couldn't fly if they got sick every time they took wing. But here's the problem. The first thing that happens is that the dragon *jumps* into the air; if you've ever jumped a horse over a huge obstacle, you'll have a very slight idea of what that feels like."

"So unless we are strapped in, we're going to go tumbling over his back," Lorryn observed dispassionately. He turned a little to look Keman in the eye. "I hope you'll forgive me, my friend, but I have a very hard time reconciling *this*—" he slapped Keman's shoulder "—with the young wizard who snored all last night."

"I did *not* snore!" Keman exclaimed indignantly.

"You did," Shana told him firmly. "Most of the night. Loudly."

He snorted, and ignored her, examining those straps of his harness that he could reach himself with ostentatious care.

"Now, at the top of that leap," Shana continued, as if she

had not been interrupted—another sign of her nervous tension—"he's going to suddenly snap open his wings and start a series of very powerful wingbeats to gain altitude. They're just like the leap; a series of surges. You're going to be thrown backward with every wingbeat, and if you don't hold on and hunch yourself over like this—" she crouched down, demonstrating the position "—you're going to feel as if your head is going to snap off the end of your spine."

Lorryn nodded, and his sister sighed. "This sounds worse than riding the worst-gaited horse in the universe!"

"It is," Shana assured her. "In fact, it's worse than riding a pack-grel. All right, at some point he's going to reach the height he needs, and that's where the discomfort *really* begins. These folks don't fly in a straight line. They swoop, like this—" She made an arcing motion with her hand. "Wingbeat, swoop, wingbeat. Your poor stomach is going to think you're falling during part of each swoop. That's where you'll get flight-sick, if it happens at all, and if you have to—well—just tell Kalamadea; he'll bank to one side so that you can—ah—straight down. And Ancestors help whatever is below you."

Keman listened with real interest; although he had carried passengers before this, he'd never heard any of them explain what it felt like to them. Of course, flying felt perfectly natural and right to *him*, but evidently that was not how it felt to those who rode his back.

"There's also turbulence up there; Keman has done side-slips, been bounced as if he was trying to buck me off, and dropped halfway to the ground, and even turned upside down by winds. I don't get sick, and I hope *you* won't, but I won't promise anything." She shrugged at their expressions of dismay. "No matter what, make sure that every strap is tight, every buckle fastened. Check them while you're flying. They are *all* that is keeping you on his back, and believe me, you need every one of them."

Mero came up as she said that, and nodded solemnly. "If we have to fly through a storm, you're going to wish you had more straps than you do," he added.

"But—the stories all made it seem as if flying was so easy," Rena said plaintively. "As if—you just got on, and off you went!"

Keman laughed. "Well, do remember that it was Myre telling you those tales, right? For us, flying *is* easy. And anyway, she wouldn't have wanted to discourage your romantic image of dragons." He thought for a moment, then added, "I can at least promise you this—it's easier flying with Kalamadea than with me. I have to take more wingbeats to stay aloft than he does, because he's bigger. Have you ever watched birds?"

At Rena's nod, he went on.

"You've probably seen the way small birds fly; it's very jerky, and it takes a lot of wingbeats. But a big hawk, now—he can glide quite a bit, and when he does take a wingbeat, it's slower because his wings are larger. That's the difference between Kalamadea and me, and you two will be riding Kalamadea, because you're less experienced."

Shana was testing every strap; the leatherworkers had worked all night on the harnesses, and Kalamadea rather approved of them. They certainly *fit* better than anything he'd had rigged up before.

"Ah—here's something else," Shana said as she came around from the other side. "Rena, Lorryn, see the pad here, that's like a saddle? *Don't* let your legs slip off it and don't ever be tempted to wear cloth breeches instead of leather. Dragonscales are very abrasive and they'll scrape you to the bone in a few wingbeats." She had them slide their hands the wrong way along Keman's shoulder, and nodded when they winced. "That's why I asked the leatherworkers to make more than two sets of harnesses and lots of extra straps, so that if some of this gets sliced up, we can just discard the pieces instead of wasting time trying to mend it."

"Would one of those extra harnesses happen to fit me?"

Keman looked up, as startled as everyone else, as a shadow slid over them all. A moment later, Dora landed in a flurry of wingbeats that kicked up dust and sent it flying in every direction.

"I saw the double-saddle on Kalamadea, but Keman is

much smaller than the Elder One, and I thought you might need an extra mount," Dora said, shyly and turned to Keman. "You were right," she said, simply, and his heart soared.

:And thank you for not—not using emotions to convince me,: she added, for his benefit only.

Kalamadea was the first one to recover, and he did so with considerable aplomb. "Keman?" he said, quietly. "Would you care to introduce us to your—friend?"

:And is this *where you've been vanishing at night, when we all thought you were hunting, you young rascal? Or were you hunting after all? Fairer game than plains deer?:* he added.

"Ah—this is Dora," he said lamely, suddenly tongue-tied. "She's from a Lair very far south, where the Iron Clans all live, and she's been watching this Clan the way we used to watch the elven lords. She didn't know there *were* any other dragons except the ones in her Lair until she saw my shadow."

"Really?" was all Kalamadea said, then he turned to Dora, every talon-length the gallant. "Welcome to our group, Dora. We are very pleased to have your help, and very grateful as well."

She ducked her head, her nostrils flushing.

"Now, if I may take command of this situation," Kalamadea continued, looking over his shoulder at the sun, "I believe we should get another harness onto our new friend Dora, and make all speed while we can. Explanations can wait until we are airborne. Lorryn, since you are riding double with your sister, who is the only one of us who cannot speak and hear thoughts, you can simply *tell* her what is being said. At the least, it will enliven the journey no end."

He clapped his wings sharply, by way of emphasis.

"Come along, my friends!" he finished. "The elven lords are sharpening their talons for our necks! It is time, and more than time, that we were in the air!"

10

LORRYN NURSED A cup of thick, too sweet red
wine in one of the many taverns he'd been frequenting since
he began this part of the "plan." This one was in Whitegates,
a trade-city administered by Lord Ordrevel—or more correctly, by Lord Ordrevel's underlings. It didn't matter where
he was, really; each of the five trade-cities looked pretty
much like the next one, and all these taverns were alike.

He should know. He'd been in every trade-city on the con-
tinent, and most of the taverns.

The taverns were all luxuriously appointed—or so it
seemed. If you looked closely, though, you saw that most of
the "luxury" was only where it could be seen. Leather upholstery extended only to the side of the cushion that showed;
satin wallpaper gave way to bare wall where the wall was
covered by furniture or something else. Velvet drapes proved
on touching to be soft, flocked paper, cheap and disposable.

These taverns all had dark rooms in the upper levels where
human slaves waited to give whatever pleasuring was required, but the rooms were so dark that neither the slaves nor

the surroundings were readily visible. They all served very cheap wine, spiced and honeyed to a fair-thee-well to disguise how cheap it really was.

And they all played host to elves who were too low in rank and status to have estates, manor houses, and concubines of their own—or young elves, leashed and collared by their lord fathers, who likewise had nothing of the sort as their own. This—and the taverns like it, in this city and the other four trade-cities—was where the "legacies," the supervisors, the seneschals and trainers, came to forget the petty insults heaped upon them by their liege lords. This was where the "extra" sons and the disregarded heirs came, to forget that there was nothing that they would ever see or touch that was truly *theirs*.

This was where the former concubines, or young girls and boys too delicate to serve in the fields, but not comely enough to grace a harem or work as house slaves, also came. It was difficult to imagine a worse life than that of a field hand, but surely this was it. Especially for the traumatized, abused creatures waiting in those upper rooms. Lorryn tried not to think too hard about them; he was already doing what he could to change their fates.

Lorryn provided a sympathetic ear, and more important, a ready purse. (Many of them were kept on meager allowances by those so-careful lord fathers, generally an amount that was less than the cost of a good dog or a field hand.) He offered his wine and murmurs of understanding. That was common enough; they all shared their grievances, those who came here. What was uncommon was that he also provided a remedy.

Word of that remedy was spreading.

He had learned something fascinating during the hours he had spent in these places, where the air was scented with perfume to cover the odor of spilled wine, and the light was dim to hide the stains on the velvets and satins of the upholstery, the serving girls, and the clientele. His worst fear had been that one or more of the seemingly disgruntled would prove to be an informant, and that the game would be uncovered before it began. And surely one or more *had* been an informant—

But whether they informed out of fear or out of greed, when he actually gave them a way to even the odds with the Great Lords, when he *showed* them how ineffective magic was against his "talismanic" jewelry, they all turned. Each and every one of them turned against the lord they had been working for, passed over the gold, hid the necklace, headband, and armbands in the breast of his tunic, and walked out without a word.

Except, perhaps, to "inform" to someone else who had a lord as cruel, as indifferent, as sadistic as his own.

He had always known that the Great Lords were cruel to their underlings, but he had never, in all of his planning, guessed that they were *so* cruel that their liegemen would turn against them at the first opportunity. He had seen the gilded facade of their world, as he walked through it as Lord Tylar's son and heir. Beneath the languid manners, the pretty magics, the idle games, was a cruelty that was all the darker for being so completely casual, a cruelty that used up and disposed of humans and elves alike as if they were toys meant only to amuse an idle hour.

He sipped his wine, and sat in his back-corner booth, and waited for them to find him.

There had been a young lord—he must be a younger son, for he did not wear livery, and his clothing was of too high a quality to be an underling—sitting at a table nearby, drinking steadily, and watching him for the past hour. Now, finally, he rose to his feet, wove his way through the tables with surprising grace (considering the quantity of drink he'd been putting away), and settled himself onto the bench across from Lorryn, empty cup still in hand. He helped himself to the wine in Lorryn's pitcher without a by-your-leave, which further argued for a high position.

Lorryn simply nodded, and pushed the pitcher of wine closer to his new drinking companion.

The stranger took that as an open invitation, downed his cup in a single gulp, and poured it full afresh.

"Fathers," he said at last, sneering, and making the word a curse. "Tell you how important you are from the time you can walk, give you ev-everything you ask for right up until you co-come of age. *Then* what?"

"You tell me," Lorryn said blandly.

"Nothing, that's what!" The stranger emptied the cup again; this time Lorryn refilled it. "You come of age, and nothing changes! You're still 'the boy,' still have to come and go as you're bid! You want to ha-have a little fun, bring in some friends, and next thing you know, *he*'s got you hauled up in front of him like you were stealing from his money chest!"

"Ah," Lorryn replied wisely. "I know. You want to have a little manor of your own, a few slave-girls, you ask for it, and hoy! He acts like you'd spit on the names of your Ancestors!"

"Oh, aye!" the stranger agreed. "And just try and walk off the path, just a bit, just for a lark! *He's* on you, he's using his power on you as if you were his slave, his property! Bad enough he crushes you down to the ground, worse that he lays the Will-Lash on you! Next thing you know, he's threatening the Change on you, to make you mind!"

"To unmake your mind, you mean," Lorryn said, in a grim voice. *Ah, so that's what's set this one off. Not that I blame him, not after what Rena told me.* "Make you into some kind of puppet, dancing to *his* tune!"

"That's ex-exactly what he said!" the young elven lord said in surprise. " 'You dance to my tune, boy, with the Change or without it, so put your mind to it!' And next thing *I* know, he's got me betrothed to some whining, milk-faced girl who can't walk across a room without having vapors, who can't say three sensible words in a row, who—Ancestors, help me!—*faints* whenever she sees a man with his shirt off! What's she going to do when she sees more than that? And I'm *stuck* with her!"

"And if you choose to leave her in the bower, and find some fun elsewhere?" Lorryn prompted.

The young lord snarled. "It'll be the Change for me, my

lad. I'm to *do my duty by her, like a proper er-Lord*, that's what!" He poured another cup of wine, but this time he didn't drink it. Instead he leaned over the table and said, in a far different tone, "But I've heard there's a remedy for that situation."

Lorryn made patterns on the tabletop with his finger and a bit of spilled wine. Filigree patterns. "There might be—so I've heard," he said casually.

"I've heard there's a bit of jewelry that can keep someone from—having magic worked on him against his will." The er-Lord looked up through his long, pale eyelashes expectantly—and a little desperately.

"There might be. I've heard that." Lorryn completed his lacy pattern. "I've also heard there's something of a craze for patterned silver necklaces, armbands, headbands. Very popular among the young lords these days, I'm told. You might begin to wonder if the cure for your troubles is in that jewelry, eh?"

The stranger nodded eagerly. "You wouldn't know where I could find a dealer for some of that—would you? A man's got to keep up with the fashions."

Lorryn pretended to think about it. "You know, I might have a bit of that with me now," he replied. "I'd bought it for a friend, but I could let you have it right now for the same price. I can go find the maker again, easily enough, but he's a hard man for a stranger to find."

"And what would that price be?" Now the er-Lord was leaning forward so eagerly that Lorryn almost spoiled the entire deal by laughing out loud. He named the price, and the stranger pulled a purse off his belt and shoved it across the table.

"There's twice that in gold there," he said, his fingers twitching, as if he could not wait to get his hands on the jewelry. "Take it, take it all!" The desperation in his eyes overwhelmed the wine. Then again, who *wouldn't* be desperate, threatened with the Change?

Lorryn did not touch the purse; he carefully took a purse of his own from his belt, one containing silk-wrapped, silver-plated ironwork from the hands of Diric's people, and slid it across the table. The er-Lord snatched it up, hiding it in the breast of his tunic, and only then did Lorryn take the purse of gold.

"You'll want to test it, of course—for its *quality* and *workmanship*," he said. "There'll be a party three nights from now in the private room above the Silver Rose. If you show up there, wearing *that*, someone who's an expert in jewelry will look it over for you, and you might hear something more that's likely to interest you. And keep it in the silk until you need to use it, hey? You know how things—give themselves away. You give the game away, and you'll hurt more than yourself."

The er-Lord nodded, obviously impatient to be gone. Lorryn suppressed a smile. *He* was able to hear this one's thoughts as clearly as if he were shouting, which, in a sense, he was. That was how Lorryn knew who the would-be informants were—and knew when he had persuaded them to his side.

This young man could hardly wait to get his prizes home. He planned to wear them constantly, as so many of his friends were, hidden beneath the silk of his clothing as like as not. And he would be at that party, another set of willing hands to aid the revolt that Lorryn was planting the seeds of. Lorryn would not even be there—

He didn't have to. The ringleader of the revolt, at least in this city, was Lord Gweriliath's seneschal, a man who had seen his precious daughter sent away as a bride to another powerful lord more than old enough to be her great-grandsire, and all to pay one of Lord Gweriliath's gambling debts. Lorryn only needed to coordinate the revolt; the ringleaders sprang up of their own accord as soon as word of the power of the jewelry began to spread.

And Lorryn had hardly been able to restrain himself when he saw, this very morning, *copies* of the filigree jewelry showing up in shops—but in gold, of course, and with none of the detail and intricacy of the genuine article. Before long, the er-Lords themselves might just start plating the silver with gold, and no one would ever be able to tell the difference between the genuine article and the copies.

Except by the effect—or lack of it.

"I wish you well, sir," he said gravely, giving the young er-Lord the signal that the interview was over. "And do enjoy the party."

"I shall, trust me, I shall." And with that, the young elven lord was out of his seat and striding out of the room with no sign whatsoever that he had put away enough wine to knock out a cart-horse.

Lorryn waited a little longer, but the hour was late, and it appeared that this was going to be his final "customer" of the evening. He paid the tavern-keeper—and paid him generously. The tavern-keeper was a human, and under his livery tunic he wore a much simplified version of the filigree-work torque, a cross between the women's jewels and the warriors' torques. These were being turned out by the clever hands of human slaves, craftsmen bought with the gold the lords were paying for the prettier styles.

They were very popular with the slaves, although Lorryn was being *very* careful whom he sold—or gave—these little baubles to. It had to be to someone who had a strong grievance against his current or past masters—and yet someone who was unlikely to be on the receiving end of his current master's power. Shopkeepers were good prospects; tavern-keepers, some overseers, a concubine or two. These, Lorryn tested himself, heart and soul.

He left the half-finished pitcher of wine on the table, and went up to the third floor, bypassing the second altogether. Here was where the tavern-keeper had his own quarters, and where the offices were. And here the tavern-keeper had made a small apartment, which Lorryn lived in with his sister and with Mero.

He paused outside the door, and sent a delicate thought-touch to the occupant. Mero opened the door for him, and he slipped inside.

"Convenient, this wizard-power, when you're building a conspiracy," he remarked, as Mero returned to the task he had left, of carefully wrapping silver-clad iron in swaths of silk, then slipping the resulting packet into a pouch like the one Lorryn had just given the young er-Lord below.

"That's precisely why the elven lords have been trying to destroy the power for so long," Mero replied, but he looked more troubled than the simple remark called for.

"What's the matter?" Lorryn asked, answering Mero's frown of anger and worry with a frown of concern.

"Shana—has her hands full," came the slow reply. "Keman and Dora went off on some quest of their own just after we left, and as soon as they could manage it, Caellach Gwain and a good half of the wizards called a wizards' Council against her, the alliance with the Iron People, and anything else they could think of. They don't *believe* that the elven lords are going to come after them—and even if they did, Caellach has the old whiners all convinced that all they have to do is give Shana up to the elves and the danger will be over!"

Lorryn did not shout his anger—but his hands clenched into fists, and a hot rage burned up in him. "They have a flexible notion of honor," he drawled. "Almost as flexible as that of the elven lords."

Mero stared at him for a moment, then his mouth twitched involuntarily. "Can I quote you on that when I talk to her?" he asked. "That's too good a line of argument to waste."

Lorryn relaxed, just the tiniest trifle. If Mero was able to see the humor in something, the situation couldn't be a total disaster—at least, not yet.

She has her allies, and she's very powerful in her own right. The other dragons will support her. If she has to, she can escape before they can make her a prisoner. "Of course," he said, "and while you're at it—remind her to tell them that if the elven lords are treacherous enough to break the treaty in the first place, they are *certainly* treacherous enough to accept Shana, then attack anyway."

"A good point," Mero agreed. "Oh, I'm worried, but right now it's only at the talking point, and all the dragons are backing Shana, so the very worst that would happen would be that Alara would have to fly off with Shana and the rest of her followers, and take them all down to the Iron People."

Since that was precisely what Lorryn had just been thinking, he relaxed a little more. It was just the thought of Shana being in any danger at all that put his stomach in a knot. . . .

We're had so little time to get to know each other—but did Mero and Rena have more? And yet—I wish I knew what she was thinking, what she thought of me. What Rena and Mero had that we had none of was time alone. She and I have to keep thinking of things besides ourselves. . . .

"But taking her to the Iron People would lead the elves to Diric's clan," Lorryn pointed out. "And we pledged to avoid that. Is our honor no better than theirs?"

Mero grimaced. "Maybe—I don't know. Shana is worried, but not in a panic, so I can't worry too much. But that means that we are going to be pretty much on our own here."

There was another tap on the door; Lorryn sent an arrow of thought out, and relaxed when he recognized Rena. He nodded at Mero, who leapt out of his seat and made a dash for the door, opening it and seizing Rena to pull her inside with something that was as much embrace as it was anything else. He shut the door, and Lorryn politely averted his eyes as Mero made it into a real and wholehearted embrace.

I'm glad they found each other, he thought, wistfully. *I just wish—*

He didn't complete the wish. He had no idea if it would even be possible. Shana was an infuriating combination of everything he had ever hoped for in a woman—and everything he found maddening in any person. She was stubborn—*strong-willed*, his conscience reminded him—opinionated—*a leader*—too quick to speak her own mind—*intelligent*—impatient—*a fast thinker*—self-centered—*self-sufficient*—

Well, the list and litany could go on for hours. He could not get her out of his mind, though. Even when he should have been thinking of other things, he often dreamed about her at night, and found thoughts about her intruding during the day. He had made the excuse to Mero that his own mental powers were too feeble to reach her from elven lands, but the real reason he did not want to speak mind to mind with her was that he was afraid he would reveal his own decidedly mixed feelings about her. She could not afford the distraction, especially not now. And he—

I can't afford the distraction either. I'm walking a knife-edge here. And—I don't want to know how she feels. Not now. Maybe not for a long time. I—I just don't want to know if she does think of me as no more than another wizard. I'd rather cherish a few illusions for a while.

Besides, it wasn't as if *he* didn't have other things to think about!

Rena coughed politely, and he turned back to face them. They stood discreetly enough, side by side, but their hands kept creeping toward one another. He kept his eyes above the level of their hands.

"How did it go?" he asked.

Her face shone with pleasure at her own accomplishments. "Perfectly," she replied. "I showed my jewelry—they'd already been seeing it, of course, at fetes, and I told them where they could find it. I told Lunalia and Merynis the truth about it—their fathers are horrid people—and I slipped them pouches then and there. It's really dreadful; this was supposed to be a prebetrothal party for poor Lunalia. Her father's pledged her to some arrogant er-Lord who seems to think she should act like his *concubine*, and not even having vapors at the mention of anything indelicate or pretending to faint when he took off his shirt made him—" She stopped as Lorryn choked on laughter, and doubled up, gasping. "What *are* you laughing at?"

He told her about his last "customer," and had to hold on to a table when she started to giggle too.

She was *not* the gentle little ineffectual Sheyrena she had been—the Sheyrena who would have reacted to his laughter with indignation, and who probably would have burst into tears at the notion that he could have found Lunalia's plight funny. She'd found that spine he had wished she would grow, and he had a notion that she'd found it somewhere back in the alicorn-hills.

She wasn't "his" little Rena anymore, though. In a way, that made him a bit sad. She didn't look to him for a partner in jokes or a source of company—she looked to Mero.

Oh, it was natural and inevitable, but it also meant that little Rena had grown up. . . .

As if to underscore that point, she sobered. "The only thing is—Lunalia was the last," she said. "We agreed that I couldn't risk the private estates, because it would be too easy for me to be trapped there. That means there is only one more place on our list for me to go."

Mero froze, and Lorryn nodded. Their own work here was well started, the last of the five cities to plant their gardens of discontent in. All of the rest had a flourishing network of tiny shops, human slave-craftsmen silver-plating the Iron People's work and manufacturing the simpler versions, all overseen by a shape-changed dragon sent to them by Keman.

I wonder—could that have been the mysterious quest that Keman has gone off on? Mero didn't seem to know any of them, but they were dragons, no doubt about it. After Shana showed us how to spot a dragon-shadow, there is no way that we could be fooled on that score. Could Keman be recruiting more dragons somewhere?

Well, it didn't much matter, not unless Keman managed to recruit most of the dragons from most of the Lairs, before the revolt took place, and that wasn't too likely.

The point was, it was time for Rena to go home.

"You don't have to go," he reminded her, although anxiety cramped his insides every time he even *thought* about his mother. She was alive, at least; that much he knew, for he had it confirmed from several sources. Her pretense that her real son had been born dead, and a "changeling" substituted by the midwife, had been accepted. Her feigned madness had been accepted as well, and had freed her from further questioning. It was a terrible scandal, but no worse than that.

And she had been confined to a single building in the garden, rather than facing the full wrath of her lord and husband—and the wrath of the law, which would permit—no, *order*—him to execute her for knowingly giving birth to a halfblood.

As yet, there were no rumors to the effect that Rena had escaped with him. In fact, the only rumors he had heard were that her mother's collapse into madness and Lorryn's own betrayal had sent *her* into a decline. She was said to have taken to her bed and refused to wed Lord Gildor until the honor of her family was redeemed. *That* was as pretty piece of fiction, probably spread about by Lord Tylar himself.

"I have to go," she told him earnestly. "We both know that. I won't pretend that I'm not afraid, but at least he can't read my thoughts—and I *will* have my own jewelry to protect me if he strikes at me in a rage."

"But not if he lulls you into thinking that everything is all right, then orders his men to haul you off to some more powerful lord for—" He couldn't say it.

She tightened her lips, and tightened her grip on Mero's hand, but only said, "That's the risk I have to take. But I'm a *much* better actress than I was before. I think that I can make this work."

He sighed, and stepped forward to hug her, freeing one hand to pat Mero's shoulder as the young halfblood showed him the face of pure agony that he would *not* turn to his beloved. "If you say you can, I will believe it, sweeting. You are not the silly little girl who used to read romances in the garden, let her birds perch on her shoulders, and then have to hide the soiled gowns from her father in terror."

"Oh, I'm not so far removed from that as you might think," she whispered bravely into his ear. "Just now I have to hide a soiled past, rather than a soiled gown. Rather easier, actually."

He had to shake his head over that, as he let her go. "All right," he replied. "We'll proceed as we planned in the morning. Right now—I've got to go meet with a few people, then I'm going to go to bed. The transportation spell is going to take a lot out of me."

He turned and went back out into the hallway without a

single backward glance, leaving the two of them alone to make their good-byes however they chose.

And he actually managed to repress his envy enough to wish them both, sincerely, well.

He hadn't told Mero about this meeting; he'd intended to, because he would much rather have had someone to watch his back, but he couldn't bear to steal a single moment of Mero's time from Rena.

This time he was going out into the streets, with the reverse of his guise of a young elven lord. He was out there, after dark, as a human slave.

He kept his eyes on the ground ahead of him and his back hunched, but his neck prickled every time someone looked at him, or seemed to look at him, for more than a heartbeat. He didn't think anyone would be looking for halfbloods among the human slaves, but how could he be sure? He wished that slaves were allowed something like a hood to cover his ears, but he would have to trust to darkness for that.

His nerves didn't stop jumping until he finally reached his goal: a plain storefront with a sign of a green leaf above the door. The place looked closed up for the night, but when he tapped in a prearranged signal, the door opened for him.

He slipped inside and his contact closed the door behind him, quickly, leaving him standing in the darkness, shivering. "Come into the dispensary," came a low whisper. "I can strike a light there that won't be seen from the street."

He followed the sound of footsteps ahead of him, barking his shin on a bench and holding in a curse. A hand touched his arm, guiding him forward, and then he heard the sound of a second door closing.

A moment later, a lantern flared into life, revealing the man he had been asked to meet, as well as the contents of the room in which they found themselves.

His nose would have told him the contents of the room: herbs, more herbs than he could identify by odor, a mingled aroma of bitter and sweet, fragrant and pungent, and just plain odd. The room was lined with shelves covered with bottles, jars, and little boxes, carefully labeled. There was a waist-high table in the middle, covered with an immaculately white cloth.

His contact was a middle-aged man, balding, with a fringe of beard, and very fit-looking. What hair the man still had was curly and brown, like the beard. The only trouble was, he was fully human.

"I was told you have something," the man said abruptly. "Something that—something that blocks elven magic."

The back of Lorryn's neck prickled afresh. "Who told you that?" he asked cautiously. "And—why are you asking?" He'd assumed his contact would be another minor elven lord—and this man's thoughts, like those of many humans, were murky and chaotic with fear. Lorryn couldn't precisely read *what* his intentions were through the emotions.

But the human surprised him again; taking a deep breath, and steadying his *own* nerves to the point that his thoughts came clear again. Lorryn almost choked; where had this man acquired that kind of discipline?

"I heard—from your good host," the man replied carefully, and nothing in his mind contradicted that. "And as for *why* I want what you have—do you know what a 'physiker' is?"

Lorryn shook his head, dumbly.

"Elves don't sicken, but humans *do*, and of course, our mighty masters couldn't be bothered with tending to a sick slave," the man said bitterly. "Nor are they prepared to deal with the sick or the injured in their own dwellings. That is when they call for me—or more often, send the poor sufferer to me. Not that I can do much, but it's better than nothing, and nothing is what they'd get without me. I take care of your host's young ladies, when one of the young lords gets too careless with his toys."

Lorryn winced at the tone of the man's voice; the suppressed anger and hate alone spoke volumes—he knew, all in that moment, that this physiker had seen things that *he* simply did not want to know about. Hearing more tales of horror was not going to get his job done any faster—but he would end up with nightmares, and he couldn't afford that right now.

"So—you want protection, because some of the lords—" he began.

The physiker interrupted him with a snarl. "Not only have they punished me because I couldn't force someone to heal faster than nature would allow so they could get on with their amusements, they've tried to force me to do—things—" He choked, and Lorryn held up his hand in entreaty and resolutely shut his mind against the thoughts that beat against it.

"Please," he begged. "I'd rather not know; I can see that your need is genuine. Here—" He emptied out his pockets of every pouch he'd brought with him, a total of three. "Take these; you may know of others who could use them. If—"

He was about to say more, but was interrupted by someone pounding on the street door.

The physiker froze, and so did Lorryn. The pounding stopped, then began again.

"Bryce!" bellowed an angry voice. *"Open up!"*

The physiker leapt into action, and shoved at Lorryn, pushing him toward a waist-high basket with a few bloodstained towels in the bottom of it. "Get in there!" he hissed, pulling the towels out and forcing Lorryn to crouch down below the level of the rim, with the three pouches dropped in after. "Don't move if you value your life!"

He covered Lorryn with the towels, draped (so Lorryn hoped) to cover him completely, then hurried to answer the pounding.

"I'm coming, I'm coming!" he shouted, as the light moved out of the room—Lorryn guessed that he was taking the lantern with him.

The door slammed against the wall as soon as Bryce opened it, and whoever it was stormed into the outer room. "Who'd you let in, just now?" the harsh voice demanded. "Somebody with a wound, maybe? Or something else he doesn't want the Master to know about?" The man's tone turned raspy and dangerous. "You remember what happened the last time you played that little game, Bryce. This time they might not let you keep that hand—"

"If you must know," the physiker replied testily, "I wasn't

letting anyone *in*, I was letting—her—out. One of the wine-girls from the Silver Rose. She has—ah—a slight infection of a personal nature." Lorryn had to admire the way the man coughed and flustered, as if he were embarrassed. "I was—ah—treating her—ah—as a favor, you might say."

The other man remained silent for a moment, then broke into a gale of laughter. "She, huh? A *personal* problem? You sly old dog, I didn't think you had it in you! Or have you got somethin' in those leaves of yours to *get* it in you?"

Bryce coughed again, and the man laughed even harder. "Next time, you ask the Master before you go treating *personal* problems. Otherwise I just might bust in here before you've let her out so I can get some of that fun for myself."

The door slammed again, and the heavy boot-steps retreated.

The light returned, and Bryce pulled the towels off him. "You'll have to go out the rooftop now," the man said, his face white in the dim light of the lamp that trembled in his hand. "He'll be watching the front. I hope you can climb—come, I'll get you out and you'll have to take care of yourself from there—"

He was babbling with fear, a fear that made him literally sick, and the images in his mind told Lorryn why he was so afraid. Lorryn swallowed his own nausea and kept his mouth shut.

He couldn't get out of there quickly enough—even if it meant a harrowing climb across the roofs. Anything was better than being in the same room with a man with *those* memories in his mind. . . .

Sheyrena dressed carefully in a purposefully soiled and torn gown, one she had prepared herself for this ruse. It had to look as if she had trekked across the wilderness in it, and not willingly, either. Instead of shoes, though, she wore a pair of worn-out old boots that could have belonged to Lorryn, with rags stuffed into the toes to make them fit. No shoes she owned would have survived the trip she was going to describe to Lord Tylar, and she would claim to have stolen the boots from Lorryn.

She and Mero had worked out every detail of her story, from the point where Lorryn talked her into coming for a morning walk with him to the point where she escaped from him, stealing his boots both to protect her own feet and prevent him from following her, and traveled alone, back along the route he had taken. Inside her gown, sewn into the body of her petticoat, she had two sets of the iron jewelry, one for herself, and one for her mother.

Myre would become, in this tale, Lorryn's willing accomplice and his contact with the wizards. Why not? It would certainly account for her presence in the boat, for a third figure had surely been seen, and it would also account for her *absence* after she fell out of it. That would also be why Lorryn had not gone straight to the wizards, but had wandered around on his own—without her, he had no guide. Anything that anyone overheard in that brief period between the moment when the pursuers had sighted the boat and the moment when it flew out of sight that might indicate that Rena had been encouraging Lorryn could easily be attributed instead to Myre.

"Are you ready?" Lorryn asked. She nodded, unable to force herself to speak. Mero was lying down with his eyes closed; that was because Lorryn was going to take all of *his* magic power and most of his own to send her straight to the border of Lord Tylar's land. The transportation spell, as modified by the wizards and taught to Mero, then taught by Mero to Lorryn, was not as "noisy" as the version Shana had used. The trick was that the person actually casting the spell had to remain behind, and the "noise" remained with him. In a big city such as this one, where there were hundreds, even thousands of spells being cast each day, another burst of magical "noise" would not be noticed.

Mero was actually better at this than Lorryn, but it was Lorryn who knew where Rena had to go, so it was Lorryn who must cast the spell, and it would take its direction from his mind.

As soon as Mero recovered, he would journey by more conventional means to Lord Tylar's estate, where he would wait for Rena and Lady Viridina with horses and supplies. Lorryn had insisted on that part of the plan, knowing that Mero would fret himself to pieces—and be all but useless—if he was not somewhere nearby, where he could help at need. It would be dangerous for him, certainly, but no more dangerous than remaining here with only half of his mind on keeping himself hidden from those searching for halfbloods.

"Take a deep breath and close your eyes," Lorryn said, and Rena obeyed him. She sensed power gathering around her, twisting and turning as Lorryn sent it through the amber globe in his hand as Mero had taught him, twisting and turning around *her.*

Then there came a flash of light so bright that she saw it through her closed eyelids.

Then, *nothing.*

No sound, no light, no air, no *floor*—she was falling, falling, she was going to fall forever! Her stomach churned as it had when Kalamadea had hit what he called an "air pocket" and plummeted three times his own length before he got back under control. She thought she screamed, but she couldn't hear herself; thought she stretched out her hands, but she couldn't even feel her own body!

Then, with no warning, she was *there*, feet planted firmly in the grass beside a tall, golden-yellow wall. She stood in the middle of a bare-earth bridle path, with grass on either side of it, in a place she knew as well as she knew her own room. She and Lorryn had been here a hundred times on their rides—there was the apple tree they always used to shade them in the summer when they stopped for a picnic meal, the grass beneath it long and rank, as if no one had tended it in some time. The leaves on the tree were just turning, a reminder that she and Lorryn had escaped in the spring, and now it was already fall.

She had forgotten how far it was to the gate from here—and she was afoot, not riding, wearing boots that were far too big for her, even with rags stuffed in the toes and more rags wrapped around her feet. She shivered as a cool autumn breeze cut through her ragged dress, and the iron jewelry felt very heavy around her waist.

Well, here I am.

And she wasn't going to get anything done by standing there.

With a tiny sigh, she trudged up the path. With luck, she might meet with some of the guards and save herself some blisters.

But no guards appeared—*of course, they never show up when you really want them to*—and her feet were sore enough to give ample evidence to the truth of her story when at last she reached the gate. She didn't *think* they were blistered, but if she got away with this, the very first thing she was going to do would be to have a good hot bath and a foot-rub!

The gate loomed much larger than she remembered it, but then again, her memory now was colored by living in the wilderness and in the tents of the Iron People. Many buildings seemed large now, compared to the tents. Made all of bronze, it boomed hollowly when she rapped on it timidly.

The gate swung open on her second knock, revealing a half-dozen fully armed guards behind it. *Elven* guards, not human, which said more than any words how Lorryn's escape had affected Lord Tylar. He no longer trusted anything important to human slaves, it seemed.

She clasped her hands before her, looked down at the ground, and said in a tired voice that did not need any acting, "Please, could I speak with my father, Lord Tylar?"

"Your *what*?" began one of the guards, as another laughed—but a third cursed and shut the other two up.

"By the Ancestors," he swore, "it's *her*! Sheyrena!"

She hadn't really hoped for gentle treatment—not until they knew she was fully of elven blood, anyway—but she hadn't quite expected to be bound hand and foot and slung facedown over a horse's back. She hadn't expected to be galloped up to the door of the manor, with the jewelry digging painfully into her skin, and her upset stomach being jounced worse than *any* dragon-flight had jostled it.

That, coming on top of the effect of the transportation spell, was just too much. When the guards reached the front door of the manor and manhandled her down off her perch, she threw up on the boots of the nearest.

She took small comfort in the fact that it was the one who had insisted on carrying her in that undignified position in the first place. He swore and kicked at her; she fell back, avoiding the kick. He aimed another at her, but before his foot connected, the sound of the door slamming open and an angry shout froze him where he stood.

"What is the meaning of this?"

Lord Tylar stood framed in his own marble doorway, glaring down at the guards gathered there. They moved aside, quickly, revealing a trembling and miserable Sheyrena huddled at the feet of one of their number.

Lord Tylar's face turned a lush crimson, which went very badly with his pale gold hair and green eyes. "You!" he spat. "How *dare* you show up here again?"

"F-f-father?" she faltered, ready tears springing to her eyes, for she really *did* feel entirely awful. "F-f-father? I—Lorryn fell asleep, and I hit him on the head and stole his boots and—"

He gestured, and the words froze in her mouth; *now* she was glad that she had insisted the iron jewelry be swathed in silk so that none of its protection would reach her. The success of her ruse depended entirely on her vulnerability to Lord Tylar's initial spells.

"You *dare* to claim to be the daughter of my body?" he spat. "We will see about that!" And with those words, he cast his second spell, which she assumed must be the one that broke illusions.

Of course, she remained precisely as she was, a huddled, wretched mess in a torn gown, dirty, tear-stained, and sick, but entirely, completely, indisputably *elven*.

And Lord Tylar, who had assumed right up to this very moment that his daughter was a halfblood just as his "son" was, stared with his mouth falling open.

But only for a moment; he recovered quickly from his

shock. He had not become the kind of power he was by being a complete dolt, after all.

And now he turned his anger on another target: the guards. *"You!"* he raged, although his face was no longer scarlet. "You imbeciles! How *dare* you treat my daughter like this! I'll see you broken to sweeping stables for this!"

And before the guards could react, he himself was down the steps and stooping to help Rena to her feet; cutting the ropes that bound her hands and feet with his own belt-dagger.

"Oh, *Father!"* she sobbed, and flung herself at his feet, to cling to them and weep into the leather of his boots. "Father, it was so *horrible!* Lorryn was—Lorryn is—"

As she had expected, since any display of emotion horrified him, and hysteria made him desert the scene of the uncomfortable outpouring immediately, he backed hastily away. "You—you—" he said, pointing at two of the guards as Rena watched covertly through her lowered eyelashes. "Take my daughter to her chamber. Instruct the slaves to attend to her every need, and gown her according to her station. *Now,* you fools!"

And he turned and fled back into the hall, leaving the poor, bewildered guards to help her to her feet again—very gingerly this time, as if they were afraid to touch her—and guide her to her own rooms.

The maids were already waiting—all new ones, which somehow didn't surprise her much—and the guards released her into their hands with ill-concealed relief. As they undressed her, Rena found the opportunity to slip the packets of iron jewelry into the old hiding place in her bed where she used to keep books. Within a few moments, Rena was sinking back into that longed-for tub of hot water, with a maid attending to each hand and two more to each foot, and another to wash and untangle her artistically tangled and dirtied hair.

It was altogether lovely, and she gave herself up into their hands with a sigh of bliss. The maids twittered to each other like a flock of her little birds, exclaiming over her roughened hands and sore feet, and the state of her hair.

"My lady!" one kept saying, as she mended the damaged

nails as best she could. "My lady, how could you do this to your pretty white hands?"

As if I had nothing to worry about in the howling wilderness except care for my nails! She had to bite her lip to keep from laughing.

Eventually they finished with her, dressed her in a gown of a soft rose color, and sent her on her way to her father's study. They had offered her a drink that she suspected was meant to tranquilize her; she accepted it, and surreptitiously poured it into a vase after pretending to drink from it. Their expressions of satisfaction confirmed her suspicion, and she took care to act relaxed and just a bit giddy when she made her way between two much-chastised guards to the study.

But as the door opened, she discovered that her father was not alone, and she was *very* glad that she did not have the jewelry on her person. She did not know these lords by name, but their faces told her all that she needed to know about them. Such arrogance only came with the greatest of power.

She made a deep, though unsteady, curtsy, and did not rise until her father gave her leave, in a voice that betrayed his pleasure at her action.

"These are two High Lords from the Council, Sheyrena," he said, speaking slowly, as if she were a child, or feeble-minded. Or both! "Tell us all what happened to you at the hands of the monster that stole you away."

One of the High Lords brought her a chair, which she sank into gratefully; in a trembling and hesitant voice, she told her story, beginning with Lorryn supposedly coming to her room with her maid to take her on a sunrise picnic, and ending with her "escape" from the terrible halfblood, stealing his boots so that he could not pursue her, and retracing the path she had memorized even in her terror.

"He was going to sell me to the wizards, Father," she cried, her voice shaking, not with suppressed tears as they supposed, but with suppressed laughter. "He told me that he was going to sell me to the wizards, to feed to their dragons! He told me that dragons would only eat maidens, and—"

She couldn't stand it anymore; she hid her face in her

hands, and her shoulders shook as she laughed silently. The three lords conversed among themselves as she strove to get herself under control again.

Finally she raised her head from her hands, and, sniffing bravely, she faced them again.

"It all fits," she heard one of them say in an undertone; her father and the other one nodded.

"You have been a good and a brave child, Sheyrena," said the one who had spoken, in a voice as unctuous as massage-oil and as sweet as treacle. "You are a credit to your father and to the name of your House."

She bowed her head submissively, and the unctuous one turned back to Lord Tylar. "By your leave, my lord, we will return to the Council with these tidings."

He nodded; they turned and left through the Portal door.

As soon as they were gone, he chuckled. Sheyrena raised her eyes, feigning shyness.

"You have done very well, Sheyrena," he said, and studied her. He blinked once or twice, as if in surprise. "I do believe that your ordeal has actually *improved* your looks, girl!" he exclaimed, in a voice full of astonishment. "By the Ancestors, you actually are *attractive!*"

"Thank you, Father," she replied meekly; she flushed with anger, but dropped her eyes so that he would assume that it was a blush of embarrassment.

"This—this all puts a new complexion on things," he muttered, and drummed his fingers on his desk. "You are of full elven blood, and now my only heir—your value as a marriage-piece is a great deal higher than when you were stolen. Hmm."

He got up from his desk, came around to her side, and put a finger under her chin, tilting it up so that he could study her face. "Hmm," he repeated, as she veiled her eyes with her lashes to hide her anger. "Add to that the fact that you're no longer a little cream-faced loon, but a handsome little thing—your value is even greater."

He allowed her to drop her head again, and stood beside

her chair. She didn't reply, but he didn't seem to expect her to.

"You may go," he finally said, abruptly.

She took him at his word, rose unsteadily, curtsied, and fled. And once she was back in the safety of her own chamber, she took the packets of jewelry from their hiding places, and quickly "concealed" them in the best of all hiding places, and the one place no man would ever look—

—in the midst of all the other jewelry in her valuables chest.

Then, and only then, did she strip off her gown without calling for her maids, slip into her bed in her petticoat, and fall into an exhausted sleep.

Her father woke her—or rather, her maids did, fluttering about, agitated beyond measure that he was waiting outside and *she* was in no state to receive him! In something of a fog, she let them gown her again, and brush out her hair; the very instant she was "decent," he swept in with all the high drama of a state entrance.

"Have your maids pack up your things, Sheyrena," he said to her. "You are moving to the bower."

She stared at him stupidly; he smiled, the smile of someone who is doing what he wants and thinks he is conferring a tremendous favor.

"You are my only right-born child, Sheyrena," he said, ponderously, and he held out a hand. She put her own in his, not really knowing what he wanted, and he set a ring of keys into it—the same ring of keys she had seen her mother wearing, for as long as she could remember.

"You are the lady of the House," he told her. "*You* now have charge of the bower and the household." At her look of naked shock and dismay, he laughed. "Oh, don't worry, child—it's only an honor and a title. The slaves really see to it all. You only need to see to it that the slaves know to come to you for their orders, and I will tell you what to tell them."

"Yes, Father," she faltered.

His smile broadened. "You are far too valuable to waste on

the likes of Lord Gildor," he said, sounding very pleased with himself. "I have sent my regrets to Lord Gildor, telling him that you are too precious to me now, and that I cannot bear to be without your comfort and company. I have dissolved the betrothal."

"You have?" She stared at him; she would not have believed that he would go *that* far!

He mistook her astonishment for dismay. "Oh, don't be disappointed, child! You are worth ten Gildors now! No, now, listen to me closely."

She shut her mouth, and kept her face carefully schooled into the appearance of attentiveness.

"I am going to find you a marriage-alliance that will put our House in the ranks of the High Lords," he told her gleefully. "*You* have a job to do, a very important one. You must *not* allow this present attractiveness to fade, and that is an order! I want you to rise every morning, put yourself right into the hands of your maids, make yourself presentable, and keep yourself that way! None of these afternoon naps, when you can't be viewed! No disappearing for long rides! Don't go hiding in the garden as if you were a child! Is that understood?"

"Yes, Father," she replied, flushing again with anger. And, predictably, he interpreted the anger as embarrassment.

"Now, Sheyrena, don't be upset," he said, in what he probably thought was a coaxing tone. "I'm not angry with you, but you aren't a child anymore, and you are far too important to the House now to play your childish games. Just do as you are told, and things will work out wonderfully for you. Just wait and see!"

"Yes, Father," she replied, still flushed.

"I have decided, now that virtually every lord on the Council knows your name and your story, to announce that you are free for betrothal at the next Council meeting. It will make a pleasant diversion for everyone from our final preparations for war against the wizards. I will be able to marshal my forces beside those of whoever becomes your lord." He beamed, as if he had thought of something terribly clever. "I shall—ah—put you up for bid, so to speak. And I do expect the bidding to be brisk!"

"But Lord Gildor—" she said, unable to think of anything else to say.

"Hah!" He laughed. "Put him from your mind. I don't know who your husband-to-be will be, yet, but you can take it as written that whoever he is, he will be as high above Lord Gildor as Lord Gildor is above the chief of my guards!"

But all that Rena could think—could hope—was that Mero would be able to read all of this from her thoughts, for she had no other way to send him this all-important message. The elves were about to break the treaty and the truce—months before any of them had thought possible!

Shana fumed, as she stood before the assembled wizards in the bare cavern they used for their meeting place, wanting very much to knock sense into several heads with a large and heavy stick! Especially the head of Caellach Gwain—and why had he chosen to take this line *now*, when he had been the one howling about the danger of the elven lords only a few months ago?

And how is Lorryn doing, and what is Lorryn doing, and why do I never hear from him, only from Mero? Does he— would he—damn it all, Shana, keep your mind on your enemies! But—he's in the midst of the worst of those enemies—

"I am telling you, I have it nearly from the mouth of one of the High Lords of the Council himself!" she growled, biting off the words savagely. "The elves know where we are, they are *going* to attack, and they are going to do it soon! They're coordinated enough to put up a Portal to bring their troops right to our doorstep!"

"Oh, please," said Caellach Gwain, waving a hand languidly. "This is an old tale, and we're weary of hearing it. *We* haven't seen any signs of this so-called mustering of troops you've been ranting about."

"That's *because*," she snarled impatiently, "the troops are all being mustered on the *estates* of three of the High Lords who *you* have been afraid to watch!"

"And who is this informant of yours?" Caellach asked shrewdly.

She didn't answer at first. They wouldn't believe her, even though they had seen Rena themselves, if only briefly. They would never believe Rena could keep her head long enough to be of any use as a spy. "I'm not about to blurt out any names when there might be a traitor among you!" she snapped.

"Oh? This is nothing more than a ruse to take our minds off the important matter of a treaty negotiated with dangerous barbarians—negotiated without permission of the Citadel as a whole, might I add." Caellach looked disgustingly proud of himself. She glanced over at Denelor and Parth Agon; the former shrugged helplessly, the latter cast his eyes up to heaven. Caellach Gwain did not have enough votes to cause her serious trouble, but he *did* have enough of the wizards on his side to embroil them in this nonsense until the elven armies were at their very door!

Once again, as she gazed out at those fat, fatuous faces, she heard Mero's voice in her mind, giving her the bad news he had in turn heard from Sheyrena. In a panic, she had spent all of the energy she dared in trying to send that same message on to Keman, but she had no real idea if he had heard, nor where he was if he had.

It would be just her luck that he and that lady friend of his had decided to flit off somewhere together out of reach of everything and everyone. Or perhaps they had gone back south to *her* Lair, to gain "courting consent" from her parents. . . .

Now, as she listened to the same idiocy that had kept her penned in this chamber, day after day, unable to accomplish *anything* productive, her temper snapped.

She stood up, right in the middle of one of Caellach's speeches, slamming the palm of her hand on the table. He stopped in midsentence, shock on his face at her rudeness.

"*You* can blather about this from now until you're cut down by elven blades, if you want," she spat. "*I* am going to try to do something about it."

"With what?" Caellach sneered.

"With us," Kalamadea replied, standing up himself, as every other shape-changed dragon in the place did the same. "Even if it is only to make plans to flee, with those who are wise enough to come with us,"

Caellach gaped at him, openmouthed at the revolt of the dragons. "But—" he spluttered impotently. "But—"

"But I don't think that will be necessary," came a voice from the door, a voice so hoarse with weariness that Shana did not even recognize it. Until she turned, and saw—

Keman. And behind Keman, a dozen, two dozen—three, four—she lost count of how many strangers there were behind him.

All of them with dragon-shadows.

"Shana, here are your new allies," he said, as Alara exclaimed in surprise and joy and ran to embrace not only her son but a tall and handsome, ebony-haired man who stood at Keman's side. "Here are dragons from our Lair, O'ordila'i's Lair, Hali'a's Lair, Teomenava's Lair—"

He named off a half-dozen more Lairs as Shana stood there, so stunned that she couldn't even speak.

"We'll form the force on the right flank," he continued. "Dora has gone to the Iron People, and Diric should be able to bring his mounted warriors in to be our left flank before the elven armies themselves show up."

"We can plant wedges of iron that will disrupt the elven plan to bring the Portal up right on your doorstep," the black-haired man said with a grin. "Our best rock-melders are bringing it up out of the earth now in fist-sized nodules, and we're flying it out here and dropping bits of it along the way. We think we'll have enough to seed the forest for a day's march all around."

"That leaves your forces to form the rear of the trap," Keman continued hoarsely, and turned to Caellach Gwain. It was at that point that Shana was struck by the realization that Keman was no longer a "boy," by any standards. He was thinking and acting for himself, taking responsibility, and willing to live with the consequences.

She saw by the look on Alara's face that the same conclusion had just struck her on the nose as well.

Her little baby is no longer little, nor a baby. . . . Like every mother, everywhere, her offspring had been a child to her long past the time when that ceased to be true.

"Now, you can do what you please, Lord Wizard," Keman continued, "and you can *believe* what you will. But an army of Iron People and another of dragons believe that Shana is right, and you fools are in deadly peril, and we are willing to help her. Now, we have a saying among the dragons—"

He stared at Caellach Gwain with a gaze as sharp as a sword-blade, and the old wizard actually shrank back from him.

"*—lead, follow, or get out of my flight-path,*" he said forcefully. "Now, which is it going to be?"

The old wizard sank down into his chair, keeping any further protests behind his teeth.

Keman bowed ironically to him, then gestured to Shana. "I believe the lightning now comes to you, foster sister," he said, with a weary twinkle in his eye. "I shall leave it to you and my friends here. *I* have done a great deal of flying in the past few hours, and I want to sleep for a week!"

"The Council meeting," Lorryn said, to the room full of quiet young elves. The tavern had been closed to outsiders for tonight; only those with an iron necklace were allowed inside. They were all arrayed on every seat, every bench, every space where there was sitting room. He alone stood, in the center of the room, and every emerald eye was on him. "Every lord of any importance in *their* eyes is going to be there, and they plan to go right into battle from the meeting. That leaves the field clear for you, all of you, to act while *they* are all stuck in the Council Hall, leagues and leagues from anywhere, with little transportation, few followers, and no way to communicate to their estates. There are only three High Lords who *won't* be there—the three who are going to open the Portals and send their slave armies through while the Council is in session."

"And all of those are sending their heirs to the Council," one of the er-Lords who had been part of the planning from the beginning chuckled. "They'll be as cut off as the rest of them when the er-Lords close *their* Portals behind them as they pass through."

"The rest of you have to manufacture excuses to be on your lords' or fathers' estates when the Council Meeting takes place," Lorryn told the rest of them. "We'll give you each a wedge of iron to spike the Portal with; after that, it will be sealed for all intents and purposes. I suggest that you hide it well; your fathers and lords may have a loyal underling or two who can't be persuaded to come over. Don't waste time trying to find them. Get to the human fighters and take them over. Throw out anyone who won't swear to you. After that?" He shrugged. "I've given you all the advice I can. Hold the estates for yourselves. You ought to be able to—anyone you shield with the jewelry will be protected from direct magic, so all that will be left to your fathers and uncles and liege lords is force. You'll have your humans; they won't. And by then, it will be too late to recall all the human fighters that were sent through the Portals."

"An even chance is all we need," said one of them, his eyes gleaming. He wasn't a young lord, either. He must have been one of those with little or weak magic, and as a result, the grudge he carried was probably centuries in the brewing. "That's all we've ever asked for."

"Aye to that," said another.

Lorryn nodded, and rubbed the side of his head wearily. Would this all work? And what was going on with Shana? The last he'd heard, through his craftsmen, Keman had recruited more dragons, but did she *know* that the armies were coming? Could even a sky full of dragons prevail against the numbers that were coming?

And for that matter, was she even in charge anymore?

It didn't matter; events had gotten away from them all. Now they had to act or be run over by them.

"You all know what to do—" he said, waving at them in dismissal. He had more of these meetings to hold, even as his draconic friends were holding similar meetings in the other four cities. "It's up to you how you do it."

And up to the rest of us to make the most of it.

Ah, Shana—I could use your stubborn good sense right now!

Rena had been a very, very obedient little girl, remaining meek and pliant in every way while Lord Tylar ordered her about. She hoped to lull any suspicions that he might have had by never mentioning Lady Viridina in his hearing, and never directly asking about her to the slaves.

He must have suspected *something*—or perhaps the habit of suspecting everyone had become so ingrained that he could not drop it even if he wanted to—for he took care that she was never alone, even though she thought she was going to scream with frustration.

Finally, though, she had a respite, if an eleventh-hour respite. He was too busy today preparing for the Council Meeting to watch her himself, and as nearly as she could tell, he had not set anyone to watch her. For the first time since she had come back to the estate, she was alone.

It might be her last and only chance, and she was going to take it.

She dared not wear her jewelry, though—she herself was going to have to work magic, and the magics guarding her mother's garden-tower were likely rigged to set off mechanical alarms if they were made to fail. So she took both packets still swathed in their insulation of silk, hid them in her gown, and slipped out of the bower with the silence of a stalking Iron Clan warrior.

Or so she fondly hoped, at any rate.

She slipped along the hallways, as cautious as a cat; she passed through the magic-barriers that Lord Tylar had placed around the bower with no trouble, although she had feared that they might stop her. Her father had told her they were *supposed* to be for her safety—in case Lorryn came after her again—but she was not going to take anything Lord Tylar said at face value.

Now she passed through corridors made more for use than for show, heading for the herb and kitchen gardens. In theory, since she was in charge of the household, she had every right and duty to go there. In actuality—it would be hard to explain her presence to anything above a household slave.

In the middle of the kitchen garden, some wag of an architect had set a prison-tower for the confinement of anyone Lord Tylar wanted out of the manor, but near enough to keep a personal eye on. It hadn't been in use in Rena's lifetime, but she'd heard of recalcitrant underlings who had spent brief but uncomfortable visits there. It was supposed to be escape-proof, provided the person kept there was less than Lord Tylar in magical power.

Or provided that the person kept there had no allies with *any* magical power on the outside.

The sun-drenched expanse of vegetables and herbs in their neat and mathematically patterned beds seemed very large as she peered out the door into the bright light. And there in the middle was the tower—very pretty to look at, all of white marble, stretching up toward the sun, a round, slender white column, fluted and sculptured, its whiteness marred by nothing like a window anywhere along its height.

But it seemed that her father had stripped every slave that he could from the household to serve in his army—evidently it was numbers that counted, not skill with weapons. There was only one slave picking cabbages at the foot of the tower, and no one else anywhere in the garden. Rena waited in the shelter of the door until the slave finished her work and hurried toward the kitchen door.

Now I know why the house has sounded so quiet, so odd. Father probably took every male slave we had and sent them off to make up his share of the forces. He may even have taken the brawniest of the females as well! No matter that they've never held anything but an eating knife; I doubt that matters to him. There are always more, waiting in the breeding sheds.

She thought about the humans she had come to know in the tents of the Iron People: Diric, Kala, the new War Chief.

She thought about the craftsmen, who were not warriors, and how ill suited they would be to fight. She thought about all those people being herded off to die like so many cattle, but without the care and dignity granted to the Iron People's cattle, and she burned with rage.

She had hated her father before, but this hatred was no longer personal—it was for everything he and every lord on the Council stood for.

She waited a moment longer, fighting her anger—both to see if the slave came back out to the garden and to get herself back under control. As long as she was this angry, she *could* be distracted; she could not afford to be distracted.

Finally the anger subsided to a slow burning in her heart; she took a deep breath and strolled out into the garden as if she had a perfect right to be there.

The door was on the opposite side of the tower from the manor; she walked with simulated carelessness up the pathways of round gravel, paced around the base, and stepped up onto the white marble stoop, all without once spotting anyone who might have been set to watch. She studied the lock to the door with her eyes closed, as Mero had taught her, but it was a lot simpler than she had expected it to be. Perhaps for a male, unused to working magic at so fine and controlled a level, it would have been very difficult to open—but for a female, well, it was easier than sculpting the feathers on a living bird.

She had it open in a moment; she slipped inside, and closed the door behind her.

The bottom story was quite empty: one echoing white marble room, with that sourceless light that illuminated most elven-made dwellings. She listened then, straining her ears against the silence, trying to determine if there was more than one occupant here. Talk among the slaves indicated that Lady Viridina was not even allowed a single body servant and had to tend to all her needs herself, but talk among the slaves was not always accurate.

She heard footsteps, faint and far above, but there was only one set of them. Someone was pacing, around and around the round wall of the tower, but it was only one person.

Silently Rena slipped up the stairs, pausing to peek over the edge of the next floor to see what was there.

This room was like the one below, except that it held a marble table, and a single chair. There was no one here, either, but as Rena moved up into the room itself, she saw a tray of partially eaten bread and a pitcher of water on the table. The bread did not look particularly fresh, and it was the coarse brown bean-bread generally fed to slaves.

Clever.

She headed for the next set of stairs, and once again paused to listen. The footsteps sounded as if they were directly above her now.

She got halfway up the stairs before the footsteps stopped, suddenly.

"Who is there?" Lady Viridina called sharply.

Rena couldn't stop herself; she ran up the rest of the stairs, heedless of the fact that her mother might not be alone.

But Lady Viridina *was* alone; dressed in a simple gown of bleached fustian, the kind a slave might wear, her hair confined in a single neat braid, with no sign of the fine lady she had once been. She stared at Rena—made a sign, and Rena felt the tingle of magic that told her a spell had just passed over her—then ran to take her daughter into her arms, babbling and sobbing as incoherently as if she *had* been mad.

Then again, Rena was doing the same thing.

When they both got themselves under control—and in a much shorter period of time than Rena would have thought—Lady Viridina held her daughter at arm's length and shook her as if she were once again a naughty child.

"What are you doing here?" she scolded. "Don't you know that *no one* is supposed—"

"I'm getting you out of here, Mother," Rena replied, interrupting her, although she did not pull away from the admonishing hands. "Listen to me—there isn't much time to explain."

Lady Viridina did listen, as Rena made a brief explanation of how she and Lorryn had escaped, how they had met the Iron People and learned of the protective power of their jewelry, and how they had finally joined forces with the wizards. "That's what I have here," she said, pulling one of the packets out of the breast of her gown with difficulty. That was the problem with fashionable gowns—there was nowhere to put anything. "Here, this is some of it. You put this on, and we'll cross the garden to where Mero is waiting and—"

"Not this time!" With a burst of power that left her nerves jangling, Lord Tylar appeared in the center of the room as if he had been brought there by magic—which, of course, he had. Rena was familiar enough now with the transportation spell to know what it "felt" like.

If his face had been scarlet with rage when she first appeared on the doorstep, it was purple now, and he came at Rena, not with magic, but with his bare hands.

She tried to evade him, but he had been a trained warrior in his youth and he still kept in practice. With a single powerful blow of his fist, he knocked her across the room and into the marble wall.

Her body hit the wall first, knocking all the breath out of her, and her head followed a moment later, sending black waves of stars across her eyes, and leaving her stunned and unable to draw in air. She lay there in pain, trying to gasp, hands clawing at the bare marble, as with a tiny part of her mind she heard the jangle of the jewelry her mother had been holding and the clatter as she dropped it to the floor at his feet.

Rena shook her head to clear her eyes, and the movement must have cleared something else as well, for suddenly she could breathe again. She pulled in a long, cool gasp of air, coughed, and pulled in a second, then looked up, trying to make her mind work again.

Her father stood with his back to her, stiff with anger. Her mother huddled against the far wall, her face white with terror and shock. There was a gleam of silk and silver on the floor under his foot.

"Now I am going to kill you, woman," Lord Tylar hissed. "I am finally going to be rid of you, and no one will say me nay—"

His hands shot out and he seized her by the shoulders before Rena knew what he was doing. In the next instant, he threw her to the floor, where she lay limp and boneless. As he turned, Rena saw his face.

It was no longer purple, or even scarlet. It was white, pale as the marble of the walls, and as controlled as if he were talking about inconsequential Council gossip among his friends. And when he spoke again, his voice was controlled, too, and so cold that it might have frosted the marble. Rena shuddered, and her mother hid her head in her arms.

"I am going to kill you," he repeated. "But I am going to do more than that. I am going to *annihilate* you. I am going to destroy you so completely that nothing of you will remain to show that you ever lived. And I am going to take my time about it."

He smiled.

And a voice echoed through Rena's mind—only now she knew who the voice belonged to, and why she had seemed familiar to the speaker.

If you can change a flower petal, what else can you change? Could you, perhaps, stop a heart?

And again from a time much nearer at hand: *It's not a power to use lightly, but sometimes—sometimes you aren't given a choice. If, by using that power, you could save an innocent life—*

Taking the first as an omen, and the second as a benediction, Rena did for her mother what she would never have dared do for herself. Lord Tylar was armored and warded against magic attack—

But his foot was touching the iron of the necklace, and the silk packet had fallen open. There was leather between him and the necklace, but it still might be *just* enough.

Rena closed her eyes, and *reached*, just as her father raised his hand to summon his power to him.

She never knew, afterwards, if it was her spell that caught

him, or the terrible effect of his own power caught so close to the iron of the necklace.

She only knew that in midreach, *he* gasped, the terrible energies he had been reaching for suddenly backwashed over him, and his body exploded into a pillar of flame.

Somehow, she got to her mother, past the pillar of fire, a thing that screamed and bubbled horribly, but seemed rooted to the spot, as if the necklace chained it there. She reached her mother, who was now quite paralyzed with fear; somehow she got Lady Viridina to her feet and down the stairs as the very marble of the tower began to burn and the stairs ignited practically on their heels. She and her mother staggered together across the garden, as slaves and underlings began to converge on the burning tower, staring and shouting and ignoring the two of them completely.

By then, Lady Viridina was able to move under her own power, although her face was still white with shock and her eyes resembled a pair of holes burned into her face. Shana led the way to the open gate—opened by patrolling guards who had seen the flaming tower and had pounded past the two escapees without a second glance. She had no idea how to find Mero, but this was the only way out that she could see, and by far the easiest.

But she didn't have to stagger around the walls of the estate to find Mero; he found them, galloping up with two horses in tow just as they reached the outside. Without a single word, he helped Lady Viridina into a saddle and tied her there in case she should suddenly collapse, since it looked as if she might do that at any moment, as Rena clambered into her own saddle, hindered by the skirts of her ridiculous gown.

"Lorryn's meeting us on the way," Mero said shortly. "Your timing couldn't have been better; the real mess is just about to begin. Let's get out of here before someone figures out we aren't supposed to be here."

Rena looked back at the burning tower, now a single impossible column of flame reaching into the sky. A portent of things to come?

She felt numb, her thoughts moving slowly, as if they were making their way through thick mud.

I'll be hysterical in a while, she realized, somewhere in the back of her mind where there was still an atom of rational thought. *Mother will be, too. We'd better be far away when that happens.*

And as he read her thoughts, Mero nodded. He turned his horse's head, and spurred it into a canter. Lady Viridina's, with the lead-rope still tied to the back of his saddle, followed with a jerk of its head.

Rena looked back one more time, shuddered convulsively, and followed both of them.

Lorryn had lost all control of his emotions by now, and his heart and mind were in as much turmoil as the land around them. Shortly after he had met up with Mero, Rena, and his mother, the countryside literally erupted all around them. He had known, intellectually, what his revolt might mean—

But it had not occurred to him what it would look like. He had galloped through madness, through scenes out of a High Lord's worst nightmares. There were armies of humans wearing bits of iron around their necks and wielding farm implements at all comers; there were armies of mixed humans led by young elves, manning the walls of besieged estates while small groups of older elves rained terrible magics down on the walls and anyone not protected by iron. There were tiny groups of human fighters, grimly protecting loot, huddled masses of slave-women—or, once, a single elderly elven woman with the look of eagles and the gentle hand of a nurturer, who wore one of his necklaces about her neck. *She* recognized them for what they were, and more, she knew Viridina on sight, and called out to them before they could pass her by.

"Boy!" she shouted, waving a restraining hand at her warriors. "You must be Viridina's—follow us, we're beating the bounds, and we'll be at my lady-keep in a trice."

By then they were all so weary, and Lorryn was so sick with worry for his mother, who had fallen into a stupor, that he would have accepted help from Jamal himself. Over Mero's objections, he did follow, and they led him to a cleverly concealed keep of the oldest sort, the kind that was proof against just about any form of siege.

She brought them in, she saw Viridina into a bed and them to a meal, and while her humans guarded and watched them warily, she got all of their tale out of them. Even out of Mero, who was not proof against her charm or her motherly manner.

"Hmm!" she said when they were finished. "My husband was a brute, my son's a beast, and my daughter got me one of these little trinkets of yours—" she caressed the necklace with one finger "—to keep me safe from his machinations. He wasn't content with having *most*, he wanted *all*, even this little corner of the world that was left to me. I got my boys here their own little amulets when I saw what they would do, and we all settled down to wait for what I knew was coming."

"You knew?" Mero said. "But how? We were very careful—"

She laughed. "When you are my age and you came from Evelon, boy, you have seen enough to be able to guess a great deal from a few signs. *I* never held with slaves, and I treated the human friends I had like the people they are, didn't I, boys?"

One of her great, grim guards crackled a smile, and put an armored paw gently on her shoulder. "That you did, little mother," he said comfortably. "Would that more were like you."

She sighed. "Well, I often said it would come to fire and the sword again, and so it has. I *think* my son is dead; my daughter and her overseer held the manor when last I heard, and those slaves that haven't run off are helping them hold it."

"That's most, little mother," said another of the guards. "You taught her well."

"Ah, well, I tried." She sighed again. "How this is all going to fall out, I don't know. I heard the army sent to kill the wizards has mostly run back home to join whatever part of

the fighting suits them best. They're full of tales of dragons
and black men, and you can tell me if those are moonshine
and madness, or truth."

Mero cleared his throat. "They're truth, as near as we can
tell you. We don't know what's happening with the wizards,
either; it's been too hard to send a message—"

He stopped, and she laughed, that peculiar, brittle laugh of
hers. "*I* know; I know the human magics, boy. I know why
you can't thought-talk now. It happened when we first came
over; the more chaos, the more thoughts in the air, the harder
it is for yours to get through, even with power behind it."

"Ah." Mero seemed at a loss for words. The old lady
looked them all over sharply.

"Sleep in a bed tonight, boy," she told him, and turned to
Lorryn. "All of you bide overnight; you're weary enough to
drop, you're about to founder your horses, and you're all sad
and sorry and sick of heart. Leave Viridina here with me; I'll
care for her and bring her out of this. I knew her mother, and
her as a girl, and if any can give her heart's ease, I think it
will be me. If any can protect her, I think it will be me and
mine."

Now Lorryn recognized her: Lady Morthena, "Lady Moth"
as he had called her as a child. She had been one of his mother's most frequent visitors, and always had hours of scandal-
ous stories to tell. He had never guessed this side of her.
Perhaps she had hidden it beneath the guise of the scandal-
mongering old lady on purpose.

His mother had never let him say a word against her,
though. Now he thought he knew why.

He looked at Rena, who nodded slightly. "Please," he said,
putting all of his fear for his mother and her sanity into the
word. Lady Moth nodded, as if she understood.

"To bed with you all, and get on with your journey in the
morning," she said only, and shooed them off to beds as if
they had been children out of the nursery. And as if they had
been children, they all obeyed her, even Mero.

The next morning she met them at the door, as her guards
brought them their rested horses, with saddlebags of provi-

sions. "Travel safely, but travel swiftly," she told them. "When the storms are over, come to me again and tell me what has happened. I think your mother will be glad to see you."

Then she smiled, and for a brief flash of enchantment, Lorryn saw what she must have been like when she was Rena's age, and her elders opened the Gate from Evelon. "And bring me some of your young wizards," she added. "I'll tell them some history, and they can show me wonders and bring me scandal."

"Scandal, Lady Moth?" Mero said, as easy with her now as Lorryn and Rena were.

She laughed. "There will *always* be scandal, boy. Maybe you and my little Sheyrena here will make some, hmm?" And as Rena blushed and Lorryn managed a smile, she waved them off. "Hurry up, now; my boys tell me there's a looting party on the road, and I don't want you to meet it. You might hurt them."

The last they saw of her was her hand, waving at them from the top of the wall around her sturdy little keep.

Two days later, and they were at the edge of the iron-seeded territory—Keman had told them about that, before he flew off with all the iron bits they could spare at the time—and Lorryn was as tight as a bowstring with tension, wondering what kind of reception they were going to get.

And what had happened to Shana through all this.

But he was not expecting to be hailed quite so soon.

"Hold!" cried out a voice, and a score of human archers stepped across their path, iron torques around their necks, and a wizard leading them. The wizard stared at them—he was an old one, and Lorryn looked to Mero, who shook his head, meaning that *he* did not recognize the old man either.

This looked bad. It looked as if Shana had won the war only to lose to Caellach Gwain. Lorryn clenched his fists in mingled fear and rage, and his horse danced as the reins tightened.

"You and you," the wizard said coldly, "are welcome. But

that—" his tone made the word a curse as he pointed at Rena "—is of elven blood!"

Mero bristled, and Lorryn reached for a sword he didn't have.

"Of *course* she is, you twit!" shouted an acidic, weary voice that made Lorryn's heart leap. "Where do you think halfbloods come from, a cabbage patch?"

And Shana brushed the wizard and the archers aside.

"Fire and Rain, I thought you'd *never* make it back!" she said, "But—" She looked them over and obviously came up one short, and paled. "Oh, Lorryn, your mother—"

"Is fine," he assured her. "Well—maybe not fine, but we left her in good hands, and Lady Moth says she'll be fine and—"

He was babbling, and he knew it, and so did she. She held up her hands and he cut the stream of words off. "Easy. We'll get to it all in time. Right now—let's get you all away from here before some idiot war party shows up and tries to kill the wizards again."

She turned away from them and the archers parted to let them through—and Lorryn's heart sank to his boots.

All of this time he had been afraid of what would happen if she lost—to the elves, or to the divisions within her own ranks. Now—

Now what do I do? She's won. She doesn't need me, she doesn't need anyone—

Black despair washed over him; in all this time he had not once been tempted to weep, and now his throat choked with tears; his chest constricted until he couldn't breath, and he picked up the poor horse's reins to send him bolting away, far away—he lagged behind them all for a moment, so that he could slip away without them noticing. In a moment they would be around the bend in the road ahead and he could escape—think—figure out what to do with his life since she didn't need him in hers—

:Lorryn—:

The single, weary word in his mind froze him in his saddle.

:Ah, Lorryn, I—I can't tell you—:

She couldn't tell him, but he felt it—that she had been as worried sick about him as he was about her, amid all the troubles and the turmoil *she* had faced. She had fretted about him, stared at the ceiling at night in sleepless concern over him—

Just as he had, over her.

:Thank goodness you're here,: she said at last, as she sensed what was in his heart too. *:I—I missed you. And Fire and Rain know I need you.:*

Then, Shana-like, the sentimental turned to practical between one breath and the next.

:And dammit, I need your help, too! You're the one who was trained to lead people, not me! I can't handle all these impossible idiots without you—look what happened with Caellach-Bean-Brained-Gwain! If you'd been with me, he'd never have given me the grief he did!:

Despair turned to joy, and to a kind of infuriated hilarity. But of course she was going to infuriate him—that was why she delighted him.

And why, he gathered from her amused thoughts, he delighted her.

:Well?: she asked. *:Are you coming to help me with this pack of fools before I kill them all out of frustration?:*

Gathering his reins up, he turned his horse's head back up the path to help her do just that.

ABOUT THE AUTHORS

FOR OVER FIFTY years, Andre Norton, "one of the most distinguished living SF and fantasy writers" *(Booklist)*, has been penning best-selling novels that have earned her a unique place in the hearts and minds of readers. She has been honored with a Life Achievement Award by the World Fantasy Convention, and her numerous science-fiction and fantasy novels have garnered her millions of devoted readers across the globe. Works set in her fabled Witch World, as well as others, such as *The Elvenbane* (with Mercedes Lackey) and *Black Trillium* (with Marion Zimmer Bradley and Julian May), have made her "one of the most popular authors of our time" *(Publishers Weekly)*. She lives in Murfreesboro, Tennessee.

Mercedes Lackey had enjoyed best-selling success with her many fantasy works, including her much-acclaimed adventures set in the fabled world of Valdemar. While much of her work lies in epic fantasy, she has enjoyed successful forays into dark fantasy, with her Diana Tregarde books, and contemporary fantasy, which includes her recently published *Sacred Ground*. She is one of the most popular fantasy authors on the scene today. She lives with her husband, artist and author Larry Dixon, in Tulsa, Oklahoma.